ISOBEL GOWDIE:

Alas that I should compare him to a man.

"The youngest and lustiest women wil haw werie great pleasur in their carnall cowpulation with him. Yea much mor than with their awin husbandis and they will haw exceeding great desyr of it with him, als much as he can haw to them and mor and never think shame of it. He is able for us that way than any man can be. Alas that I sould compare him to an man."

ISOBEL GOWDIE'S 3RD CONFESSION 15TH MAY 1662

CHAPTER 1: ISOBEL DANCES.

Jean Martin's bridal e'en. 9th September 1657.

And ance it fell upon a day
A cauld day and a snell,
When we were frae the hunting come,
That frae my horse I fell,
The Queen o' Fairies she caught me,
In yon green hill do dwell.
And pleasant is the fairy land,
But, an eerie tale to tell,
Ay at the end of seven years,
We pay a tiend to hell,
I am sae fair and fu o flesh,
I'm feard it be mysel.
The Ballad of Tam-Lin

Isobel dances within the hearth of her own home, cheered on by the raucous encouragement of her neighbours and friends. The womenfolk gathered for Jeannie Martin's bridal e'en. The menfolk dutifully out of the way. They have saved a month of ale for this celebration, loud and intimate within the small dark house. The firelight illuminating Jeannie's youthful beauty. A shawl from her mother, a new penny from her father in her shoe, a crown of bluest catnip adorning her golden hair, a blessing for fertility. The firelight illuminating Isobel's shining, smiling eyes. Her auburn hair, normally covered for work, allowed to flow wildly free. All within know the magnitude of taking a man as husband, can recall themselves in Jeannie's innocent eyes. All wish her well. There have been songs and stories and the earthy humour of women safe among their own.

"Hush now!" commands Elspet Nishie, "Oor very ain bard o' baillie will gie us a ballad. Hush now! Listen a'!"

Isobel dances. Shorn of her work-a-day plaid she wears only a linen sark that allows her every movement to accentuate her slender, womanly body. Before the hushed gathering she is limbs, breasts, sparkling eyes, flaming hair and oxters. The firelight illuminates the sinews and hollows of her oxters as she raises her bare arms. Isobel dances above the daily drudgery of her life and as her ballad begins, her lowly home is for her listeners transformed into an enchanted forest in the Scottish Borders. A place where none of them have been, except within the magic of Isobel's words.

"Oh I forbid ye, lassies a', that ha'e gowd in your hair" Isobel recites, as she runs her fingers through Jeannie's golden locks. "Tae cam or gae by Carterhaugh, for young Tam-Lin is there." Isobel steps back from the seated gathering of women and transforms her body into the cocksure pose of a handsome man. Her friends and neighbours cheer and whistle.

"There's nane that gaes by Carterhaugh but leaves him a wad, either their rings or green mantle" Isobel moves to Janet Breadheid and strokes her index finger as she mimes removing her brass wedding band. She steps back and slowly shrugs a strap of her sark off her shoulder to signify a mantle being disrobed. She stops just before her breast is exposed, the women call encouragement for her to go on, "or else they maun gie him their maidenhood!" Isobel calls out the final price demanded by Tam-Lin, the fingers of her right hand curve under the hem of her sark, her eyes locked on Jeannie's, her body arching, as would a woman riding a crest of pleasure with a man.

Firelight, shadow, warming alcohol, shared experience drives the performance on. Isobel shifts her body, her being, yet again to convey a young maiden, full of yearning. Her eyes fixed once more on the bride to be. "Jeannie sits in her lonely room, sewing a silken seam, looking oot at Carterhaugh, abune the roses green and Jeannie sits in her lonely bower, sewing a silken thread," Isobel is on her haunches, her right hand rising and falling as a seamstress, her head uplifted, her slender neck exposed, gazing outward, her lips and breath conveying sexual imminence "and she longs tae be in Carterhaugh, abune the roses red."

The moment of longing is held. The audience hushed. Then the moment is broken as Isobel casts the imaginary needle to the ground. The time of decision is now. "She let's the seam fa' at her heel, the needle tae her toe and she has gone tae Carterhaugh, as fast as she can go. She hadnae pulled a rose, a rose, a rose but ainly yin, when then appeared a bonny man, soncy young Tam-Lin" and for all her overt womanliness, Isobel appears as a man once again. The strut of the step, the shrug of the shoulder. Her Tam surveys all the ladies present, walking round in judgement of their beauty. Some in the crowd shrink back, others brazenly seek to match Tam's gaze. It is, of course, in front of the bride-to-be that Tam finally stops. Isobel's hand caresses Jeannie's cheek. "What maks ye pull the rose, the rose, what maks ye touch my tree?" Her hand goes down to the hem of her sark, pulling out the fabric to show the "tree" that has been touched and illustrate the effect. The onlookers hoot and call. The fabric is dropped and Isobel licks intimately into Jeannie's ear "What maks ye come tae Carterhaugh, without the leave o'me?"

Isobel steps back. Becomes woman again. She is Jeannie and Jeannie is strong. "But Carterhaugh is nae yer ain, roses there are mony, I'll cam and gae sic I please and no ask the leave o' ony!" The watchers cheer and shake their fists in the air, until Isobel calms the crowd, walking the semi-circle of seated women, stooping to present a finger of admonition, of warning to each. "But there's a'ways a price tae pay, tae gaze on a soncy face, and Jeannie wanted sair tae pay, tae ken sweet Tam-Lin's ways."

To all within, Isobel's house is Carterhaugh forest and Isobel is now Tam and Jeannie both, seamlessly moving from taking by the hand and being laid down. "And he has tak her by the hand, tak her by the sleeve, and he has laid his Jeannie doon, abune the roses green,"

All are enraptured. The room is silent. Only the fire crackles until Isobel, lying on the hard floor reaches up an arm, her body undulating as if in bliss, because she is in bliss. Where she is most herself. Most free. Tam and Jeannie both. "And he has tak her by the arm, tak her by the hem," her hand slowly pulls up the hem of her sark revealing tantalising inches of shapely thigh "and he has laid his lassie doon."

Isobel creates magic with her words.

CHAPTER 2: NOWHERE, NOTHING. VICTORY.

Aberdeen 13th September 1644

"There was little slaughter in the fight but horrible was the slaughter in the flight, fleeing back to the town was our townsmen's destruction, whereas if they had fled and not come near the town, they might have had better security but being commanded by Patrick Leslie, Provost, to take to the town, they were undone. Yet himself and the prime Covenanters, being on horseback, won away safely. The Lieutenant (Montrose)follows the chase into Aberdeen, his men hewing and cutting all manner of men they could overtake within the town, upon the streets and in the houses, as our men were flying, with broad swords and without mercy. Their cruel Irishes seeing a man well clad would first strip him to save his cloaths unspoiled, then kill the man. Montrose had promised them the plundering of the town for their good service but he stayed not but returned back to camp, leaving the Irishes killing, robbing and plundering at their pleasure and nothing was heard but pitiful howling, crying, weeping and mourning all through the streets. Some women they pressed to deflower and others they took per force to serve them in camp. The men they killed they would not suffer to be buried but teared their cloaths off them, then left the naked bodies lying above ground. The wife durst not cry nor weep at her husband's slaughter before her eyes, nor the daughter for the father, which if they did and were heard, then they were presently slain." **The History of the Troubles and Memorable Transactions in Scotland in the years 1624 to 1645 by John Spalding, Commissary Clerk of Aberdeen.**

I can name the day God died for me. Friday 13th September 1644.

In the summer of 1644 I was enamoured of two people, Patrick Gordon and Peggy Strachan. Patrick was my greatest friend and idol. His family had sponsored me to attend Marschial College, taken me as apprentice in their legal practice, raised me up from poverty. I loved him and aspired to be like him. Peggy, my landlord's daughter, I loved in more natural ways and she loved me. Given time and my new found status we would have married.

Patrick and I were both eighteen, he a Catholic and I an episcopalian, which was as close to him in religion as I could countenance. We spoke of joining the Earl of Huntly in his resistance to the Covenanting Kirk party, who were eroding the authority of the King and suffocating our nation with their drab sanctimony. Somehow the time was never quite right for our dream of joining the great events of our age but Patrick kept two horses, with a pair of swords and dragoon pistols ready, should the opportunity ever arise.

First came the rumour, the ripple of disbelief and hope. An army for the King risen in the west, led by the Marquis of Montrose, the Covenanter turned Royalist and a wild half-Irishman, Alasdair MacColla. The Covenanting armies had seemed invincible, yet on 1st September, at Tippermuir, outside Perth they were smashed, some of their number who had fled, limping into Aberdeen with tales of an irresistible Highland charge of sword and dirk. The listeners were supposed to be appalled. Patrick and I were thrilled.

The Royalist army marched north-east, passing Dundee heading for Aberdeen. There was frantic activity on the streets, levies called for and a real prospect we may be pressed to fight for the wrong cause.

"We will never get a better chance than this, you and I!" Patrick exclaimed as he clasped each of his hands on my shoulders. "If we take not this opportunity to serve both country and King, we will ne'er be able to face ourselves."

I felt like a lover being asked to elope. Peggy viewed it much the same. She knew I was leaving her.

The night of the 12th she shared my bed, the softness of her flesh and the warmth of her body almost unbearable to be parted from in the morning. I asked her to come with me but Peggy rejected the offer with both sadness and anger in her eyes.

"It is madness, Archie. I cannot leave my father, my family. Your cause is hopeless. You will die or be ruined. What is so wrong with biding here, with me?"

Peggy pulled back the bed sheet in final appeal. A woman offering the wonder of her body and of her embrace. For God and King, I told myself I had to choose the more noble cause.

There was scarce another horseman in the army we joined. James Graham, Montrose himself, welcomed us, eager as he was for any sign of wider support, particularly among the gentry of the north-east, which I was now considered to be a part.

"Is it not wonderful?!" Patrick called to me, his sword brandished in his hand, "We finally will be able to put all our practice to use."

Practice and youthful dream are no match for the reality of war. The ugly truth dawned early on 13th September. The 12 year old drummer boy we sent forward to beat parley and offer the city the terms of surrender, was shot in the back as he returned to our lines. The boy had been the son of a McDonnell Captain. Anguished cries of vengeance bellowed out from the angry men around us. I speak Gaelic and Scots and understand "No Mercy!" when I hear it.

The killing of the drummer boy had been madness on the part

of the garrison of Aberdeen. The men they had enraged had been born into Ireland's endless blood feud. The madness was compounded when Lord Burleigh did not defend the city walls but led his army out to confront us on the plain. He must have been blinded by his greater numbers on foot and on horse. Shore porters and shopkeepers cannot be compared to the warriors I was to fight alongside that day.

The Covenant army attacked first with their cavalry. It was a rash and ill co-ordinated assault. MacColla opened his ranks, encircling the unsupported horsemen, whereupon his soldiers hacked and hauled at the trapped foe.

Patrick saw our chance, kicking his horse into the fray. His quest for glory lasted only seconds, a Covenanter dragoon pistol blasted into his face. Only for a moment did I watch in horror as my friend fell. Something inside me changed. I did not turn to Patrick's aid but plunged forward with my horse, striking my friend's killer with my sword. Amid the swirling mass I recall a surge of pride as one of MacColla's men gave me a grin of surprised acceptance. I pressed forward, withdrawing my own pistol. A Covenanter horseman tried to surrender, I shot him with my pistol at close range.

The Covenanter cavalry were destroyed. The two armies closed for a bitter hand to hand fight. This was when the Highlanders and their Irish cousins could show their well-honed skills. The enemy should have kept them at a distance with musket fire. Once broadsword and dirk were allowed near enough to taste blood, that was all they were born to do. The defenders of Aberdeen broke and ran, Royalist swords, my own included, slashing down on their backs as they did.

In those minutes I became someone else. I saw a gate open to let those retreating escape within. In an instant I knew my horse and I were best placed to prevent the door from closing, giving the men around me time to exploit the breach. "Patrick!" I roared as I pushed my poor frightened horse into the gap between gate and wall. I swiped down against men desperate to push me back. MacColla's men pressed in beside me, the gate pulled open wide. I had a few seconds to understand I had succeeded, when a pike thrust caused my horse to rear in pain, throwing me violently backward, where I was rendered unconscious on hitting the ground behind.

I must have been pulled away from the fighting at the gate. I did not wake until the dawn of the next morning. I awoke with a throbbing head but no other signs of injury. I awoke in a room I recognised, the refectory of Marschial College, filled with injured men, like myself.

"Have I been captured?" I asked of a man I took to be a surgeon's mate.

"Captured?" The man replied in Gaelic. "We were told you were one of the young gentlemen from the town who rode out to join us. Told you fought with courage to secure the gate. The men who brought you, esteemed your actions so highly, they ensured your trappings were brought also." He said, pointing at the pistol, powder and sword by the bench I had been lying on. I continued to look at the man in confusion. "You have not been captured, young sir," he explained, "the town is captured."

"Good God." I intoned softly, not joyously, trying to piece together what the information might mean. "I am one of the young men who rode out to join you. Do you have news of the other?" I asked in Gaelic.

"Dead, sir. Killed near the start of the fight, so I was told. A friend of yours? He helped the King's cause prevail."

Patrick dead. So swiftly, there seemed so little glory in it and such random chance that it was him not me. The city taken. My clearing mind began to comprehend. Peggy! I must see that she has come to no harm.

I moved to pull on my boots. The surgeon's mate put his hand on my shoulder with a questioning look. "I have a friend in the town, I must see she is unharmed."

"Then you had better take these." Replied the man, reaching for my scabbard, pistol and crossbelt, a look of concern on his face. "The city refused terms. You must be prepared for what you find."

• •

I stepped out into dawn's half-light. I stepped out into nightmare. Streets I knew and so recently had felt at home in, strewn with corpses. Windows smashed, fires smouldering. As I walked toward my lodgings, Peggy's home, I saw the naked corpse of a man, slumped at the hearth of his house. Behind a half-shuttered window, the anguished eyes of a woman stared out at him. I knew at once, some injunction had forbidden her to bring his body into their home. Something made her cower away from the window in fear and I realised it was me.

I quickened my pace to a run. I was an apprentice lawyer. I knew the convention that a victorious army could plunder a town that refused an offer to submit. I had never understood the terrible truth of these words. Never seen the horror enacted on streets and people I knew.

I ran past windows from which I could hear stifled screams. On the cobbles outside Peggy's father's house I slipped on a slime I realised was vomit and blood. Two Highlanders came out the door, one wearing a plaid but the other adjusting the cord that held up his trews. I saw a stain on the fabric below the cord. The men were laughing.

"All yours." Joked one, in Gaelic, as they pushed past me.

I leapt the stairs up to Peggy's room. I saw disorder and madness in the gloom. Her father was slumped dead on the floor by her bed. His outer garments stolen, his body punctured by stab wounds. Peggy was by his side, cradling his lifeless head. Her shift was ripped and bloodied. She looked up from her vigil with despairing eyes.

"You!" she flared in recognition.

"Peggy, I…"

"You aided them!" she spat. I wanted to take a step forward.

To comfort her. To explain. To explain what? My hesitation betrayed my guilt. "Don't you dare come near me!"

She rose in obvious pain. Her thighs bruised. She pulled a butcher knife from under her mattress. She looked like a wraith. "Get awa' from me, Archie." She said softly, the knife uncertainly held in front of her. For the briefest second I thought I could see who we used to be.

"Peggy, will you come…"

"GET AWA' FROM ME!" she screamed, wailed like a banshee. Her grip on her knife stiffening, its point moving closer. I backed out the room.

"Peggy, I'm sorry." I said from beyond the door.

I sat all day in front of the house door, my pistol and sword ready. I deterred all who may have entered. Late afternoon, one of MacColla's men, one I recognised as the man who had acknowledged my first kill, spoke to me in solicitous tones.

"We must away. Our army is too small to hold this town." He looked around at the corpses and violated homes. "It will not be safe for you to stay."

Slowly I raised my head and looked around too. I briefly looked back at Peggy's closed door. I had started the day before with God, friendship, ideals, hope and the warmth of a woman's love, now I had nowhere and nothing. And I had been on the victorious side. That made me smile bitterly to myself. Hollow-eyed I followed the Irishman.

CHAPTER 3: ISOBEL CRIES.

Maggie. 4th August 1655.

"An alder lord will twist an oak tenant." **Gaelic proverb**

"They willna tak this bairn. Nae this bairn." Isobel cries. "No like they took the others. No like they took them a'!" She rocks the swaddled babe gently in her arms. "See! she's got your e'en, John and my smile. We gi'ed her a name. Does that no mak her baptised in the e'en o' a loving Lord?! I willna let her go!"

John Gilbert, Isobel's husband, shifts uncomfortably by his wife's bedside. He curses himself for thinking, *at least there will be one less mouth to feed*. When they are all so hungry. When all around are so hungry. Isobel tries to press the nipple of her breast into the unresponsive mouth of her child.

"Christ gi'e me strength, John!" Isobel cries. "My paps are but empty sacks. Come, my wee darling, your mither's here for ye. Sook Maggie, sook. Christ! If I wisna sae weak. If we a' were nae sae weak."

In the four months before Maggie's birth seemingly incessant rain has ruined crops, fouled roads and slowed trade. John and Isobel's home stinks of wet thatch and acrid smoke from wood not properly dry. Amid the hunger, the grim shadow of death has stalked, causing the community of the neighbouring fermtouns to turn inward. The gatherings that bound neighbour to neighbour, now so much harder in the unnatural, incessant rain. The minister in the Kirk preaches of God's judgement and even the English soldiers in the back pew know that for once, he is not talking about them but about the rain.

In the month before Maggie's birth, John and Isobel's landlord, the Laird of Park and Lochloy, took almost all they had. The Laird and his father before him, have always been in debt. When his creditors growl, the Laird bites at his tenants. Three capons, 2 cuts of yarn, 10 bolls of barley and the only Scots pound they owned. Isobel and John chew on straw and thin cabbage broth.

"In a land o' plenty an' a'!" Isobel suddenly cries. "No this godforsaken year but every ither. A land o 'plenty a' aboot, yet John Hay wants it a' tae himself. Maggie, Maggie, ma bonny bairn, wake up. Wake up. Your ma's got milk for ye." Isobel looks up at her husband as she squeezes painfully on the teet of her breast. "Look, John, can ye no see it?"

John Gilbert stretches out his hand and places it on his wife's shoulder. With his other hand, he reaches under the swaddled babe and begins to pull her away from her mother's fierce embrace. "She's gone, Isobel." John says, at first his voice is flat, then filled with loss and entreaty. "Please, my love, ye must ken it. She's gone, like a' the rest."

Isobel stares up at her husband. The bonny face that drew admiring glances from all the young men for miles around, is creased with grief, wild with pain. "No!" Isobel cries. "I willna let you. Ye willna tak my bairn!"

John is insistent. A man who husbands livestock through all the challenges of life, including death. A man who loves his wife. "Hush now, Isobel. Let me tak oor bairn. Let me hold her just a peery while." John eases the silent baby out of his wife's arms. He kisses his daughter on the forehead. "Maggie, ye would ha'e been the bonniest o' bairns."

Isobel looks at a father holding a dead child.

Her dead child.

Isobel cries.

CHAPTER 4: MIDDLETON AND GOWDIE

Edinburgh 18th June 1662

"There came then to Inverness one Mr Paterson who had run over the kingdom for trial of witches, and was ordinarily called the Pricker, because his way of trial was with a long brass pin. Stripping them naked, he alleged that the spell spot was seen and discovered. After rubbing over the whole body with his palms, he slipt in the pin, and, it seems, with shame and feare being dasht, they felt it not, but he left it in the flesh, deep to the head, and desired them to find and take it out. The accused were barbrouslie tortured, by waking, hanging them up by the thombes, burning the soles of their feet at the fyre, drawing of others at horse taills and binding of them with widdies about the neck and feet and carrying them so alongst on horseback to prison, wherby and by other tortur one of them hath become distracted, another by their cruelty is departed this lyfe, and all of them have confest whatever they were pleasit to demand of them." **Reverend James Fraser, Wardlaw, Strathglass, June 1662.**

I value my freedom, as only one who has lost it, can. Seven years an indentured servant amid the stinking swamps of Bermuda, after capture at the Battle of Worcester. Ten of my company made that journey in chains, only three of us came out of it alive. I had a long time, aboard ship and in the fields to think on what God's purpose for me was and whether I could discern His hand at all. Yet I survived, God or no, my own imperishable core, my own drive to get back. And when I did, she was dead. There is no plan, just what we make and lose, for ourselves.

I value the truth also. That which I can weigh with my own hands. I hear the words all around me, all so strident, so certain that God is on their side. For years, across this land, they have been proclaiming it, each more certain than the next. Now I see only the man speaking the words, hear only their ambition, feel only their prejudice and superstition. I mostly keep my own counsel, which serves me well. For what I have become, the strident ones, would hate me most.

I was a lawyer, a Public Notary, an educated man, a leader of men, a Captain of Horse yet still they set me to the fields. To cutting drainage ditches, so the cane might grow. Only the last two years did it dawn on them to use me as bookkeeper, secretary and scribe. I ingratiated, I served a purpose, I subtly stole, I survived. 1660 I purchased a passage to return. I could have stayed on as an overseer but I could not thole the thought of treating the poor blacks even more savagely than I had been. No seven years for them. No white skin. Yet still they looked like men to me. I saw no reason to doubt their claim, as good as mine, to an immortal soul.

I did grieve for my loss, Kathryn my wife and Mary, my daughter both dead. I was told it was the pox four years into my servitude. I had been praying , in my captivity, to their memory, trying to keep their image alive in my mind's eye, for five years, without knowing they were dead. I do not regret it. I drew upon their love longer in death than I had shared with them in life. I value love. I know that it must be cherished whenever it is found. My life goes on, as I know it must but I will always revere my Kathy and Mary for loving me, in life and sustaining me, even after death.

Whatever fortune or fate swirls around us in this most bewildering of times, it smiled on me when I returned to these shores. I stepped off the ship In Greenock just as King Charles was restored and as I had fought for him and ofttimes near died for him, I found myself in favour. Even more so when my old General, John Middleton, swept into Edinburgh as His Majesty's Lord High Commissioner to the Scots' parliament and as Earl of Middleton, Lord of Clermont and Fettercairn, no less. The General, or should I say, My Lord, has seen fit to employ me in legal work here in Edinburgh and now, on 18 June 1662 he has summoned me to his sumptuous quarters at the Palace of Holyrood.

I travel down the Royal Mile with my man-servant Wattie Garland, from Fochabers on the Moray coast. A trooper with me at Dunbar and Worcester. Somehow, he won his way back to Scotland, when I was captured. I judge him a canny man for that. Wattie is better at the coarse work than I. He clears a path through the crowds that throng the streets and vennels, with his common tongue, fearsome glare and strong right arm.

"Gentleman coming through!" Wattie bellows, his cudgel raised to ward off a beggar, pressing an unhealthy hand too close.

We pass through the Tollbooth at the Netherbow Port. I glance up at the decaying, yet still recognisable skull of James Guthrie, a dirty black corbie pecking at the remains of his flesh. "The man was a prick!" I remember My Lord exclaiming to me, with more anger in his voice, than I ever recall him using, even deep in his cups. "He cried me unworthy. After all that I had given. All that I had done. Wha's unworthy now?! Prick"

To pass through the Netherbow, we must also pass the former home of Guthrie's idol, John Knox. How high the Kirk party rose and how low they are cast. The hubris of man, not God, I think. The corbie takes another desultory bite and Reverend Guthrie's head nods in accusation as we walk below.

Beyond the port, we pass the world's end. The limit of the city. The seething mass reduces as we move into the Palace precinct beyond. Why we are content to cram ourselves into upper and lower tenements of the overcrowded town, I know not. Wattie exhales deeply as we near the Palace, the looming mound of Arthur's Seat above. Wattie a'ways exhales at this point of our regular journey. It is an article of faith between us. The throng left behind. Aye there are folk still hawking their wares around Holyrood but not the swaying, interconnected of the town. If you have ever seen a murmuration of starlings or a shoal o' herring, you will ken what we have just left behind.

Palace guards recognise us, as surely as we recognise them. Wattie with his expansive gap-toothed grin, "Fit like, Geordie? Fa's the wife an' bairns?" Myself, with a more restrained nod and a polite word of thanks as the iron gates are pushed open to allow us within.

Within the Palace itself, we are shown immediately to the banqueting hall where my Lord Middleton likes to hold his court. I allow Wattie to make himself useful with Geordie and others of the household, enquiring after their bairns and other morsels of more pertinent gossip. Round the council table I see four men, one of whom, My Lord Middleton, rises to greet me in his usual loud and unsteady manner, "Archie! What kept ye! Sit yourself down. I ha'e but little time."

I take a seat. I recognise my superior, Advocate-Depute, George MacKenzie of Rosehaugh, the brightest legal mind of our generation. The other two, Highland, gentlemen, I know not. In truth, one of them, with an eagle's feather bonnet setting off his antiquated gear, is little more than a youth. I cannot place what council this is or why I have been summoned to it.

My Lord Middleton leads the proceedings as he always does, as, of course is his right. "May I introduce Archibald Kellas from the Cabrach in Strathdon but more recently from further climes, Bermuda in the Indies tae be exact." My Lord says these words with a flicker of penance in his eyes. "Archie, ye ken Rosehaugh but this fine young man is the MacLean o' MacLean, Sir Allan of Duart and this other his guardian, Sir Rory of the same."

I nod acquaintance to all three men but choose to say to the two Highlandmen, "Sir Allan, Sir Rory, the fame o' your family precedes you. I was not at the Inverkeithing fight, I was already headed south with My Lord and General Leslie but I have heard great tales of the courage of your kin, "Another for Sir Hector!" did not seven brothers cry? No greater measure of devotion could be asked or given." I said in greeting and in genuine admiration of the sacrifice of the personal bodyguard of the MacLean chieftain, eleven years before, trying to prevent Cromwell crossing the mighty Forth.

"Fear eile airson Eachuinn" The older Highlander replied, "Another for Hector, indeed. A noble but dreadful business. I thank you for your remembrances."

"And I also." The younger man joined. "I became Father to my people that day, although I was but a boy. Hector was my elder brother."

The shared bond of those who had fought and at times lost, filled the room. My Lord Middleton, who knew it also, indulged it for a few moments, before he reached to refill his claret cup. "Aye, we ha'e all sacrificed for our Noble Sovereign but I needs must bring us tae the matter at hand. I may not have much time. I have often wondered why my Lord Lauderdale did not oppose my appointment as the King's High Commissioner tae the Scots Parliament. Now I jalouse he wanted me far away from His Majesty's ear, so that he might constantly whisper in it wi' his viper's tongue! I must go tae London soon, tae correct the many lies." My Lord Middleton gripped the table to supress the anger he felt when he spoke of his enemy Lauderdale.

"Kellas, what think ye of witchcraft?"

I confess I was bemused by My Lord's sudden change of subject and his directing this question at me. I briefly looked in puzzlement at MacKenzie, the Advocate Depute, who indicated with slight wave of his hand that I should answer.

"If Satan does indeed recruit here on earth, he picks a guy poor class o' follower and grants them the most ineffective powers."

"God's teeth, man! You cannot claim tae deny it all!" George MacKenzie interjected with a thump of his palm on the table. "This very year I ha'e convicted witches in league with Satan. What does that make their executions? What does that make me!? Kellas, you are but a junior Notary, what gi'es you the right to presume tae ken mair o' the law than me? Tae ken the designs o' Satan!?"

I hesitated in my reply, uncertain of the purpose of this meeting, Middleton came to my aide, "Mister MacKenzie, I asked the man tae speak. Archie was e'er the bravest and maist forthright of my Captains." I exchanged a look with the Lord High Commissioner that told me we were both, in that instant, thinking back to Worcester, when he, as my General, ordered the rearguard to *"shift as best ye can"* as he himself rode away. It is always the network of human obligation that I see, never the hand of God or of Satan. My Lord was in hurry to get to London and he knew the debt he owed me. He quelled the Advocate Depute's objections and drove the meeting on.

"My friends," Middleton continued, "we are no here tae debate the truth o' witches but whether in this past year we may ha'e allowed the zealots and the unscrupulous tae go too far. George, you, yourself, ha'e confided in me your doubts about the activities o' certain notorious "prickers". Men wha' get paid for every witch they find. What mair dae ye need to ken!? What mair fertile ground for miscarriage o' justice could there be? We ha'e twa cases in hand. Sir Allan will shortly explain the matter which has aroused his concern. I earnestly believe we have gone too far this past year. We maun need rein them in. I was sent back tae Scotland by His Majesty tae restore Peace and Order tae the land. Tae show the hail community o' the realm the benefits o' returning tae obedience o' His Majesty's writ and law. God's Truth, men, we ha'e all seen the great harm that too much dissent and disorder can bring! The unleashing o' madness and bloodletting that Civil War can cause tae o'erflow. As King's Commissioner I ha'e pardoned all wha would return tae the King's Peace. Pardoned men wha spouted the maist foul treason. Only the maist recalcitrant ha'e suffered the full force o' the King's law and their heids serve as examples tae us all." All in the room had an image of Reverend Guthrie's severed head, as Middleton spoke. "I want this witch burning tae stop, just as I want Ministers wha will not accept the return of Episcopacy tae stop. They baith reek o' a land yet riven wi' superstition and dissent. Too many folk wha' claim tae tak their lead direct fae God or the Devil, when all in this Realm, all in this Realm, mark you, should abide by the law o' the King and the King's law only. A Happy Land can ha'e only one Law! I was chosen by His Majesty tae bring Conformity and Law tae this sick benighted land and By God I shall!"

My Lord Middleton had a wonderful direct passion when he had just the right amount of drink to make him inspired, yet still coherent. This mid-morning meeting seemed to be one of those happy occasions. "Gentlemen, we ha'e little time. This fever for witch hunting has spread like a fire in a dry-summer forest. From the Lothians, tae Fife, tae Forfarshire and now beyond. I represent the King's Law and Good Order. I ask ye tae go out tae these mair Northern places and be a fire-brake. Find out what is happening and commend the local Bailies and Kirk sessions tae pause or desist. Sir Allan, I would oblige ye tae set out again the petition that brought ye from Mull tae myself and the Privy Council."

All eyes in the room turned to the thin youthful features of MacLean of Duart . The young man exchanged the briefest of glances with his kinsman, Sir Rory, who indicated, with an inclination of the head that the young Chieftain should proceed. "I am not long in my majority as Taoiseach. I could not let the injustice that was presented to me pass. In the vale of Strathglass, by Beauly, MacLeans have lived for over three hundred years, these last years as tenants of the Chisholm of Warldaw." Young Allan's cheeks flushed red with anger as he mentioned the name of the tormentor of his people. "He coveted my kinsmen's land, yet found no legal means to dispossess them, until he heard of witch trials to the south and a wandering pricker whispered in his ear. All this was told to me by John MacLean who travelled the many hundred miles from Strathglass to Duart to appeal to me on behalf of his wife, Christian, accused and most vilely confined and tortured.

Some of the accused, my people, have already died so severe has been their questioning. I jalouse this John MacLean to be an honest man. A desperate man. He fears he will obtain no justice from a Commission granted to Chisholm, his cousins and his cousins' cousins. Please My Lord I beseech you, reach out your hand to aid my innocent people, foully accused."

There was a murmur round the table after Sir Allan concluded. Rory MacLean placed his hand on the young man's back and told him, *"Well said, Taoiseach"*. George MacKenzie exclaimed indignantly, *"If this Wardlaw has used torture, it is against the express ordinance of the Privy Council after a motion I, myself, introduced this very April."* Myself, I did not speak but felt certain I had been summoned to travel to Strathglass to use my legal eye to uncover the truth and act as My Lord's "firebrake", if all was as young MacLean described.

Middleton responded, "Sir Allan, your concern for your kinfolk does ye proud. Your appeal has no' fallen on deaf ears. We will dispatch an investigator, wi' letters o' authority from myself and Advocate Depute MacKenzie, on behalf o' the Privy Council." I waited for My Lord to turn and confirm the commission on me. "George, who did you ha'e in mind?"

"John Neilson, a sound man. Notary from Dingwall, not far from this Strathglass."

"Capital!" Middleton exclaimed, "Sir Allan, Sir Rory, our business concluded, you will join me in a glass?" My Lord said as he proffered the claret jug, topping up his own cup as he did.

"What of myself, My Lord?" I asked. "Why was I required at this council?"

Middleton turned his head briefly to MacKenzie of Rosehaugh, as he poured the remaining claret into the glasses in front of each MacLean. I saw a momentary darkening crease My Lord's brow, "George, be sae kind as tae explain."

MacKenzie coughed as he looked down at a folio of papers in front of him on the table. There was a moment's tremor in his hand, before his palm came to rest on the small pile, which he pushed across to me. "Mister Kellas, we ha'e a second report requiring an honest legal mind." His hand seemed to hesitate, as he contemplated the final release of the pages into my care. "In front of you, sir, is the maist extraordinary account. Mair detail o' demonic practices than I ha'e e'er encountered in my career. Two confessions o' witchcraft from Auldearn, by Nairn." My mind raced back at the name, a place I had been 17 bloody years before with My Lord Montrose. MacKenzie hesitated further, "After hearing your opinion, Kellas, I am nae sae siccar you are the right man." MacKenzie released his hand from the bundle.

"What you will read in these papers may well be true."

Middleton had finished his act of hospitality with the MacLeans. He resumed his seat next to me more sombrely than was his wont. "You need not doubt him, George. Archie is the right man for this job. The bravest o' my Captains. I ha'e perused these confessions. Janet Breadheid and the other, Isobel Gowdie. A guy queer business if true. A guy queer business if no'. Be my eyes and ears once again, Archie and report back tae me what ye find."

And so it was that I first encountered the name that was to haunt my dreams for weeks to come.

Isobel Gowdie.

• •

CHAPTER 5: ISOBEL SINGS

Threshing the big field. 3rd September 1646
"Come butter come
Come butter come
St. Peter stands at the gate
Waiting for a buttered cake
Come butter come"
Song to accompany rhythmic churning of butter

Isobel sings to the women passing round a water jug as they prepare to return to the threshing. Each woman has a basket and a scythe. Some, like Janet Breadheid, have their newest babes wrapped close within their plaids. As the women pause for a few minutes' rest and Isobel sings, Janet takes her baby boy out to suckle on her breast. It is a fine late summer day and all hope that this year, unlike the last, the crops they reap will not be taken by any army.

Isobel is a lithesome lass of 16. The sunlight glows in her long red hair as she finishes the ballad of the Elfin Knight.

"When ye've done and finished your wark,

Blaw, blaw, blaw, winds blaw,

Ye'll come tae me, love, and get your sark

and the wind has blown my plaid awa'"

"Weel done!" Elspet Nishie commends, "Could ye sing us a song tae help us as we cut?"

"I dinna ken," Isobel demurs shyly. "I'm sure yin o' you…"

"Nonsense lass," Janet interjects, as she moves her baby son back into his protective sling. "You ha'e a lovely voice, lass. Could ye lead us in "Fie we cut the barley now"? Whitever ye like for the verses."

Isobel smiles a brilliant smile. She has wanted to be asked all along. "I ken my mither says I've been dreaming songs, sine afore I could walk."

Janet reaches out her hand for Isobel to help pull her and her baby up. Her eyes fixed intently on the younger woman. "Thank ye," she says as she reaches standing, then whispers quietly into Isobel's ear, "You'll be fine, lass. Just sing whatever your dream tells ye."

The eight women each assumes their position at the head of a row of barley, scythes in hand. The stalks rustling in the light, refreshing breeze. Isobel has to improvise a verse and the other women will join with the chorus. For a few moments Isobel stops in thought. She glances behind her at the Auldearn woods. As her voice rings out the women start cutting.

"A sojer cam tae me fae the war
Meikle strang and meikle braw
He had the brightest Irish eyes
But his lips could tell me ainly lies."

The older women smile as their voices unite in the chorus, each moving along cutting as they sing.

"Fie we cut the barley now!
Fie we cut it doon!
Our lives are but stalks o'corn
When the reaper comes aroon."

Isobel has had just these few seconds to invent the next verse but the rhythm and the mischief flows through her, bursting to be set loose.

"The sojer he cried, "Bide lass
In my forest bower"
I ainly went tae sae fareweel
But bided mony an hour."

Isobel hugs her own shoulders to indicate what happened in those hours. The women smile again, as they bring in the chorus and cut with renewed vigour.

"Fie we cut the barley now!

Fie we cut it doon!

Our lives are but stalks o'corn

When the reaper comes aroon."

Momentarily Isobel bites her lip as she decides on the final verse. It is not the words that give her pause. It is the confession.

"Lassies, a' things ripen

We maun reap what we sow

My sojer he is gone now

But my belly starts tae grow."

Janet looks up at the young singer but cannot linger long, as the rhythm of the chorus drives the women on.

"Fie we cut the barley now!

Fie we cut it doon!

Our lives are but stalks o'corn

When the reaper comes aroon."

Later, when the rows are cut and collected, Janet comes and sits by Isobel. She hands over her four month old baby James into the younger woman's embrace. The baby beams back as Isobel strokes his cheek. "He's richt bonny," she tells Janet. "Aren't you a bonny boy?" she tells James.

Janet smiles, then places a hand on Isobel's arm. "Your song wasnae jist words was it?" she asks. "How far are ye gone?"

Isobel's smile for the baby shifts to a more pensive frown. She looks into Janet's eyes, deciding if she can trust her secret to her. After a few seconds, she says, "It's been mair than twa month sine my last bleed."

Janet reaches over and gently retrieves baby James. "Then you maun marry lass. Plenty o' lads ha'e looked your way."

Isobel looks over her shoulder, back toward the woods. "Oh, but he is such a man!" Isobel places her hand on her breast as she inhales deeply. "I'll wait for him, as lang as I can."

Janet regards her companion with compassion and intrigue. She places a final hand on her shoulder. "So be it, lass. If you wish no tae be wi' bairn, come and see me. I ken how tae help. You're no alone, lass. Niver forget that. Now we maun baith be hame, afore yonder clouds turn tae rain."

Isobel thanks Janet. The women's journey home takes them opposite ways. As Isobel carries her basket back toward her mother's house, she looks longingly into the dark woods and sings.

CHAPTER 6: THE CONFESSION OF JANET BREADHEID

"*Confession of Janet Breadheid spouse of John Taylor, in Balnakeith. At Inshoch, the fourteenth day of April 1662 yeiris. In presence of Patrick Dunbar, Sheriff Principal of the Sheriffdom of Elgin and Forres ; Hew Hay of Newtowne , Archibald Dunbar, in Meikle Penick; Archibald Dunbar, in Lochloy; Walter Chalmers, in Balnaferrie ; James Cowper, in Inshoch ; John Weir, in Aulderne; and ane great multitude of all sortis of other persons ; Witnesses to the Confessions and Declaration efter set down, spoken furth of the mouth of Janet Breadheid, spouse to John Taylor, in Balnakeith. The quhilk day, in presence of me, John Innes, Notary Public and Witnesses and, the said Janet Breadheid, protesting repentance for her former sins of Witchcraft, and that she had been over long in the same service; without any pressure proceidit as follows, to wit.*

First, I knew nothing of Witchcraft until I was mariet with my husband, John Taylor ; and it was he, and Elsbet Nishie, his mother, that enticed me to that craft. And the first thing that we did was, we made some drugs of dogs flesh and sheep's flesh, against John Hay, in the Mure ; and thereby took away his corns, and killed his horse, cattle, sheep, and other guidis and layed it about his house, to tak away his own life; and therefter, he shortlie died. Only my mother-in-law and my husband did this, to learn me ; and this was my first lesson from them. When they got me to consent to this craft; first they had me to the Kirk of Nairn, in the nycht tyme; and the Devil was in the Reader's dias, and a book in his hand." **Confession of Janet Breadheid, confined in the dungeon of Inshoch Castle, as recorded by John Innes, Notary. 14th April 1662.**

Why did it have to be Auldearn? I am a hypocrite when I write and speak of My Lord Middleton's drinking. That evening, in my chambers, perusing the documents entrusted to me, thinking back on Auldearn, I reached for strong liquor as I had not done for nine years. It is one thing to recall with righteous indignation the murder of innocents by the enemy, such as Cromwell at Drogheda or Monck at Dundee but where is a man to hide his memories when he was part of an army that did the same? What if I can still see Peggy's anguished face and hear the accusation in her voice?

I pour another drink so I do not have to remember. The man I no longer wish to be.

I have accepted a commission, I must force myself to go back to Auldearn.

I must forget guilt and alcohol and focus only on the facts. Within a day or two I would travel north with a writ from the King's Commissioner and the Advocate Depute to interview the principal witnesses. Before I did so I must understand what facts these documents contain. Even the next morning my head swam, as I contemplated them, not simply from my indulgence the night before. I believe in scientific law. Law not based on prejudice or superstition but based on principles that apply equally to all. A discovery of what actually happened and a proportionate apportioning of blame and punishment. The words in these papers rebelled against my precious reason. If I were to take them at face value, I would need to find and interview the Queen of Faeries. I would have to believe that elf arrows can be flicked from fingers to maim or kill. That humans can change their bodies into animals or birds, gather as a murder of crows then transform themselves back again through the chanting of a few words. Incantations written down before me.

I have seen men, women and children, myself included, in wartime, in the greatest extremity of pain or fear. Not wanting to die, or even more powerful, not wanting loved ones to die. In that extremity, no-one has ever turned into a rabbit or a crow to escape. No-one has flicked elf-arrows when powder or shot was in short supply.

God's truth! Satan, where are your battalions when your true servants are being tortured and burnt!?

If I am to believe these words, I am to believe that Satan walks this earth and involves himself in the most petty of matters. He and his followers can enter the bedchamber of a Minister who has offended them and make him more ill. Not kill him, just sick for a few more days than he might have been. Satan can break into a banqueting hall and steal a Laird's meat and drink. Satan can curdle milk and sicken a neighbour's sow.

Satan, why are your ambitions so limited? Why do your ambitions appear as limited as the narrow aspirations of your followers? Even as I scratched this question into my own Notary's notebook, I knew I had given my own answer.

I must also confront the numbers. This Janet Breadheid has named some three dozen. She has explained initiations going back generations. I could only imperfectly remember the land from seventeen years before but there could hardly be a farmtoun for miles without a witch within it. How can you keep such a secret? Neighbours in small villages have nothing else to think on or talk about. I should ken, it was why I had to get away. Neighbours can tell before you can whether your man has been at the hochmagandie ahent your back. How on earth would they not know about repeated orgies of carnal pleasure with Black John, the Devil, in their own Kirk!?

Christ's wounds! Were there no Christians in Auldearn, Lochloy and Inshoch!

What I first wrote, what I first accepted as fact, was this. Isobel Gowdie was kept in Auldearn Tollbooth and interviewed on 13th April. Janet Breadheid was held some miles away in

Inshoch castle and interviewed on 14th April. They were both confined, no possibility of communication.

Hah! I laughed almost bitterly. No communication that an ordinary person might accomplish. Perhaps they met as crows on the night of the 13th and put themselves back in gaol the next day.

With no possibility of communication these two women produced confessions remarkably similar in detail. In the procedure of their initiation, in the names of those involved, in the names they wished to harm. Where the names differed, it actually made me believe them more. Not identical but Janet, being the older woman, a longer established member, recalling folk that Isobel would not have known. If they had agreed a story before their confinement, would they have thought of that?

George MacKenzie in his most recent treatise on Scots' Law is most fond of the word, "corroboration". Rely not on a single testimony but feel the strength when two strands of evidence combine. I could think of only three reasons why the confessions of Janet Breadheid and Isobel Gowdie might so strongly corroborate the other. Firstly, they had shared these stories together before their imprisonment, although God alone knew they were hardly stories that in anyway served to save them. Except perhaps their immortal souls. Secondly, the stories were led and shaped by the inquisitors, or even the recorder, John Innes. The similarities were a creation of what the accusers wanted to find and hear. Why they wanted to know how huge was the male member of Black John was beyond me. If these words were the creation of the most respectable and important men in the district, what did it tell me about them? God help us. My head swam again.

Thirdly and here my hand trembled as I recorded my thoughts, perhaps the stories were so similar because they expressed a kernel of a shared truth.

What had MacKenzie said to me as he handed over the folio?

"What you will read in these papers may well be true."

As I sat at my table with the neat pages of Janet Breadheid's confession, next to the less ordered pile of Isobel Gowdie's four confessions, I knew I preferred Janet. Isobel seemed a hallyrackit creature to me. Whatever led these women to interrogation, I could not help feeling that once she had her audience, Isobel was enjoying shocking them. Enjoying showing off. Poor John Innes could not keep up at points in his recording, noting only "etcetera, etcetera".

Janet, on the other hand, fantastical subject matter excepted, seemed sober and matter of fact. I could almost imagine her as housekeeper. Imagine her as wife. A dread thought stopped my quill in my hand. Why had Janet only the one confession? I would have gone back to her, were I seeking confirmation of certain facts. Could it be she had only the one confession for that very reason. Those leading the interrogation did not wish confirmation of certain facts? Was she yet living to give a second confession or had she been quietly disposed of in her dungeon cell?

"Johne Taylor, my husband, was then Officer; not Johne Young, in Mebetoune, is now Officer to my Coven

Quhan I cam first there, the Devil called them all by thair names, on the book; and my husband,

then Officer, called thame at the door. And when that was done, Bessie Wilson, in Aulderne,

sat down next the Devll;- Bessie Hay, thair, sat next him, on the other side; Janet Burnet sat

next her; and Elspeth Nishie, spouse to the said Johne Mathew sat next Bessie Wilson, her mother. She was the Maiden to her mother's Coven. All the rest sat down as they came.

The next thing, after what was done that night, the Devil lay with them all about. And then

for me, my husband presented me, and he and Margaret Wilson, in Aulderne, held

me up to the Devil to be baptised: And efter I had put my hand to the soles of my foot,
and the other hand to the crown of my head, and renounced my baptism, and all betwixt my two hands to the Devil, the Devil marked me in the shoulder, and sucked out my blood with his mouth, at that place ; he spouted it in his hand, and sprinkled it on my head. He baptised me therewith, in his ain name, 'Christian.' And then immediately thereafter, they all returned each to their ain houses. Within five days thairefter, he cam to me to my house, quhan my husband was furth, in the morning, at the plough, to see the mark which he gave me ; and he did lye with me in the naked bed, and had carnal copulation with me; and gave me ane piece of money, like a testain. He was a meikle, rough, black man, cloven footed, very cold ; and found his nature within me as cold as spring-well-water. He promised to see me again, within eight days, quhilk he did, and had carnal copulation with me again, and gave me another piece of money, lyk the first ; bot they both turned red, and I got nothing for them. He cam again within twenty days, and then once in the twenty days, and lay with me at each time continually.
We met in the palace of Darnaway' next that, and thair we did eat and drink
The first thing that we did, except the taking of meat, was taking of the cornis of Drumdewan, and then pairted that amongst us. Secondly, Agnes Grant, who was burnt on the Hill of Downie, got here from Elspet Munro, to destroy the Lairds of Park and Lochloy, and their posterity. And then I and my husband, Elspeth Nishie, and Bessie and Margaret Wilson, in Aulderne, convened ourselves with the Devil, in Elspeth Nishie's house ; and then took dogs' flesh, and sheepis flesh and baked it verie small.
We were upon our knees, our hair about our eyes, and our hands lifted up, and we looking steadfastly upon the Devil, praying to him, repeating the words which he learned us, that it should kill and destroy the Lairds of Park and Lochloy, and their male-children and posterity. We did it to make that house heirless. It would wrong none else but they.

And it was Kathryn Souter, that was burnt, that shot William Hay, the last Laird of Park's brother, for Gilbert Kinley. It was only that bag that was the death of both the last Lairds of Park.
Also, four yeir since, I and my husband, Isobel Gowdie, spouse to Johne Gilbert, in Lochloy, and
Bessie and Margaret Wilson, in Auldern, made a picture of clay, like the Laird of Park's eldest
son. My husband brought home the clay in his plaid neuk. It was made in my house and the
Devil himself with us. We broke the clay very small and sifted it with a flew, and
poured in water amongst it, with words that the Devil learned us in the Devil's name. I
brought home the water, in a pig, out of the Rood (Holly Cross) well. We were all upon our knees and our hair about our eyes, and our hands lifted up to the Devil, and our eyes steadfast looking upon him,
praying, and saying words which he learned us, thrice over, for destroying of this Laird's male
children, and to make his house heirless.
All which of the premises, was spoken and willingly Confessed and declarit furth of
the mouth of the said Janet Breadheid"

I spent the first night of my commission far more with Janet than with Isobel. Whether or not charms, shaped in the image of a child, made out of rye-dough had the power to harm the intended victim, I knew not. The sad earth of this world is filled with the corpses of children, my own child included. Children die, it is the way of the world, we need not spells and charms to explain it. I wrote in my book that I must find out if the Laird of Park and Lochloy had suffered the loss of many children. Then I stared again at Janet's confession and copied the following words, "We were upon our knees, our hair about our eyes, and our hands lifted up, and we looking steadfastly upon the Devil, praying to him, repeating the words *which he learned us*, that it should kill and destroy the Lairds of Park and Lochloy, and their male-children and posterity."

The Devil learned them the words. The Devil initiated this very precise desire to kill not only the Laird of Park but his male children also. What did I know about Satan? He was a fallen angel, once at the right hand of God in Heaven. He aspired to challenge God for dominion over all creation and was cast out. Why should he care who inherits a minor Scottish estate in a northern back of beyond? My quill was busy again. Who would inherit if the Laird of Park and all his male children were removed? What did I keep telling myself?

See only the motivations of men, never Satan or God.

Janet Breadheid, I must fly north as soon as possible to ask you, who the Devil is the Devil?

CHAPTER 7: ISOBEL LAUGHS.

Finding a husband. 6th April 1647.
"What's for ye, will nae go by ye." **Scots proverb**

Isobel laughs and although William Bower thinks she looks even more beautiful when she does so, he feels uneasy. It is not a friendly laugh. "Foreby why should I gang oot wi' you, Willie Bower?"

Her slender, yet all too womanly body tantalises him. They are both seventeen but Isobel seems years older. "My faither holds mair strips in Moyness than ony ither." William blurts.

Isobel pouts and arches her body to make her breasts beneath her shift rise even more alluringly. "Then for your father's strips, I shall gi'e ye a kiss, Willie Bower."

William feels the bliss of her woman's body pressed against his. She is a tall lassie, he barely needs to incline his head for his lips to find hers. Luscious lingering moments. Her arm draped over his shoulder. Her other hand, for the love of God, searching to feel his cock. William blinks as Isobel disengages from the embrace and steps back. "When can I see ye again?" he asks, breathlessly.

Isobel laughs. A short dismissive laugh. "Willie Bower. Willie Bower. I ha'e kent full grown men. I ha'e nae use for a boy!"

William thinks to speak in anger or entreaty but Isobel raises a slender finger to his lips. "Hush now, Willie Bower, there are plenty mair sheep in the field."

With a flourish of her long auburn hair, Isobel spins away.

Down the track, mending a wooden fence, twenty year old John Gilbert watches as the beautiful vision passes by.

The last thing either man hears is the sound of Isobel, amused with herself, laughing.

CHAPTER 8: THE CONFESSION OF ISOBEL GOWDIE.

"At Auldern , the thirteenth day of April, 1662. in Presence of Master Harry Forbes, Minister of the Gospel at Auldern; William Dallas of Cantray, Sheriff Depute of the Sheriffdom of Nairn; Thomas Dunbar of Grange; Alexander Brodie the Younger of Lethen; Alexander Dunbar of Boath; James Dunbar appeirant thereof: Henry Hay of Brightmoney; Hugh Hay of Newtown; William Dunbar of Clune; and David Smith and John Weir in Auldearn; Witnesses to the confession after specified, spoken forth from the mouth of Isobel Gowdie, spouse of John Gilbert, in Lochloy.
The which day, in presence of me John Innes, Notary Public, and the abovenamed witnesses, all undersubscribed, the said Isobel Gowdie, appearing penitent for her heinous sins of Witchcraft, and that she had been overlong in that service, without any compulsion proceeded in her Confessions in the following manner, to wit: As I was going between the farmsteads of Drumdewin and the Heads I met the Devil, and there made a sort of covenant with him. I promised to meet him during the night here in the Kirk of Auldern, which I did. The first thing I did that night was deny my baptism. Then I put one of my hands on the crown of my head and the other to the sole of my foot and renounced all between my two hands to the Devil. He was in the reader's desk with a black book in his hand. Margaret Brodie from Auldern held me up to the Devil to be baptised by him. And he marked me in the shoulder and sucked out my blood from the mark and spat it into his hand, and, sprinkling it on my head, said, "I baptise thee Janet, in my own name!" Next time I met him was in the New Wards of Inshoch and he had carnal copulation and dealing with me. He was a meikle, black, roch, man, very cold and I found his nature as cold within me as spring well water. Sometimes he had boots and sometimes shoes on his foot but still his foot was forked and cloven...The last time our coven met we and another coven were dancing in the

Earlseat Hills. The other coven was in the Downie Hills so we went over to join them, and met up near the houses at the Wood-end of Inshoch. When we sneak in to a house, we steal food and drink and we fill up the barrels with our own piss again. We put brooms in bed beside our husbands until we return to them again. We were in the Earl of Moray's house in Darnaway Palace. We got plenty there, and ate and drank only the best, and took some away with us....John Taylor and his wife Janet Breidheid from Belnakeith, Bessie Wilson from Auldern, Margaret Wilson who's married to Donald Callam in Auldern and myself made a clay image to kill the Laird o' Park's male children. John Taylor brought the clay home in a fold of his plaid and his wife broke it up very small, like meal. She sifted it in a sieve and poured water into it, in the Devil's name, and kneaded it hard until it looked like rye dough, and made an image of the Laird's sons. It had all the parts and features of a child – head, eyes, nose, hands, feet, mouth and little lips. It wanted none of a child's features, and its hands were folded down by its sides. Its texture was like a crab or a scraped and scalded piglet... All the multitude of our number of witches of all the covens kent all of it at our next meeting after it was made. And the witches yet that are untaken haw their ain poweris and our poweris quhilk we haid before we were takin, both. Bot now I haw no power at all."

First Confession of Isobel Gowdie ,13th April 1662(as transcribed by Archibald Kellas, removing some of the more fantastical claims)

Had I not in my possession the only account of Isobel and Janet's confession I would have marked them with my quill to aid my understanding. I would have scored through all the passages that did not accord with my experience of the world. Treated thus, Isobel's four confessions would be reduced to the size of Janet's one. I would have marked "JB" on Isobel's confession where the two accorded and

"IG" on Janet's. What would be left would be two confessions filled with great similarity. If the confessions were not based on some shared truth, how could this be true? If I was being tortured to reveal the secrets of a Society to which I did not belong, I could name no names and describe no activities. Janet and Isobel described identical baptisms, the touching of head and foot, giving all in between to the Devil. The biting of the soft flesh by the shoulder, until blood is drawn and the spitting of that blood onto the palm, to be used to anoint the head. The carnal copulation does not accompany either ceremony but follows later, when the husband is away. The Devil described in almost the exact same words. A big, black, rough man. If there was no truth, how could both claim John Young to be Officer? If I was to shout a name through torture, the chances are not high of it being the same name shouted by someone else being tortured five miles away. The Devil stood at the Reader's dais with a black book in hand. If there was no similar ceremony, how could both women recall that detail? Both women broke into Darnaway Palace and stole food and drink. There are many fine houses in the area, why did they, in their separate interrogations, agree upon Darnaway? Almost identical accounts of making a clay image to wipe out the male line of the Laird of Park. If Isobel and Janet had agreed a story before their capture, they would have agreed one that proved their innocence. These commonalities spoke only of their guilt.

Either some shared truth or the similarities were the invention of the interrogators and John Innes who wrote them down. I looked at the names of those who had attended on both 13th and 14th April. Only three, Harry Forbes, the Minister of Auldearn, a tenant called John Weir and John Innes, the Notary. Members of the local gentry, Hays and Dunbars attended each day but different forenames, different people. When I made my journey north, I would need to speak with Innes and Forbes for certain. John Weir attended every session, perhaps he was the Tollbooth keeper and gaoler for Auldearn. I would find out soon enough.

It was late on my second evening with the confessions. I had not drunk quite so much this second night. Wattie had prepared horses and baggage for our ride north and we would leave the next day. I had written in my notebook as if rational jurisprudence could make sense of the words before me. My faith, which in truth is in the evidence of my own senses, had allowed me to discount many paragraphs of incantations, shape-changing and killing with a flick of the thumb. Yet I was still troubled. Perhaps worse than troubled, seduced. There were passages where Isobel seemed to come alive both to recount with true passion and also to give comical, mundane details that no interrogator would have thought to put into her mouth. So mundane they had the ring of truth. *"I shot at the Laird of Park as he was crossing the Burn of Boath but, thanks to God now, that he preserved him. Bessie Hay gave me a great cuff because I missed him."*

I could envisage that cuff. Perhaps not even anger but two women laughing at their shared pretence to have more power in this world than anyone would otherwise give them credit for. I have ridden through villages at the front of an army in wartime. I have seen the sullen, fearful faces and given them little thought. We soldiers were the shapers of destiny, the faces we rode past were but part of the landscape. These women dared to believe that their covenant with the Devil raised them to a higher level. Power of life and death over friend and foe alike, unseen controllers of their community.

There was another passage within Isobel's words that simply leapt out as memory. Not details the inquisitors wanted to hear, nor would they have invented, were they directing the replies. Through Isobel's description, I could imagine the different characters within the coven, from timid Alex Elder to foul mouthed Bessie Wilson, as they each confronted the Devil's domineering temper. *"Sometimes, among our fellows, we would be calling him ' Black Johne,' or the like, and he would ken it and he even then come to us, and say, ' I ken weill enough what ye were saying of me!" And then he would beat and buffet us very hard. We would be beaten if we were absent any time, or neglect anything that would be appointit to be done. Alex Elder, in Earlseat, would be very oft beaten. He is but soft and could never defend himself in the least, but greet and cry, when he would be scourging him. But Margaret Wilson, in Auldern, would defend herself finely, and call up her hands to keep the strokes off from her; and Bessie Wilson would speak crudely with her tongue, and would be telling against him stoutly. He would be beating and scourging us all up and down with cords and other sharp scourges, like naked ghosts and we would be still crying, ' Pittie ! pittie ! Mercie ! mercie, our Lord !' But he would haw neither pittie nor mercie. When he would be angry at us, he would girne at us like a dog, as if he would swallow us up. Sometimes he would be like a stirk, a bull, a dear, a rae, or a dog and haw dealing with us; and he would hold up his tail until we would kiss his arse."*

I need beg forgiveness before I write this next. My Kathryn was the most devoted wife. She presented me with my darling Mary. She acted with wifely dignity when my conscience demanded I accept a commission from General Middleton to join the army to defend the realm and the new King. In all things my Kate was sweet and demure. "If this is what you want." she would say, when I craved the intimacy of our marriage bed. "I would wish you wanted this too." I replied. "Oh, my husband, I am happy that you are happy."

I hate myself, Kate, for writing what I now write. For betraying your memory. For betraying you with a mad woman I have never met. Isobel's carnal freedom excites me. "*After that he had carnal copulation with me in the New Wards of Inshoch and still thereafter from time to time at our pleasure.*"

Not "his" pleasure but "our".

"*Alas that I should compare him to a man!*" In my mind this was the truest, most impassioned utterance in all the confessions.

A woman recalling the delight of carnal relations, without shame. "No shame" she repeated the phrase several times. "*And within a few days he came to me, in the New Wards of Inshoch, and there had carnal copulation with me. He was a very meikle black, roch man. He will lye all heavy upon us, quhan he does carnal dealing with us, like a malt sack. His member is exceeding great and long; no man's member is so long and big as his is. He would be amongst us like a stud-horse amongst mares. He would lie with us in presence of all the multitude; neither had we nor he any kind of shame; but especially he has no shame with him at all. He would lie and have carnal dealing with all, at every time, as he pleased. He would haw carnal dealing with us in the shape of a dear or any other shape that he would be in. We would never refuse him. He would come to my house-top in the shape of a crow, or like a dear, or in any other shape, now and then. I would ken his voice, at the first hearing of it, and would go furth to him and haw carnal copulation with him. The youngest and Iustiest women will haw very great pleasure in their carnal copulation with him, yea much mor than with their ain husbands; and still will haw a exceeding great desire of it with him, as much as he can haw to them, and more; and never think shame of it. He is abler for us that way than any man can be.*
Alas that I should compare him to a man!"

In my zeal to strip out all the magic, as I felt compelled to do, what I was left with was a man or a creature, who controlled a group of mostly women through imparting to them a sense of power and through carnal freedom. "*The Maiden of the coven sits above the rest, next to the Devil and serves the Devil, for all the old people he cares not for and are weak and unmet for him. He will be with her like a stud-horse after mares and sometimes as a man but very wilful in carnal copulation at all times and they even so also wilful and desirous of him.*"

I had thought, aided by a bottle or two of claret, to think or dream myself into the reality of Isobel's words. That night, alone in my bed, I rubbed myself.

CHAPTER 9: ISOBEL DREAMS

Sidhe. 1st October 1646

"I was in the Downie Hills and was dined there by the Queen of Faerie – more food than I could eat. The Queen of Faerie is finely clothed in white linens and brown and white clothes {etc}. The King of Faerie is a fine-looking man, well built and broad faced... {etc.} ... and there were elf-bulls rollicking and roistering up and down and they scared me." **Isobel's first confession. 13th April 1662**

Isobel dreams. Isobel has always dreamed. Her mother always knew her dreams were stronger than hers. Stronger but not so different. Isobel's mother would hold both her hands and laugh, "Forget them. The self-important world of men, of ministers, lairds and kings. They are but mumbling on the surface. We can't hear them and they can't touch us down here. Here in the older, deeper world. Here among the sluagh, with the faerie queen. Hah !" she laughed, " what do they know, my beautiful girl ? The most important war, since the last most important war. The truest word of God, since the last truest word of God. Look at the ruined monasteries, once so powerful now fallen so low. Their stones used for cow byers. There is an older, deeper truth, we people of the soil, have always known. The old people, our ancestors and the sidhe beyond that. Learn to ride with them. To feast and love with them. Not the empty prattling of the men, so far departed from the true nature of their souls. So lost in their own greed and self-importance. Come. Come. Dance. Sing. Laugh. Cry. Love. Ride with us. We are all that has gone before. The people of the land. Of the Faerie mounds. Who forged the first elf arrows. Who hunted here before even farms were known. Who listened to the whispering of the trees and the singing of the grass. Who know the magic of herbs and mushrooms. Who can ride with the wild hunt and divine the future. Laugh, my daughter, at the ministers, lairds and kings with their empty vanity. They cannot touch us here. We swirl about them, like the wind. We were before, we will be after. Join. Join. Join. Feel. Feel the bliss. They think you nothing. Less than cattle. Not here. Not here. Not with this host. Here we are beyond. Beyond. Outside. Before. After. Older. Wiser. Dance, my beautiful daughter. Dance with the faerie host and feel the joy and power of being free. These men would cage you. The ministers, lairds and kings. With us, they cannot. Believe in your own freedom. Your own dance. Your own song. We have lived upon the land for longer. We have danced and dreamt before their God was even born. Kings and lairds are but tomorrow's dust. Not so our dance. Our dance is eternal. Our dance is ours."

Isobel awakens lathered in sweat, somewhere between pain and ecstasy. Her head aches and spins as she tries to piece together her memories. The dream was so vivid and blissful. Alas that she could not be in that realm all her days! The wonderous dance. The ancient ones and the faerie. The faerie queen had shone with beauty and power and Isobel just knew that in her realm, she did too.

Now, though, she was somewhere else. The darkness of her mother's house. Pain in her stomach. Terrible gripping pain. Wetness between her legs. Was that from the dance? Memory begins to jostle with the dream and take shape. She can see again in the darkness. Her mother is holding her hand and Janet Breadheid is using a damp clout to mop her brow. "Welcome hame, beauty," Janet says softly, with a smile, "the worst is done, the work is done."

Isobel remembers. She could wait for her soldier no longer. Though she went to his hiding place in the woods whenever she could, he was no longer there. She could not have a child now, not after the land had been scoured by the army last summer and all were so hungry still. She had gone to Janet for help, as Janet had offered. Her mother was understanding too, sick though she was herself. Janet had given Isobel crushed pennyroyal mixed with ale and something for the pain, she said, to ease the journey, redcap mushroom, fly agaric. With a start, it all came back and Isobel suddenly, in a panic, raised up her torso to see what caused the wetness between her legs. Janet had moved to the end of the bed and was bundling up bloody rags. "You'll ha'e nae bairn this time, my sweet." Janet said. Isobel's mother coughed uncontrollably, shaking the connection of their hands but when she could compose herself, she said, "It's for the best, my love."

Isobel remembered. This is what she chose. These women had helped her. These women who loved her. The bairn gone from her. Isobel closed her eyes and shuddered. "I'm sorry" she whispered. Her mother, by her side, heard and squeezed her hand. "I ken, lass, I ken." Gently and discretely Janet took the bloody rags out the house.

The two older women bathed Isobel with a cloth dipped in a bucket of rain water. They wiped away the blood and the sweat. Isobel's own hand wiped away a tear. "I ken" she said, "it's for the best." Then with an uncertain smile, "There will be others, when the time is right"

Isobel sat up, washed, loved and pregnant no more. The pain was beginning to ease but the strange thoughts in her head would not depart. She could not shake the memory of the bliss. The deeper knowledge. Her dance among the spirit world, among the sidhe. Janet came back in the house. She saw the look on Isobel's face.

"You've been there, lass, ha'e ye not?" the older woman said, reaching out to touch Isobel's hand. "Tell me whit ye saw. Ye've been among the faerie-folk ha'e ye not!?"

CHAPTER 10 : AULDEARN. 9TH MAY 1645

"I am in the fairest hopes of reducing the kingdom to your Majesty's obedience. And if the measures I have concerted with your other loyal subjects fail me not, which they hardly can, I doubt not before the end of this summer I shall be able to come to your Majesty's assistance with a brave army" **Letter from Marquis of Montrose to King Charles I, February 1645.**

"I acknowledge to my great grief and shame that 15 years since I denied father, son and Holy Ghost in the kirk of Auldearn and gave over my body and soul to the Devil." **Confession of Isobel Gowdie, 1662**

Hollow-eyed I followed the Irishman and he led me into the very pit of Hell. I could not remain in my old life after the slaughter of Aberdeen. I followed the Irishman. I followed Montrose. They led me ever further from the dream of war. We moved ever Westward that autumn, it is said to seek out clans that may be loyal to the King but, in truth, we were moving to enact a further chapter in an ancient blood-feud between Clan Campbell and Clan Donald. What we did was thought impossible, to penetrate into the Campbell stronghold of Argyll and puncture the illusion of invincibility. What we did was bold and daring. What we did was bitter and cruel.

I count myself fortunate that I am an excellent horseman. I stole a horse from Aberdeen and I was deployed often as scout or messenger, carrying some of the many letters My

Lord Montrose wrote to implore Lairds and Chieftains to join the King's cause. I attached myself to a group of Farquharsons of Strathdon, with whom we Kellases are believed to be kin. I avoided the worst but I could not avoid that our purpose was to lay waste the lands of the Campbells. Crops destroyed, livestock stolen or slaughtered, menfolk murdered whether they offered us defiance or not. The men should have concealed themselves in the hills at our approach but what man would leave his womenfolk to our army?

It was said we were showing that the mighty Duke of Argyll could not protect his own and this would send a message to the many clans who had lost territory to the Campbells over the years. I spoke Gaelic. I spoke with MacColla's men. "Dioltas" "Revenge" was what they mostly spoke of. They were hard men but cruel. I became a hard man too.

I will not dwell on our miraculous march through snow laden passes to come down upon the Campbells with both surprise and dreadful ferocity at Inverlochy. Gaelic bards rightly sing the praises of our valour that day. The MacDonald bards also sing of the slaughter. It is the currency of their songs. One season you are in the glorious ascendant, the next your bard composes a lament for cruel and treacherous loss.

After the slaughter of the Campbells we headed back East. We re-entered Aberdeen in March. The city had learned its lesson and paid us to behave. I knocked on Peggy's door but was told she had gone away. Our army had won three great victories and fought for the King but still our numbers were smaller than those who opposed us. We could stay nowhere long. On 4th April we called on the citizens of Dundee to surrender and when they did not, we stormed the city walls. We had little time to enjoy the spoils before a larger Covenanter force entered the town from the west. I was one of the first to exit the city through the gate named for martyred Reformer

George Wishart. Some others were too drunk, greedy or stupid to escape Dundee in time. I saw it as the consequence of their folly, while most of the citizens knew it was the righteous punishment of God.

North again, sometimes chasing the army of General Hurry, sometimes being chased by him. He sought the safety of Inverness and on 8th May we made camp by the village of Auldearn. I remember little of the layout of the place. I remember words, one of MacColla's Irishmen, O'Dea, saying his ancestors must have been here before as the village was named for Old Erin.

We arrived in a dreadful downpour and elected to avail ourselves of the hospitality of the locals. A hard-faced widow called Bessie told us "I'm no afeared o' ye! You'd maun tak no liberties, sine it'll be worse for ye." We laughed, we Gordon and Farquharson horsemen and told her "You're nae wrang there, quine. Thank the Lord we're no MacColla's Irish." Then Bessie's whole countenance changed, her face softened as she ladled us some thin soup. "Is he a fine, wild man, this MacColla?" she asked, "I've heard tell he is the very Devil himself." "He is a fearsome warrior." I replied and Bessie regarded me as she filled my bowl. "What's a young man, wi' soft hands daeing wi' men like these?!" and I blushed, while noticing with a shiver that Bessie's hand brushed mine as she moved away.

That night, as we all lay sleeping, Bessie came to me. "Hush, young Sir. Dinna mak a sound." Her hands and mouth were soon upon my member, which rose in surprise and appreciation to meet her. She looked younger in the near darkness, as she mounted me, her curving shape silhouetted by the thin moonlight as she rose and fell on my manhood. Her hand pressed upon my mouth, I thought to stifle any sound but perhaps as a gesture of control. "Dinna fash, young sir," she whispered, "we may baith be deid in the morn." From thinking nothing of her, I believed her to look beautiful, in the moment she ground and pushed down for the final time to rip me of my seed. A smile played upon her lips, as she released my mouth and slipped me out of her most intimate embrace, my libation within her. "Beautiful." She said, as if reading my mind. Then she rose and was gone.

I believe I only had minutes of dazed bewilderment, wondering if what I had experienced was real before the world erupted. "To Arms! to Arms!" A Captain was calling. He pushed open the door breathlessly. "The enemy are upon us! Rouse yourselves! Make haste!"

Hastily dressed, I was making for the barn where my horse was tethered, when MacColla himself took hold of my arm. "Kellas, ride to My Lord Aboyne, camped tae the South. Tell him I am holding here wi' what force I have. Tell him, make haste! For we are like tae be sair press'd"

As I made to head for my horse, I saw MacColla give John Forbes a similar urgent instruction to ride to My Lord Montrose and bring him hence. As I was leading my horse from the barn, men all around me pulling on doublets and sword belts, Bessie suddenly appeared at my side and pressed into my hand a small knot of straw, shaped like a crude child's plaything of a man. "Tak this, young Sir. It'll keep ye safe" I had not time to register either surprise or thanks before, without saddle, I was on my horse and away. I looked back to see our leader bellow out "MacColla! MacColla!" to rally all waking men to his Standard. Bessie had disappeared.

Sore pressed they were indeed. For near on an hour MacColla's 300 stood against Hurry's 3,000 amid the dykes and houses of Auldearn. Toward the end, in desperation MacColla even charged the enemy, the better to get at them with sword and dirk. Then My Lord Aboyne's horsemen, myself included, clinging on for dear life to the reins and bridle on my saddleless horse, crashed into the Covenanter right, scattering their horse and slashing down at their infantry. At the same time Lord Gordon's cavalry assaulted the enemy left, while the appearance of Montrose with the rest of the army, advancing in good order, completed the turning of the tide and after much stiff fighting, General Hurry's men began to break and flee.

You do not turn your back on sabre wielding cavalrymen or claymore wielding Highlanders, especially not men who a short while before were fighting for their lives. This is when the butchery began, when victory was made complete. We harried them south and west. I was among a group of Gordon horsemen and Highlanders that chased some of Lawers Regiment down a dark tree-lined path to the door of an old fine house. "Brightmoney" said Lewis Gordon, who knew this area, "property of Hugh Hay, the Laird's uncle." At the door of "Brightmoney" stood a tall, bearded man with jet black hair and piercing eyes. Beside him, an uncommon sight, a tall, muscular negro.

"You will come no further!" Hay commanded. "These men have sought sanctuary." For some moments, three horsemen and ten fierce McDonnels, who minutes before had been ending lives without thought, were stopped in their pursuit by the stern, unnerving presence of this man. Until Lewis Gordon remembered his courage and called out "This is no church, Hay! Bring out the men within or join them." Further seconds passed in which Hay seemed to cause our swords to waver through the ferocity of his glare, then he conceded. "Very well. John, go tell them they must come out." As the negro departed into the house, Hay had the final word. "Lewis Gordon! I ken ye. Nae harm must come tae these men. Be warned. No harm."

I saw five wary Campbells step out of the house but I did not see their fate. Lewis Gordon turned his horse, "Come Kellas, let's us away. Time we found your saddle!" For all our haste, we could not help but hear the screams as we sped down the dark lane.

The Irish McDonnels , the Clanranald MacDonalds and we north-eastern cavalry came together in shared celebration of victory that night. All had shown their courage and each had rescued the other. MacColla through holding until the main army was ready, Montrose through bringing his men forward at the right time. My new friend, O'Dea, hailed me "the bravest man with the sorest arse!" for fighting on a saddleless horse for three hours. MacColla remembered too, "Thank you, Kellas, you brought the Gordons just in time." I looked for Bessie, amid the firelight and shared flasks of whisky but I did not see her.

A woman in the dark of the morning, the acceptance of men in the dark of the evening. I was not yet nineteen. I was content.

ISOBEL GOWDIE

CHAPTER 11: ISOBEL LISTENS

Auldearn Kirk, 10th June 1656

"There shall not be found among you anyone that maketh his son or his daughter to pass through the fire, or that useth divination, or an observer of times, or an enchanter, or a witch. Or a charmer, or a consulter with familiar spirits, or a wizard, or a necromancer. For all that do these things are an abomination unto the Lord: and because of these abominations the Lord thy God doth drive them out from before thee. Thou shalt be perfect with the Lord thy God."
Deuteronomy 18: verses 10 to 13

Isobel listens to Reverend Harry Forbes as he preaches. She tries to place what she feels in the Kirk. "They think they ken it a' but they dae not" is her recurring thought. Judgement. They control such power of judgement, she thinks as she watches Agnes Forgie forced to kneel before the Minister's dais and do public penance for selling ale to English soldiers on the sabbath. Agnes is lucky she is not fined but Reverend Forbes explains the Kirk Session took into account this was her first offence and wish Mistress Forgie to use repentance as the way back to not only dutiful but also sincere observance of the Lord's day. Captain Lofthouse of the Nairn garrison shifts uneasily in his seat, aware that the men who bought the drink have been condemned to no censure.

Isobel stands at the back of the kirk with the lesser folk, her husband John by her side. The pews at the front, closest to the Minister, are reserved for the land-owning gentry, Hay, Brodie, Dunbar, Rose and Dallas being the leading local families.

The English Captain sits alongside them. Behind the leading citizens in the pews are several rows of tradespeople seated on stools they bring to the kirk. Agnes Forgie, the brewster, is in this group, as is Bessie Wilson, school mistress. Standing at the back, for the two hour service, are the tenants and cottars of the fermtouns, those who scratch a meagre living from the land. Their relentless work of the six days not reserved for the Lord is devoted to the rent or fields of their temporal Laird, with a small strip of land allowed for themselves. Auldearn kirk, sitting high on auld castle hill, is one of the few high roofed, finished stone buildings Isobel has ever been inside. She has never been in service in a big hoose. All her life has been in the fields, byers, workshops and dark, low houses of the fermtouns. Isobel forms the thought that tells her how she feels within the kirk. In the fermtouns, among her ain, she is known, admired, a bard, a seer and a bonny, sharp tongued quine. Here in the kirk, she is silent, sullen, packed in the throng of those less close to God. Those so often judged and scolded by their betters. Her legs suddenly feel weak and she has to grab John's arm to steady herself and use his strength to bring her mind back onto the words of Reverend Forbes.

"I take the lesson today from Deuteronomy Chapter 18 verses 10 to 13 : There shall not be found among you anyone that useth divination, or an observer of times, or an enchanter, or a witch. Or a charmer, or a consulter with familiar spirits, or a wizard, or a necromancer. For all that do these things are an abomination unto the LORD: and because of these abominations the LORD thy God doth drive them out from before thee. Thou shalt be perfect with the LORD thy God" Forbes preaches from the pulpit, "I have been your Minister, your spiritual guide, for a little over a year now and I would like to think that, in that time, you have come to know me, as I have come to know you. There is great zeal and virtue for the Reformed faith in this parish and the Lord exulteth at its discovery but, I fear, there are practices and practitioners, where the hoof of the anti-Christ might yet be seen. Not just those who cling to Romanish adulation of saints and idols but also those who were a blight upon the god-fearing in the days of the Holy Prophets and a danger to our great mission of Reformation even now. The diviners, necromancers, consulters of familiar spirits and witches."

A ripple of heightened attention runs through the congregation. Avid interest from the lairds at the front and an uncomfortable shifting among the standing cottars and farm folk at the back. Isobel inhales deeply and schools herself to betray nothing. Encouraged by eliciting a visible reaction, Forbes risks a personal elucidation of his point. "I myself, no stranger to lax and dissolute parishioners in my previous charge, felt a profound difference when I was called to Auldearn. In this parish of Auldearn, the Lord has seen fit to make the most-learned in Nairnshire the most perfect in His adherence and the Devil, in his jealousy, has chosen to re-double his efforts in the seduction and corruption of those less well educated in the works of Our Lord. I, myself, have felt myself lifted and tossed within my own bedchamber. My own bedchamber. By forces that I felt sure were the occult manipulations of those who feared having a man of true faith, standing here, in your pulpit, as your spiritual guide."

Captain Lofthouse, willing to give local kirk and lay authorities their place but wary of any resurgence of Covenanting subversion of the Protectorate, feels compelled to take the unusual step of interjecting. "And such claims were found without substance by the local Magistrate."

Forbes momentarily freezes in shock in his pulpit, as he takes- in the interruption. He has a commanding position to maintain, he cannot let the issue pass. "Thank you, Captain" he replies through gritted teeth, "that was indeed the verdict of the, current, temporal authority on the matter but I am not here to debate law or evidential thresholds, I am here, as your Minister, to tell you that within our land is a battle greater than any fought in recent years. A battle for your immortal souls. A battle between the purity of God's word and the filth and degradation of superstition and the insinuating whisper of Satan himself. Do not allow yourselves to be fooled or seduced, my brethren. Do not tell yourself, *"it is only a charm"*, *"it is only an offering at a Holy well"*, *"it is only a curse made in anger"*, *"it is only a divination seen in dream."* In all these things a door is opened to Satan. In all these things, Satan works to tighten his grip. I am a man of God. A God of compassion and love. A God of Repentance. I offer all the chance to loosen the grip of Satan on themselves or, where they see it upon their neighbours. Come to me where you see the hand of Satan upon your friend or neighbour. At stake is their immortal souls. And yours! I return to the word of the Lord, as found in his Blessed Book the Bible, "For all that do these things are an abomination unto the LORD: and because of these abominations the LORD thy God doth drive them out from before thee. Thou shalt be perfect with the LORD thy God." Choose wisely this day, my friends and all days forward yet to come. Chose to expose and confront these abominations, so that they might be driven from our midst. For those that give good service in the discovery of corruption, shall be judged perfect with the Lord thy God."

Forbes is energised by his recovery of control. The congregation has never responded with such thoughtful attention. The Cromwellian regime has had little time for accusations of witchcraft but he is sure their writ will not run forever. He will watch, listen and wait. At the end of the service, he sweeps down the central aisle, Bible firmly in his grasp, his black gown flowing behind him. He wants to study his flock, as they exit the kirk, more avidly than usual, for signs of those who are enthused by his words and for those who appear discomfited by them. Watch, listen and wait. He found that the visceral thrill of judgement on such a supreme matter has made his manhood rise to full hardness within his breaches. He moves his Bible lower in his grasp. Out the multitude file, some to press Forbes's hand and thank him for his words, others slipping out, eyes cast down.

One strikingly tall red-haired woman, as tall as Forbes himself, tries to move silently past. "Miss Gowdie, is it not?" Forbes says, arresting her departure with his hand. Isobel's eyes widen in response. "I do not see you often in the kirk. Perhaps I might assist you in some private instruction in catechism, at your home or up at the manse?"

John Gilbert, Isobel's husband, had been a few yards behind. John was normally a man of few words, whose silence masked a pride in his hard-earned talent in literacy. His dour demeanour also covered a fierce, protective nature. John pushes forward through the crowd to draw next to his wife. The hackles on his neck rising. He hooks his arm through his wife's curved arm. "It is Mistress Gilbert" he informs Forbes, quietly but forcibly. "And ye wid better preach fae Malachi chapter 3 verse 5, "And I will come near to you to judgment; and I will be a swift witness against the sorcerers, and against the *adulterers*, and against false swearers, and against those that oppress the hireling in his wages, the widow, and the fatherless, and that turn aside the stranger from his right, and fear not me, saith the LORD of hosts."

For the second time in an hour, within the threshold of his own domain, Forbes momentarily freezes before recovering himself. "Ah, a student of the Scriptures, Mr Gilbert. I will watch out for you at future service, make no mistake!"

Isobel's entwined arm pulls John away, as she and the Reverend nod utterly false wishes of "Good day." Forbes, armoured by his robes and Bible, can smile untroubled at the next parishioner. Isobel departs the kirkyard in a much more disturbed frame of mind.

CHAPTER 12: JOURNEY BACK TO AULDEARN, JUNE 1662

Lord God, to whom vengeance belongeth; O God, to whom vengeance belongeth, shew thyself. Lift up thyself, thou judge of the earth: render a reward to the proud. Lord, how long shall the wicked, how long shall the wicked triumph? How long shall they utter and speak hard things? and all the workers of iniquity boast themselves? Understand, ye brutish among the people: and ye fools, when will ye be wise? He that planted the ear, shall he not hear? he that formed the eye, shall he not see? He that chastiseth the heathen, shall not he correct? he that teacheth man knowledge, shall not he know? The Lord knoweth the thoughts of man, that they are vanity. Blessed is the man whom thou chastenest, O Lord, and teachest him out of thy law; That thou mayest give him rest from the days of adversity, until the pit be digged for the wicked. For the Lord will not cast off his people, neither will he forsake his inheritance They gather themselves together against the soul of the righteous, and condemn the innocent blood. But the Lord is my defence; and my God is the rock of my refuge. And he shall bring upon them their own iniquity, and shall cut them off in their own wickedness; yea, the Lord our God shall cut them off. **.Psalm 94**

The evening before my departure north, Advocate Depute MacKenzie called on my lodgings.

"Kellas, the letter I now gi'e tae you will make you an additional Commissioner, alongside the local gentry already appointed by my fellow Advocate Depute Colville. They will ha'e tae co-operate wi' you and you will ha'e the power to defer any final decision before ye report back to me but you will not have a casting vote. You will be but one voice among many. We ha'e been at great pains tae restore local Justice after the abuses of English rule, do ye understand?"

I took the letter and indicated that I fully understood the delicacy of my task and the need to respect the Nairnshire Commissioners already appointed. MacKenzie yet felt the need to clarify my role even further. "If a confession is founded on torture, or pricking and is no freely given, you ha'e the right tae challenge it. If the conviction rests on a so called "witch's mark" on the body, you may challenge it, for I have it on the best medical authority that the body may be afflicted by many such marks, all perfectly natural and all better considered God's work rather than the Devil's and lastly, accomplices named under interrogation, without any corroborating evidence against them, cannot be presumed guilty through that naming alone. God knows which names any of us might call out under such extremity!?" MacKenzie fixed me with his penetrating stare. "Kellas, you understand? I am telling ye also that the opposite be true. This injunction I fear may be even more necessary tae you. If the confession is freely made, if the names of accomplices are accompanied by solid evidence or if the curses or compacts are corroborated by witnesses, you must urge conviction. I am wanting commissions against witchcraft tae be justly undertaken, with the most modern knowledge, not through out-dated superstition, mair suited tae a mair barbarous age. Do ye understand?"

Again I said that I understood the evidential and judicial task. MacKenzie gripped my arm. "Kellas, I ken ye ha'e seen much in your lifetime. Fought in winning and losing campaigns, been indentured in the Indies and yet returned but even for a' that, keep your mind open that there may be forces at work even beyond your ken. I ha'e admired your work here in Edinburgh, scientific justice o' the best modern kind but remember there are dark, ignorant, secret places in our clachans and fermtouns. Places where the enlightenment of either science or the word of the Lord is yet tae reach. Ye maun be open tae the evidence o' mair than your ain eyes."

"George," I replied, "I was born in such a clachan and would be there still had fate not intervened. In Barbados we were made tae bide with mulattos and negroes. I ken something of dark corners and lingering superstitions."

"Be on your mettle is all I ask," MacKenzie continued, "and be prepared for more worldly opposition. All the Nairnshire lairds, Brodie, Dunbar, Hay and Rose remain zealous for the Covenant. They will soon learn that you are the "Bluidy Kellas" that rode wi' Montrose. Your connection with Lord Middleton will be viewed with suspicion also, given he is thought by them to be a man who abandoned the Covenant, he once swore to uphold. My letter grants you the authority of the Privy Council but for God sakes, Kellas, use it wi' care!"

I protested that the name he had given me was ill-deserved. I had been a youth in 1645, guilty of little other soldiers had not done. "That is hardly an endorsement," interjected MacKenzie wryly, "You were at the burning of Auldearn and Nairn? You foraged with menaces among the lands thereabouts?" I had to signify agreement to both. "Then you will understand why your intervention may not be wholly welcome. Restored monarchy or no. Hell hath no fury as a Covenanter whose God appears to ha'e scorned him!"

The next day, on the journey north, I brooded on MacKenzie's words. So much so that Wattie was driven to exclaim, "Christ's banes, Master Archie, you're poor enough company at the best o' times but you've no said a word frae Queensferry tae Cupar!" True enough, all through Fife I struggled in my mind with two troubling thoughts, the first about the man I had become in the bloody crucible of 1645 and the second, a lost, dark barely remembered fragment from my boyhood in the desolate Cabrach.

After my brave conduct at Aberdeen, Inverlochy and Auldearn, I was made a cornet in Lord Aboyne's cavalry. Although a great honour, I felt a keen pressure being now promoted over older, wealthier men. I could not help but be shaped by the brutal savagery of that year. On 2nd July we hammered another Covenanter army at Alford. Just when we thought our victory was complete and the enemy to our front surrendering, some of their musketeers fired and slew Lord Gordon and my great friend Lewis Gordon. We were enraged. I was enraged and knew also I must prove myself to the men around me. "No Quarter!" I yelled, as I pointed my sword forward. Our horses crashed into the musketeers as they laboured to reload. Our swords ensured they laboured no more. On we rode after all who fled, all entreaty ignored, even calls of wealth and ransom. A Captain of Lord Elcho's Regiment raised one hand, his sword lowered in submission. "I crave Parole!" he called. I heard the words and even had time to observe the richness of his attire, none of it halted the slashing of my sabre. Across the field, the Highlanders and Irish also pursued our foe. The Covenanters would blame them for the slaughter but my aching arm and bloodied mount were testament to the ecstasy of killing that had overcome me. By the time our vengeful lust was slaked, my troop regrouped on my command and we each looked upon our blood and gore streaked visages. "Huzzah for Bluidy Cornet Kellas!" trooper Thomas Grant called. My acceptance was complete.

I took a lover that summer, or rather I should say, she took me. Sorcha one of the Irish camp followers, whose man, Sean Curtis, had either been lost or had deserted after Auldearn. Sorcha wished the protection of a new warrior and I was happy to oblige. She had the darkest Irish eyes and we may have been happy for even longer were it not for a tragic mistake. Our victorious force pressed south seeking to engage the last Covenanter army between ourselves and Committee of Estates now sitting in Perth, away from plague-ridden Edinburgh. We advanced too far and in our retreat back to Dunkeld some of our women were caught by the enemy in Methven wood. The women who escaped told me that Sorcha had been one of those killed in the Covenanter attack. I blinked once and thanked them for taking the trouble to tell me. That year it was blood upon blood, blood for blood. I no longer shed tears.

A week later I had my chance to avenge Sorcha. We met that last Covenanter army in Scotland at Kilsyth. They were fools who failed to learn. I was told later their General had been cajoled by kirk ministers and Committee of Estates Lords to move his army against his better judgement. We caught them marching across our front. On a hot August day, the Highlanders and Irish cast off their heavy plaids and tied their white shirts between their legs. Every one of them knew their survival depended on the speed and ferocity with which they weaved their patterns with sword, targe and dirk. Patterns carved in flesh, painted with blood.

On a hill to the north of the battle, Aboyne's cavalry rode to the rescue of Gordon's, destroying the enemy right flank. Everywhere the Covenanters began to flee, so many were untrained levies. Not blood hardened killers as were we. As I had become. So many more died in the pursuit than ever died in battle fought face to face. Five great victories and I had not accepted a single prisoner. I deserved the name, "Bluidy". I did not deserve what fate had in store.

If God died for me at Aberdeen on 13th September 1644, great men died for me on 13th September 1645 at Philliphaugh. From almost nothing, Montrose and MacColla had conquered all Scotland, in less than a year. In less than a month, through division and vanity, they lost it all. With no more armies to oppose him Montrose ceased to be a challenger to authority, he now had to show that he could rule. With plague in Edinburgh, we entered Glasgow and Montrose had to win over Lowland doubters at the expense of the plunder the Highlanders and Irish believed was their hard earned right. The army fractured, the McLeans and MacDonalds went home north-west, the Gordons north-east and MacColla west to pursue his blood feud with Argyll. I stayed because I had known only victory and knew no other Lord. In September, my Lord Montrose led us south in the hope of recruiting in the Borders. I was 19 and looked with scorn at the few, as green as I had been but a year before, who came to join us.

We all heard the rumours, the lowliest pikeman, the grim young Cornet and our Lord and General. The Scottish army fresh from the English Parliament's great victory at Naseby, was rushing north to see what real veteran soldiers would make of the upstart Montrose. We heard also that the Border Lords, Hume, Roxburgh and Traquair had promised themselves to the King to avoid their lands being plundered, not to fight and die. Yet still we lingered, hardly even an army, a pitiful exposed rump, waiting to be loved when all we could expect was to be plundered ourselves. Without MacColla, my Lord Montrose was worse than a fool. His vanity led him to be dismissively careless of his responsibility for our lives. We swore to serve him, he did not have the courtesy to lead us. Even the remaining Irish, named savages by friend and foe alike, stayed out of faith and duty, when they must have known the price of defeat. It was hardly a battle, more a rounding up of lambs to the slaughter. I should have died that day.

I first met my Lord Middleton at the end of a sword at Philiphaugh. In comparison to my Lord Montrose, General

Middleton was a man of the world. "I am empowered tae redeem those misguided wha would be redeemed" he said. I looked around at the dead or dying or the sullenly defiant. I no longer knew what or who I was fighting for. "I will be your faithful man from this day hence, if that is what you ask." I replied. I have never seen such a smile. Like the sun coming out from behind a cloud. "Good man!" he roared. "I shall hold ye tae that, mark my words, Archibald Kellas." Then, My Lord Middleton looked wistfully out toward the junction of the waters of Yarrow and Tweed and said, "I know not what service ye might yet gi'e, nor for which master, but I will hold ye tae your personal oath tae me." I had only moments to consider the meaning before My Lord Middleton lowered his sword. "Kellas, your life is spared."

For well or ill, I have been his faithful servant ever since.

That night, on the road back to Auldearn 1662, we rested at the Inn at Pickletillum before attempting the crossing from the Ferrytoun of Portincraig to Broughty in the morn. I told much of the story of 1645 to Wattie once again. It reassured us both to recall how I had earned my elevated position through the blood of the King's enemies. That night, I had an even darker dream. I was a child of five in the Cabrach, terrified by my mother's unnatural sleep. "Dinna dare disturb her, lad" my father warned, "She's seeking whaur the lost kine are. If they dinna tell her, we'll a' starve." I knew I hated the memory. I longed to be two years older and away to Reverend Forest's school or two years older than that and away as stableboy to the Gordons of Mortlach, where I discovered my love of horses and Patrick Gordon both. My last vision, in dream, was of my mother saying, "When ye go, boy, ye'll think you're better than us, Archie. You'll forget your ain." That night I realised for the first time her words were neither an entreaty nor a warning, they were a prophesy.

We crossed the Tay, skirted Dundee and headed north to Forfar, where years before I met my Kate and we made our life until my Lord Middleton called me back to armed service to resist the English Parliament's invasion. I owed him my life and had to heed his call, when it came, even though it lost me my freedom and my family.

The journey was pleasant in summer. Ever north, through Glen Isla, then Glenshee, the brooding bulk of Lochnaggar telling us we had crossed our nation's great divide from lowland to highland. By Cockbridge, deep in the Cairngorms we had to stop again for the night and I knew in the morning, if I did not take the road north, I could head east to Kildrummy and the bloody battlefield of Alford or even head to the strath beyond, the Cabrach of my childhood. I am a man of reason and do not normally dream vivid dreams but that night I was once again riding down the enemy at Alford. My dragoon pistols reloading themselves, my sword arm never tiring, the men my host slew powerless to resist. We fell upon them like a whirlwind, driven by the joy of conscienceless killing. My horse was no longer a normal flesh and blood steed but one that seemed to fly across the land. The Wild Hunt, a deep corner of my memory told myself, until I forced myself awake. Breathing heavily, my heart racing in panic, I wrestled with my dream. I do not joy in killing. I am not that man anymore. I have seen the price. Paid the price. We did not ride down the enemy through any unseen force. Their Generals made mistakes and we punished them. *I AM A MAN OF REASON*. My heart was still racing long after we had breakfasted and resumed our journey. I am not that man anymore.

We urged our horses up the steep, steep slope to Tomintoul, then the descent back into fertile plains. In truth Scotland is not straightforwardly divided into Lowland and Highland. An enclave of the coastal northeast has ever been more low than high. Speaking English not Gaelic, trading with Flemings or the Baltic states, not Ireland and now in 1662, a stronghold neither of Anglican or Catholic faith but of the Kirk with a direct and personal Covenant with God. The same men who had told me, after I had left my wife and young child to join them, that I was not worthy to serve with them at Dunbar. The Committee for Purging the Army. The name still caused my bile to rise, even though their sanctimonious stupidity had probably saved my life. "Bastards still let me go to Worcester" I found myself muttering out loud. Wattie was not perturbed, as he knew me so well and had been on that same journey. It was not the most diplomatic frame of mind in which to descend into a hotbed of Covenanters. *Were there too many bitter memories for us to heal as a nation?* I asked myself.

Evening was upon us. We intended to room in Nairn, so that I might present my credentials to Sir Hugh Campbell of Cawdor, Sheriff Principal of Nairn but I could not resist a diversion into Auldearn. I was not sure I could recognise Bessie's house, after all these years but I did remember the church on the hill. We tethered our horses at the gate and walked up to the door.

"Locked" Wattie said.

"Indeed" I replied. "We will have to find out how long it has been locked in the evenings and who has a key."

We looked down at the nearest house, close to where our horses waited. A light came on and a face appeared at the shutter, presumably curious about our presence. "How could thirteen people and the devil gather here without being seen?" I asked Wattie, who shrugged.

"Be on guard. They will try and show us spectres and demons but I wish only to find flesh and blood."

CHAPTER 13: ISOBEL CONSOLES

Fermtoun of Inschoch, 7th November 1660.

"I found out the occasion for it to be conversing with one highly reputed for piety, who took a liberty in his conversation which I could never go in with, but having such an esteem of the person, his practice had some secret influence upon me, that put me out of that degree of tenderness the Lord had brought me to. (This was Mr Harry Forbes, minister in Auldearn, whose wife had troubled Mrs Ross so to leave that place and the said Mr Harry fell in adultery with his servant afterward.)" **Memoirs of Katherine Collace Ross, pious Covenanter and needlework tutor to the daughters of the Laird of Park in mid to late 1650s (with commentary by the editor of her memoirs)**

"In winter 1660 quhen mr harry forbes minister in auldrearn wes seik we maid an bagg of the gallis flesh and guts of toadis , pikles of pairings of the naillis of fingeris and toes the liewer of ane hair and bitts of clowts...satan wes with ws and learned ws the wordis to say thryse ower; he is lyeing in his bed and he is lyeing seik and sore, let him lye intill his bed two months thrie days more..quhen we haid learned all the wordis from the divell..we fell all down upon our kneis with owr hear down ower owr showlderis and eyes and owr handis lifted up and said the forsaidis wordis thryse ower to the divell striktlie against master harry forbes" **Isobel Gowdie second confession 3rd May 1662**

Isobel consoles her friend, Margaret Brodie, dismissed from service with Reverend Harry Forbes after her pregnancy revealed the relationship between Reverend and housemaid. "It's sae guid of ye tae tak me in, when ye ha'e little yourselves. I cannae thank you enough. As soon as the snaw clears fae the roads, I'll be oot yer hair and awa' tae my uncle's in Balmore."

"Tak as lang as ye need, Maggie" Isobel says. The two women are seated on stools, side by side, carding wool, from a fleece John brought in from a sheep that had died. Although Isobel's hands are constantly moving to tease the wool and switch the wooden carders from side to side, she stops to place a hand on Maggie's arm, turning her head to look upon the younger woman. John is away cutting peat. Isobel and Maggie see each other's faces, illuminated only by the diminishing fire light. The single window in the low, primitive dwelling, adding little on an overcast winter's day. Yet still Maggie can see the glistening of sincerity and charity in Isobel's eyes. Maggie is moved to share her emotions. Her hands on her carders cease their movement as she exclaims in a heartfelt wail.

"He said he found me sae desirous, he was willing tae forsake his vow tae his wife and God baith!" Maggie's words cause Isobel to also stop her working of the wool. She takes both of Maggie's hands in hers. "I kent it was wrang but he was sae insistent, sae fierce in the protestation o' his desire. I thoucht it was love!" Maggie wailed again. The recalled emotion overwhelming her. Isobel pulls Maggie closer and Maggie sinks into Isobel's embrace.

"I'm sorry, lass, I truly am." Isobel comforts. Her hands now stroking Maggie's hair. Her fingers gently dividing the strands, as if in a continuation of the carding the women had been working on moments before. Maggie is crying now. Isobel can feel her tears on her chest. Her fingers move from Maggie's hair to wipe a tear from her cheek. "There now , lass, ye can let it oot. Speerit tae me, if it helps."

"I dinnae ken, Issy. I kent it was wrang, I was risking a guid position but Mr Forbes was so fu' of passion. Dae ye ken what I mean? When we had carnal copulation, he would say things like, "How can this be wrong, when ye feel sae sweet?

This must be God's will." He would cry out when his moment came, "This must be thy will, Lord!" and he would be fu' o' tenderness, "The Lord must have sent you as a blessing to me, my sweet Maggie. I should not say this but when my seed fills inside you, does it not feel like a baptism of sorts?" I was too happy tae think. I just said "yes". "Oh Maggie," he said, " I would that I could baptise thee a thousand times."

Isobel held Maggie for long moments, as she helped the hurting woman to express both the good and the bad of the relationship, so recently sundered. Maggie sniffed loudly, then moved on.

"But when we were found oot, he became sae cold. It was as if a' the words he had said had nivver been said. A' we had shared had nivver been. That's what hurts the maist. The coldness. He denied me utterly. "She bewitched me," he told his wife. "We can save our position in this community, if she is sent away immediately and knows the virtue of keeping a silent tongue." The same eyes that had looked at me wi' such love, looked at me wi' pure hate. "But Harry," I cried, "I carry your child." "It cannot be my child. The Lord would not allow it." He said. He didna sae much as look at me again, except tae whisper a last word intae my ear, "If you breathe a word of this to anyone, I will call you witch and liar and who, then, do you think they would believe?" "Harry!" I said "You canna mean it."

A' tenderness had gone fae his face. "You have been paid and your goods collected. Go." As I walked awa' I looked back tae see if he would gi'e me a last glance o' pity but he jist closed the door."

"Bastard!" Isobel exclaims. "Holy Wullie or nae sae Holy Harry. I feel richt sorry for ye, Maggie." Isobel holds onto her friend, until Maggie feels ready to raise her head.

"I can help in otherways, ye ken." Isobel says. Maggie's heartbroken face looks at her with a question in her eyes. "I ken ways tae make Mister Harry feel some o' your pain. Gi'e him a taste o' what it feels like tae be us. It'll dae ye guid tae fight back

"

Maggie sniffs again and wipes her hand across her nose. "You're the best friend, Isobel and the wisest woman. What did ye ha'e in mind?"

CHAPTER 14: ONE KINGDOM, ONE LAW.

Investigation begins Friday 27th June 1662. Nairn.

"Rescissory Act 1661 :Act rescinding and annulling the pretendit parliaments in the yeers 1640, 1641 etc.

The estates of parliament, considering that the peace and happines of this kingdome and of his majesties' good subjects therin doth depend upon the safety of his majesties' persone, and the mantenance of his royall authority, power and greatnesse, and that all the miseries, confusions and disorders which this kingdome hath groaned under these tuentie-three yeers have issued from, and been the necessary and naturall products of these neglects, contempts and invasions which, in and from the begining of these troubles, wer upon the specious but false pretexts of reformation, the common cloak of all rebellions, offered unto the sacred persone and royall authority of the king's majestie, and his royall father of blessed memorie; and notwithstanding that by the sacred right inherent to the imperiall croun ,which his majestie holds immediatly from God Almighty alone and by the antient constitution and fundamentall lawes of the kingdome, the power of convocateing and keeping assemblies of the subjects; the power of calling, holding, proroguing and dissolveing of parliaments and makeing of lawes; the power of entering into bonds, covenants, leagues and treaties and the power of raiseing armies, keeping of strenths and forts are essentiall parts and inseperable priveledges of the royall authority and prerogative of the kings of this kingdome, yet such hath been the madnes and delusion of these tymes that even religion it selff, which holds the right of kings to be sacred and inviolable, hath been pretended unto, for warrand of all these injurious violations and incroachments, so publictly done and owned, upon and against his majesties' just power, authority and government, by makeing and keeping of unlawfull meitings and convocations of the people; by entering into covenants, treaties and leagues; by seizing upon and possessing themselffs of his majesties' castles, forts and strengths of the kingdome, and by holding of pretendit parliaments, makeing of lawes, and raiseing of armies for the mantaining of the same, and that not only without warrand, but contrary to his majesties' expresse commands. And forasmuch as now it hath pleased Almighty God, by the power of his oune right hand, so miracoulously to restore the king's majestie to the government of his kingdomes and to the exercise of his royall power and soveranity over the same, the estates of parliament doe conceave themselffs obleidged, in dischairge of their duetie and conscience to God and the king's majestie, to imploy all their power and interest for vindicateing his majesties' authority from all these violent invasions that have been made upon it and, so far as is possible, to remove out of the way every thing that may retaine any remembrance of these things which have been so enjurious to his majestie and his authority, so prejudiciall and dishonourable to the kingdome and distructive to all just and true interests within the same. And considering that besides the unlawfullnes of the publict actings dureing these troubles, most of the acts in all and every of the meitings of these pretendit parliaments doe heighly encroach upon and are destructive of that soverane power, authority, prerogative and right of government, which by the law of God and the antient lawes and constitutions of this kingdome, doth reside in and belong to the king's majestie, and doe reflect much upon the honour, loyaltie and reputation of this kingdome, or are expired and serve only as testimonies of disloyalty and reproach upon the kingdome and are unfit to be any longer upon record; thairfor, the king's majestie and estates of parliament doe heirby rescind and annull the pretendit parliaments keept in the yeers 1640, 1641, 1644, 1645, 1646, 1647 and 1648, and all acts and deids past and done in them, and declare the same to be henceforth voyd and null. And his majestie, being unwilling to take any advantage of the failings of his subjects dureing those unhappie tymes, is resolved not to retaine any remembrance thairof, but that the same shall be held in everlasting oblivion, and that all difference and animosities being forgotten his good subjects may in a happie union under his royall government enjoy that happines and peace which his majestie intends, and really wisheth unto them as unto himselff, doth therfor, by advice and consent of his estates of parliament, grant his full assureance and indemnity to all persones that acted in, or by vertew of the said pretendit parliaments and other meitings flowing from the same, to be unquestioned in their lives or fortunes for any deid or deids done by them in thair said usurpation, or be vertew of any pretendit authority deryved therfrom, excepting alwayes such as shall be excepted in a generall act of indemnity to be past be his majestie in this parliament," **Act of Recission 1661**

Sir Hugh Campbell, 15th Thane of Cawdor was surprised to see me. He turned over in his hand the letter of Commission that was appended by the seal of the Advocate Depute and Royal Commissioner both. "Well, Mister, er, Kellas, we would appear to have no choice but to add you as an extraordinary Commissioner, though I find it hard to conceive why Holyrood should wish to concern itself with a matter, surely more suited to the local authorities, who know the temper of their tenants and neighbours far better than Edinburgh. What next, eh? Shall we see My Lord Middleton fixing the price of herring in Elgin harbour?" Campbell looked into my expressionless face and chose to discontinue his list of local matters. "Well, what can we do for you, man? What does an extraordinary, additional Commissioner require?"

"Thank you, Sir Hugh, just access to all the principal witnesses and a period of grace to communicate my findings to the Privy Council before a final judgement is made."

"And what if your findings do not correspond with those of the original Commissioners, who is to have precedence?" Nairn's

Sheriff Principal asked.

"That I cannot say. Advocate Depute MacKenzie was at pains to instruct me that I was but one Commissioner within a group. I would hope that as, all being reasonable men, we might come to view the matter similarly."

Campbell smiled, a not unfriendly smile, "Who in this country has seen things similarly this last thirty years? Kellas? Your name is familiar to me but not in a legal context. Are you not the bluidy Captain Kellas of Lord Gordon's cavalry?"

As he had asked disarmingly, I replied truthfully. "Lord Aboyne's cavalry and I was never more than a Cornet, until I joined with General Middleton to enter England on behalf of the King."

Campbell studied me for a few seconds. I could imagine his mind conjuring the fragments of reputation attached to my name. I had already calculated that he was younger than me and unlikely to have been more than boy in those bloody years. "Indeed. Your fellow Commissioners will be most gratified to have your identity confirmed. A word of warning, Kellas, I jalouse that attachment to General Middleton may once have been a mixed blessing to you. It may be so again. His *drunken Parliament* has not been without its critics. His star, though bright this last year, may soon be on the wane. More senior, and dare I say, sober, men have been restored to his Majesty's favour, no matter what their allegiance in our recent troubles. Tread carefully," Sir Hugh handed my letter back with a light flutter of the paper, "this seal does not carry as much weight as you might think."

I took the letter and carefully folded it. Beneath my studied calm, I found ugly, unwelcome thoughts welling back to the surface, *"if this were the field of battle, I could cut you in half."* I thought. Instead, I smiled thinly, "I thank you for your warning, Sir Hugh. Fortunes have indeed fluctuated for many in recent times. You should know that I assisted the Lord Advocate, Sir John Fletcher, in drafting the Act of Rescission. I understand the forgiveness of past misdemeanours at its generous heart but I also know that the path to future prosperity, for individuals and this country alike, lies with accepting one King, one law. No more Covenants, National or secret. I jalouse there will be some in these parts who will find that harder to abide by than others." It was Campbell's turn to smile thinly. I pressed my advantage. "I would be obliged, Sir Hugh, if you would pen, as Sheriff Principal, a note I can show to my fellow Commissioners, expressing your acceptance of their need to co-operate with my investigation. Sir Hugh, if you would be so kind?"

I left when I had the letter signed and sealed. I met up with Wattie, who had returned after finding us lodgings in Auldearn itself. "Good man, Wattie," I commended. "Now we must move with haste. This will be like a cavalry charge, we must strike hard today because I fear as time goes on the local lairds may combine to work against us. I will go to Inschoch Castle. I want to find out why Janet Breadheid has been so silent, while Isobel has been naming familiar demons by the dozen. Wattie, I want to understand what Isobel means when she says she shot a man with a fairy arrow. We have these confessions but no-one is commenting on whether they are true or not. Do they correspond with real events or the ravings of a mad woman? In her third confession she was moved to say *"bot the death that I am most sorrie for is the killing of William Bower in the milltone of moynes."* Go to Moyness and find out if William Bower is alive or dead. I will meet you back at our lodgings at 4 in the afternoon. And Wattie, go carefully about it, people may be afeared we are trying to implicate them."

As we mounted our horses, Wattie gave me his sunniest grin. "You ken me, maister Archie, I dinna gae aboot rubbing people up the wrang way like you do!"

CHAPTER 15: ISOBEL PRAYS

The Holy Well of St. Ninian, Foynesfield. 28th May 1657

"The sins forbidden in the first commandment, are, Atheism, in denying or not having a God; Idolatry, in having or worshipping more gods than one, or any with or instead of the true God; the not having and avouching him for God, and our God; the omission or neglect of anything due to him, required in this commandment; ignorance, forgetfulness, misapprehensions, false opinions, unworthy and wicked thoughts of him; bold and curious searching into his secrets; all profaneness, hatred of God; self-love, self-seeking, and all other inordinate and immoderate setting of our mind, will, or affections upon other things, and taking them off from him in whole or in part; vain credulity, unbelief, heresy, misbelief, distrust, despair, incorrigibleness, and insensibleness under judgments, hardness of heart, pride, presumption, carnal security, tempting of God; using unlawful means; and trusting in lawful means; carnal delights and joys; corrupt, blind, and indiscreet zeal; lukewarmness, and deadness in the things of God; estranging ourselves, and apostatizing from God; praying, or giving any religious worship, to saints, angels, or any other creatures; all compacts and consulting with the devil, and hearkening to his suggestions; making men the lords of our faith and conscience; slighting and despising God and his commands; resisting and grieving of his Spirit, discontent and impatience at his dispensations, charging him foolishly for the evils he inflicts on us; and ascribing the praise of any good we either are, have, or can do, to fortune, idols, ourselves, or any other creature."
Westminster Larger Cattechism 1648, accepted by the Kirk in Scotland.

Isobel prays, "Blessed St. Ninian, patron and protector o' this toun, grant your protection, as ye ha'e gi'ed it tae our forefathers for lang years sine by. I tak your holy water and anoint the croon o' my heid, as I tak your holy water tae the soles o' my feet and offer ye the devotion of a' my body betwixt the twa, as I beseech ye to extend your protection tae a' betwixt the twa, including this bairn, wha grows inside me. Blessed Ninian, perhaps ye ken my four bairns that are wi' ye in heaven?" Isobel looks up from the well-side where she is crouched. Her hair is hanging free, the water from the well yet wet and cool upon her forehead and feet. She smiles at her last words, the thought of her children who died young, in heaven with the saint. "D'ye ken them Ninian? I ken ye'll look after them if ye dae." The image of her children, older than they ever lived to be, yet still cherubic, being watched over by a kindly man, a saint no less, fills Isobel's heart and mind for long seconds, before her mood darkens. Her faith falters. "Help me, Ninian! Help me God! I fear sae greatly for this bairn. I yearn sae badly yet still they are a' taken awa'. Ye cannae still be punishing me for the bairn I didnae ha'e!? Please Ninian, please God I was but a lassie. I will dae anything ye command, if ye but let this bairn inside me live. Anything, Lord." Isobel falls to the ground by the well. Her eight-month pregnant body curves and writhes on the grass. "Anoint me, Lord! Anoint me, Ninian! Bless me, Lord! Bless me, Ninian! For the bairn's sake, Lord, nae mine. For the bairn's sake, Ninian. Reach oot one hand o' blessing. One finger! Please Lord, I couldna bear the loss o' another. Please blessed Ninian. I renounce a' others save you. Tak a' that I am for this one thing. I beseech ye in your name. Learn me what tae dae. Grant me your grace. Please, Ninian. Anything. I would gi'e anything. Let my bairn live."

Isobel lies still upon the ground for long minutes. The breeze whistles through the hedgerows and through the scant remains of the saint's chapel that once stood at Bognafuaran. Isobel waits for a sign. She touches her forehead and foot to check the water can still be felt. She does not want to fail for want of belief, yet she knows she hears nothing, sees nothing, feels nothing. It feels like punishment. It feels like fear. "GOD, I BELIEVE!" she yells. "Believe in me. Notice me. Love me," she whimpers. Isobel is curled in a ball now, as best her belly will allow. "Please Ninian, please God, take me to be thine."

One month later the child is stillborn.

CHAPTER 16 INSCHOCH CASTLE 27TH JUNE 1662

"In the presence of.....James Cowper in Inshoche, Johne Weir in Auldearn and a great multitude of all sortis of uther persones, witnessis to the confessione and declaration efter sett downe spokin furth of the mowth of Janet Breadheid, spows to Johne Taylor in Belmakeith. The quhilk day in presence of me Johne Innes notar publict and witnessis abow namet undersubsrivand said Janet Breadheid professing repentance for hir former sines of witchcraft and that she haid bein owerlong in the divellis service without any pressuris procedit as followes to witt..." **Janet Breadheid's confession 14th April 1662 at Inschoch Castle.**

I could not help but think that people looked up from their work with surly suspicion as I picked my horse through the middens, barns and houses of the New Wards of Inshoch. As men, women and children tended livestock, took advantage of the fine weather to weave in the light, they glanced briefly at the stranger riding by. Perhaps I was a new pricker come to drive my long steel pins into Janet in the dungeon of the castle. If they suspected I was a new inquisitor come to join the witch hunt they would little suspect that I came with an open and generous mind. How must it feel in a community when one neighbour's word might condemn another? Where a grudge could find the perfect weapon, an accusation so fantastical that it cannot be disproved.

I tethered my horse in the castle compound. Those tending the physic garden next to the castle would now see that I walked with a rapier hanging from my belt. I knew it was foolish. Did I think I might have to fight my way in or out of the castle? I knew it was an affectation that gave me comfort as I moved within this hotbed of Covenant fanatics. *I cut you to ribbons once, as you ran.* I thought. I never had thoughts like this in Edinburgh. I shuddered at the visceral violence that welled up inside me. I was repeating it too often these days. *I am a man of reason.*

The door was answered first by a porter and then by James Cowper, Chamberlain of Inshoch Castle. I asked if he could read, then showed my letter from Sir Hugh Campbell. "Of course, I can read, how dae ye think I keep note of the rents fae this lot?" he asked, waving his arm out toward the door. "An additional Commissioner tae assist? Ye best come through."

Cowper led me into a small room close by the great hall. I saw or heard few people within the castle. Whatever it once was, it felt reduced in grandeur now. I accepted a flagon of ale. My theory that these first days of the investigation might prove most fruitful, before any word of warning spread, appeared to be proving true.

"What service can I be tae ye, Mr Kellas?"

"I would like to interview Janet Breadheid. To hear what else she might have to say."

"Ahh." Cowper squirmed uneasily in his chair. "That mayn't be sae easy."

"Why not, man!"

"Mistress Breadheid died twa months past."

I had feared this. Sensed it in my gut even, when I had compared the two confessions. Why go back to Isobel four times for flights of ever greater fancy, when you had Janet naming every witch for thirty miles and for the past thirty years? My instinct then had been that for someone, Janet's silence was of more value than her further testimony.

Still, I had to hide all this from Janet's gaoler, James Cowper. I needed to distract him, divert him from my true intent.

"Saved on the hangman's fee, then" I commented gruffly, taking a swig of ale.

Cowper inclined his head, a slight smile playing on his lips, before he too took a drink from his flagon. "We still burnt her mortal remains tae ensure she couldnae be raised back."

In every other respect Cowper appeared a stolid, sensible man, proud of his literacy and his position. Yet here he was telling me they burnt the corpse to prevent satanic resurrection in the exact tones he might say we left the lid off the barrel to catch the rain.

I made myself look comfortable in my wooden chair. "Mr Cowper, as I am no longer able to speak with Mistress Breadheid in person, it would help me if you could tell me something about her. I recall also from Mr Innes' statements that you were one of those named as being at Mistress Breadheid's confession. Is that not so?"

"I was, as Chamberlain it was my duty. I brocht her up tae the Hall here."

"Did she speak freely or did she have to be coaxed to confess?"

Cowper began to show the first signs of unease at my interview. "She wasna tortured, if that's what you mean. She had little food or drink in the days leading up and they telt me tae set out a trestle wi' victuals. Tae reward her if she spake the truth, ken?"

"Clever." My mind raced to get the picture of events, without provoking Cowper's suspicion. If I failed I would have to remind him of my authority. "Who led the questioning?"

"I thocht your letter said ye were an additional Commissioner. Surely ye ha'e spoken wi' your fellow Commissioners and got a' this fae them ?"

"I am sorry Mr Cowper for not explaining better. I am new arrived from Edinburgh. I have not yet had the chance to meet my fellow Commissioners. I went first to Sir Hugh Campbell, who gave me the letter I showed you." The time seemed right to emphasise his need to co-operate. I reached into my coat breast pocket and pulled out the original letter from the Advocate Depute. "I am sent by the Privy Council and the King's Commissioner to the Scots Parliament. We are assisting in several such trials to ensure...to ensure a standard approach."

I carefully turned the Advocate Depute's letter and pushed it toward Cowper for his inspection. The seals of Mackenzie and Middleton appeared to convince him. He relaxed back in his chair.

"The twa Ministers." Cowper said. "Mister Forbes and Mister Rose. They led the questioning. Mister Forbes especially. He visited Breadheid several times before the day. Tae help her ken what tae expect and tae remind her what was at stake."

I wasn't sure if Cowper had made a little joke, using the word stake. I smiled and asked "What do you mean?"

"Her immortal soul. Mister Forbes is a very diligent Minister. Often oot visiting his parishioners. A'ways helping them seek the Godly path. He wanted Janet, Mistress Breadheid, tae see that only a full confession o' her sins would help her tae repentance. Back tae God's grace. Aye. Mister Forbes led the questioning maist o' a'"

I remembered the words written by Notary John Innes *"protesting repentance for her former sins of Witchcraft, and that she had been over long in the same service".* Thinking of the confessions of both Janet and Isobel I recalled they both expressed penitence, among the many striking similarities between them. I knew that was a puzzle I needed to solve.

"I am a lawyer, Mister Cowper. Sometimes when we have two accused, accomplices you might say, a clever thing is to play one against the other. Tell one that the other has already confessed to their involvement, so they may as well tell the truth themselves. Is this what worked with Janet, being interviewed the day after the other?"

Cowper smiled a conspiratorial grin. "T'was that way indeed, Mister Kellas. Mister Forbes and Mister Rose as well, they telt Breadheid *"Isobel has already telt us how you a' covenanted wi' the devil. How she renounced her baptism and swore tae serve the devil. Fae the croon o' her heid tae the soles o' her feet. We know this now. We ha'e your name fae Isobel. Was that how it was wi' you?"* and Janet looked all sad and uncertain and I swear she looked at the food that was to be her reward for confessing, then she says in the quietest of voices, *"yes"*. "Record that, Innes!" ordered Mister Forbes. Mind, maist the rest was a' her ain words."

"She confessed freely?"

"Aye, free enough. If ye count starving and being in fear o' your immortal soul as free. We didna torture or prick her as I ha'e already said. We were telt tae no let her ha'e much sleep in the weeks afore. Mister Forbes telt us it would mak her mair likely tae return tae God. When she was examined and she was slippin awa' fae a' the questions, Mister Forbes would be very comforting, gi'e her a sip of ale fae his ain cup and whisper tae her *"Remember what we said Janet. Remember your only true way out."* Mister Forbes had a way wi' her. Like they were old friends. I suppose he was her friend, seeing as he was trying tae save her soul."

"He was doing her and the country a great service, I can see." I lied. I now had a much clearer picture in my mind's eye of the way in which the confession was drawn from Janet. "Tell me, James, how did Janet die?"

Cowper's face clouded over, the engagement of the previous moments suddenly gone. "No by my hand, if that's whit your saying!"

"Not at all," I reassured. "Was it illness? Was it fear from her examination? Did anyone get to see her after her first examination?"

Cowper was still wary but wanted to take his chance to clear his name. "We gi'ed her enough food and water tae stay alive. No' a lot but enough. I dinna ken, it was sudden like. Mayhap a week after she spoke. I went tae gi'e her some breid and she was deid."

"Did anyone see her the day before?"

"Now, Mister Kellas, King's Commission or no, whit dae ye want tae ask that for? We're no on trial here."

I knew I was losing Cowper but I had to press this point while I could. "Mister Cowper, you are right to remind yourself of my Commission from the Privy Council. My letter from the Sheriff Principal, the Advocate Depute and His Majesty's Representative in Scotland. Do you want me to tell them that James Cowper would not answer a simple question!? Who had access to Mistress Breidheid, aside from yourself, before she died?"

Cowper thought for a few seconds. I saw his eyes flicker toward my two letters that yet lay upon the table. "Mister Forbes came back to see Janet after her confession and ...naw, nane other."

"Mister Cowper! I can assure you, men have been hanged for less. You will give me the name!"

Cowper was a burly man but he looked genuinely frightened. Instinctively, I gripped the handle of my rapier. It wasn't that he was frightened of . "No-one saw Mistress Breidheid, except Mister Forbes and the Seneschal o' this Castle."

"The Seneschal of the Castle? John Hay of Park and Lochloy?"

"No man! The Seneschal o' Inshoch is his uncle, Hugh Hay o'

Brightmoney. My maister."

My mind slipped back seventeen years, to the memories that had been stirring since I was given this commission. Hugh Hay of Brightmoney. I had seen him that bloody day. "A tall, man with jet black hair and piercing eyes?" I found myself saying.

"Aye, that would be him a few years back. The hair's white now. For love o' God, Mister Kellas, you'll no tell anyone what we talked of here today?"

"You have my word. Thank you, Mister Cowper. You have been most helpful. One last question. I would like to form some idea of who Janet Breadheid was in life. Did you know her.... before?"

Cowper's sudden agitation had eased a little but he still pushed his chair back and rose to usher me out. "Aye, I kent wha she wis. Afore. She was a comely woman. I didna ken her weel."

We were both on our feet now, only seconds remaining of my interview. "Her husband, John Taylor, did he try to see her? Or to protest?"

We were stepping toward the front door, James Cowper's arm showing me the way. "Now, Mister Kellas, he could hardly dae either o' these things. No' wi'oot risking being chairged wi' being in league."

I was walking as slowly as I could but Cowper's hand was on the great brass handle. "Mistress Breidheid, Janet, did she have any children?"

Cowper looked at me with a puzzled face, as he pulled open the castle's thick wooden door, "I believe she had four that lived. Some full grown and a babe no long born. Taylor took them tae Inverness tae bide wi' kin, when she wis apprehendit, early

March. Why? What's that tae dae wi' whether she's guilty or no'?"

As I stepped through the door, I gave James Cowper my only honest answer of the last half hour. "Nothing. Nothing at all." I said. "Thank you. Thank you again for your time and for your care of the suspect. All that you said will be only between us."

I rode away from Inshoch not thinking of the information I had gained. Hardly picturing the scene of interrogation and confinement that Cowper had allowed to grow in my mind. Instead it was pity I felt. Pity for the four children. What story could they have been told? What sense could they ever make of their mother's fate? Whatever was happening in Auldearn, these four were surely innocent.

As I helped my horse pick and weave its way through the cottages and fences of the New Wards, I glanced at the men and women, in their homes or in the fields, living their meagre lives and I knew I felt pity for Janet also. Her life quietly extinguished. Her mortal remains turned to ash with no friends or family to say any last farewells. Her final months of life, denied sleep, barely fed, kept in complete isolation with her tormented thoughts. Visited only by a persuasive Minister telling her over and over that her only hope of salvation was a confession that might save her soul.

And visited by one other. Hugh Hay of Brightmoney.

CHAPTER 17. ISOBEL SOARS

Lochloy 30th March 1649

"Ye Hielands an ye Lowlands

Oh whaur hae ye been?

They hae slain the Earl o' Moray

And lay'd him on the green.

Now wae betide thee, Huntly

And whaurfor did ye say

I hae bade ye bring him me

But forbade ye him tae slay?"

The Bonnie Earl O' Moray

Isobel soars with the faerie folk. Higher than the houses, higher than the trees. Caught in the faerie wind. Horse and Hattock awa'! The breeze in her flowing red hair, the breeze through her shift, cool on her skin. Though the winter past has been bitter, she feels warm as never before. Exhilarated, ecstatic, warm and free.

They curve with the course of rivers, racing the water to the sea. They skim over beaches and soar over hills. They swoop down , laughing, to cast elf arrows at anyone below. Some land, some miss, as fate decrees.

Red Reiver is with her. His dark eyes sparkling above his mischievous grin. He rides a bean shoot, while Isobel is astride a stalk of corn. Tossed by the air, they roar with laughter, tumbling and turning, out-doing the other with each spin, while all the time, holding the gaze of each other's shining eyes. Though they whoop in no known language, each knows the sounds mean, *I love you.*

They swoop down again. Isobel rides three times about, widdershins, the dye-works of Alexander Cummings. Knowing she has stolen the strength from the vats, until the only colour they can make is black. Cummings is paid back for the dye he sold Isobel that ran in streaks upon her cloth.

They fly on. Masters of the air. Lords of a landscape so familiar. In any house they can slake their thirst on the drink and appease their hunger on the beef. They fly on to somewhere new. A palace no less. The Earl of Moray's castle at Darnaway. They soar among the great high beams of the banqueting hall.

The host descends. Janet is there too. Oh what a feast is set before them! The winter's hardship all but forgot in a single repast. The spirits of the departed are pleased to see them. The Bonnie Earl welcomes them and he is truly such a well-favoured man, the scars carved by Huntly all vanished away. Flaming Janet Kennedy is there with her man, Jamie the Fourth. She and Isobel laugh as they compare their long red hair. *We could be sisters, you and I* laughs Janet. *We could indeed* replies Isobel, her equal at this gathering. Wherefore should they not be equal, beautiful flame-haired women both.

Everyone dances. Giddy from the swirling once again. The maidens of Forres sing and Isobel is seen and known for her grace of movement and her lithesome form. Jamie the Saxt is there also but he is a melancholy presence, grieving for his son and mother both. *Leave sad wee Jamie*, calls the Reiver *and dance again with me.*

No-one wants to leave but they must to their homes return. Horse and Hattock Go Go Go! Horse and Pellatts Ho Ho Ho! The host disperses. Isobel descends to re-enter her own home, her own marriage bed. She glides in complete silence back beside her sleeping husband. The besom that had lain in her place, falls without a sound to the floor. John places an unknowing hand upon his wife and Isobel smiles. She is in bliss.

That morning Isobel and Janet Breadheid meet on the path to a cloth waulking meet. There is the briefest second where each searches the other's eyes, before each senses the happiness, the radiance. They burst into grins and embrace. "Sister from another mother," Isobel exclaims, "you *were* there too!" "Darnaway" Janet says. "Yes, yes, yes!" Isobel confirms, spinning in a pirouette of joy, showing a lightness of movement little seen through a grim, hungry winter and a slow, still cold spring. "Such a feast!" continues Isobel, "and the dancing, the welcome, the Bonnie, bonnie Earl!"

Janet steps back, her face changing to a serious expression, as she takes in the meaning of Isobel's words. "They welcomed you? Danced with you? My host stole in after a' were gone. Oh Isobel, I ken I learned you the way but you, you hae far surpassed me! I see the empty hall, you see the banquet in full flow! I am a thief in the night, you are a honoured guest." Janet gazes at her friend. There is no jealousy in her voice. Janet reaches out her arms and embraces Isobel once more. "Sister from another mother, I love ye! I am sae happy for ye!"

When they pull apart and resume their journey, Isobel is keen to reassure her friend. "I must hae seen the Bonnie Earl because I sang that song and Jamie the Saxt maun be there because a' this talk o' his son, the King, being killed."

Janet puts her hand out to stop her friend. She is smiling.

"Dinna fash, Isobel. It's a' right. We a' ken ye hae the words and the dreams. You are our bard o' baillie. If I aided ye, then I was John the Baptiser and ye were Jesus Christ!"

"Janet! Ye canna talk like that! Someone might hear!" Isobel replies in all seriousness. They see their destination. The women gathered to waulk Bessie Hay's cloth. Their long daily grind stretches before them, a day filled with none of the riches they tasted the night before. Yet both feel joyful and revived. Just before the reach the waiting women, Isobel says softly, "Sister from another mother, I love ye too. Oh but it was such a feast!"

CHAPTER 18 : REVEREND HARRY FORBES

Auldearn 27th June 1662

> *"God doth not leave all men to perish in the estate of sin and misery, into which they fell by the breach of the first covenant, commonly called the Covenant of Works; but of his mere love and mercy delivereth his elect out of it, and bringeth them into an estate of salvation by the second covenant, commonly called the Covenant of Grace. The covenant of grace was made with Christ as the second Adam, and in him with all the elect as his seed. All that hear the gospel, and live in the visible church, are not saved; but they only who are true members of the church invisible. The members of the invisible church by Christ enjoy union and communion with him in grace and glory. The union which the elect have with Christ is the work of God's grace, whereby they are spiritually and mystically, yet really and inseparably, joined to Christ as their head and husband; which is done in their effectual calling. The imperfection of sanctification in believers ariseth from the remnants of sin abiding in every part of them, and the perpetual lustings of the flesh against the spirit; whereby they are often foiled with temptations, and fall into many sins, are hindered in all their spiritual services, and their best works are imperfect and defiled in the sight of God. True believers, by reason of the unchangeable love of God, and his decree and covenant to give them perseverance, their inseparable union with Christ, his continual intercession for them, and the*

Spirit and seed of God abiding in them, can neither totally nor finally fall away from the state of grace, but are kept by the power of God through faith unto salvation. The communion in glory with Christ, which the members of the invisible church enjoy immediately after death, is, in that their souls are then made perfect in holiness, and received into the highest heavens, where they behold the face of God in light and glory, waiting for the full redemption of their bodies, which even in death continue united to Christ, and rest in their graves as in their beds, till at the last day they be again united to their souls. Whereas the souls of the wicked are at their death cast into hell, where they remain in torments and utter darkness, and their bodies kept in their graves, as in their prisons, till the resurrection and judgment of the great day." **The Larger Westminster Cattechism 1648**

Wattie bursts into our shared lodgings shortly after the agreed hour of 4.

"I found him!" he exclaims, happily. "Willie Bower. I found him."

I look up from a table upon which I had been writing some notes, "Found him? Found him where? In the grave or in the flesh?"

"Alive and weel, maister. Alive and weel. "*Willie Bower*" quoth I "*did ye ken Isobel Gowdie?*" He was a muckle, daft-like loon, for a' he is overseer at his faither's mill. Afore he could think he grins like a wee boy and says *"I kent her weel eneuch one nicht!"* They were childhood sweethearts o' a sort. Then, just as ye jaloused, Maister Archie, Willie gets a' concerned about why I'm asking. *"She's no named me as an accomplice!?"* He cries, a' wild-eyed. I tell him no' at a'. *"Oh Dear God and Saint Michael, she's no named me in her testimony as one she has shot!?"* Noo, I'm nae siccar what tae say here, sine he's hit upon the truth. *"Whit if she has?"* quoth I. *"Then I maun surely sicken and die."* William Bower says, the fear clear wi'in his een. Having caused his upset, I feel it is ainly richt I dae my utmost tae reassure. *"William Bower! Look at yirsel, man! Mair hail and hearty I hae ne'er seen! I hae charged Cromwell's pikes, man and survived. Ye think they didna curse me, as I hacked them doon? Gang tae yer Minister for a protection prayer. Ye didna even ken she had named ye. Does that no show her words hae nae power?"* Willie looks at me, my hand on his strong shoulder. His eyes look like they want tae believe but as I leave him I hear his wail, *"But noo I ken!"*

"What can it mean, Wattie?" I ask. "In testimony, at risk of her very life, she expresses heartfelt sorrow at killing William Bower from Mill of Moynes, yet you find he is not dead. Why is she saying these things? If they are but her dreams, her fantasies, how has the Kirk Session found out and why do they care? What are we chasing here, Wattie?"

"You're a bricht man, Archie but awfy dim for a' that. Dreaming, wishing is nae sae far fae plotting and how are we supposed tae ken the difference between idle talk and real hairm? The Kirk canna hae fowk praying tae or covenanting wi' other spirits. Mind the first commandment, "Thou shalt hae no other Gods afore me." Onyway, whit did ye find oot fae Mistress Breadheid?"

"That she died for her dreams." I reply, still feeling the sorrow of her quiet disappearance. "She died before her second examination. Her gaoler says he does not know how. I found out more about how they treated them in confinement and how they questioned them. Starved and kept from sleep but not tortured, I think. Offered food and intercession for their immortal souls if they confessed. The Minister, Reverend Harry Forbes, seems very active in all this. Leading the questions, working on the women in between examinations and another man, whose name I cannot get out my head. Not the Laird of Park but his uncle and tutor, Hugh Hay. I don't know his role in this but he had access to Janet before she died." I slap the table to mark the shift from contemplation to renewed action. "Let's press on, Wattie. We can have a bite to eat, then I will call on Reverend Forbes and you seek out the husbands. Janet's man, John Taylor, may be gone with his children to Inverness but Isobel's husband, John Gilbert, he is like to be hereabouts."

• •

I knocked on the door of the manse of Auldearn at 7 in the evening. After some minutes a very elderly housekeeper answered the door. A woman in her 70s at least. I give my name and explain I seek a meeting with Reverend Forbes, if he would be so kind as to see me. The housekeeper does not even have time to seek her master before Reverend Forbes enters the hallway. At the landing of the stairs I can see the curious faces of a wife and two children.

"Mistress Cunningham, thank you. I will receive Mister Kellas." Forbes says, although I am sure I did not give my name loud enough for someone in a closed room down the corridor to hear. "If you might bring us two glasses of claret, I would be most gratified." Forbes shows me into the study he has just emerged from. He is a man in his 40s, older than me. Handsome and well proportioned, even though he wears the vestments of a Minister of the Kirk. The study has shelves of books, a desk with papers stacked and two leather padded chairs by a small table, where I take a seat.

"Mister Kellas, I will tell you I aspire to be honest with everyone, from first utterance to the last. Having you in my home makes me think of Psalm 26."

"Mister Forbes how is it…" but my question is interrupted by the housekeeper with great slowness and fragility filling each of our glasses. I tell her thanks, as does Forbes as she leaves the room. It is Forbes who speaks next.

"Psalm 26. Gather not my soul with sinners, nor my life with bloody men."

I have had more cordial greetings in my life but most galling was the knowing smirk that played on Forbes's lips. "Mister Forbes, do you claim to know me, sir?"

"Archibald Kellas. Sir Hugh has sent word of your arrival. However, it is true that we have met before."

I was genuinely non-plussed. Of all the memories I had searched, Harry Forbes had not appeared in any of them. I indicated my uncertainty, inviting Forbes to explain. "The Committee for Purging the Army 1650, before Dunbar. I had not yet a parish and conceived it my higher duty to serve the Kirk's National cause. You probably saw me as one Minister among many but I remember you, Bluidy Kellas."

I knew that Forbes was trying to unsettle me but he had stirred the wrong memories in the wrong man. "Reverend Forbes. I thank you for your permission to speak freely and your explanation of how you claim to know me. Your sanctimonious Committee did untold damage that day. Good soldiers, like myself, were driven from our Nation's army. Through the ignorance and prejudice of men like you, thousands of Scottish patriots were sent to the Americas and Indies into indentured servitude and if you truly know anything of me, you will know that I understand only too well what such servitude involved! Mister Forbes, since you say you value frankness, let us dispense with any pretence, do you know my Commission and by whose authority I am sent here?"

Forbes blinked twice, the only outward sign I had discomforted him. "Sir Hugh's messenger explained your letter from the Advocate Depute and the King's Commissioner, although the messenger could not explain to us the reason nor the necessity."

"I have been sent because there is concern that witchcraft examinations have been contaminated by torture and the dubious activity of certain notorious prickers."

Forbes suddenly rose to his feet, exclaiming, "Then Hallelujah, your work is done. Neither pricking nor torture have taken place here. You have my word on that. You may return to Edinburgh and reassure the Privy Council."

The Reverend even outstretched his arm, showing me the way to the door. I sat firmly in my seat. "Reverend Forbes, these were but examples of the malpractices that might occur. I am not leaving until *I* am satisfied and until I have sent my report to Advocate Depute MacKenzie and the Royal Commissioner." It was my turn to gesture with my arm. "Pray be seated, I have some further questions to ask of you."

Forbes slowly regained his seat. I continued "Reverend Forbes, it matters not who we were in 1650 or 1645, what matters now is that justice is done. Tell me, what do you believe to be the truth in this case?"

The Minister sat and regarded me for a few moments. "You wish the truth, Mister Kellas? Church Divine to soldier turned lawyer? You have asked me to contemplate that you, yourself, endured indentured servitude, I did not know. I am sorry for you. I do not know your career well enough to know the occasion."

"After Worcester, for seven years, in Barbados." I said and I sensed a strange, disarming sympathy in Harry Forbes' voice and demeanour.

"It cannot have been easy for you. Not easy at all. I praise the Lord you came through. I imagine some you knew did not."

I confess I was utterly disarmed by his empathy. I fought to tell myself it was a ploy but found myself saying. "I had friends who died on the plantation and when I returned to Scotland, my wife and child were dead."

Forbes leaned forward in his chair, his two hands on the table, available if I wished to take them. "I grieve for you, my son, I truly do. So much loss in those difficult years. Perhaps so hard to comprehend?"

For a second or two I thought to tell him my feelings. He was offering himself as a man who understood pain and loss. A man who cared. I forced myself to remember that God had died for me at Aberdeen many years before. "I thank you, Reverend Forbes, for your concern. Many have suffered loss, perhaps even yourself? Please return to your answer, you were about to speak to me man to man, or Minister to lawyer at least."

"Minister to old soldier. I find it hard to move beyond your previous renown. You have fought in battles, then picture, if you may, the battle I have to fight here. In Auldearn. I, who am charged with spreading the word of the Lord, amid a land where the ordinary people of the fermtouns and clachans yet cling to savage, ignorant ways. Not just the vestiges of Catholic idolatory but even older superstitions and beliefs. Faeries, familiar spirits, seers, protective charms. None of it sanctioned by the Bible. All of it fertile ground for Satan to play. I do not know what you think me, Mister Kellas but I am neither an uncaring man nor a fool. I have no more wish to see the innocent suffer than do you." Reverend Forbes fixed me unerringly with his stare. "Mister Kellas there is something deeply troubling and Satanic occurring here."

"And your evidence is?"

"Good Lord man! You have read the confessions have you not!? John Innes, our Notary is a most scrupulous man. The others who set their signatures to attest to the authenticity, myself included, my colleague Hugh Rose from Nairn, the leading men of this parish, they are all pious, honourable men. Would we perjure ourselves to convict two lowly women? From their own mouths, in their own words, they have Covenanted with the Devil, renounced their baptism and joined with Satan in most evil deeds. I have sometimes wondered about the course of my career, why God's plan for me should send me so far from the larger events of our time but perhaps it was to discover this coven and to expose its corrupt malevolence to the cleansing Light of the Lord!"

My mind reeled from the force and conviction of Forbes' words, strengthened as they were by the truth that the confessions did say exactly what he claimed and with detail, such as nicknames of familiar spirits, that surely only came from Isobel herself. I groped for a question that might test Forbes' certainty. "Mister Forbes, I am told you visited Mistress Breadheid and Mistress Gowdie several times during their imprisonment, why was that and what was the nature of your discourse?"

Forbes took a sip of his claret, his features trying to retain civility while suppressing righteous anger, "Mister Kellas it is a Minister of the Lord's ceaseless duty to be intimately acquainted with his parishioners, even more so in a lax and backward place such as this, where there is such a divide between the learned few and the ignorant multitude. God's infinite love must penetrate the darkness, through me, His poor vessel. Should I not tend to my flock in their hour of need and when they have strayed from the fold? Our Lord Jesus Christ was such a shepherd and I am His humble servant. I spoke with these women of repentance."

I had an overwhelming sense that Forbes meant all that he said and it caused in me a growing doubt that I would achieve much in this interview, "Why repentance, surely if they have done even half they are accused of these women are damned already?"

A condescending smirk played on Forbes' lips, "Oh Mister Kellas, surely you are familiar with Luke 15.7 *"I say unto you, that likewise joy shall be in heaven over one sinner that repenteth, more than over ninety and nine just persons, which need no repentance."* I cannot save them from eternal damnation but can hope that through repentance their torment may be assuaged somewhat and that by their example others may more clearly see their path out of wickedness."

Forbes put down his glass and rose to his feet, "Archibald Kellas, the hour is late and you have informed me of your Commission. I might say it is a pleasure to be re-acquainted with you but my honesty forbids it. There is no more either of us can do this night."

I did not disagree and rose to my feet also, allowing Reverend Forbes to show me to the door. For some reason, despite the many more pertinent to the case questions I could have asked, I found myself saying to Forbes, as I stepped out "One last question. The Devil presides over the fires and torments of Hell. Evil doers are sent to Hell. Why does the devil torture those who have served him faithfully? Does the Devil in fact work for God in punishing evil doers?"

"Mister Kellas, you surely do not presume to question me on theology?"

"Well, Mister Forbes, twelve years ago, as you have reminded me, you did presume to question me on my military ability to fight for my King and country. Good day to you, sir."

CHAPTER 19: ISOBEL HEALS.

Lochloy . 19th August 1659

"Quhan we would heall any sore or broken limb we say thryse over: He put the blood to blood, till up stood; The lith to lith, till all took with; Our Lady charmed her dearlie Sone; with her tooth and her tongue; And her ten fingeris in a waist; In the name of the Father, the Sone and the Halie Gaist! And this we say thrice over straiking the sore and it becomes heall. For the boneshaw or pain of the haunch, we are three Maidens charming the boneshaw: Be Man of the Middle earth, blow beaver, land fever, maneris of stoors, the Lord flegged the Fiend, with his Holy Candles and yard, foot , stone. There she sits and here she is gone! Let her never com here again.

For the fevers we say thrice ower. I forbid the quaking fever, the sea-fever, the land fever and all fevers that ever God ordained. Out of the head, out of the heart, out of the back, out of the sides, out of the knees, out of the thighs, from the points of the fingers to the nebs of the toes, out fevers go. Some to the hill, some to the stone, some to the stock. In Saint Peters name, Saint Pauls name and all the Saints of Heaven. In the name of the Father, the Sone and the Halie Gaist." **Isobel's second confession. 3rd May 1662**

Isobel heals with the intercession of the best spirit for the charm. Saint Peter, Saint Paul, Our Lady, the Father, Son and Holy Ghost. All the Saints of Heaven. They fill her hands with healing fire to glide over sores, drawing out sickness, so it can be cast into the earth or taken in dream to be passed onto the first creature seen. She is consumed when she heals, awake but all her being given to the task, the fight, the driving out.

Her husband, John Gilbert, falls while repairing thatch on the roof. His back and pelvis are hurt sore. He lies on his stomach upon his marriage bed, groaning and barely conscious. Isobel and John have been married for twelve years, many people do not get near so long. She loves him as a strong and silent man, her partner in the daily struggle to survive. She does not love him as she loved the man she met between Drumdewin and the Heads, the year before she met John but the love she has for John is fierce, proud, protective. She loves him enough to keep half her life secret from him.

"I willna lose you, John Gilbert." Isobel tells herself, as she works her hands over the knotted muscles of his back. A bowl of animal fat helps her fingers sink deeper into the sinews. Her words, at first promises, then later charms and rhythmic chants, drive her tired arms on. "No after a' we've been through and a' we still hae tae dae." John shows no sign of hearing, she would say the exact same even if he could. "I couldna gie ye bairns, John Gilbert, and for that I greet sair every day but I can dae this." Isobel holds up her greased hands, reddened from the exertion. "Was that my bargain, Lord? Ye gied me these instead o' wee ones tae my breast." Isobel feels again the choking sadness. The guilt and the regret. She moves down to her husband's calves, making a circle, a waist, of her two hands as she slides them firmly up his legs. "I will rub every inch o' ye, as I hae lo'ed every inch o' ye. I willna rest till ye are hail again." The sadness and fear well again. "It's the least I can dae for ye, husband o' mine."

"He put the blood to blood, till up stood; The lith to lith, till all took with; Our Lady charmed her dearest Son, with her tooth and her tongue; And her ten fingers in a waist; In the name of the Father, the Son and the Halie Gaist! Be Man of the Middle earth, blow beaver, land fever, manners of stoors, the Lord frightened the Fiend, with his Holy Candles and yard, foot, stone. There she sits and here she is gone! Let her never come here again. Pain be gone!"

"I feel ye dearie Oh! I feel ye loosening. You will be hail again. I canna lose you." When you love someone enough you will call on anyone to help. When you love someone enough, you want for them the best. The most effective spirit for the job. Somewhere in Isobel's knowledge of things, she knows there were spirits in this land before the churches. The faerie have told her. Red Reiver has laughed and said "and wha'd ye think I am?" The Reiver is good for mischief and flying, not for healing. The Saints are good for healing, Our Lady too. Isobel calls on Saint Bride but as Brigid, her ancient triple name. Isobel works so hard on every limb, every finger, every toe, she sees the three Maidens, the youth, the mother, the hag, the three Brigids assisting her. Thank Bride, Isobel feels John getting better. She did not want to call on the other. *"He will recover"* Brigid tells her. *"Your love and power have healed him."*

Isobel pulls off her shift and lies naked on top of John, her breasts to his back, her fundament to his buttocks. She feels his breathing and knows her breath is moving to the same time. "I would hae taken it from ye, if I'd had tae." She whispers, with love, in his ear. "But I'm glad I dinna hae tae."

Isobel heals. It is another of her powers. Isobel heals with the intercession of many spirits. It is what you do when you love.

CHAPTER 20 : AULDEARN.

Late evening Friday 27th June 1662.

"Quhan my husband sold beef, I used to put a swallow's feather in the hide of beef and say thryse: Put out this beef in the Divells name, that meikle silver and good price com hame. I did ewin so quhenevir I put furth either horse, cow, webs of cloth or any other thing and still put in this feather and said the same wordis thrice ower to caws the commodities sell weil." **Isobel's second confession 3rd May 1662**

I was in a melancholy mood when I returned to my lodgings from Reverend Forbes. I had allowed him to get under my skin and found out precious little as a result. I was refilling my claret cup when Wattie came back in.

"Cheer me up, Wattie. Tell me some good news!"

"Cheer you up, Maister Archie? I'm a faithful gillie, no' a sorcerer!" Wattie laughs and I am brought to a smile.

"Forbes claimed to be one of the Committee for Purging the Army who deemed me unworthy before Dunbar. I fear I could not think straight after that and came away little the wiser. How fare ye with Mister Gilbert?"

Wattie shrugged off his coat and with an inclination of his hand that asked, *"May I?"* took a seat and a glass of claret both. The pause was infuriating, as Wattie well knew, made worse by an elongated "Aye, weel, ye ken."

"Ye ken what? Spit it out, man!"

Wattie's smile warmed me before ever his words did. He was so much that I was not. "Ah found John Gilbert. Wasna easy and wasna easy tae get him tae talk, neither. No' surprising, his wife set tae burn, her best friend deid a'ready an' him fearing every stranger just wants tae tak him for a witch as weel. Just as weel for ye, Archie, I could talk Saint Symeon doon fae his pillar!" Wattie flashed me his smile again, as he refilled his glass. "Ah had tae tell him, we were fae Edinburgh and here tae see justice done. Which is richt enough. Ah dinna blame him for no easily trusting me. One wrang word and anyone could be taken. Ah'm beginning tae see this your way, Maister Archie. They a' seem like ordinary fowk. Trying tae gang aboot their ain business. There's something no' richt here."

I refilled my own glass and poured the last of the bottle into Wattie's cup. I could listen to his stories at the best of times but now I was desperate for the consolation of his news. Wattie could read people. I had to thole him milking my eagerness.

"He was afeared but he was sad also. Afeared for his wife. John Gilbert cares for Isobel Gowdie I can tell ye that. *"Can ye help? Can ye truly help us?"* he asked, the desperation, the disbelief, and, aye, the love, in his voice. *"Wha was she, your wife? Isobel Gowdie spouse o' John Gilbert in Lochloy, tell me wha she wis?"* He sits there his heid in his hands, then he pulls his face tae face mine, *"Ye want tae ken, ye truly want tae ken?"* It was one o' they moments when ye ken ye hold a man's life in your hands. When they ken it too and they're nae siccar whether they can trust in ye. *"Ye can trust me."* I say and I give him my smile. Weel, whit could he dae? *"Isobel thoucht I didna ken but you're no married tae a'body for fifteen year an' no ken a quine. She wis a bard o' baillie, a teller o' tales, wonderful tales. You should hae seen ma Isobel, Mister Garland, sic a wonderful teller o' tales. She... she became the story, so that the listener micht become the story too. Dae ye ken?"*

"I would hae lo'ed tae hae seen her, Mister Gilbert. Ah tell ye that true" Quoth I and ye ken, I wisna tellin' him nae lies. The Isobel he showed me wi' his words, wi' his love, I wanted tae ken. *"Her body, her body, Mister Garland, it moved wi' the wind, it moved wi' whatever she maun dae. Ah canna explain. Fowk just wanted tae watch her gang by. I lo'ed tae watch her gang by. Though she wis a bissum mair than hauf the time!"* Ye ken Maister Archie, ah'm nae siccar I could hae strung him alang wi' lies, after that. Just as weel we are on his side. *"She was a healer."* Gilbert said, *"and a quine fowk cam tae if they wanted tae ken if their man was haeing hochmagandy oot wi' their ken. She a'ways got an egg or a boll o' yarn for her troubles, so I wis pleased for it. Proud o' her. My Isobel. My wife. Fowk cam tae her for other things an a'. Revenge or tae richt a wrang. Ah wisna a' ways sae siccar."* John Gilbert's face changed as he spoke tae me. Fear. Fear mair than the fear o' arrest. *"She had these dreams, ah truly dinna ken. She thocht I didna ken but some nichts ah couldna raise her, though ah would shake her, fit tae raise the deid. She wisna just asleep, a husband kens, Mister Garland. A husband kens."* I asked him, "Dreams o' what?" but he shook his heid, *"Ah dinna ken. God's truth, ah dinna ken. She kept that place awa' fae me."* Then for the first time I saw tears in his ey'n. *"Ah didna dare tae pry. Ah hate masel. Ah didna dare tae pry. Whaur did ye gang, ma Isobel? Whaur did ye gang?"*

I knew better than to interrupt Wattie when he was telling a story and clearly, so did he. "Gilbert's face changed tae cold, steely anger. *"Ye ken wha tells ye, ye can trust him but turns oot tae be a viper in the sack? Ken wha?"* I shook ma heid, wanting him only tae gang on. *"Reverend Harry Forbes that's wha! He says he wants tae ken his flock, we a' ken whit he means by that!"* "No, I dinna ken" Quoth I. Gilbert looks at me as if I'm a gormless fool. *"Ah'm no' fae hereaboots."* I hae tae explain. *"Ah canna be the one tae tell ye. He doesna just want tae convert his flock wi' his words is a' I can say."* Gilbert turns tae pure fear from then on. Even ma coaxing canna bring him back. I leave him five groats. *"It canna be easy for ye, Mister Gilbert."* I say, kenning ah mean every word. Just as ah'm ganging oot his door he cries oot *"It wis ne'er the de'il, Mister Garland! As far as ah ken. The faeries, aye, but ne'er the de'il. That wis a' Mister Forbes, ah tell ye. He's the de'il, if ye ask me."* I went back in but Gilbert waved me awa'. *"Ah've told ye too much a'ready"* He sobbed. I put my hand on his shoulder. *"If ye want tae tell me mair, ah'm at Mrs Mcilravey's in Auldearn."* He looks up at me wi' such pain in his ey'n. *"Why canna they just leave us in peace? Why? My Isobel."*

I puffed out my cheeks as I exhaled. "You could give Isobel a race for her money as a storyteller, Wattie."

"I think that's why ah'm growing tae like her sae much." He replied, in all seriousness. Then he looked about to see if there was any more ale in the house. After Wattie came back to the table with two bottles of porter, I showed him the notebook I had been writing in.

"I'm beginning to see it, Wattie. Not all of it but some. Look here," I pushed a scribbled note under his nose, that truthfully only I could decipher. "Isobel talks about her healing, then she talks about getting fish from the fishermen in the Moray Firth and I can just see the Inquisitors seething with impatience. John Innes, the Notary, has not included their words, their questions, their inducements, their threats. *"These quaint cures are all very well, Mistress Gowdie, but tell us when you first went out with your coven to do harm?"* The whole story changes. It doesn't follow. They forced her down certain dreels. Now, if what John Gilbert told you is true, they didn't much care to hear about faeries but wanted to always hear about devils. No, not devils. The Devil. In some of this testimony. Look, Wattie, look." I said in desperation, as I pushed the papers under his nose. "Look here, she's hoping her husband sells a bit of beef for a decent price in the market, "*Quhan my husband sold beef I used to put a swallows feather in the hide of beef and say thryse, put out this beef in the divells name, that meikle silver and good price come hame.*" Christ's banes, Wattie, nobody talks like that. "*Satan, gi'e me strength,*" you might say in your darkest hour but not to get a few pennies more on a cut of beef, no matter how poor you are. I just know, they made her add those words. Isobel could be telling them anything but they are just looking for the Devil. Forbes especially."

Wattie nodded his head to show he understood, until I pushed the matter too far. "Christ knows, Forbes saw the devil in me. Bastard!"

"Let the past be, Maister Archie. We hae enough tae get on wi' here."

As so often, Wattie's wise words shook me out of my determination to wallow in the past. "You are right, the morrow we must test what we have found. I must seek out John Innes, the Notary. By reputation I believe him to be a scrupulous man. I need not ask him if he recorded Isobel's words truthfully but I can ask him about the interrogators' words he missed out. No-one speaks as he has written Isobel speaks, long, disconnected stories, without prompting to change subject. We need to see the Laird of Park too, to find out if ill-fortune has befallen his male heirs or who might have wished such. That interview must be mine but Wattie, you could take him a note I will write asking for an interview on the day after the morrow. We also need to see Isobel, apart from all else, to make sure she is still alive. We could both go to see her the day after the morrow. Tomorrow, if you could visit the house next to the Kirk gate, the light we saw the first night? Ask if they have seen any unusual gatherings in the church. Does that sound like a plan?"

Wattie shook his head in his own distinctive way, when he was talking to me. "Aye, Maister Archie. Except one thing. Ah swear ah dinna ken if ye live in this land or no'. The day after the morrow is the Sabbath. We'll no get much work done that day! Christ kens, ah dinna want tae be hauled afore Harry Forbes' Kirk session!"

CHAPTER 21: ISOBEL REMEMBERS.

Auldearn 1st July 1645

"Somtyms we wold be calling him Black John or the lyk, and he wold ken it and heir us weil aneughe and he ewin then com to us and say I ken weil aneugh what ye wer saying of me and then he would beat and buffet us werie sor, we wold be beaten if we wer absent any tym or neglect any thing that wold be appointed to be done. Alexander Elder in Earlseat wold be werie oft beaten, he is but soft and could never defend himself in the least but greet and cry quhen he wold be scourging him but Margaret Wilson in Auldearn wold defend herself fynlie and cast up her handis to keep the strokis off from her and Bessie Wilson wold speak crosslie with her tongue and wold be belling again to him stowtlie. He wold be beating and scourging us all up and down, with tardis and other sharp scourges, lyk naked ghaists and we wold be still crying Pittie, pittie, mercie, mercie owr Lord bot he wold haw neither pittie nor mercie. Whan he wold be angrie at us, he wold girne lyk a dowg as if he wold swallow us up. Somtym he wold be lyk a stirk, a bull, a deir, a rae or a dowg and haw dealing with us and he wold hold up his tail until we wold kiss his arse and at each tym quhen we wold meet with him we behoovit to ryse and beck and mak owr curtsie to him and we wold say, Ye are welcome Lord and how do ye do Lord."
Isobel's third confession 15th May 1662

Isobel remembers her father, as they lay him in his grave. She does not grieve. He was an evil man with the drink and a harsh man with the tawse on Isobel and her sisters' bare backsides. Isobel recalls a beating when she spoke to her sisters afterward, holding back the tears but determined to respond with defiant humour. "Yes father, no father, three bags fu', father!" Except he had followed her and overheard. A second six strokes were administered to punish Isobel's cheek. Still, she did not cry. He would not break her. It is one of the reasons she does not cry now, as they bury him.

Her father had been looting the dead and dying after the great battle. A Highlander caught him and ran him through with his sword. Isobel remembers saying a prayer of thanks to the Heilanman. Her father lived on in pain and fever for six weeks before succumbing. *"Ye will hae tae find a man now."* Isobel's mother tells her fifteen year old daughter. Soon after the funeral she meets a man as she walks between Drumdewin and the Heads.

Isobel sometimes remembers her father in her dreams.

CHAPTER 22 . JOHN INNES.

Nairn . Saturday 28th June 1662

"The Quhilk day in the presence of me Johne Innes, notar publict and witnessis all under-subscriwand, the said Issobell Gowdie appearing to be most penitent for hir abominable sines of witchcraft, most ingeniouslie procedit in her confession thereof in manner efterfollowing. …..He is able for us that way than any man can be.(Alas that I sould compare him to an man). Pittie, pittie, mercie , mercie….ye ar welcome owr Lord and how doe ye my Lord etc….alace I deserw not to be sitting heir, for I haw done so manie ivill deidis, especiallie killing of men etc. I deserw to be reiven wpon iron harrowes and wors if it culd be devysit…"
Excerpts of the detail written by John Innes during Isobel's third confession 15th May 1662

I found John Innes at his notary office in Nairn. I am happy to relate that he displayed little of the hostility and suspicion I had encountered in my interviews with Sir Hugh or Reverend Forbes. I conceive this to be, in part, due to John Innes being proud of his work in this case and his conviction that he had recorded faithfully the words of Isobel and Janet. By the end of my hour with Mr Innes I shared his conclusion. I do not believe the fantastical claims of either women were invented or even significantly altered by an honest lawyer, such as I found Mr Innes to be.

It helped that Mr Innes knew of some of my recent work from notary circles. It was a pleasure to me to be spoken to as the man I aspired to be and not as Bluidy Kellas from over a decade ago. I had worn my rapier to the meeting but found myself, ceremoniously, unbuckling it and setting it aside, as I relaxed into John Innes' company. "*A habit from an older time*" I explained, as I set the sword down. "*Indeed*" Innes observed, in such a way that conveyed that he both knew something of my reputation and had no need of discussing it further. Thus disarmed, my approach was flattery, or perhaps, more accurately, honest admiration and inquiry.

"John, over and above my Commission to report on these proceedings, I confess I was both appalled and ….enthralled by the account you produced within the testimonies. The pictures painted were so vivid, full of life and even mischief. How did that come to be?"

"Thank you, Mister Kellas, Archie, I fully understand your observation. Appalling and enthralling at the same time, an apt summary. I strove to keep up with the torrent of images and words." Innes gave a short laugh. "Hah! Mayhap you saw my "*etc*" when my hand could not keep pace?"

"Yet you managed to capture so much"

"I believe so. It was my duty after all. Mistress Breadheid was much more studied in her responses but Mistress Gowdie, Isobel, when she took flight, so to speak, I tell you, she soared. I did ask Reverend Forbes and he explained she was considered a bard of sorts, a singer of ballads and ancient lore by the firesides of the fermtouns. Tales that fill the dark winter nights within their lowly homes."

I had a flash of momentary memory, just such a performance in my family home in the Cabrach. Though it was the life into which I was born, my mind conceived it a dark and smothering world, from which I longed only to escape. "She was permitted within the interrogation to perform?" I asked.

"Yes there were times when she found the strength not only to regale us but also to leap and dance almost, whilst giving her confession."

"Extraordinary. I have been captured twice, my life in others' hands. I do not recall much leaping about. Why do you think she was like that?"

Innes sat back and stroked his chin. "Truly you ask such interesting questions. I have been fearful to speak to any other as I find myself speaking with you. For fear of seeming too taken with a witch's words. What I am trying to tell you is, it was not the words that enraptured me, it was the woman herself. Her movements, her glances, her knowing laugh, as if she believed she knew more than we. Her betters. If I had to inquire into her motivation, I would hazard three things. Repentance, a genuine earnest desire to return in some small measure to God's Grace. Reverend Forbes worked tirelessly to bring her to that path and to keep her upon it. Reward. The more she spoke, the more she kept to the subject matter of her charges, the more food, drink and promises of small comforts she was given. The promise of the opposite, if not. And finally, I would say animal pride, primitive hubris. She was a bard in front of the most elevated audience of her life."

"I did wonder when I read your words *"ingeniously proceeded"*. Thank you. Now I can picture so much more clearly., Were they her own words or were some suggested for her?"

"Mister Kellas! I thought you understood the character of the man before you! And of all the good men of this county. They attested that these were her words. I did not record such vows lightly, nor were they lightly given."

"I am sorry, John, if that is what you took my question to mean. What I intended to ask is this. Your recording reads as a single narrative from the mouth of the accused but it cannot have been so. There must have been questions that prompted answers. Answers that the interrogators were less interested in and therefore discouraged and answers that they pushed the accused to develop further. I crave your help, John. I have been tasked to join this inquest. I did not seek the Commission. I do but seek to understand the testimony my fellow Commissioners have already gathered."

John Innes relaxed a little, recovering his previous sympathy. "Archie, you are trained to the law. The questions asked were those any prosecutor would ask to establish the case. The law is most concerned with those who make a pact with the Devil. Who renounce their baptism. Who call on the Devil to help them perform maleficum I would say these questions were pursued and the other answers, the charms recounted, the names of the familiar spirits, these were indulged but were known to add little to the establishment of guilt. There was interest also in crimes against the Reverend and the Laird. I could see the anxiety in Reverend Forbes' face when he heard of the many efforts to harm him. He had long suspected but now he was hearing actual proof. It cannot have been easy for him. I conceived it my principal duty to record the words of the accused, not of the accusers. If you wish to picture the questions that I did not write down, then think on the subjects I have just expounded."

"Again, thank you. I begin to see. All four of Isobel's confessions start with an account of her first pact with the devil. Did she recount this anew every time?"

"No. She was questioned precisely to explain it the first time and thereafter it was read to her that she previously agreed these facts and she assented. Similarly, what Isobel had described was read to Janet and she was asked if she agreed. Some things she did and some she did not. Some of the new detail given by Janet was then put to Isobel and she assented or otherwise to what she heard." Innes looked up to make sure I could see his eyes. "But you must understand, although I have honestly explained the questioning, I equally honestly tell you that these two women freely gave their own answers to the questions and even gave answers to questions that were not asked. My mind has not the words to make up the descriptions they gave!"

I had only one question left in my mind. "Do you believe them guilty, John?"

Innes again made sure I was studying his face as he answered. "With all my heart I do. Although I admired Isobel's rustic storytelling and her sense of mischief, her accounts of desired harm and demonic compact were utterly appalling. Such evil cannot be permitted to reside within our midst. It must be rooted out! Do you not agree?"

John Innes deserved my honest reply. "John, pray permit me to delay an answer. I have not yet gathered all I need to pursue. You have, truly, been a great help to my understanding of events. I hope we may meet in our mutual line of work at some future date."

Innes concurred. Just as I was rising to leave, I asked. "Why was Janet interviewed but once? Was there a plan to return to her before some mishap prevented such?"

"Indeed so. I was appointed to record her second interview shortly after Isobel's second. I believed we would continue to build on the mutual detail each gave but she sickened suddenly and died. I know they were not tortured, you have my word on that but I concede they were not well provisioned in their captivity, perhaps that had an ill-effect on Mistress Breadheid's health. She was not long delivered of a child, that may have caused her to weaken also. However I urge you not to lament. She was guilty also."

I left John Innes' offices in a deeply thoughtful mood. I could now picture the interviews that had produced the testimonies I had read. The similarities between the first two confessions, only one day apart, were no longer the work of mystery but largely a reading across from one confession to the other. The questions not on the paper suddenly leapt into my head. No doubt both women were cajoled and coaxed to talk of the Devil but even great deprivation and pressure could not explain the personal detail in the answers they gave. I knew in my heart that I had wanted Isobel and Janet to be innocent so that I could ride to their rescue. The more I learnt, I wondered if John Innes' explanation may be correct. They were both guilty as charged.

CHAPTER 23 ISOBEL WEAVES

Lochloy 3rd May 1660

"If it wasna for the weavers what would ye dae
Ye wadna hae a cloth that's made o' woo'
Ye wadna hae a plaid o' black an' blue
If it wasna for the wark o' the weavers" **The wark o' the weavers**

Isobel weaves. The warp of the wool thread pulled through the weft. The deft return of the wooden shuttle, her hands a practiced blur. This hour she weaves while the light is still good. Another hour she may card fleece, churn butter, milk the kine, collect kelp, cut peat, hunt for cockles, weed the herb patch, knead the dough, sew repairs, wash at the burn, tend the fire, feed the chooks, collect their eggs, waulk the cloth, dye the lint, suckle a bairn. Only this last labour has been denied to Isobel. In her heart she has accepted the bargain she struck all these years ago when she took Janet's pennyroyal and redcap and exchanged her unborn child for her first wonderful dream. It was fitting she had dreamed that day of Elphane. The faerie took her unborn child and left in his place the power Isobel now has to return often to their realm, to fly with their host, to feel herself wild in their abandon. Although she grieves sorely for every successive child surrendered, she welcomes the wisdom and power she receives in return. In this world she is changed also. Neighbours come to her with their ails and their fears. Neighbours sometimes look upon her with fear.

Perhaps as great as the dreams is the dance and the song. Perhaps it is all the same power. To soar above the relentless drudgery, the endless hunger and frequent cold. To feel her body inhabited by the ballad. To leap, writhe, contort, smile, cry and yearn as the song demands People love her for it, seek her out, notice her and speak of her as she passes by. The folk of the fermtouns for miles around will talk of her when she is gone.

Isobel passes the warp under the weft without a thought for her hands. They know where to go, when to turn. Her mind is on another thread, one that stretches from Elsbet Nishie to Janet Breadheid to Isobel Gowdie and now Isobel nurtures her ain maiden, beautiful Jeanie Martin. Isobel wonders how far back that thread winds back into years lang syne. She had been told of Agnes Grant and Catherine Souter. None would have invented the wisdom from only the breeze. Isobel was sure the thread went back and back. She smiled as the thread pulled through, back before the churches. They think they know it all but they do not. They hardly even see us and understand us even less. If lecherous old goat Harry Forbes knew what Margaret Brodie and Isobel did with his clay image, it would wipe the smug smile off his face on a Sunday.

Isobel weaves. She thinks of Harry Forbes and her thread snags.

CHAPTER 24: AULDEARN. SATURDAY NIGHT.

28th June 1662.

"Among other things I am desiring this day to lay to hart the prevailing of the Devil by witchcraft. Oh! that's a sad token of displeasure, quhen Thou permits him to deceav, tempt and to prosper and that his visibl kingdom taks issue expressli As if thou hadst given up that place where I had my residenc and the inhabitants of it, to be the Devil's propertie and possession, what comfort can I hav in it? Shall I not bemoan Satan's success, the spreading of sin, the destroying of so mani immortal souls? And even in that place quhair I live. What does this say to me? Oh teach! Teach for Thy name's sak! Discover in the meantym mor, and destroy as Thou discovers Satan's works. Let the land be purged and not given over, for Thy nam." **Diary of Alexander Brodie of Brodie, Nairnshire Laird, neighbour and friend of Laird of Park, June 1662**

"I hae your appointment wi' the Laird o' Park on Monday" Wattie explains "but no' until fower in the afternoon, so I took a daunder doon tae the Tollbooth an' hae us baith an appointment tae see Isobel Gowdie hirsel at the back o' ten"

"Good man, Wattie. I'm glad I saved your life at Worcester, for you are the truest blessing tae mine"

"An' there's me thinking it wis me that saved yours" Wattie smiles. "Mind there wis a lot ganging on that day. Dinna thank me too soon, Archie, there's mair tae ma day than filling yer appointment book!"

We were eating our evening meal at our lodgings, a simple repast of bread, cheese, a few cuts of pork, all washed down with ale. Wattie had wanted to explore the local tavern but I had preferred to stay in our rooms, so I could talk through the day's discoveries. I wanted peace to piece together.

Wattie tells me what more he has to say. "Ah went up tae the kirk as ye spearit me tae. Hector Bowie has the house abune the kirk gate, the yin we saw thon nicht. We were chewin the fat, Hector an' me, aboot the weather and the times and he wis sore impressed wi' a' the high an' michty people I hae met. *"Nae yon turncoat Middleton, ye ken him!? An' Archbishop Sharp, another wha changed his tune as soon as advancement came knocking. Ye hae guy queer freends, Mister Garland."* Quoth Mister Bowie. *"An' ye are michtily well informed!"* Quoth I. *"Well, I coulnae bide nixt tae a kirk and no ken the ins and oots."* Quoth Bowie." Wattie beamed his most pleased with himself smile. *"Exactly whit I maun spearit ye aboot."* Quoth I. *"Hae ye seen any strange meetings in the kirk, mayhap of an evening or late at nicht? Ony fowk that gang there often, no' countin the Minister?"* We were staundin at Hector's doorway and damn me but just as I asked, twa fowk came oot the kirk. A strappin' muckle negro and a bonny slip o' a lass. *"Well, talk o' the de'il, "* quoth Bowie *"there's they twa for a start an' their maister, Hugh Hay o' Brightmoney, the kirk beadle. The negro is cried John, a dinna ken his surname, if he has yin, and Jean Martin is the bonny lass . They baith work for Hay o' Brightmoney."* Now, I decide tae press ma luck and ask," *Are there times when there's meetings o' aboot thirteen fowk, mostly women wi' yin or twa men?"* *"No, I dinna ken aboot thirteen, no' that I've seen."* An' that wis aboot that wi' Mister Bowie"

"Wattie, indulge me for a minute. Let me tell you what I found in Nairn. Coming back after meeting with John Innes I saw women coming back from the shore with great baskets of kelp and others with baskets of cockles and mussels on their backs. Nearer the village I saw men and women with baskets of peats, hard at work in the fields. Poor, hard working folk. This is what I can't understand. The women in their confessions say the Devil has been coming to Auldearn for years, at least fifteen according to Isobel and even more years before that if Janet was recruited by her husband and mother-in-law. The Devil, Wattie, Satan himself. Isobel names other spirits, her own Red Reiver included, so she knows the difference between spirits, the faerie king and queen and the Devil. The Devil consorts with these people for years and none of them are any the richer. The women name two people the devil wants to harm, Harry Forbes and the Laird of Park and both are alive and well. The Devil, Wattie, who can take any form he wants, helps his followers enter homes, teaches his followers how to turn into hares or crows and, as far as I can see, the only thing either the Devil or the women have got out of all this is pleasurable carnal copulation." I looked at Wattie with genuine consternation written across my face. "Wattie, in these years, a King has been murdered, Puritans have seemed set to rule for 100 years, yet managed only ten, the same so in Scotland where Covenanters believed the Lord had made Scotland his own chosen country, yet now the Bishops are restored. Great national events, yet the Devil comes every quarter day and many others besides to have carnal copulation with cottars' wives in Auldearn." I jabbed my knife with a chunk of pork impaled upon it toward Wattie. "What can it all mean?"

"The cottar's wives in Auldearn are awfy bonny?"

I replied to Wattie with an exasperated shake of my head, although I did not discount his words entirely. John Innes had imbued his description of Isobel with a primitive allure. I pressed on to more fully explain my dilemma. "John Innes was helpful to me, pleasant even. I judged him to be an honest man and not stupid. He swore that neither Janet nor Isobel were tortured and that his records were a truthful account of their words ……and he thought they were guilty of compacting with the Devil. It does not make sense. Janet has already died, perhaps through maltreatment or even murder. Isobel is set to be strangled and burnt. Sensible, proud people, who judge themselves pious in the conduct of their lives, view this as a most heinous matter, one for which they are prepared to condemn and kill, yet to me it is incomprehensible nonsense. Help me, Wattie, why did the women say what everyone says they said?"

Wattie had a talent for sympathy when he knew someone was in difficulty. He scraped his hunk of cheese off his knife but kept his knife in hand to emphasise his point. He pursed his lips for a few seconds and tapped his knife to show he was giving my question full attention. "The women werna tortured, they're no mad and they're no' sae dumb as tae no' ken their words will see them burnt." I nodded in agreement. Wattie shifted his knife to his other hand. "The fowk investigating are otherwise learned and maistly honourable men. They havna just invented a'thing Innes wrote doon." I nodded my head again. "An' you are no keen tae just put a'thing doon tae the Devil being a useless but randy old bugger!" I rolled my eyes but nodded again. Wattie tapped his knife lightly on his plate to signify concluding thought. "Perhaps the women told something that felt true tae them and the investigators twisted it just a peerie bit tae something closer tae what they wanted tae find."

I had been about to take a sip from my cup but I placed it down. "Christ's bones, Wattie, I think that might be it! No-one's completely lying, they're just describing slightly different things. Sometimes I ken why I keep ye on! I think we know fine what Forbes and the Lairds want to find. They want to twist everything to a pact with the Devil. Innes told me as much and

Forbes did too, in his own way. Now we've got to work out what it was the women thought they were saying."

Wattie refilled his cup because he knew he had earned it. "If they are ha'eing carnal copulation, wha are they ha'eing carnal copulation wi'!"

CHAPTER 25: ISOBEL AWAKENS

Lochloy 15th May 1660

"And within a few days he came to me, in the New Wards of Inshoch, and there had carnal copulation with me. He was a very meikle black, roch man. He will lye all heavy upon us, quhan he does carnal dealing with us, like a malt sack. His member is exceeding great and long; no man's member is so long and big as his is. He would be amongst us like a stud-horse amongst mares. He would lie with us in presence of all the multitude; neither had we nor he any kind of shame; but especially he has no shame with him at all. He would lie and have carnal dealing with all, at every time, as he pleased. He would haw carnal dealing with us in the shape of a dear or any other shape that he would be in. We would never refuse him. He would come to my house-top in the shape of a crow, or like a dear, or in any other shape, now and then. I would ken his voice, at the first hearing of it, and would go furth to him and haw carnal copulation with him. The youngest and lustiest women will haw very great pleasure in their carnal copulation with him, yea much mor than with their ain husbands; and still will haw a exceeding great desire of it with him, as much as he can haw to them, and more; and never think shame of it. He is abler for us that way than any man can be.

Alas that I should compare him to a man!" **Isobel's third confession . 15th May 1662**

"**N**o shame, lass, we baith ken there's nae shame in it. Come!"

Isobel advances, she is entranced by the dark eyes and the devilish smile. There is no other word for it. The devilish smile. The smile and the eyes of one who is licking his lips at the thought of her woman's body. Who is anticipating the glory of undressing her, caressing her, possessing her.

"Tak off your shift. Let me look on you, for ye ken ye are the maist beautiful o' a' women tae me."

Isobel reaches for her hem and pulls her shift up and over her body.

"I love e'en that. The sight o' your arms o'er your heid, your oxters exposed, your sinews stretched."

He steps forward and lifting her arm inhales deeply from the pit of her oxter, then licks hungrily across her breast. He steps back and pulls down his own breeks. It is no longer just his dark eyes and devilish smile showing appreciation, his member rises in adulation. In desire. He is huge pressed against her. He is huge inside her.

They shapeshift and take so many forms. He is a great bear on top of her, an eager dog from behind. She mounts and rides him as if he were a stallion, sometimes grinding blissfully, other times bouncing as if they are galloping wild. They kiss and coo like two turtle doves, they tumble in playful embrace like two fierce wee kittens. When they each reach their moment they roar from the depth of their throat and chest, like two rutting beasts. When he is spent, he lies on her heavy like a great sack of malt.

"Come on, lass, ye maun be getting hame. Nae shame, mind. Nae shame."

"Nae shame." Isobel whispers.

Isobel awakens, moist and pulsing between her legs. Her husband lies in bed beside her. Asleep, oblivious, irrelevant, to her bliss.

CHAPTER 26 : AULDEARN KIRK.

Sunday 29th June 1662

"Unto thee, O Lord, do I lift up my soul

O my God, I trust in thee: let me not be ashamed, let not mine enemies triumph over me.

Yea, let none that wait on thee be ashamed: let them be ashamed who transgress without cause.

Shew me thy ways, O Lord; teach me thy paths.

Lead me in thy truth and teach me: for thou art the God of my salvation; on thee do I wait all the day.

Remember, O Lord, thy tender mercies and thy loving kindnesses; for they have been ever of old.

Look upon mine affliction and my pain; and forgive all my sins.

The paths of the Lord are mercy and truth unto such as keep his Covenant and his Testimonies.

For thy name's sake, O Lord, pardon mine iniquity; for it is great.

What man is he that feareth the Lord? him shall he teach in the way that he shall choose.

His soul shall dwell at ease; and his seed shall inherit the earth.

The secret of the Lord is with them that fear him; and he will shew them his Covenant.

Consider mine enemies; for they are many; and they hate me with cruel hatred.

O keep my soul, and deliver me: let me not be ashamed; for I put my trust in thee.

Let integrity and uprightness preserve me; for I wait on thee.

Redeem Israel, O God, out of all his troubles" **Psalm 25**

"Margaret Kyllie is one of the other coven. Meslie Hirdall who's married to Alexander Ross in Loanhead is one of them. She has a fiery complexion. Isobel Nichol from Lochloy is one of my coven. Alexander Elder from Earlseat and Janet Finlay his wife are in my coven. Margaret Hasbein from Moyness is one. So are Margaret Brodie, Bessie and Margaret Wilson from Aulderne and Jean Marten and John Mathew's wife, Elspeth Nishie. They all belong to my coven. The Jean Marten I mentioned is Maiden of our coven and John Young from Mebestown is its Officer. One time, Elspet Chisolm and Isobel More from Aulderne, Margaret Brodie and I got into Alexander Cumming's dye-house in Aulderne. I got in in the shape of a jackdaw and Elspet Chisolm was in the shape of a cat. Isobel More was a hare, and Maggie Brodie a cat, We took a thread of each colour of yarn in Alexander Cumming's dying vats and tied three knots on each strand in the Devil's name, and stirred them about in the vat, widdershins. That way we completely took away the strength from the dyes and made sure they would only dye black, the colour of the Devil in whose name we stole the strength of the right colours that were in the vats." **Isobel's first confession 13th April 1662.**

As someone who had read and re-read the five confessions over the previous ten days, I was more than intrigued to take my place in Auldearn Kirk on a sabbath, surrounded by so many of the principal characters, so vividly described by Isobel and Janet. I was exhilarated. Facing us all was Reverend Harry Forbes, chief instigator, interrogator and cajoler within the investigation. He had greeted the surprise entry of Wattie and myself, with only a momentary look of discomfort. His practiced composure had quickly reasserted itself.

All around us, arrayed in their social stratification of educated Laird, middling trades people and impoverished tenantry was the whole citizenry of Auldearn. I sensed the brooding tension of a community in the midst of a period of mutual suspicion and recrimination. Within this one building, standing together in communal worship, were people with relatives accused of witchcraft. There were others who had been named as fellow coven members within these confessions and others still who had been named as victims of the coven's activities and in the leading positions within the kirk, were the Lairds and the minister, who held Isobel's fate in their hands. They could move on to arrest the others named by Isobel and Janet. The Lairds and Minister who had already allowed or caused, a local woman to die in their care.

I whispered to Wattie, "*I wish we had been here a day or two longer, then we may have known who everyone was.*" "*Aye, if I had been here a day or two earlier, yourself, Maister Archie, I would say one or twa months!*" Wattie replied.

Still, we could piece together and speculate. "Thon's the Laird o' Park." Wattie said, nodding toward the front pews. "An' behind us, thon's John Gilbert, Isobel's man."

I thought how brave John Gilbert must be, to come into this place, in these circumstances, to face the man who was accusing his wife and who could easily move on to accuse him. Perhaps that was why he was here. John Taylor, Janet's husband had fled to Inverness. John Gilbert was declaring he had nothing to hide, before the eyes of his community and the eyes of God. How many in the small crowded kirk wondered how John Gilbert could possibly have lived alongside Isobel Gowdie and not known, or shared, in her activities?

I recognised with a shudder a tall white haired man in a long puritan coat, Hugh Hay of Brightmoney, the Laird of Park's uncle. I recognised also the even taller man, the negro manservant, who stood by his master. The last time I had set eyes on these men, they were reluctantly surrendering Lawer's Campbells to be slaughtered by MacColla's McDonnels. I was hardly blameless, I had not participated but I had known what was going to happen, as I turned my back and rode away.

Wattie nudged me and directed me through whisper, to look upon a pretty young woman behind us. "That's Jean Martin, house maid tae Brightmoney." *And also Maiden of the Coven, if Isobel is telling the truth,* I thought.

Good Lord, I thought, *there are women in this very building who have had carnal copulation with the Lord of Darkness, Satan, himself!* I suddenly felt light-headed, the same feeling I got when I recalled my own dark and primitive childhood in the Cabrach. Panic at the clawing grip of constricting superstition. *If Isobel is to be believed, there are people standing just behind me, who have travelled around this village in the form of a cat or a hare.* I thought. The atmosphere was too oppressive to allow me to laugh, instead it made me feel sick. *If Willie Bower's good health is taken as an example, there may well be people in this building whom Isobel alleges to have killed with elf arrows. Others fired such arrows too. The victims may even be standing next to the very people Isobel says killed them!*

Given our uncertain status in the community and my humble origins, Wattie and I had taken seats among the middling people. The man next to us had introduced himself as

Alexander Cumming and I recognised his name as the man who had his dye works broken into and all his dyes turned to black. Perhaps standing not far from him were Elspet Chisholm, Margaret Brodie and Isobel More, who were alleged to have helped Isobel Gowdie do the deed. As I glanced behind me, I fancied I saw a timid looking man and I wondered if he might be Alexander Elder from Earlseat and the large woman next him, his wife Janet Finlay. *"Mercie, mercie, pittie, pittie!"* I thought, as I remembered the description of the soft man who would greet and cry after being beaten, whereas Margaret and Bessie Wilson, from Auldearn, would stoutly and with crude language defend themselves. Were Margaret and Bessie somewhere in the crowded kirk? Was "my Bessie" somewhere in the building, though it had been dark and seventeen years before?

Was there ever such a congregation as this?

It was, truly, the most extraordinary kirk gathering imaginable. Victims of witchcraft, relatives of witches, alleged witches and prosecutors of witches all gathered under the one roof to worship God and even more extraordinarily, despite all the simmering tension of a community consumed within a witch-hunt, the darkest looks and most audible muttered comments came from the Lairds, directed at the presence of Wattie and me. Reverend Forbes decided to address our visit.

"Dearly beloved, we have an unexpected guest attending our Holy service today. Pray stand to be recognised, Archibald Kellas," I rose uncertainly to my feet, "sent from Edinburgh, no less, to assist in our commission to root out from our community the sin of compacting with the Devil." I was about to resume my seat, when Forbes extended his arm to make even more pointed reference to me, "Of course, this is not Mister Kellas's first visit to Auldearn. He was here with Montrose and MacColla's papist Irish, when so many of our homes were destroyed and our loved ones killed!"

I stood exposed as Harry Forbes had planned. The murmuring grew more general and I found myself having to half-turn to look around to better gauge the threat. A sudden violent thought erupted in mind and I saw myself with my two dragoon pistols loaded, responding to Reverend Forbes *"Aye, an' now I've come tae finish the job!"*

Fortunately, my rational self asserted its control. "Reverend Forbes, I thank ye for asking me to stand and be known to the good people gathered here. We live in a nation with one King and one law and I represent that law. I would say I did the same when I was here, seventeen years ago. But surely this is a house of Our Saviour Lord Jesus Christ and the better path for all of us, in Scotland now, is forgiveness. Whatever our allegiances in the unhappy civil strife, now thankfully peacefully resolved." My arms were outstretched, my palms open in a placatory gesture. I now motioned for Wattie to join me in standing. " We are here to report on the allegations of witchcraft and to ensure all is investigated correctly, within the law. If any of you good people have any information on this matter, my companion, Walter Garland and I can be found at Mistress McIlreavey's lodging house."

"Well done." Wattie said under his breath, as we resumed our seats, the murmuring subsided and as I sat, I fancied I caught the eye of John, Hay of Brightmoney's negro. Was he responding to my request for those with information to come forward? I had little time to dwell on the matter, as the service, proper, began. I will say this for Reverend Harry Forbes, whatever reaction he had to my defence of my character, he did not let it show. This was his church, his parish, his stage and he intended to dominate it, as all good Ministers should.

After we sang Psalm 25, Forbes ascended the pulpit to deliver his sermon. "My brethren, let us consider the words we have just sung in praise of the Lord. "O my God, I trust in thee: let me not be ashamed, let not mine enemies triumph over me. The paths of the Lord are mercy and truth unto such as keep his Covenant and his Testimonies. Consider mine enemies; for they are many; and they hate me with cruel hatred. The secret of the Lord is with them that fear him; and he will shew them his Covenant."

"This is not the sermon I had planned to preach today, the words I speak now are the words our current plight demands and I pray the Lord guides me in what I choose to say unto you. I wish to speak to you about Covenants. The Covenant made by God with man. The Covenants men and women make with God and the Covenants some misguided people make with the Devil.

Let us consider firstly the most perfect Covenant, that of God with men. The Lord made the most perfect world for Adam and Eve, a place of rest and plenty. The Garden of Eden. This was God's Covenant of Works. Were it not for Eve's surrender to temptation, mankind would be in Eden still but Satan whispered in Eve's ear and for the many generations since, mankind has wandered from God's path. Mired in sin and destined for damnation. The Lord our God is a kindly father. He could not leave His creation in such a state of hopelessness. He sent His son, Lord Jesus Christ, to show us the way back to God's Grace. The Covenant of Grace. Our Lord Jesus permitted himself to suffer and die on the cross, as a man. Making the fullest sacrifice of his Divine self to save the souls of pitiful men and women like you and me. Think on it! The Lord Jesus Christ made this sacrifice of love for you and me! For Love of you and me."

Reverend Harry Forbes was speaking with intensity and passion. He then did something I had not seen within a service before, he descended from his pulpit, to talk with even greater intimacy with his congregation. "My dearest Brethren, let me now consider the Covenants that men and women have made with God. After God has offered us such a perfect Covenant, how can our personal Covenants with God offer anything less in return? We must offer ourselves to the Lord with all that we have, body and soul. For it is a *personal* Covenant, such was the great discovery of the Reformed Church. Men do not need the intercession of priests, bishops, archbishops or Popes. Their elevation is nothing but a form of false idolatry. We people of Scotland saw this truth clearly in 1638, when men and women in vast numbers signed the National Covenant to defend our Faith from the corruption of bishops and other papist notions. When this Covenant was sworn it was not simply a bond between men, it was a bond sworn by each individual with God. Our Psalm told us to *"be not ashamed"* in the face of our enemies. Each and everyone of us must "be not ashamed" even in this time of darkness, when the twin threats of episcopacy and Devil worship threaten our Kirk and our land." As Forbes was walking up and down the narrow aisle within the crowded kirk, his appeal to "each and everyone of us" was intimately personal. He stopped next to Wattie and myself, when he said "Mister Kellas's two masters, the Marquis of Montrose and the Earl of Middleton both signed that Covenant. No-one compelled them. They swore an oath to God then broke it. They may have dreamt of worldly glory and gain but in breaking their Covenant with God, they perjured their very souls. Our travails here on earth are but fleeting, our days in the afterlife without number. Which of you would wish to risk perjuring your very soul?" Forbes reinforced his personal appeal through waiting long seconds for an answer. Many felt compelled to call out "No!" and "Never!" Wattie and I sat tight-lipped. Forbes walked slowly and deliberately back toward his pulpit, ascending the steps like a friend reluctant to leave.

"Let me address another aspect of what a Covenant between

man and God must endure. The Psalm tells us there will be times when our enemies appear to triumph over us, when their hatred of us is hard to endure. Our Covenants must be strong enough to survive both times of Glory and times of distress. I was privileged, two years back, to attend the final service conducted by the great martyr, the Reverend James Guthrie of Stirling. Reverend Guthrie knew the forces of iniquity were gathering to plan his arrest. He did not flee. He attended his kirk and ministered to his flock, as any good shepherd would. He was not ashamed! My brethren, heed me! This is the courage we must soon display ourselves. Reverend Guthrie took as the subject of his last sermon, Matthew Chapter 14, verses 22 to 24. The Lord fed the multitude with but a small number of loaves and fishes. A miracle that sent everyone who witnessed it homeward, rejoicing. Then the Lord bade his disciples board a fishing craft and sail upon the lake. Their craft was beset by a great tempest. A storm so great, even the most experienced fisherman feared he must surely die. Then the Lord calmed the tempest. Why did he send it at all? I tell you, dearly beloved, my eyes were opened when Reverend Guthrie spoke. The Lord sends tempests to test us. We do not Covenant with the Lord expecting to dictate the terms. Expecting that we can instruct the Lord to ensure we suffer no ill. No, my friends, man does not tell the Lord what rewards he expects, man beseeches the Lord to grant him favour, to acknowledge his faithfulness, to let him know that the Lord has included him within his elect. The Lord decides. The Lord chooses his own. If the Lord sends us tempests or times when our enemies appear to triumph it is but a test of our devotion. At such times a true believer must not abandon his Covenant with God, he must strengthen it, re-double it. Proclaim it to the very heavens. Be not ashamed of it! I proclaim it to the very heavens! Whatever the forces of iniquity demand of me, I, Harry Forbes, will be not ashamed!"

I was not sure if the crowd behind me understood every

word Forbes uttered but they understood the intensity of his personal oath. They understood the emotion. To my surprise, I found that Forbes' appeal to an intimate, personal relationship with God quite unsettling, as it challenged the hierarchy of King and bishop that I had spent so many years serving. Forbes continued his description of a personal relationship with God and he reinforced the intimacy by descending his pulpit once again. "Understand, my brethren, the perfect covenant of God with man and the perfect devotion to God we, all, must aspire to in return. The Lord Jesus Christ is the most perfect husband, the Bridegroom of Souls. His concern for all who compact with Him is constant, as is His compassion, as is His Love." Forbes was now among the throng and looked particularly at a group of women, which included Jean Martin. "Imagine a husband who knows your every grief and ailment. Who listens to your heartfelt concern. Who listens with the most perfect love and compassion. Who whispers to you softly, that all your answers can be found through trusting in his Love. Is it not glorious!? Is it not miraculous!? That the King of Heaven should offer Himself as such a companion to people such as us? What should we not do for such a Lord? We, all, can do no other than offer him all that we are. Body and Soul."

Forbes had walked back to the front of the congregation. I could see a bead of sweat on his forehead from his outpouring of passion. He spread out his arms to their extremity, to embrace all, then lowered his arms again. "Dearly beloved, in the loving embrace of such a perfect husband as Jesus Christ, how dreadful is it that some among us reject that Love? Betray that perfect husband, through renouncing their baptism and Covenanting with the Devil. People who have accepted communion, Holy Sacrament, which is nothing less than a marriage vow with the Lord. Those who compact with other spirits are like a woman who breaks her marriage vows! This is why we must maintain our eternal vigilance to discover and root out such dangerous betrayal." Forbes reascended his pulpit. "There are many among you who recall a sermon I preached when I first came to this parish, warning of just such dangers. I am not an insensible man. I could see the sullen faces, hear the muttered dissent, *"Why is he being such a killjoy, it was only a faerie curse"* Believe me, my brethren, the Devil is a great deceiver. He can enter our world in many forms, to tempt us ever deeper into his mire. A man or woman who seeks protection through a charm, who hangs a wishing-rag on a clootie tree, who dreams of riding with the faerie, is like a man or woman at the top of a slippery slope. They can feel the Godly hands that reach out to return them to true devotion but, my brethren, some take one step too far, slip beyond the outstretched hands, and descend, descend, descend into the very pit of Hell!"

Forbes closed his eyes and leant his head upon his folded arms, resting upon the ledge of the pulpit, like a man exhausted. I believed him to be a man exhausted after the passionate exertion of his words. The moments he stayed in that position, also gave everyone in the building the chance to reflect, privately on his words. My thought was *whatever is happening in Auldearn it is not a cynical land grab as described by McLean of Duart, Forbes truly believes he is battling for the souls of his parishioners. Perhaps he is.*

Reverend Forbes raised his head and opened his eyes. "Dearly beloved, I have spoken to you of the three Covenants. I wish you to remember my words today, to take with you in your hearts. Reject always the abomination of the Covenant with the Devil and the slippery slope that leads the foolish toward it. Remember always the perfection of God's Covenant with man. The Covenant of Perfect Love. Aspire, each and everyone of you, my brethren, to your own Covenant with God in your own heart." Forbes placed his two hands upon his own heart, like the most earnest lover. "You must own your Covenant with God. You must feel it in the depths of your heart. A man or woman who feels it not, is but a carcass of a Christian, an empty shell, repeating words without meaning or feeling." Forbes extended his arm to point at all the assembly in a sweeping arc. "Dearly beloved, I tell you this final thing. Each and everyone of you who makes a true Covenant in their heart with God will never foreswear it. Never be ashamed of it. Never betray it. No man of conscience ever could. No matter what tempests lie ahead. No matter what temptations the Devil may set before us. Hold to your Covenant with God and the Lord will see you safe through any tempest, any storm!"

There followed long seconds in which everyone in the kirk believed the sermon was concluded, until Forbes shuffled uncertainly through some papers within his Bible. He held up a single sheet, with trembling hands and a look of human consternation on his face. "Here, my brethren is my test of conscience. My test of the truth of my Covenant with God. A letter I received yesterday. In the name of Archbishop Sharp, no less. Instructing that all parish ministers have three months to swear their acceptance of the authority of their local bishop or to consider themselves ordained no more. I commune directly with God and help you, in my own imperfect way, to that same direct knowledge of God. What need have I of a bishop to tell me how to Love my Lord?! What need have any of you? Yet if I do not swear, I cannot be your Minister anymore! I will have no livelihood. My wife and children, no provider." Forbes set down the letter. "I will pray on the matter and ask that you also pray for me, although I already believe I know the answer my Covenant with God must dictate. Thank you, my brethren, for listening. Mr Hay, the next reading, if ye please."

There was silence as the congregation considered their Minister's words and emotion, followed by a spontaneous outpouring of murmured comments, accompanied by some shouts of "No!" "We willna allow it!" "Stay!"

In the lowest murmur of all, I said to Wattie, "I helped draft the Act that voided all ordinations made after the King was first opposed." "Aye, weel, I'd keep that tae yersel in the current company" Wattie replied, then added. "Y'ken I almost feel sorry for Harry Forbes."

"I think that is what he intended" I replied, then I realised that while Harry Forbes' theology may well be that which impressed the educated Lairds, he reached out to the common folk with his physical attractiveness and the power of his emotion, be it fear, love or sympathy. I had a sudden image in my mind of Forbes meeting with Isobel, alone and unobserved in the Auldearn Tollbooth after her apprehension. How might the strong personalities of the entrancing, local bard and the Minister who instructed his flock in the Bridegroom of Souls, combine and interact?

At service end, Reverend Forbes was thronged with those wishing to offer him support, which allowed Wattie and I to slip quietly out. Except we were stopped by the imposing presence of Auldearn Kirk's beadle, Hugh Hay of Brightmoney and his muscular negro, John. Hay fixed me with his unnerving stare, "Ye should not be here" he said, although as he spoke, I saw that John looked down at the ground.

CHAPTER 27 ISOBEL WORRIES

Lochloy. 17th April 1661

"He would send me now and then to Auldearn some errands to my neighbours, in the shape of a hare. I was one morning, about the break of day, going to Auldearn in the shape of a hare and Patrick Popley's servants, in Kilnhill, being going to their labouring, his hounds being with them, ran after me being in the shape of a hare. I ran very long, but was forced, being weary, at last to take to my own house. The door being left open, I ran in behind a chest and the hounds followed in, but they went to the other side of the chest and I was forced to run forth again and ran into another house and there took the leisure to say,

"Hare, hare, God send the care! I am in a hare's likeness now, But I shall be a woman even now, Hare, hare, God send the care!"

And so I returned to my own shape, as I am this instant, again. The dogs will sometimes get some bites of us, when we are in hare's shape, but will not get us killed. When we turn out of a hare's likeness to our own shape, we will have the bites, the tears and scratches on our bodies." **Isobel's third confession, 15th May 1662.**

Isobel worries about John, her husband and everyone who is tenant to the Laird of Park. The rents have increased again. The Laird pleads poverty and pressure from creditors, yet the Lady of Park leads an extravagant life, a new sewing instructress recently employed for their six year old daughter. The Laird pleads pressure from his creditors, when a'body for miles around kens he has never paid a penny back, unless forced.

Isobel worries about John. The evening light is fading and he is still working on the fields of the Laird's Home Farm. The men and women who labour there will never see a single bushel of the crops they grow, except for that which the Laird sells to them. John will come home and will insist on tilling their own small strip, guided only by the light of the stars and moon.

Isobel is out by the peat fields, gathering sphagnum moss, to staunch the flow of blood from her time of the month. She has reconciled herself to never carry a living child. She spies Jean Martin also filling her basket with moss. Isobel had such high hopes of Jean but has seen so little of her, since she went to work in the big House. The two women kneel by the same clump,, their knives moving deftly to free the moss from the soil. A flash of fellow womanhood passes between them. *"On yer rags?" "Aye, I've been feeling like roarin' an' greetin' a' day!" "Ken"* Both women smile.

The task is almost done and Isobel feels a surge of panic that Jean is wiping her knife to leave.

"Jeanie, I've missed you" Isobel confides.

The brief up-turn of Jean's lips in response is so muted it is less a half smile and more a gesture of regret. "I hae been sae busy. They fair mak ye work!"

Isobel reaches out her hand to rest her palm upon the back of the younger woman's hand. It is Jean who moves her hand away first. Isobel feels her pulling away. She risks reaching out in another way. "I feel the need tae ride tonight. Micht I see ye there?"

Jean has collected her tools and all the moss she needs.

Brightmoney lies down a different path from Lochloy. "Perhaps. I dinna ken" is Jean's non-committal reply, as she moves to depart.

Deep in the wee sma' hours of the night, as John snores by her side, Isobel seeks the host. Jean is not among them. There is no compensatory revel that night, no triumph over Laird, Minister or neighbour. Isobel is sent as a hare and immediately chased by baying hounds. They come so close they scratch her, as she twists and turns in desperate evasion. The pursuit is relentless. Closing in. Finally, she is able to return to her woman's body again and awake next to John, her heart beating, mind unsettled, her forearms raked by her own nails. *Why could she not soar and overcome? Where was Jean? What is this pursuit closing in?*

Isobel worries.

CHAPTER 28: ISOBEL AND THE LAIRD OF PARK AND LOCHLOY.

Monday 30th June 1662

"*Be it kend till all men be thir presentis, me David Hay of Lochloy was in my minoritie and being under the government of uncles Walter and Alexander Hay of Kynnudie, then my curators, transportit me fra the county of Moray...towards London..to the effect that I micht see and understand guid manneris and fashions...unto the time of my marriage, of the quhilk charges debursit upon me the said Sir Alexander received but eight score pounds, being thocht meetest by lawyers, that I should be servit heir to my brother quha was invest in the lands, to the effect I micht eschew to be heir to my guidsire...and to eschew his deed, because it wantit the King's consent, my hail landis and baronies of Lochloy and Park fell under the recognition of the said Sir Alexander. Having taken the same upon his charge and credit..would, in effect, overthrow me in my estate, if I should have peyit for the composition according to the rigour. Likewise the said Sir Alexander having lyine out of his money four or five yearis, he resignit the samye hail landis and baronies pertaining to me... and recoverit to me the privileged of my woods, quhilk was the pleasure of my estate.*" **Testimony of the Laird of Park's grandfather, David Hay, regarding how he fell under obligation and debt to his uncle Sir Alexander Hay of Kinnudie in the early 1600s.**

"*Agnes Grant was apprehendit for the murder be sorcerie and witchcraft of David Hay of Park and John and William his sones. This wretchit creature has been ever, and yet is of an, exceeding evil reporte and there have been mony vehement presumptiounes exhibited to us that she has been accesorie to diverse devilish practices."* **Petition for a Commission to try Agnes Grant for the murder by witchcraft of the Laird of Park's grandfather, father and uncle, 1643.**

"Agnes Grant who wes burnt… got hired from Elspet Monro to destroy the Lairds of Park and Lochloy…and it was Kathryn Sowter that was burnt that killed William Hay, the last Laird of Park's brother." **Janet Breadheid's Confession, 14th April 1662 with remembrance of events from 20 years before.**

"Alasdair was hard pressed by Hay of Kinnudie but tricked him by calling out, "I'll not deceive you, my men are coming up behind you." As Hay turned to protect himself from these new, imaginary, enemies, Alasdair cut him down." **Bain's History of Nairnshire, telling of the death by ruse of the elderly Sir Alexander Hay of Kinnudie at the hands of Alasdair MacColla during the Battle of Auldearn, 9th May 1645.**

"That it is not unknown what great sufferings the petitioner has lain under these late years, as first in the year 1662 he was fined in the great Act of fining without so much as being called or any cause signified in the sum of £200 sterling and albeit in the former times of our troubles, upon the account whereof these fines were said to be imposed, the petitioner was under age and had no meddling and at the same time had his grandmother and mother two life-renters of no less than forty chalder of victuals yearly, living upon his estate." **Petition written by the Laird of Park in 1690 to obtain more time to repay debts.**

"Forasmuch as the king's most excellent majesty, out of his tender respect and love to his people and from his desire that all animosities and differences among them be buried in oblivion, and that his good subjects may now, after so long trouble, enjoy happiness, peace and plenty under his royal government, has been pleased to declare his resolution to indemnify all persons for their actings during and in relation to these troubles, excepting

such as should be excepted by his majesty in this parliament... But considering that by these troubles and rebellious courses many of his good subjects have been under great sufferings and liable to great loss for their affection and loyalty to his majesty, therefore, in order to their reparation, and for diverse important considerations of state, his majesty, with advice and consent of his estates of parliament, has thought fit to burden his pardon and indemnity to some ,whose guiltiness has rendered them obnoxious to the law and their lives and fortunes at his majesty's disposal, with the payment of some small sums....In the Shire of Nairn : Sir Ludovic Gordon of that ilk, £3,600; Alexander Brodie of that ilk, £4,800; Patrick Campbell of Boath, £600; Brodie of Lethen, elder, £6,000; Brodie of Lethen, younger, £1,200; Hay, tutor of Knockawdie, £360; Hugh Hay, tutor of Park, £1,200; Francis Brodie of Belivat, elder and younger, £3,000 equally between them; the laird of Grant, £18,000; Campbell of Caddell, £12,000; Colonel Innes of Boage, £1,200; Mr John Campbell of Moy, £600; Patrick Nairn of Alchrosse, £1,200; Patrick Hay in the North, £2,400; John Innes of Conrock, £1,000; Robert Stewart of Lethernie, £360; Alexander Anderson of Garioch, £1,200; John Tulloch in Nairn, £600; John Falconer of Tulloch, £1,200; Alexander Dunbar, commissary clerk of Moray, £1,200; and David Brodie of Pitgairnie, £1,200." **Act containing some exceptions from the Act of Indemnity and Oblivion 1662, with no mention of a £200 fine for John Hay of Park but does include £1,200 fine for Hugh Hay, Tutor of Park.**

"Christ's wounds, man! Tis a damned disgrace, that's what it is!" I shout in indignation at John Weir, keeper of Auldearn Tollbooth. I toss the filthy lump of blue mould covered rye bread onto the table. "Is this, is this all you hae being gi'eing her tae eat!?"

"Why waste guid breid on a witch?! She was no tae be fed unless she spake the truth. Since she has confessed, we hae been keeping her alive on that." Weir gestured defiantly with his hand toward the mouldy lump. "Keepin' her alive, till she burns!"

"Alive! Alive! What I have just been shown was a woman mair deid than alive!" My two fists were planted on the table, barely containing my anger. Wattie, my trusty lieutenant, had moved round the table to loom his imposing bulk over John Weir. "On whose instruction have you been starving this woman, now poisoning her with mould ridden bread!?"

Weir was beginning to reconsider his defiance and, at Wattie's menacing presence, flinch. "Reverend Forbes. Reverend Forbes, he determined how the prisoner was tae be treated. When rewarded and when…when pressed mair sore."

I had in my mind the image from a few minutes before of a painfully thin woman, filthy in rags, quaking and convulsing on her wooden bench. She may have had the auburn hair and statuesque beauty described by Notary John Innes but that hair was thinning and matted now, any beauty, contorted and lost beneath skin disfigured by grey blotches and a face caught somewhere between despair and madness. *"John, my jo, is that you?"* she had plead when we entered her cell, then she had convulsed with pitiful, manic laughing, followed by eerie child-voice singing, *"John, my jo, tak me hame, John, my jo, ma dearie, John my jo tak me hame, tak me hame ma dearie"*. *"I'm not John"* I had said, hoping it would bring her back to the present. It was a mistake. She had shrunk back into corner of the room, hugging her knees and rocking. Even Wattie could not bring her back, for all his couthy charm. That was when we signalled our wish to leave the cell, to remonstrate with her gaoler, John Weir.

In truth I was more than angry, I was thwarted. Not just in my wish to speak with Isobel but she had grown in my mind and my dreams, through her shameless copulation in her confessions and through Innes's evident attraction to her poetic, testimony and her primitive flair in bringing it to life. I had entered the tollbooth with a fantasy of sparring with a flame-haired, feisty native bard. I had allowed my thoughts to stray to insinuations that I could help her argue her case, perhaps for a price. We stepped into the stinking cell, her bowl not changed for days, her rotting food, thronged by ants, her body wrecked by filth and hunger, her mind wandered through disease and despair.

"Mister Weir, I have shown you my letters of Commission from the King's Commissioner to the Scottish Parliament, from the Advocate Depute and the letter instructing all to co-operate with my investigation from your own Sheriff Principal of Nairn. You will listen tae my instructions and heed them well. My man, Mister Garland, will bring food to Mistress Gowdie every day. She will be given it all. I will purchase and bring new clothes and blankets. She will be given them all. I will return to speak with Mistress Gowdie in four days, if she is not recovered in her senses, I will report you to the Privy Council for interfering with the King's principal witness." Now I stood to press my angry face close to Weir's. "Do you understand!? If I return to find a corpse, I swear, you will swing for murder. If I return to find her as I found her today, I will...I will charge you with obstructing justice. No matter if Harry Forbes or any other tells you to disobey me, remember who is sent from the Privy Council and who is sent from the King." I paused to let Wattie whisper, menacingly, in his ear. *"Best dae as he says, man. Mister Kellas, wasnae a'ways a lawyer." "I ken who he is. We a' dae."* Weir had replied, his resistance crumbled.

"Good. Mister Weir is there a physician in Auldearn, or failing that a curewife of good, not ill, repute?"

"The nearest physician is in Nairn but Agnes Duncan in the village is guid wi' herbs and assists at births, wi' no praying or charming." Weir replied, now only too eager to help.

"Excellent. You will tell Wattie, Mister Garland, where to find Agnes Duncan. Mistress Gowdie will be washed, her hair combed out, her sores treated, her body rested, her piss-pot removed twice a day, for God's sake! If I cannot talk with her on Friday, I will hold ye tae account, Mister Weir. Do you understand what must occur?"

Weir nodded, Wattie slapped him on his back. "We will bring the first of the food today. Wattie, see that all is arranged. I will go to meet with the Laird of Park."

On my way out of Auldearn Tollbooth, I took a final look through the opening in the cell door. Isobel lay rocking on the floor, her body curled into herself, as if her own embrace could comfort or protect. *"Well, she can be sure that neither God, nor the Devil, will lift a finger to help her."* I thought, as I headed out. *"There is only me. Only Wattie and me."*

• •

I skirted the woods of Kilnhill as I rode toward the old mansion house of Park and Lochloy. I knew Isobel's confessions so well that I thought, *this is where she was chased as a hare by Peter Popley's hounds.* Followed by my inevitable bitter, almost taunting, thought, *you will not turn yourself into a hare to escape your degradation now, will you!?* My mind yet reeled as I sought to grapple with all I had discovered. People who covenanted with the Devil, yet gained no power or aid from doing so, now imprisoned by people who covenanted with God, who would happily starve, torment and murder them. Wattie had grabbed me just as I was set to depart, to tell me what he had gleaned from local gossip about the Laird of Park *"Ye ken he's up tae his ears in debt. No-one kens why. A grippit, mean , slippery Laird, for a' that he's just a young man "* And, as I was moving beyond earshot, " *Folk say his father and grandfather were killed by witchcraft as well!*"

Some folk called me the devil, as my reputation grew in 1645. They said I never once took a prisoner. Only I knew that to be God's honest truth.

As I rode through the home farm of Lochloy, I tried to recall what I myself knew of the Hays of Park. I had added some paragraphs to the Act of Indemnity and Oblivion, George MacKenzie had praised my turn of phrase, but I had no part in the Act of Exceptions, my long years in servitude in Barbados, not equipping me to know whose guilt deserved fining. Yet I had sought out a copy prior to my departure from Edinburgh. John Hay, Laird of Park, had not been fined but his uncle, in the role of Tutor of Park, had been. This was an Act from earlier this very year. Why was John Hay yet under a Tutor, when he was old enough to have children that Janet and Isobel, and the Devil, wanted to kill? I could not make sense of this place or this case. It made the machinations of Montrose, MacColla, Middleton, Argyll and Lauderdale seem like child's play in comparison. At least I could understand their earthly motivations.

If Inschoch had looked crumbling and in need of repair, the House of Park and Lochloy was similarly so. A forbidding ancient tower, extended in all directions by annexes and outbuildings. I was met, as I approached the outer gate, by a man who identified himself as Mr Popley, the Laird's chief woodsman and keeper of the grounds. He told me I was expected as he asked me to dismount.

"Mr Popley, your accent it is not from around here, I jalouse." I said.

"No, Mister Kellas. I hail from Hampshire, south of London. Came here with Colonel William and stayed on after he died."

Mr Popley replied, as I walked my horse toward the stables.

"Ah, Colonel William Hay, the present Laird's uncle. How did he die, Mr Popley?"

"Is you going about your investigations, already?" said Mr Popley with a smile, while he handed my horse to a stable boy, as an energetic pack of hounds bounded out to greet their master. After greeting and calming the dogs, Mr Popley returned to my question. "The bloody flux. Dreadful pain, rotten bowels. Though some say it was witchcraft. You Scotch have more time for that sort of thing."

I thanked Mr Popley as we reached the great wood and brass door. "I will leave you here, Mr Kellas. I'm sure Matilda will see to you." He glanced at the hounds yet slobbering and thronging by his legs. "The mistress and the old mistress oh, an' the dowager mistress, don't care for the dogs in the house."

Matilda, the maid, showed me into the house. I can only say that the interior was strangely cluttered, as if different, mostly female, tastes were vying to fill every wall with a tapestry and much of the floor space was crowded with furniture from every decade from the last one hundred years. Grippit but in debt, I was beginning to see why.

Whatever sense of multiple influences I obtained from the house, it was dwarfed by the overwhelming peculiarity of the reception committee that greeted me when I entered the Laird's hall. Seated round a table was John Hay, Laird of Park, a man in his mid-twenties, his wife Marion Campbell, his mother Jean Cumming, his grandmother Mary Rose and most unsettling of all, his uncle, Hugh Hay, Tutor of Park. "We all wanted to see the monster. The man who rode and murdered with Montrose and MacColla, Mister Kellas take a seat."

It was one of the most extraordinary introductions of my life.

John Hay was but a youth and the presence of his elders, suggested weakness but his manner and the mocking tone of his words, spoke more of bitter entitlement. A man who felt hard done by his own accumulation of debt. I guessed the family had gathered to intimidate me through a display of pedigree. As I sat, I realised that the three generations in the one room was ideal for my purpose, with the fourth generation, presumably being cared for by a nursemaid upstairs. According to Janet Breadheid's confession, the Lairds of Park and their offspring had been under demonic threat for decades, throughout the lives of all the generations now in this room.

Before I could frame my first question, John Hay spoke again. "Why should we assist you, Mister Kellas, for nothing in return?"

I signified that it was a reasonable point and countered, "What is it you think I may be able to do?"

"You work with the Lord Advocate in Edinburgh, do ye not? You must know this family has been most unjustly fined, for alleged disloyalty during the late troubles. You could petition for mitigation or defrayment."

I knew my best chance lay in flattering the hopes of these declining minor gentry, despite knowing the Act of Exemption was a Parliamentary matter and way beyond my ability to influence. "I could certainly present your case, particularly if I can also report that you gave good co-operation with a Commission from the Privy Council."

"There is, of course, another reason why Mister Kellas should help us" intoned Hugh Hay sternly, "The Lord kens it should be the crown paying compensation to us, for the rape, destruction and murder of the savage Irish and afterwards the brigands of Huntly and Glencairn. I believe you know I speak the truth with regard to the former, do ye not, Mister Kellas?"

As his eyes burnt into me, I was once again outside his house of Brightmoney, seventeen years before, the pleas and screams of Lawer's Campbells in my ears. "I acknowledge a personal reason to argue your case when I return, although we all must submit that all armies cut a trail of destruction in that sad war. It is why we must eschew further civil strife, where we can."

Perhaps I should have omitted these last words but my sense of justice would not let me stay silent. The assembled generations of Hays, by birth or marriage, demurred through each emitting a low grumbling sound, though none pursued the matter further. John Hay was more interested in confirming the bargain struck. "Very well! We have your word of honour that you will assist our petition for a reduction in penalty. How may we assist your commission to investigate the witches of Park?"

"Thank you. May I take you back to a time before the current accusation of witchcraft, to a previous. I ask because the confessions I have read suggest your family and your House have been the target of sorcery and witchcraft for some time. Perhaps, if I may, a question for Lady Mary, why would Janet Breadheid say *"Agnes Grant who wes burnt on Downie Hill got hired from Elspet Monro to destroy the Lairds of Park and Lochloy"* ?"

For all she was in her late seventies, Lady Mary Rose Hay flared up with something more than indignation. With venom and hatred. "Elspet Monro! Elizabeth Monro! how dare ye mention that name here! Sir Alexander was a'ways kind tae my Davie but his wife, that viper. Now there wes a witch, if ever I saw yin!"

"Mother, please.." Hugh Hay attempted to calm his mother, whether to silence her or out of concern, I could not tell. Either way, Lady Mary would not be silenced. "Not one o' ye told me that Breadheid said that! Elizabeth Monro, Elspet was what the family cried her, she was ay jealous that my Davie was the senior Hay o' the line, *"After a' my Sandy did for him in London!"* she would say. Covetous bitch!"

"Please," I said as disarmingly as I could, "I do not know the events from this time, could someone explain?"

Hugh Hay placed a hand on his mother's arm as he spoke. "When King Jamie the Saxt became James the First, every likely Laird in Scotland went south to London to try his luck at court or in society. My father was no exception. Sadly he ran up debts, that his uncle, my great uncle, Sir Alexander Hay of Kinnudie defrayed at interest. It is a debt that bothers this Household yet."

"No, no, ye've got it a' wrong!" Lady Mary scolded her son, "Sir Alexander was ay guid tae us, it was his wife wha wanted the lands of Park!"

"Tell me, if David Hay and his male heirs failed, who would have inherited?" I asked.
John Hay replied. "I was looking at that charter but recently, *"with the remainder to himself and heirs male of his body, which failing, to Mister Alexander Hay of Kinnudie and heirs male of his body."*

Suddenly, it was Jean Cumming Hay, who stood up in consternation. "It was my John who died afore his time! Before his own father! Mother, your David, lived three score years, my John did not reach two, I had so little time wi' him! If there was sorcery it was against my John."

It was now John Hay, Laird of Park's turn to comfort *his* mother. After he had moved to hold her and whisper *"Hush now, ye must not upset yourself"* he turned to me with anger in his voice. "Mister Kellas! Is there a point to this upset you are causing. How concerns these ancient wounds with the matter in hand!?"

I was thankful that my reason for resurrecting the memory of the previous alleged witch attack was quite genuine and well founded. I had simply to set it out. "Please, I did not intend to cause upset but you must see there is a peculiarity in these recent confessions, a theme that should concern you all. Isobel Gowdie describes flying on beanstalks with the faerie folk shooting innocent people with elf arrows. Her victims seem random, people who happen to be in the path of the host but she and Janet Breadheid talk over and over about one maleficent crime they work hard to perform. They are instructed by the Devil to perform. To destroy the Laird of Park and his male heirs. Not random, precise and calculated. Why?"

Now it was the turn of the present Laird's young wife, Marion Campbell, to swoon. She would have fallen from her chair had her husband not caught her. "Mister Kellas, for Love of God, these are our children you are speaking of. William and Elizabeth are safe upstairs but our first child, darling wee John, he died after only a few days. You do not believe these vile witches had a hand in our John's death!?"

"You do not?"

My question hung, unanswered, in the room. I could see each of the assembled family in front of me, considering their loss, considering also its cause. Lady Mary, two sons and a husband alleged victims of Agnes Grant and Kathryn Sowter. Certainly the allegation was sufficiently believed to see the two women burn. Lady Jean, a husband lost in the prime of his life. John and Marion, a baby son.

John Hay, Laird of Park, broke the thoughtful silence, with a stern conclusion, "Then thank Christ one of them is already dead and the other soon to follow!"

Hugh Hay rose to his feet and spoke next. "Mister Kellas, we have given you quite sufficient co-operation and you have caused the ladies, in particular, quite regrettable upset. I believe this interview is at its end."

I held Hay's gaze whilst schooling my voice to sound as artless as it could. "One final question, I pray. If the male line of the current Laird fails, who stands to inherit then?"

"Mister Kellas, I forbit it!" Hugh Hay roared, his hand planted hard upon the table. The other family members looked around at each other anxiously. John Hay chose to answer. "I am not sure I like what you may mean by the question but since you are sworn to help us with the Privy Council, I will tell you that I have delayed being declared my grandfather's heir on advice of my lawyer, in light of considerations such as the recent fine. If I and my son were to die, my uncle Hugh Hay, standing beside me, is my curator and tutor, he would inherit all."

"I hold but in trust!" Hugh Hay spluttered. I then rose from my seat.

"Thank you. You have all been most helpful. I promise I will do all in my power to plead your case when the opportunity arises."

If the three generations of Hays of Park had sought to intimidate me with their display of pedigree, I left them as a tableau of concern, as fractured and unhappy as I suspected their relations to be.

CHAPTER 29: ISOBEL TRIES

3rd July 1661

"And if a child be forspoken (bewitched) we tak the cradle belt throw it thryse and shake the belt above the fyre then put the belt down to the ground till a dog or cat go over it, that the seikeness may cam into the dog or cat." **Isobel's second confession. 3rd May 1662**

Isobel tries, of course she tries. It is her friend's sister's child. Wee Donald, son of Sarah Martin, Jean's sister. His mother so very frightened. The times when he stops and stares, cut off from folk around him as if they are not there. Or worse when he convulses on the ground, biting his gum and tongue. Not even George, his strong father or Sarah, his loving mother can calm him. He must shake and be departed until the spell is done.

No-one knows who or why. *"He's just a bairn!"* they cry. *"Tak me, no the bairn!"* his father pleads, to no avail. Jean recommends they send for Isobel. The parents are not sure. *"She is as like tae hae caused it, as cure it."* Sarah gives voice to a well-kent concern. *"Not Isobel, trust me, sister."* Jean reassures.

Isobel is wary. These are not her people. The Fermtoun of Boghole is a ten mile walk there and back. Jean has come to live and work among Isobel's folk but Sarah, she hardly knows. She has no true idea what ails the child. If he truly is bewitched, she has no idea who by or why. How can you counter a curse if you cannot penetrate its meaning? A further thought troubles Isobel's mind as she walks amid the summer evening, she will be bard to her ain, curewife to her ain, charmer to her ain but the mair she moves among strangers, who kens what stories they might tell. Tell Harry Forbes or Hugh Rose.

"*I'll dae this for Jean.*" Isobel tells herself, because she knows she is losing Jean.

The only message that Isobel sends before she agrees to attend is, "*if ye hae a cat mak siccar it's ben the hoose when I call.*"

Donald does not look sick, nor forspoken when Isobel arrives. The last time was the day before. Isobel has cured many or tried. She is not sure how she will know if she has succeeded if the spell is not upon him now. If it never comes upon him again. Donald does not look sick but he does look frightened of the strange woman who bades him lie down.

Isobel takes the cradle belt, the wrap his mother wore around the child and herself to carry him, as a babe, close to her heart, as she worked. Isobel ties the belt so it forms a circle and she moves the bairn so the belt passes three times over his whole body. She invokes Father, Son and Haily Ghaist to assist with each passing of the belt. She invokes no other spirit, not when she is not among her ain. She has the strangest thought, that it would help if she knew if Sarah and George believed. Believed in her. She cannot blame their worried faces, the faces of a father and a mother, she just cannot read what they think about her.

"I will cast thee out, awa from this bairn, awa from this place, I will cast thee out, in the name o' Father, Son and Haily Ghaist!" Isobel chants and she throws the belt three times above the fire. Then she sets the belt on the ground. Sarah hands the cat to Isobel, who sets it down next to the belt. The cat walks over. "Go from this bairn, whate'r thou art, go from this bairn, into this cat!"

Who could have done this? Isobel still does not know. Often after she heals or performs a ballad, she is left exhausted her whole body spent. This evening she feels empty. She is not sure anything has passed from her, let alone from Donald into a cat. She asks the boy if he feels better and he runs to bury his head in his mother's embrace.

Isobel is given four eggs and a jug of ale. Sarah and George are polite enough but everyone in the small house knows they wish their guest to depart as soon as she has finished her task. "Jean will let me ken" Isobel says as she leaves and realises she has admitted she does not know the outcome herself.

She has tried. Isobel tries for Jean's sake. She hopes it is enough.

CHAPTER 30 : MONDAY NIGHT, TUESDAY MORNING.

Auldearn: Tuesday 1st July 1662

"Quhen we goe to any hous we tak meat and drink and we fill up the barrels with our own pish." **Isobel's first confession 13th April 1662**

"By the rivers of Babylon, there we sat down, yea, we wept, when we remembered Zion….O daughter of Babylon, who art to be destroyed; happy shall he be, that rewardeth thee as thou hast served us. Happy shall he be, that taketh and dasheth thy little ones against the stones." **Psalm 137**

"When he shall be judged, let him be condemned and let his prayer become sin, Let his days be few, and let another take his office, Let his children be fatherless, and his wife a widow, Let his children be continually vagabonds and beg, let them seek bread out of desolate places, Let the extortioner catch all that he hath, and let strangers spoil his labour, Let there be none to extend mercy unto him, neither let there be any to favour his fatherless children, Let his posterity be cut off, and in the generation following let their name be blotted out." **Psalm 109**

As Monday turned to Tuesday, I had a vivid dream. When I was first indentured in Barbados, we indentured Scots were kept in cabins and further toward the swamp the negro slaves had their cabins. We were not supposed to fraternise and some among us did not wish to but I went, at times, to go close, at first to listen and later to enter and befriend. When I listened, I heard them singing and chanting in their heathenish tongue and I knew they were singing of home, praying for deliverance, imploring for a better life for their children and demanding their Gods exact revenge. Exactly the same as we indentured white men were doing. God knows my fellow Scots in my cabin knew many Psalms of Revenge.

In my dream I was lying in the dark bushes listening as the negros sang, except in my dream they sang in English, a language they were yet learning and sang a Psalm from a religion they had not been taught. "By the Rivers of Babylon, there we sat down, yea, we wept, when we remembered Zion." Then the singing turned to rhythmic chanting, the further verses of Psalm 137, "Happy shall he be that taketh and dasheth thy little ones against the stones."

I forced myself awake to escape the menacing sound. As I returned to Auldearn, I realised the houses of the fermtouns were little different from the cabins of the indentured or enslaved and the hopes for deliverance and the dreams of vengeance would also be the same. Isobel and Janet may well have muttered darkly against a Laird who pressed them hard through labour and rent. They may even have invoked greater powers to aid them. Listen to the Psalms! It is not vengeance the Kirk stands against, it is asking the wrong spirit for aid.

I found myself suddenly laughing. I was not sure that Isobel had truly done anything she said, not even replacing stolen beer with her ain pish. The only pish was the words that had come out of her mouth. You cannot burn a person for harbouring evil thoughts. There would be no-one left alive on God's earth.

I dozed off again and saw the negroes on the plantation dancing round a fire. I had a remembrance of their long, powerful limbs and how, when we saw them bathing or lined for inspection, their manhoods often seemed longer and thicker than ours. What had Isobel said "huge nature, he is abler for us that way than any man can be"? My waking mind began to speak louder than my dreaming. I had though the description of the Devil, as a "black, roch, man" had meant a swarthy man but what if it meant exactly what the words said, a black skinned man? Hugh Hay's servant was called John. Could he not be "Black John"? All the pieces of information from the last four days began to fall into place. Not a mystery, a straightforward description. Even though diseased and befuddled in her mind, Isobel had asked for John when I saw her. I had assumed she meant John Gilbert, her husband but what if it was her great lover, Black John, that she was calling out for?

I kept my eyes closed. It helped my mind find its way without distraction. It came racing into me like an inrushing tide and as a tide, it could not be denied. If "Black John" was the Devil's carnal incarnation, perhaps wearing an animal mask to compliment his long limbs and "huge nature", then his master, Hugh Hay, was the demonic high priest, the man who had found the alchemy to combine the sexual prowess of his black servant with the ancient folk beliefs of the local women. The Devil's only precise demand in all the confessions, repeated in Isobel's and Janet's both, was that the Laird of Park and his male children, his posterity, be destroyed. Who would inherit then? The curator and tutor, Hugh Hay. Who had lived through the 1640s when everyone in Auldearn believed two of Hugh Hay's older brothers had perished through witchcraft? Perhaps his father also. Perhaps at the behest of Elspet Monro, to help her husband inherit. Yet Hay of Kinnudie had been cut down by MacColla's cunning. No longer in the Laird of Park's Charter of Confirmation. Who did all these untimely deaths clear the way for? Two older brothers dead, if the eldest brother's male line could be extinguished, only Hugh Hay of Brightmoney would be left! After all his hard work acting as Tutor and mentor to a spoilt young brat. Hugh Hay, the only adult male left alive amid a sea of bereaved women and a whining child. Good God! Hugh Hay had been an adult when his brothers John and William died. I had seen him and feared him in 1645. Could he have commissioned Agnes Grant and Katherine Sowter, while sowing the seeds of blame on Elspet Monro? Could he have felt the success of these curses and sought out the next generation, Janet Breadheid and her protégé, Isobel Gowdie and conscripted them to work their Devilish maleficium to destroy the surviving male line of his older brother John? What had George MacKenzie said in law lecture, *"who's problem is it, who's gain is it? There, most commonly, is your answer!"*

Good God in Heaven! Hugh Hay had both the reason and the means. As beadle of the Kirk he had a key to allow entry to night-time carnal ceremonies with his servant Black John and the women with faerie belief. As Seneschal of Inschoch Castle, he visited Janet Breadheid just before she died. Just after he had attended Janet's first confession, where she had appeared to be lucidly able to tell her inquisitors exactly what was going on. Until she died. Hugh Hay attended Isobel's confessions and saw that her mind was wandering to the Lord knows where. Her removal could wait. Perhaps wait until the public garrotting and burning that would mark the end of this whole affair. Lo! See the demonic guilty party! Not Hugh Hay, loyal uncle, conscientious Tutor, elder of the Kirk, pillar of the community.

Bastard! I thought. He damned well killed them all. His father, his two brothers, his nephew's oldest son, his accomplice, Janet Breadheid, with four children left without a mother.

Well, he damn well won't kill Isobel! No' when Bluidy Kellas is riding him doon!

Then I opened my eyes. Then I sat up. Did what I had just

thought still seem real? Did it stand the test of the spreading light of day? I searched my mind in that place where waking reason drowns out the fantasy of dream.

This was no fantasy. This was pure, cold blooded, fact.

I had a final thought of Isobel, healthy, laughing, squatting over a barrel, her thighs spread, the dimple where each leg opened from her fundament, the flash of hair above her cunny, as red as that which tumbled in cascades from her head, her mysterious womanly places libating with moisture, filling the barrel with her gushing pish. I had a final thought that I would like to see that.

Alas that I should compare him to a man. Perhaps I had been sent here to help both Isobel and her Black John to escape and be together once more.

CHAPTER 31: ISOBEL. HEAVEN AND HELL

28th February 1662 Balmakeith

"And all the witches yet that are untaken haw their poweris and our poweris quhilk we haid before we were takin both but now I haw no power at all." **Isobel's first confession 13 April 1662**

"Janet Breadhead professing repentance for hir former sines of witchcraft and that she haid bein owerlong in the devil's service without any pressuris proceidit." **Janet Breadheid's confession 14th April 1662**

"I'm getting too auld for this!" Janet gasps with grim humour, between contractions. Isobel is assisting at the birth, as is Janet's fifteen year old daughter, Moira, who is herself eight months pregnant. "I'm glad my bairn's coming first" Janet had opined between earlier pushes, "Wouldnae dae tae hae the auntie or uncle younger than the niece or nephew!" "Dinna mak me laugh, ma, ye might stert me aff!" replies Moira. Janet pushes into another wave of contractions, her female helpers encourage her through. Her husband John, her sixteen year old son Jamie and twelve year old William are out repairing fences damaged in the previous night's winter storm. Jamie ran the three miles to fetch Isobel, then straight after went out to join his father at work. Birthing is no place for a man. This pregnancy is a late surprise for forty-two year old Janet. "Someone tell John Taylor this is definitely the last time!" Janet calls out amid the next crescendo.

Isobel moves between her friend's legs and calls out "No' long now, Janet. I can see a heid!" Isobel gently reaches to feel the skull of the nearly born babe. "Definitely a heid, you beautiful woman, is your ma no clever, Moira?"

Even as Janet prepares herself for the next most crucial and painful contractions, she is able to share a look of love and respect with her friend. Tinged with a half-smile of sadness that Isobel will never know a child who survives. Even as Isobel busies herself to coax and encourage her friend for the most difficult pushes, the crown of the head and the shoulders beyond, she sees and understands Janet's sympathetic look. Janet cements the moment by reaching out her hand to squeeze Isobel's. No words, just deep understanding and love. We a' maun get on wi' whate'r the Lord ordains for us. Friendship, skill and calling compel Isobel to help at her friend's seventh birth, three in the grave, two out with their father and one holding her mother's other hand. It took all Janet's wifely persuasion to have Isobel at this birth and not her formidable but now frail, mother-in-law, Elspet Nishie. "*Ye ken, John, her shakes are so bad, she's like tae drop the bairn!*" John had acquiesced but he still hoped his slighted mother wasn't muttering darkly against this birth, as a result of her exclusion. Childbirth is difficult enough for mother and babe at the best of times but at Janet's age and mid-winter, both needed all the protection and absence of ill-intent, they could get.

Janet cries out as she rides the next wave. It is a cry of pain and triumph both, of ancient physical energy. The timeless cry of what is needed to get the child born, so that the whole of humanity might live on. Isobel's fingers barely have to guide either side of the crown of the head, as Janet's love and power drives the new-born's head through the dilated lips of her vulva. Janet roars from the deepest animal heart of her chest and soul. A huge multiple push. The bloodied, purple, angry head, followed instantly by the shoulders slipping through. Isobel's deft fingers move from the head to the out-rushing torso. *"I see it, ma! I see the bairn!"* Moira cries in wonder, as a whole, unique human being, head, limbs, body, cord emerges, intact and alive from her mother's womb.

"It's a lassie!" Isobel calls out as she holds the babe up for all to see "A beautiful baby girl!"

"Oh, ma, I love ye!" Moira says in admiration as she lowers her head to kiss her mother.

Janet pulls herself to sitting. Her shift bloodied, her breathing ragged but ecstatic. Her older daughter supports her back, as Isobel clears the babe's mouth and nose. The new-born cries out, a sweet shuddering squawk. The three women beam with smiles of satisfaction, wonder and relief.

"Gi'e her here!" Janet commands, from the most important throne of all. "Bring me baby Isobel."

The three women look at each other and Isobel Gowdie gently places the baby on Janet's chest. In a few minutes, she will use her knife to cut and tie the cord but in the seconds after setting down the child, she places the palm of her hand on her heart. A hand that is bursting with love for the compliment of her friend's choice of name.

"Coorie doon, my beautiful Isobel." Janet coos to her babe. Moira has tears in her eyes, which Janet sees and she motions for her oldest daughter to put her head on her chest also, close to her sister. Isobel wants to be about her work of cutting the cord and helping Janet push out the placenta, for its reverent removal. Janet doesn't want her friend excluded from the crush of female love, she motions with her free hand and Isobel lowers her head to rest it close to Janet's cheek. *"I love you."* Isobel whispers. Janet twists her neck to kiss her friend Isobel's forehead. Mother and baby safe. Three of the people she most loves in the world, pressed against her in the most wonderous embrace, Janet feels in bliss.

Perhaps there was a sound. A hammering of fists on the door or the howl of inrushing cold air.

The men enter.

James Cowper, steward of Inschoch Castle, John Weir, keeper of Auldearn tolbooth, Tamas Dunbar, William Fordyce and Reverend Harry Forbes. Dressed in their long winter coats against the February cold, their eyes adjusting to the dim light of the smoke filled home. If their steps faltered as they realised they had encountered as yet uncompleted childbirth, Harry Forbes made sure they did not desert their purpose. The women were momentarily uncertain until Reverend Forbes' words changed heaven into hell.

"Isobel Gowdie. We are here tae arrest ye for witchcraft! Ye will be taken furth tae a place of safekeeping until the Kirk session can examine ye! Mistress Breadheid, we are here for you also but given your circumstances, we will permit ye a few hours tae compose yourself and seek a wet nurse." Forbes looks at Moira's pregnant form, "Though it seems ye may hae just such close at hand."

"No!" Isobel leaps forward, the knife to cut the cord in her hand. "Ye canna dae this! Are ye monsters! She is no' yet fully delivered. The bairn's cord no' yet cut. This is surely agin Christ's law!"

Cowper and Weir each have a thick wooden cudgel that they bring forward at the sight of Isobel's knife. Baby Isobel begins to emit a pitiful wail, sensing the change in her mother's breast. Moira cries, "No, ye'll no' tak my mother!"

Forbes steps between Cowper and Weir. He is inches from Isobel's outstretched arm and knife. If she lunged now, she could stab him before anyone could intervene. Some power stays her hand. Common decency and something more, a deep buried certainty that this day might one day come.

Forbes senses the women's waning resolve and their imperative to complete the birth. Janet's body gives her no choice as a fresh wave of contractions compel her to push the placenta out. Her roar this time is pure anguish and pain. Isobel yet stands with her knife pointing at Reverend Forbes. For seconds she stares into his eyes, as she withstands her friend's primeval scream.

"Finish it." Forbes says quietly but firmly. "Attend to your friend. Cut the cord and surrender your knife. If you do not, my men will cut the cord instead of you."

Isobel feels a flood of power seep out of her. In a single moment she is no longer loving midwife attending her friend's birth. No longer the greatest ballad singer in Nairnshire. No longer the darkest charmer. Her whole body wilts. She is exactly what Harry Forbes sees in her, a powerless and deluded woman. Isobel cannot understand it. Her hands begin to shake, as tears course down her cheeks. Tears. She has so rarely cried all her life. She has been inured and fortified against it. This powerlessness, she knows she is letting herself and her friends down. *"I'm sorry, Janet."* Isobel says as she turns away from Reverend Forbes and back toward the mother and new-born child. The women dissolve. The dark powerful women dissolve and shrink. Janet feels tears falling from her eyes. *"I'm sorry tae"* she says, knowing she led Isobel down the path that brought them both to this day. Moira shouts at the men, *"Hae ye nae decency, avert your eyes!"* but Forbes holds out a hand commanding his men to stand their ground. *"We durst not. Wha kens what devilry ye might concoct if we do."* Fumbling fingers, great sniffs of regret, Isobel cuts the cord between baby Isobel and her mother and ties it off. Janet's placenta oozes out. Isobel could reach forward but a few inches and end her friend's life. It would have been better if she had.

Isobel collects the placenta and makes sure it is free of Janet's womb. She feels a surge of defiance. "This gave life tae a bairn! Ye only bring death!"

At a nod from Forbes, John Weir reaches under the placenta to remove the knife from Isobel's hand. In the scuffle that follows, James Cowper moves forward and wrenches the placenta out of Isobel's hands and casts it down to the ground. The women would have given a prayer of thanks over it had the men not arrived. Weir brings his cudgel sharply down on the back of Isobel's head and she falls senseless to the ground.

"The Lord Jesus Christ is the only bringer of life!" Forbes intones. "You should have remembered that, before ye consorted wi' the Devil!"

Janet has lived through famine, pestilence and war, the loss of three children. She cannot quite place this moment. The surge of joy at the safe delivery of her child. The perfect consummation of love as Moira and Isobel shared in the embrace with mother and child. The absolute shattering. Her friend knocked unconscious to the ground. The implacable stare of the men. There is no escape from this. Her dreams and her charms always gave her an extra strength. Helped her survive. Helped her carry on amid the endless desperation and grind. Now they seemed powerless and foolish. All she could do would be to get herself ready to go. Go with these men. With the greatest surge of strength in her life, Janet pulled herself to sitting, adjusted her bloody shift and latched the babe to her breast. With the greatest surge of strength in her life, Janet prepared to let go her life.

"Moira, ye maun wash me doon and fetch my clean dress and plaid. Gentlemen, will one of ye gang tae my husband and sons at the Home Farm and tell them where I have gone."

Moira looks appalled. "No, ma!" she cries. "We cannae let them tak ye! Ma!"

Forbes puts his hand on the girl's shoulder. "Do as your mother says, lass." His voice is soft and reassuring. "You'll hae the babe to look after and soon after that your own. If your mother is innocent, ye hae nothing tae fear."

"Please, Moira. It is for the best." Janet tells her daughter. Numb with shock, Moira reaches for the wooden bucket and begins to wipe down her mother's legs with clouts.

"Take her to the tollbooth." Forbes commands to Weir and Fordyce, who lift Isobel's body. "Tamas will seek Mister Taylor, once we have you safely removed, Mistress Breadheid. I will allow ye five minutes for your washing and dressing, no more. Miss Moira, you must be the woman of the household when your mother is away."

No-one turns into a crow to fly away. No-one even fights back with the knives or implements close by. A newly born babe whimpers at her mother's breast, her older sister wipes blood and placental matter from her mother's thighs in bereaved disbelief. Isobel is being hauled out the door by two men, who do not wish her well. Janet feels strangely calm. For the briefest second all she can feel is baby Isobel sucking the first gulps of life from her breast. "Clever girl." she tells her daughter. It will be the last words she ever says to her. From the day twenty-five years ago when she first let her mother-in-law Elspet Nishie talk to her about the lore, it has all been leading to this.

Minutes later, Moira completes her ministrations. Her mother is cleaned and clothed. Her best plaid pinned at her breast. Moira cannot stop the tears from falling. Her own unborn child kicks inside. Janet has finished giving baby Isobel what little milk she can take from the breast at this early stage. Janet hands the swaddled babe to her daughter. As she does so she places her hand on Moira's tear stained cheek. "Look after her. Tell her who her mother was." The two women place their forehead's together, their breathing sorrowful and uneven. Forbes must have the last word in face of such female grief and power.

"Take her!" he instructs Cowper and Dunbar. His final words are for Moira, babe in her arms, as her mother is led away. "You need not follow your mother's path." Forbes places his hand on Moira's forehead, as if in exorcism of her mother's so recent touch.

"The Lord shall preserve thee from all evil, he shall preserve thy soul. The Lord shall preserve thy going out and thy coming in from this time forth and even for evermore."

CHAPTER 32: JEAN, THE MAIDEN AND BLACK JOHN

Auldearn Tuesday 1st July 1662

"The maiden of owr coven Jean Mairten, we doe no great mater withowt our maiden" **Isobel's second confession 3rd May 1662**

"Quhen we ar at meat or in any uther place quhatever, the maiden of each coven sits abow the rest nixt the divell and she serves the divell for all the old people that he cairis not for and ar veak and unmeit for him, he will be with her and us all lyk a weath horis after mearis and somtymes a man bot werie wilfull in carnal cowpulation at all tyms." **Isobel's third confession 15th May 1662**

I awoke with such a feeling of certainty about my nocturnal deductions, that I was disappointed in Wattie's cautious response when I discussed it with him at breakfast.

"I can see how it might all be as you say, Archie but it might not. Isobel and Janet said they met the Devil, no just a man wha was black and surely they would ken Hugh Hay, the Laird's uncle and the man who ran the estate when the Laird was a boy. They would ken he wis a man and no' the De'il?"

I ruffled my hair in exasperation, "How am I supposed to know exactly how it works!? Perhaps they know Hay is a man but he's a powerful, persuasive man. I felt that in him when he spoke to me seventeen years ago. He stayed with me, in my thoughts, despite all the other things I saw and did that year. Perhaps Hay leads them like a Preacher and he calls on Black John, who leaps out with a roe deer's mask on and has carnal dealings with the women using his huge nature?"

Wattie shrugged. Part of me shared his unease, whenever I tried to picture this clearly, it was never quite an exact fit. It was not *the* Devil, I was sure of that but if it was a man, why didn't Isobel and Janet just say so and where did all the fantastical flights and shapeshifting come into it?

Wattie asked a more practical question. "So how dae we prove this? We cannae just accuse one o' the town's leading men. You're unpopular enough here as it is. We could haul doon Black John's breeks and if his "nature" isnae huge then he's no' our man! Or our De'il!"

"Hopefully it doesn't come to that." I replied, accepting what I assumed was Wattie's attempt at levity. "It would be good to speak with John and explain we mean him no harm."

"That will no be easy" he replied, "*we think you pretend tae be the De'il so ye can hae copulation wi' a' the wives in the village!* That's no harmless where I come fae!"

"I'll find a way." My mind kept repeating the thought that my task was to help Isobel and her lover, John, to be together. I had not voiced this to Wattie. "I will go to Brightmoney. I would like to speak with Jean Martin, housemaid there, the one Isobel calls the Maiden of the Coven. If I get a chance for a word with John, all the better. Your task, Wattie, is to do all you can to bring Isobel back to health, at least enough for us to speak with her again this week."

• •

And so I rode back down the avenue of trees that led to Hugh Hay's house of Brightmoney. Seventeen years before I had driven the fleeing men of Lawer's Regiment before me, hacking down with my sword at any who lagged behind. I knew the truth. I may not have taken part in the killing of the men Hugh Hay reluctantly ordered to be brought out but I killed others that day, who offered me no harm. I had such a dreadful schooling in war, I came to think that was how it had to be. A boy, my age or younger, tried to surrender to me. Pled for his life. I had my dragoon pistol loaded and blasted him at close range. Lewis Gordon was appalled. *"Men should not go to war, if they do not ken what to expect."* I said, as if I was a sage of man's inhumanity, not a boy of eighteen. Perhaps after Aberdeen, the harrying of Argyll, Inverlochy and now Auldearn, I was both.

Perhaps it was there or there, I thought, as I walked my horse slowly. *Where I ended a life for no reason, other than I could.*

I had a sudden thought, who among all the people named in Isobel and Janet's confessions had actually killed someone? Maliciously, as I had done. Perhaps none. Even the old witches, Agnes Grant and Katherine Sowter, convicted of killing through witchcraft, Hugh Hay's two brothers, perhaps it had just been the bloody flux, as Mister Popley suspected and the only people murdered had been the two women. Of all the people involved in this investigation I might be the only one who had killed in wanton cold-blood.

I tethered my horse and knocked on the door. After waiting several minutes, the door was answered by the exact two people I wished to see, Jean Martin, the housemaid and the man I could not help but think of as Black John.

"The Master is no at hame," Jean explained. "He's awa on business tae Nairn. He was nae expecting ye."

I could not help but notice that John looked protectively at Jean and suspiciously at me. I needed to state my intention persuasively. "Mistress Martin, is it not? And Mister John. Ye ken I am part of the commission of investigation. Sent from

Edinburgh to make sure justice is properly done. I think you both could be able to help me. I just want to ask a few questions. I promise I mean neither of you any harm."

"You should go." John said. On hearing his voice, I was surprised to detect a Scottish accent but when I thought on it, he had been here for seventeen years, at least.

I had not persuaded them, I knew that. What happened was something else. Jean had a slight smile on her lips, even as she tried to look concerned. A hint of mischief or something darker. She wanted to talk. "Thank ye, John" she said, placing an appreciative hand on his arm, "I will speak with this man. It is best that he kens."

John frowned uncertainly but permitted the pretty maid to invite me in. "Very well but I will stay near, tae mind for anything asked that should not be."

They led me through the house, past the public rooms and the kitchen to a live-in maid's room at the back. Just a bed, a chair and a chest, upon which a bible rested. I was offered the chair, Jean moved the bible and sat upon the chest. John stood dutifully by the door, where he could observe us both.

"You have been reading this?" I said, picking up the bible, surprised, as literacy was not usual among the common people.

"John is teaching me." Jean said, looking over at John with evident gratitude and pride. If I could see his colour change, I could have sworn that John blushed. I had to supress also my surprise that John could read and teach.

I replaced the bible on the bed saying "Excellent, a great gift. I, too, came from humble beginnings but was given the opportunity to learn my letters and now I am a lawyer." I patted the bible, "Who knows where this will lead for you. Jean, Mistress Martin, what was it you thought I should ken?"

Jean inhaled deeply, then broke down weeping, her words expressed in a sorrowful wail. "I gave the names o' Isobel Gowdie and Janet Breadheid tae Mister Forbes. I had tae! They were my friends, I ken but they were trying tae drag me deeper intae their ways. Isobel especially. I had tae!" I saw real tears but still something made me wary of Jean's display of emotion. John appeared convinced and concerned, he stepped forward and placed his hand on her shoulder, saying "There, Miss Jean, you don't have to do this, if you don't want to." Jean briefly touched John's comforting hand, before sniffing and saying she wished to carry on. John stepped back.

"What "ways" did they try to teach you?" I asked.

Now Jean looked frightened, "I dinna ken if I can say! Mister Forbes has promised me the Lord's salvation and his protection, if I spoke the truth. Do ye promise tae protect me also?"

Jean leaned forward to press her question. I caught a disconcerting glimpse of cleavage as she did so, beneath such a pretty face. I was going to grant her safety even before that moment. "I am sure if you have confessed already to Mister Forbes and he has seen fit to not condemn you, then neither shall I. Please, help me understand."

"They consort wi' the devil. They invoke his name and others tae work their charms, for good and ill. They wanted me tae join wi' them. Isobel telt me their wisdom stretched back through the ages, Janet tae her, Elspet Nishie tae Janet, Agnes Grant tae Elspet Nishie and others for mony years afore. She called me her Maiden, their name for the next in line."

John stepped forward again. His voice conveyed an urgent

appeal that I should understand, "Miss Jean came forward before their corruption took hold. She came forward in time. Mister Forbes and Master Hay are both quite certain, she came to us in time."

I nodded at John, to acknowledge the vehemence of his concern and his certainty that Jean could and should be saved. For the moment I had to force to one side that his words clashed with my belief that he and Hugh Hay might be orchestrating this all through the mantle of the Devil. John's intervention prompted a question I might not otherwise have asked. "Jean, can Isobel Gowdie be saved? Should she be saved?"

For the first time in the interview I sensed Jean's emotions to be real, confusion, pity, resolution all crossed her face. "I feel heart-sorry for her, because she wasnae all bad and at times even kind tae me but no, sir, Isobel Gowdie cannot and should not be saved. She is too lang in the service of the Devil."

"What does she do in the service of the Devil? What is the worst she has done?"

"The worst! The worst! Is consorting wi' the De'il no' bad enough!" Jean cried out. "She has worked spells tae harm people who she says hae done her wrong and she has ridden wi' the wild faerie host, marking folk wha are set tae die. Is that no' bad enough for ye!?"

"It certainly sounds bad but I still don't understand. How do you know this? Did she tell you this or were you shown?"

Once again Jean was dramatically uncertain as to whether she should answer, "I dinnae want tae say. Aye, she told me. Told me o' her spells and her corp creadh, wee mannies made o' rye dough that were said tae bring harm tae the person they were formed for. She told me o' her journeys wi' the faerie but" Jean buried her head in her hands before raising her head free, "but she tried to show me also. Tried tae tak me wi' her."

"How tak ye wi' her? You met with the faerie host also?"

Jean hesitated and I saw her glance briefly at John. I believed I saw genuine confusion in her eyes. " I…I…dinna ken. It felt.. it felt sae…true." Jean grabbed the sleeve of my jacket between two of her fingers. "As real as this but I'm nae siccar. It started as a dream. A special dream Isobel wanted me tae share. I tried tae gang wi' her but it affrighted me and that was when I kent I had tae speak wi' Reverend Forbes"

"And thank the Lord she did." John chimed in. "Returned to the Lord in time."

"Jean, you talk of riding with the faerie but you say Isobel served the Devil. Did you see the Devil? Did you see Isobel with the Devil?"

Before Jean could answer, John stepped forward more forcibly than before. "You will not ask that, sir. We have helped you more than enough. Can you not see that Miss Jean is tormented to think back? We should not have allowed you in Master Hay's house. You must leave and Miss Jean will answer your questions no more."

I did ask myself if I could out-wrestle the formidable man looming over me. The men I had killed had been shot or slashed while I was mounted on a horse. I also calculated I yet needed to respect the hospitality, such as it was, of the folk of Auldearn. I could not out-stay my welcome. I showed the palms of my hands in a gesture of acceptance of the caution I had received. "Very well. John. Mistress Martin, permit me a few final questions, which I promise will not tax Miss Martin too hard. Did any of your meetings take place In Auldearn Kirk?"

Jean looked immediately at John. "She will not answer that either!" he replied for her. "It is time you must leave!"

I rose to stand, as did Jean but before I agreed to step toward the door, I asked, "John, did you know Isobel Gowdie? Do you want to see her burn?"

The question hung in the room, as both Jean and John could not conceal a show of mixed emotions on each of their faces. "I knew Mistress Gowdie." John replied cautiously but respectfully. "Difficult not to in a small village such as this. The world can be a cruel place and I have my own reasons to not want to see folk suffer." John moved toward the bedroom door, ushering us all out. "But if anyone deserves to burn, it is Isobel Gowdie!"

We stepped into the kitchen, John and Jean both urging me out. I moved slowly. I could not let John's answer go unexplored. "And if she could be saved, John. If Isobel could be declared innocent in the eyes of the law. Would you welcome that?"

John stopped. His brows furrowed. He stared at me intently, his eyes searching mine. I sensed Jean's intense interest in the exchange also. "If you could truly do that. If she is truly innocent. I would welcome that."

"Thank you, both, for your time." I said, as I allowed myself to be directed out of Brightmoney House.

CHAPTER 33: ISOBEL NEEDS.

Auldearn Tollbooth 3ʳᵈ March 1662

"Quhen we goe to any hous, we tak meat and drink and we fill up the barrellis with our own pish and we put boosomes in our bedis, with our husbandis, till we return again to them. We wer in the Earl of Moray's house in Darnaway and we gott anewgh ther and did eat and drink of the best and brought part away with us, we went in at the windows. I haid a little horse and would say "Horse and hattock in the divellis name!" and then we would fly away where we would be even as straws wold flie upon an hie way, we will flie lyk strawes quhen we pleas wild strawes and corn-straws will horse to us when we put them betwixt oor foot and say hors and hattock in the divellis nam, and quhen any sees these straws in the whirlwind and does not sanctify themselves, then we may shoot them dead at our pleasure. Any that are shot by us, their soul will go to Heaven but their bodies remains with us, and will flie as hors to us als small as straws. I was in the Downie Hills and got meat there from the Queen of the Faeries, more than I could eat. The Queen of the Faerie is brawlie clothed in white linens and in white and brown clothes. The King of the Faerie is a braw man, well favoured and broad faced. There were elf bulls crowtting and skoylling up and down there and affrighted me." **Isobel's first confession 13ᵗʰ April 1662**

I sobel needs to remember who she is but somehow it keeps slipping through her fingers. Three days and nights of no food, no drink, no sleep, her slop bucket unemptied, no water to wash. No visitors. Just the stony presence of John Weir and young Tamas. They have said nothing to her. No response to her pleas, her entreaties or even her anger. Tamas once pulled open the wooden shutter on the little viewing window built into the door and caught Isobel squatting to piss over her bucket. Instinctively, Isobel lurched forward and hissed. Tamas pulled the shutter closed. Later, amid the endless hunger and silence, Isobel wished she had kept her cool, pulled her filthy shift up higher, enticed his eyes in, to establish some connection.

Isobel needs to remember what worked for her before but so little of it seems to work for her now. She recalls the feeling as soon as Forbes and his men invaded Janet's home. Her power deserted her. Fled through her flesh. No dream of escape can breach these walls. She knows her captivity would mock her flight. She might dine with the Queen and King of Elphane, yet still wake up in silence and starvation, next to her own filth. No clever words or rhyming couplets will move John Weir to grant her a flicker of human concern.

Isobel does not know that Reverend Forbes has instructed Weir and Tamas closely. *"No-one is to speak with her, feed her, bring her comfort until I arrive. She must see that her path to salvation, earthly and heavenly, lies through me. She must long for my visits. She must long to talk with me. She must be taught to long for me."*

Isobel cannot forget how she left Janet, her calling as healer not yet completed, her charge yet bleeding and in pain. Oh God! How great must Janet's pain be, torn from her child within moments of her birth? Isobel searches for a spirit or a saint or a demon that might help Janet but somewhere deep in her mind, she knows there is none. Go into a crow, go into a hare. She could say the words thrice and in the devil's name and know they would only mock her. I am sorry Janet. I cannot help you. I promised to see your new-born baby safe, the baby you named for me, yet now I cannot know where or how she is. Isobel recalls that moment of absolute consummation, when she and Moira each held Janet, while baby Isobel lay upon her mother's breast. The memory only causes her to cry. That moment was not meant to be the pinnacle. It was not meant to be the end of anything. It was the promise of mother to daughter, female friend to female friend. It was meant to be the beginning of baby Isobel's shared life.

Isobel lies in the implacable silence of Auldearn Tollbooth and knows she and Janet may never see baby Isobel again.

Help me Lord Jesus! Help me the faither, son and Haley Ghaist! Help me, all the saints! Saint Ninian, I hae knelt afore your well! Saint Bride, I hae honoured ye as Brigid and Bride both. Help me Red Reiver! Ye were swift enough tae appear quhen pickings were guid! Help me Satan. Oh Christ, I hae ne'er had much truck wi' ye, Satan, but if ye will help me now, I would change a' that.

Silence. Emptiness. Growing disbelief. Weir pulls open the shutter. Isobel tries. Tries to do what? She cannot even formulate. The shutter closes. Silence. Emptiness. Growing despair.

Isobel needs a rescuer.

Reverend Forbes enters the cell like the first warm spring day after winter. "In the Lord's name, this is unacceptable! Mister Weir the stench is unbearable. Remove that slop bucket immediately. Mistress Gowdie, Mistress Gowdie, Isobel, what can I do to aid you? Tamas bring water and bread and a basin of water so Mistress Gowdie can wash herself. For pity sakes, she is almost wasted away!"

Isobel swims back to consciousness, although the torpor from her weakness is hard to overcome, she sees the bustle around her, hears the authoritative concern in Reverend Forbes' voice and for the first time in 3 days her senses are energised by hope. "Thank ye, Mister Forbes. Thank the Lord! Thank ye!" she manages to say. Isobel painfully moves herself off the board that serves as a bed and kneels at Reverend Forbes' feet. She raises her two hands in supplication, her long untended hair, falls about her face. "Thank ye!" she says again as her fingers grasp the hem of Forbes' frock coat. Forbes, in the same moment, is both thrilled and appalled by the sight. Filthy, pathetic woman, yet not so long before she had been a striking, well-kent member of the community. Forbes had always been stirred by the sight of her, not just the memorable red hair but by the challenge and mystery of her poise and social exchange with her peers. Isobel Gowdie had a standing with the farm labourers of Auldearn that was not derived from her betters. It came from the fire in her eyes and the mischief in her smile and whatever magic she commanded with her words. *Well, ye are brocht low now, Isobel Gowdie!* Forbes thought, as he gently prized her grasp from his coat. *Now, ye shall be brocht back tae your proper obedience!*

"Weir! Bring me a chair. Mistress Gowdie is there anything else I can seek for your comfort?"

Isobel is biting desperately on the bread set before her and washing it down with blessed water. "A comb," she manages to say between gulps "and some rags and moss, for I fear my time of the month will be upon me soon."

John Weir sets down a wooden stool that Harry Forbes sits himself down upon. "Thank you, Mister Weir. Pray close the door and leave us undisturbed until I call for you."

The heavy door closes, the scraping of the iron bolt announces that Isobel, accused witch and Harry Forbes, Minister of the Reformed Kirk in Scotland, are alone and unobserved in the small cell.

"Isobel, my child, I have always thought of you as a seeker after spiritual truth. Is that not so?"

Isobel felt some of her strength return, though her mind was yet sluggish and confused. Harry Forbes' manner was so disarming and he had taken her side against the implacable John Weir. Isobel knew that she had to nurture and please Harry Forbes, the first person to treat her kindly since her arrest. "How d'ye ken me , sir?" she asked.

Forbes reached into his coat pocket and pulled out an object wrapped in paper. Once revealed it was shown to be a small pastry, filled with mincemeat. Forbes handed it over to Isobel, "From my own kitchen" he explained. Isobel took the gift and devoured it, desperately. It tasted like the most marvellous morsel she had ever eaten. Forbes watched her patiently, a slight smile upon his lips. "You are part of my flock. Have shared in divine service at my kirk. A guid Minister kens a' his sheep. How else can he guide and tend them? I always knew you were special, Isobel but now your friends have told me all about you. About your gifts. Jean Martin has spoken with me, at length. Tell me about your flights, Isobel."

Isobel's mind reeled. Jean, her maiden, had spoken with Forbes. Jean had betrayed her, after she had such high hopes for Jean. Feelings akin to love. She had wanted Jean to learn all that she had learnt. Oh God in Heaven!Jean had spoken to Mister Forbes. Janet taken too, in a weakened state. Janet who had taught Isobel. How soon before she spoke? Isobel could not think, she had to play for time. "I dinna ken what you mean, Mister Forbes" she replied. She could not help but speak the lie with a hint of insolence in her tone.

Instantly Forbes sprang forward and slapped Isobel hard upon the cheek. The unexpected violence was in such contrast with his previously benevolent demeanour that it caused Isobel to lose her balance and her mental calm also. Isobel put her hand to her stinging cheek as she pulled herself back to her sitting position on her plain wooden bed. Forbes followed up his blow with passionately delivered words,

"Isobel Gowdie! I will not be trifled with! Understand this and understand it well. I am your only hope of salvation. In this world and the next. You have a clear choice of paths ahead of you, these coming days. Speak with me. Tell the truth and I will ensure that you are well treated. No more hunger and thirst. I will also help you meet your inquisition with a penitent heart. This will be taken into account by those questioning you and, more importantly, will also be known by God." Forbes reached forward and placed his own hand on the cheek he had just slapped, stroking it gently with his fingers. "Speak honestly with me, Isobel, and I will do everything in my power to help you." Forbes removed his hand from Isobel's cheek and held it, shaking, inches, from her face, as if about to strike again, " but chose the wrong path. Chose to lie, dissemble, remain obstinate and un-confessed in the service of the Devil, then you will know only pain, aching hunger, maddening isolation, as your final days play out in torment before you descend into the even greater torment of Hell. We have your accomplices, Isobel. I do not need your confession to convict you. I need your confession to help save your soul." Forbes let the tension subside in his threatening hand as he gently placed it on her cheek again. "Heed my words, Isobel. I am your only hope."

Isobel closed her eyes. She was not deranged, nor ignorant or uncaring about her fate. She could not think who to call upon who might help her in this cell. Her power no longer existed once apprehended. No earthly power could save her either. Although she feared Forbes, had never fully accepted his spiritual authority, she had a sense that what he said was true. He was her only hope in this world and the next. The pain from the hunger had been so great, the relief to eat and drink again, even greater. Only Harry Forbes could help her. Isobel opened her eyes and put her fingers to her cheek, remembering both the slap and the touch. She looked Harry Forbes boldly in the eye, even as she knew she had no choice. He was her salvation and condemnation both.

"When we go to any house," she began, "we take meat and drink and we fill up the barrels with our own pish and we put brooms in our beds, next to our husbands, until we return again to them, so that they do not notice we are gone. My husband kens nothing of my flights. Once we went to the Earl of Moray's house at Darnaway and we did eat and drink of the best and brought part away with us. I flew on a little horse and would say "Horse and hattock away!" and then we would fly away wherever we pleased and we would be even as straws or even corn-straws will be as a horse to us when we put them between the toes of our foot and when any sees these straws in the whirlwind and does not sanctify themselves, then we may shoot them dead at our pleasure. Any that are shot by us, their soul will go to Heaven but their bodies remain with us, and join us, on horses as small as straws. I was in the Downie Hills and got meat there from the Queen of the Faeries, more than I could eat. The Queen of the Faerie is brawlie clothed in white linens and in white and brown clothes. The King of the Faerie is a braw man, well favoured and broad faced. There were elf bulls crowtting and skoylling up and down there and I must admit, it affrighted me."

Harry Forbes was a master at masking his true feelings. He felt a surge of triumph as he realised Isobel was going to give him the confession he needed. He must yet nurture and cajole, for her words were primitive and not wholly to the point. He would need to win her trust even further, for her to allow him to shape her testimony. Of all things, she most needed to understand what he next had to say.

"It must have been quite splendid but also quite frightening,

Isobel, I can see that and what wonderful powers, who hasn't yearned after the sumptuous tables of our Lords and masters, when our own hunger is most severe? But Isobel you must heed my next words and reflect on them, in your solitude, before my next visit." Forbes leaned forward again, to physically emphasise his point. "Just as I told you that you had a choice of paths, so too does mankind have only one choice." Forbes placed one hand upon Isobel's bare thigh, just above her knee, "God. The Word of the Lord and all things Righteous and" his other hand came down upon Isobel's left thigh. "the Devil. The Devil takes many forms, Isobel. There are no powers in-between, Isobel. No faerie King, no ancient Goddesses, no Saints, well certainly not the craven images and deceitful bones the Papists would have us worship. You have been seduced by the Devil, Isobel. All these other forms, all these powers, if they come not from God and I know they do not, then they must come from the Devil. Think on that, my child. Think of how you first compacted with the Devil. How you first let him into your life. I will reward you even more splendidly than I have today if you show to me, next time, that you have understood that your master was the Devil, all the time. You will do that for me, Isobel?"

Isobel found that Reverend Forbes' hands had each moved an inch up her thighs and in the vehemence of his speech he had pushed her legs wider apart. Naked and exposed under her shift, Isobel found the strength to move Forbes' left hand from her leg, while also giving him what he said he wanted. "I will think on your words carefully, Reverend Forbes. I thank ye for your kindness and will reflect on what you have told me of the Devil. I am fatigued now and would wash myself before Mister Weir thinks better of allowing me this basin and cloth." Forbes accepted Isobel's cue and removed his right hand from the flesh of Isobel's thigh. As he adjusted his coat for leaving. Isobel pressed her case. "Food when you come again, Mister Forbes and clean clothes if you can spare them. Knowing you will bring these things, I will think hard on all that you have said."

Forbes rose to his feet. He would like to watch Isobel wash herself but he knew he had achieved as much as he could have hoped and more, this visit. All in good time and he would soon be able to play Isobel's and Janet's testimonies off against each other. He had waited years to uncover Satan's handiwork in Auldearn. He could wait a bit longer to ensure it was all brought to light. All in God's time.

CHAPTER 34: THE DEVIL, LIKE THE LORD, WORKS IN MYSTERIOUS WAYS.

Auldearn: Wednesday 3rd July 1662

"I aknowledg to my great grief and sham that fyftein yeiris since I denyed father, son and holie gost in the kirk of aulderne and gaw over my bodie and sowll to the divell." **Isobel's fourth confession 27th May 1662**

Wattie reported back on the day's visit to Auldearn Tollbooth. John Weir was not opposing the improved conditions. Isobel had been washed and freshly dressed by Agnes Duncan, who appeared to be a couthy and caring woman, prepared to put helping the sick above any fear arising from tending a witch. Mistress Duncan diagnosed rye-mould sickness and prescribed boiled garlic and hawthorn to thin the blood, a thickening of the sanguine humor being a symptom of ingesting too much mould. Wattie reported that Isobel was still delirious and barely sensible but her skin was improving and her physical health responding to more regular food and drink. "We micht no' be able tae speak wi' her on Friday but she'll certainly look mair bonny when we dae" was Wattie's medical opinion.

Wattie did not know if Weir had informed Reverend Forbes of our intervention. I did not think it mattered whether he did or not, as my credentials trumped any Kirk session authority. Wattie said Isobel still asked for John but whether it was her husband or Black John from her confessions, he could not say. Then Wattie asked to be permitted to be absent the rest of today and much of tomorrow. He wanted to ride the 28 miles to Fochabers to see family. "It being a crying shame tae be sae near and no' visit" he explained. "Ye'll hae tae oversee Isobel's food the morrow" he added. I granted him leave, we had interviewed all the principal witnesses and keeping Wattie near would not influence the speed of Isobel's recovery one way or another.

Twenty eight miles due east on the Forres Road to Fochabers. About the same distance south from Auldearn to the Cabrach. Why did I not take my chance to see what family of mine yet remained? I had been running from that place since the day I was born. After Wattie departed I sat at my table to pen my report to Advocate Depute MacKenzie. Setting out in writing my findings to one as learned as Mackenzie would help me sift the wheat from the chaff. I had prepared my notes and ink, when there was a knock on the door. I was not expecting anyone and my sense of unease amid this shire filled with previous enemies made me pile my notes under a book and ensure that my rapier and dragoon pistols were close by.

The rapier posited by the door and the pistols left on top the dresser seemed ridiculous when I saw the man at my door was John Innes, a man I had admired for his decency and honesty on our first acquaintance. Innes agreed to come inside and take a seat but I could tell he was ill at ease.

"Mister Kellas, Archibald, I am er instructed to tell you that your fellow Commissioners are convening on Friday this week at 2pm at the Sheriff Principal's Rooms in Nairn to give verdict on this case. You may attend and share in the deliberations, as requested by the Advocate Depute. The Commissioners feel you have had quite enough time to investigate and have been granted exceptional access to the principal witness."

"God dammit, John! You must know that the principal witness, Isobel Gowdie, is sick in mind and body, through starvation and poisoning and the second principal witness, Janet Breadheid has been cared for so poorly in custody, she has died. This is an outrage! I have been here less than a week. How long did Harry Forbes have access to the witnesses, when their minds were whole? Months. This is not justice and you know it!"

Innes cast his eyes downward in a sheepish manner. I knew he was the message boy in this matter, rather than the main protagonist. He had the decency to say, "Mistress Gowdie is unwell? I saw that she was deteriorating, I would say between third interview and the fourth. She was quite magnificent in the third interview! How is she now?"

"John, I will answer your question and any others that you may have of me. All I ask in return is that you offer the same courtesy to me. As Brothers of the Bar. It is surely not too much to ask?"

Innes continued to look discomforted but at least he raised his eyes to meet mine and said," As I do not know your questions, I cannot give an unequivocal reply. If I can answer, I will."

"Isobel suffers from ill-effects of starvation and rye-mould poisoning, whether deliberate or through callous treatment of a prisoner, I know not. She was incapable of coherent answer when I met with her two days ago. I have been funding a restorative regime of food and care. I will visit her again tomorrow and I hope to find her improved, at least sufficiently to speak with me." I explained. Innes said he was glad she was improving. I continued on to my questions. "John, you explained to me the last time we spoke, that question and assent was sometimes used during both women's interviews, for example, each of Isobel's confessions starts with an account of how she met and compacted with the devil, I presume she did not retrieve this memory afresh every time but was asked *"you have previously described how you met and compacted with the Devil, is that not so?"* To which Isobel only had to nod her head or say *"yes"* for you to record the original testimony again. Is that correct?"

"I believe I have already told you as much." Innes replied, cautiously.

"And now you have told me that between Isobel's third confession on 15th May and her fourth confession on 27th May her health had visibly deteriorated. The fourth confession is by far the most repetitive, the least enlivened by idiosyncratic detail. Two questions, John, was the fourth confession largely a *"tidying-up"* through question and assent? and what was the purpose behind arranging the fourth interview at all?"

"Archie, I can best answer you as I answered you last time. Isobel's second and third confessions were wonders that I shall remember all my life. Enthralling performances. When the Devil beat his acolytes as they pled for mercy, all who witnessed the description were in Auldearn Kirk with the protagonists also. She exuded such passion, she would cavort as the domineering Devil, then cower as the more timid victims, then stand with fists bunched as the women who defended themselves. It was extraordinary, Archie. My greatest fear is that when Isobel was most herself, most dramatic, I was so enraptured I was able to record the least. Oh, I did my duty as best I could but there were charms and detail of the Faerie domain that I did not capture and now cannot recall. The fourth confession was nothing like the previous. Now that you tell me that Isobel has sickened to the point of incoherence, then I must say that the 15th of May, when she *performed* so magnificently for her interrogators, that the 15th of May was the last day she was truly alive." John Innes looked genuinely saddened and reflective. The next was said with a sympathetic laugh. "It was, I suppose, both the apex of her life and the moment she condemned it utterly." We sat in contemplation of that moment in the life of Isobel Gowdie, a woman we had both come to strangely admire. I felt a pang of jealousy that Innes had known her at such a moment, whereas I could visit only the husk. After a few seconds of silence, Innes answered my second question. "I believe the fourth interview was to cast some light on when exactly Isobel covenanted with the Devil, if it had been twenty or more years before it may have linked back to some older Devilry in the area but she said fifteen years, which accorded with her age, as she would have been a child, when the last Laird of Park died."

"Ah yes, the previous witches condemned and burnt, Agnes Grant and Katherine Sowter." I then made a dreadful error and let the past well-up again. "Much as I have every reason to hate Lord Protector Cromwell, for how he treated prisoners such as I, his regime at least supressed the nonsense of witch trials."

"Mister Kellas! How can you say such?! How can you impose on my good nature to question me closely, when you already conceive the whole issue to be "nonsense"!? I see there is no need for me to answer any more questions."

Hard as I tried, there was no way I could retrieve the connection I had created with John Innes. "I am sorry, John, that was a tired slip of my tongue. Of course, it is not nonsense but please, before you depart, answer me this. Witchcraft is a crime like no other. As one lawyer to another, how do you convict someone who claims to have killed people who are not dead? William Bower. Isobel regrets most killing him, yet he works and breathes still at his Mill of Moynes. How do you convict people for committing crimes while in the shape of a hare or rook, yet in captivity, they show no ability to assume these forms? Why does Isobel not charm herself into a mouse to escape?"

John Innes had risen from his chair. I believe it was both his decency and his inquiring mind that bade him engage with my questions, no matter how troubling he may have found them to be. "I am no expert Mister Kellas but I would say that the Devil, like the Lord, works in mysterious ways, not always discernible to mere mortal men. Perhaps Reverend Forbes, once he had Isobel and Janet apprehended, rendered their powers inviolate, through prayer and Divine intercession. You must allow the Lord has powers also?"

I must train my face not to betray my inner-most thoughts. I allowed too many seconds to pass before I answered John, with a lie, then another question. "Undoubtedly. Is not Auldearn Kirk, consecrated ground? How in God's earth could the Lord permit the Devil to hold his initiations and his orgies there?"

"Mister Kellas, I refer you to my previous answer. I am not a theologian. But is it not all the more reason for us to take swift, decisive action to protect our community knowing that the Devil has found ways to penetrate such sanctuaries?"

Innes had collected his walking cane, in a further indication of his desire to depart. "John, is it possible that a man might assume the guise of the Devil and entice these poor women into rituals, motivated to achieve a much more common-place and understandable outcome? Why else would the Devil, a fallen Angel, a former celestial being, care to destroy the Laird of Park's posterity?"

John Inness fidgeted for a few moments upon his cane as he considered his answer, "Mister Kellas, in the last few minutes you have given me reason to believe you not only doubt the existence of the Devil but of God also. Now you wish to shift a straightforward admission of covenanting with the Devil, into some unwarranted allegation against a leading member of our community. You had best watch your step, come Friday!

You too have a reputation to consider. If there had been some common-place conspiracy, as you suggest, I am sure Reverend Forbes would have uncovered it in his many sessions with the accused."

"God's teeth, man! What hope have we as a modern country or even as lawyers dedicated to scientific law, if people can not state a case openly. If certain prejudices are unchallengeable. Reverend Forbes had no interest in anything, other than finding these women in league with the Devil!"

"Mister Kellas, I have delivered my message. I have with civility answered your questions and given you my personal warning regarding your conduct and unwarranted reasoning. Good day to you, sir. I can do no more. Reverend Forbes, I will have you know, is a Divine of high reputation and Godliness. I warn you to cast your aspersions elsewhere."

With these words, John Innes left my lodgings and I was left ruing letting Wattie depart, losing both his diplomacy with people and his counsel for my jangling thoughts.

CHAPTER 35: ISOBEL REPENTS

Auldearn Tollbooth: March 8th 1662

"Isobel Gowdie appearing penitent for hir haynous sines of witchcraft and that she haid ben ower long in that service without any compulsitoris proceidit in her confessione" **Isobel's first confession 13 April 1662**

"Isobel Gowdie professing repentance for hir former sines of witchcraft proceidit in hir confessione" **Isobel's second confession 3rd May 1662**

"Isobel Gowdie appearing to be most penentent for hir abominable sines of witchcraft most ingeniously proceidit in hir confessione." **Isobel's third confession 15th May 1662**

For two days after the visit of Harry Forbes Isobel found that John Weir and Tamas were grudgingly solicitous of her welfare. She had meals of oatmeal, cheese and even bacon. As good as she ate at home in lean times. She was given a comb, which she worked to untangle the knots in her hair. Her auburn curls had long been her pride and joy, only the slightest flecks of grey now appearing. She was allowed the basin with water to wash and her bucket was removed once a day. No-one banged on her door at night to keep her awake and she was given rags and moss to staunch the flow of blood from her monthlies, which came upon her the day after Mister Forbes left. She knew that the Reverend had spoken for her and caused the change and in her many quiet moments, she thanked him for it.

She could not see the street beyond her thick wall, there being only a small high window in her cell. In one of the few times that Weir had spoken to her, he had told her emphatically that no-one would be allowed to visit her, for fear that she bewitch them or conspire with them. She would see only her gaolers and the Reverend, who would prepare her for her questioning by the kirk session. Isobel worried about John because she knew he would be sick with worry for her. All she could do for him now was make sure his name was kept out of anything she said, which was not difficult, as he was truly innocent of everything, except loving her.

Isobel prayed, to whoever might listen, for Janet, apprehended minutes after giving birth. She prayed for baby Isobel and could not help but break down with anguished weeping, as she rolled upon the cell floor, as she realised her curse had caused her to lose yet another child while new-born. She would have been godmother to baby Isobel. Janet should have known better than to have chosen her, she told herself, amid bitter, inconsolable tears.

She had lost her Maiden, Jean, also. That was not so much losing a child, as losing a dream. Someone she had such high hopes for and had only ever wanted to help. She had poured her soul into Jean and, as Isobel lay on the cold stone floor, she knew that made her utterly vulnerable. If Jean had gone freely to Hugh Hay or Harry Forbes her only way to save herself would be to say that Isobel enticed her, tried to lure her in and she broke away before it was too late. It was not only the sensible thing for Jean to do, it was the truth. Always, when you love someone, Isobel thought, comes the possibility of loss, of heartbreak and betrayal. Would she rather she had never known the joy of thinking Jean would follow her path? That was like thinking she wished she had never been herself.

On that cold stone floor, tears upon her cheeks, Isobel

could still remember herself. True, in this cell, since her apprehension, she had felt her power desert her. No prayers or charms that made any sense but she could recall when these same charms made her a woman of importance in the cottar houses of the fermtouns. How she held her head high when she walked and higher still when the people she passed, talked about her. Isobel Gowdie, Bard o' Baillie, charmer and healer. She could smile and throw back her hair when people frowned, she could hiss then laugh at small children when they cowered. This, she could still recall, the dreams and spells that made her, herself.

"*A buddy needs something tae keep themselves agither in this accursed place*" her husband John had said to her, when he acknowledged the little of her work he knew. "*Otherwise we just work hard for a pittance, then we die.*" John was not daft. "*My but ye're a special one, alright*" another voice said in her head.

As Isobel lay on the cold cell floor, she could not un-be who she was, even though it had taken her to this prison. She did not want to. Was she so far from God? She had always given Him his place. What more did He want? *Christ,* she realised with a smile, *He is a jealous God, no' content tae share e'en a puir wretch like me*! Isobel stretched out her hand to touch the rough wall of her cell. *I canna run from Him, I maun run tae Him,* she thought. *If I am ever tae get oot o' this place.*

6th of March everything changed. No more food, her bloody rags from the last day of her monthly and her brimming pisspot, uncollected in a corner of the room. She sensed John Weir, silently, watching her more closely, sometimes through the shutter but other times, furtively, through the keyhole. Hear his breathing as he tried to make no sound, notice the slight change in light as he tried to be unobserved. *Whit are ye keeking for, ye auld bastard?* she thought.

7th March still no food. This day she was given the water basin, to drink or wash with, or both. She immersed her face in the blessed liquid and drank. Later she used a cloth and some of the water to cleanse her most intimate areas. Was she unobserved? *Whit can I dae?* she thought. *Let the auld cunt look upon the young cunt,* she said to herself, with a smile.

The key ground within the lock, John Weir entered. "Right you whore, ye are going tae gi'e me what ye gie a'body else!"

Three strides and he was across, a hammering low punch to Isobel's stomach, a big hand gripping her by the throat pushing her back, hard against the wall, banging her head against the stone. Isobel yelled for him to stop, it merely caused the fist that had punched her to unclench and reach under her shift, between her legs, coarse fingers seeking to penetrate. Weir's hate-filled face inches from her own. "No-one can hear ye, witch! Nae cunt'll believe ye. Tell a soul and it'll just be mair o' your devilish lies. Tell a soul and ye'll get plenty mair o' this!" The hand that had been pushing fingers into her was pulled out so the fist might be clenched close to her face. The left hand still gripping tightly to her throat. "Are ye going tae behave, or dae I hae tae gie ye some mair?"

Isobel wanted to resist. Her eyes flashed, her legs flailed, she managed to dig her nails into Weir's gripping hand. His right fist smashed into her face. Weir let go his choke-hold. Isobel crumpled to the ground. She wanted to resist but felt so weak. So alone. Weir pulled up her shift and raped her. Isobel barely conscious. Isobel not nearly unconscious enough. *Tak me, Red Reiver, if e'er ye maun heed ma call. Tak me someplace awa' fae here.*

How long Weir grunted over her, Isobel no longer knew, she only remembered him withdrawing after spending his seed inside her, tying his breeks and saying, "Mind dinna tell a soul.

Nae cunt'll believe ye"

Isobel lay on the floor, her cheek and jaw throbbing. She remembered He was a jealous God and she had promised to turn to Him.

Please God, get me awa' fae here!
• •

Next day, Reverend Forbes came. He brought some fresh pastries and most blessed of all, clean new clothes. Forbes once again instructed Weir to close the door and leave them alone. At first Forbes withheld the new clothes, patting the garment on his lap. "Do you remember what you promised to do, if I brought this?" Then he saw both the distress and the bruise on Isobel's face. "Lass, oh lass!" he said, with sympathy and concern.

Isobel fell to her knees and wrapped her arms round the Reverend's legs, her face coming to rest on his knees. "Help me, Mister Forbes! I'll dae a'thing ye say. Help me! In this cell, I hae seen the error o' my ways and I will gie masel only tae God, just keep Weir awa' fae me!"

Harry Forbes leaned forward in his seat and reached out to gently touch Isobel's left cheek. "Mister Weir, did this?" he asked. "Without provocation?"

Isobel raised her head, so her eyes could meet the Reverend's, "And mair. Please Mister Forbes, mak it stop. I'll dae whit e'er ye ask."

Forbes shifted in his chair to gently help Isobel to a seating position on her bed. Tenderly, he placed the simple but clean dress by her side. As he resumed his seat he said, "It must have been terrible for you. I will do what I can." Then more confidently he said, as he pulled his stool close to Isobel, "No. I am sure I can speak to Mister Weir and make it stop and no more of these either." The Reverend's fingers once more reached out and touched the bruised cheek.

Isobel sniffed amid her subsiding tears and gave a smile of thanks. It was Reverend Forbes who spoke next. "Isobel, what I most require of you is that your repentance be genuine. Otherwise, I cannot help you. I do not mean I won't help you, I mean I cannot. I cannot intercede on your behalf with either man or God, save that I believe you to be truthfully penitent. Do you understand?"

Isobel's chin had briefly fallen and Forbes reached forward again to lift her head, so this time, he ensured her eyes met his. Isobel nodded her head and gave the slightest sad smile of agreement. Once more it was Forbes who spoke. "For me to know, to truly believe, that you are penitent, you must give up what you were before. All that was not of God. You must confess to me what that was, so that I can help you understand it and help you put it aside." Forbes leant close again and took both Isobel's hands in his. "Everything depends on this, you understand? My ability to speak for you, to help you in your captivity. My ability to do what I can for your immortal soul. Trust me, Isobel, it is the only way. Let me guide you. Let me be your Minister and friend."

Isobel withdrew one hand and wiped it across her nose. She could not think straight. She could not tell if she was pretending to agree or truly agreeing. Either way, she knew it was her only hope. "Oh Mister Forbes, I dinna want tae be here. I wish wi' a' my heart tae repent."

Reverend Forbes explained that Janet had already confessed to renouncing her baptism and covenanting herself with the Devil. "You must remember, Isobel, what I told you before, even if you thought it was a faerie or some other spirit, it was but the Devil in one of his many forms. If you tell me one of your charms, you must know it was a charm in the Devil's name and insert those words into every spell. You must think on the spirits you met and remember when you first compacted with them, except you must recall it for what it truly was. A compact with the Devil." Forbes moved his stool even closer and squeezed both of Isobel's hands as he rubbed each thumb across Isobel's fingers. "Isobel, Isobel, my precious child, you cannot let Janet appear to be the truly penitent one, the one who attracts the sympathy of the kirk session. You cannot appear obstinate in their eyes. Isobel, tell me when you first met the Devil."

"I first met the Devil as I wes going betwixt the towns of Drumdewin and the Heads. This is where I covenanted with him and promised to meet him in the night time in the kirk of Auldearn. You werena the Minister then, Reverend Brodie was. The Devil stood in the reader's dais wi' a black book in his hand, quhair I cam before him and renuncet Jesus Christ and my baptism and all betwixt the soul of my foot and the crown of my head I gave freely up and over to the Devil."

• •

Isobel and Reverend Forbes spoke for over an hour that day. Isobel spoke more of her craft than she had done to any man. Forbes did not rant, scold or condemn but interceded only to point out when he saw the Devil's hand, in disguise, among what she described. At the end he thanked her and said that they should pray together. He pushed back his stool and they both knelt, facing each other, on the floor, their clasped hands touching. "Dear God in Heaven, who sent His only begotten Son, the Lord Jesus Christ, to give his own life so that our sins might be forgiven. Harken now, to this your child, Isobel Gowdie. Strengthen her heart, fill her spirit with your loving power, so that she might renounce and repudiate her compact with the Devil. Help her name and cast out all her previous wicked practices. Guide her, O Lord as ye guide me, your humble servant, in aiding her. See, O Lord the growing penitence of this woman before ye and give her the strength to cleanse her soul. Send O Lord your loving strength so that she might continue the task she has begun with such courage today. Great God in Heaven, cast your blessing upon this, your sinner, Isobel Gowdie and love, protect and cherish her in the journey she has ahead. In the name of the Father, Son and Holy Ghost, Amen"

Isobel found she did feel comforted by Reverend Forbes' words and the thought of God's strength and protection being extended toward her, at this her time of greatest need. Long after the Reverend departed, as she enjoyed the kiss of the fresh clothes he had brought, she continued to feel a glow from the promise of God's love. That she might be saved. *"Ower lang in the wrang service"* she thought.

She may not have felt so cleansed or hopeful if she had witnessed Harry Forbes' exchange with John Weir just before he left the Tollbooth. "Best day's work I hae ever done in the Lord's name." Weir said with a wink and a smile. Forbes did not reprimand him but simply raised an index finger to his pursed lips to remind his collaborator to keep silent.

CHAPTER 36: SEVEN YEARS

Auldearn, Thursday 4th July 1662

"Her skirt was o' grass green silk, Her mantel o' velvet fine, At ilka tett o' her horses mane, Hung fifty sil'er bells and nine.

True Tamas taks off his hat, An' bowed doon tae his knee, "All hail the Queen o' Heaven, For your like on earth I ne'er did see."

"Oh no, Oh no, True Tamas" she says, "That name doesna belong tae me, I am the Queen o' fair Elfland, And I cam tae visit thee."

"But ye maun gang wi me Tamas, True Tamas, ye maun gang wi' me, For ye maun serve me seven years, Through weel or ill, as chance may be."

The Ballad of Thomas the Rhymer

Entering Auldearn Tollbooth I was met by Agnes Duncan coming out. "Is she recovering?" I asked, as I gave Mistress Duncan some coins for her labours. "Aye, sir, slowly. Her fever is broken, her skin improving every day. Her mind is still wandered and she is afflicted by spasms from time tae time. She was far gone when ye called for me." I gave Mistress Duncan my thanks and asked her to return again tomorrow. I knew I was not committing myself beyond the Commissioners meeting on Friday and I wondered if my show of concern would end if the Commission sentenced Isobel to death. One complication was that the allowance Lord Middleton had given me had all been spent and anything after today was my own money. Would my passion to see justice done survive such an imposition?

John Weir insisted on checking the basket of food, which contained, bread, cheese, some ale, carrots and mussels. *"She's getting better fed than I am"* he commented bitterly, though, in truth, he appeared reconciled to the new arrangement. I asked for some minutes alone with Isobel to see if there was any improvement in her sense. A sneering smirk passed across Weir's face. *"Oh, aye. Time alane is it? Whitever ye say, Mister Kellas."*

Isobel was lying lethargically upon her wooden bench when I entered and Weir pulled the door closed behind me. She was transformed from when I had seen her on Monday, the clean dress and the reduction in the flare of red blotches on her skin being the most obvious improvements. Her long red hair was combed and tumbled over the edge of the bench. My breath caught and my heart jumped, as I saw for the first time the lithe, strikingly attractive woman she had once been, perhaps could yet be. *Shall I fight for you all the harder because I now think you bonny?* I thought. *Is it never for justice alone?*

I set down by her bench the basket of food and drink. I was in the act of moving back to the stool, when her eyes opened and I gave a startled response, as if I felt I had been trying to wrong her as she slept. *"Mistress Gowdie, Isobel. Do ye remember me, Archie Kellas? I visited the other day."*

Isobel stretched, as she came to sitting. The elongation of her limbs, the exposure of her oxters and a hint of curving breast escaping the confines of her simple dress, captivated me. Her face registered something deeper than confusion. Befuddlement. Absence or perhaps more accurately elsewhereness. A smile came upon her lips and eyes, as she reached out her right hand to my cheek. "Jeon, Jeon. Is that you my love?" she said, sounding the name not exactly as "John". Then her hand came back to touch her own lips as she giggled, "You're no' Jeon" she said, "though ye smell a bit like him."

"Mistress Gowdie, Isobel, I must speak…."

"Shhh!" she indicated with a finger to her pursed lips and then she weaved toward me and placed that finger at right angles to my lips to request my silence. "Shhh! Let me see. Let me see" she said, as she regarded me unsteadily, before she placed the fingertips of each of her hands upon the temples of my head. "What can Isobel dae for ye? You're a guid man, I jalouse." Her fingertips stroked down from my face, over my shoulders, down my arms to my hands, which she turned to open palm. "Though not a' guid, I see. These haunds hae done some herm."

I motioned to speak but she commanded my further silence with another "Shhh!" with her finger back to her own lips, as she stood up, taking a step back from me. I can only describe it that she acted like a woman who was pleasantly drunk, though I knew that could not be the case. Disinhibited but not beyond herself. "I ken. I ken. Isobel kens the song for thee."

She stroked her hands over the curve of her dress "Her shirt was o' grass green silk." She stretched her right arm languidly over her left shoulder to pluck at the material on her back. "Her mantel o' velvet fine." Isobel rocked an undulated her body as if riding. *Both kinds of riding*, I thought. "At ilka tett o' her horses mane, hung fifty siller bells and nine."

Isobel stepped back. I cannot explain, her body shape and face changed to that of a man, she took off a cap and bowed on one knee. "True Tamas taks off his hat, an bowed doon tae his knee." Isobel knelt in front of me and looked in my eyes with admiration, worship, even. "All hail, the Queen o' Heaven! For your peer on earth, I ne'er did see." Isobel took my hand and kissed it, as a man might kiss a woman's. She rose and stepped back, becoming woman again, smiling, shaking her head fondly. "Oh no, Oh no, True Tamas, she says, that name does no' belong tae me," Isobel allowed her body to fill with regal splendour, her bosom swelling. "I am the Queen o' Fair Elfland and I cam to visit thee."

Isobel knelt in front of me once more, clasping my right hand in both of hers, as her eyes searched mine, "But ye maun gang wi' me, Tamas, True Tamas, ye maun gang wi me." I felt Isobel's two hands pulling me from my chair, although I knew also that I had not moved. "For ye maun serve me seven years, through weel or ill as chance may be."

Isobel let go my right hand and stroked my cheek with the palm of her left hand. Her face had changed again from performer to woman. "Seven years," she whispered soothingly. "Seven lang years, puir Archie."

I grabbed her hand. What did she know of me? How could she know of my seven dreadful years of indenture? As unable to escape as True Tamas trapped in Elfland. "What do ye ken o' me, woman!?" I said with frightened harshness.

Isobel shook her head and recoiled. She retreated to her bench, shrinking her body, hunching it in upon itself. Shaking. Her hair falling like a curtain to obscure her face. I regretted my harsh tone. I am always regretting how I speak to people, after it is too late. I moved forward and knelt in front of Isobel, one hand upon her shoulder. The shuddering I could feel was not voluntary. My arm vibrated in sympathy. "Hush now. Hush now. I'm sorry. I did not mean to startle ye. I just wondered why you said seven years. It is a span o' time that means something to me. Can you tell me? Why seven years?"

While yet shaking, Isobel pushed her long hair away from her eyes, to look out from her protective curtain. Her eyes bulged with fear. Her breathing was rapid and loud, lapsing into sobbing. I put both arms around her in the hope that my embrace might convey safety and concern. She rocked, sobbed and shook within my arms. "Isobel. Isobel. Hush now. Hush now. I mean you no harm. Quite the opposite. I am here to help ye. Wattie and I are the only ones who can help ye." I had started talking hoping to calm her but now I was talking to calm myself, in the hope that though she could not speak, she may be able to hear. "We will look after ye as long as we can. I will look after ye as long as I can. Do whatever I can. But I need your help Isobel. I need ye tae regain yourself, as much as ye can. If not today, then tomorrow morning when I will come back. We will come back. Ye maun speak wi' us then, Isobel. It's more important than you'll ever know. You must speak with us tomorrow. Please Isobel." I found that I had pressed my lips to her hair and kissed. "Please, Isobel, please. It is later than you think. The Commission, the people judging you, meet tomorrow. Can you understand?" I squeezed my arms tighter around her, "Please Isobel, if you are in there, please find yourself tae speak wi' us."

I held her tightly until I sensed her quaking subside and her breathing and mine fell into the same deep, slow rhythm. Then I felt Isobel push out with muscles of her arms and shoulders, wishing me to release my grip. I did so and moved back, hoping she might look at me and speak, instead, she stared at me once, with dreadful, fearful eyes then fell sobbing and shaking again upon her bench.

Behind me the door opened. "That's enough time!" Weir barked. "Hae a nice wee cuddle did we, Mister Kellas?" Weir said, with his sneering smirk.

Perhaps I should have punched him immediately or damned

his eyes for his impertinence. Instead I pulled myself to my full height and grasped his collar, while speaking softly in his ear. "You will dae well tae remember what I telt ye before. If she is no' improved tomorrow, I will report ye for denying the Crown a witness or worse. Who has friends in higher places, myself or Harry Forbes? Ask yourself that, Mister Weir"

Weir brushed my hand away and stepped back. He did not appear frightened when he replied. "That a' depends on what ye mean, Mister Kellas." Weir cast his eyes to the ceiling. "Reverend Forbes has friends in guy high places."

Behind us, yet bunched and shaking on her bench, Isobel lay. "*Christ*" I thought as I exited the door, "*the Commissioners meet tomorrow, and I will have but one chance to speak with Isobel before that. Let her be improved, Lord.*" Then as I stepped out of the Tollbooth altogether, Weir's hostile arm shutting the door, "*Where's Wattie when I need him?*"

CHAPTER 37 ISOBEL CONFESSES

Auldearn, 13th April 1662

"All qwhilkis of the premissis swa spokin and willinglie confest and declarit furth of the mowth of the said Issobell in all and be all things as is abow sett downe." **Isobel's first confession 13th April 1662**

For six weeks Isobel has known only two voices. Her own, within her head and Harry Forbes'. Weir and Tamas do not speak with her, neither to explain the days when they permit her food nor the days when they do not. Nothing Isobel does can move them. Neither entreaty, nor anger. At least Weir has not raped her again.

The only thing Isobel feels she can control is how much she pleases Reverend Forbes. He is swift both to chide and to bless. It is not just the material rewards of food and drink. When Isobel prays with him most fervently or remembers to acknowledge that all the spirits who are not of God must be of the Devil, Reverend Forbes rewards Isobel with his blessing, sometimes his smile, other times his pleasure that she is working to cleanse herself most fully and prove her repentance through confessing her past crimes and mis-allegiance.

Isobel wants to please him. She has no other outlet for either her hope or her talents.

The regime of solitude, except for the visits of Reverend Forbes, has been absolute since her arrest, until 13th April. On

11th April the Reverend visited and heaped praise upon Isobel for her honesty and her penitence. *"It is for the best, my child. Soon you will be questioned by the Kirk session, you must show them what you have shown me, a woman over long in the Devil's service, determined to repent her former ways."* Forbes not only brought food that day but three daffodils, a vivid reminder of the colourful spring erupting in the world beyond Isobel's prison walls. The gift brought tears to Isobel's eyes, not just regret at the world of nature that was no longer her home but also tears of gratitude toward Reverend Forbes. That a man such as he could be considerate to a woman such as she.

A woman such as she. Isobel found as the weeks of captivity went on, her dreams were changing. She could see more clearly than ever before, it was the Devil she had compacted with. She may have visited the elf boys to obtain their small flint elf arrows but now in her dreams she saw it was the Devil who oversaw the whytting and dighting of the arrows. Now whenever she remembered a charm she inserted the words, "In the Devil's name", even though sometimes she still heard the words being spoken in Reverend Forbes' voice, as he clasped her hands and prayed with her, entreating God to give her the strength to say what she must say.

On 12th April, John Weir spoke to her for the first time since he had raped her. "No food or water today. You will only be fed again if ye speak as the Reverend has counselled ye to the Session tomorrow."

That night she was denied sleep by Weir loudly hammering on the door every hour and once, when he was uncertain of her response, he entered the cell, saying harshly into her ear, "Wake up, whore!"

Weir should not have bothered. Isobel could not sleep. She tried to make sense of the fragments of her life as they shifted and slipped away. Regret. So much regret. The wife she had been to John. Not giving him a child. The Christian she had been. So long and often invoking other powers. The pride that had sustained her. Her pride in her charms and her soaring, wild dreams. All the things that set her apart from the downtrodden crowd. All the things Reverend Forbes now told her came from the Devil and had brought her to this point when she must, for the sake of her repentant soul, confess. Must confess. Isobel could not quite forget the ecstatic thrill of a flight with the host. Of the joy of taking food, the strength of the land, of taking lives, without compunction or redress. Until now. Now the redress. Now the dreadful regret. Isobel prayed, as Reverend Forbes had taught her to pray. "Dear God and Lord Jesus, give me the strength to say what I must say."

Just after noon she was led out of her cell for the first time in over 40 days. Into the crowded quarters of the tollbooth keepers. A man sat at the table with a quill and pen, all around men stood. Isobel blinked and stumbled as John Weir prodded her into the centre of the crowd. She was given a stool, which Weir pushed her down onto. Three chairs set in front of her, where sat Reverend Forbes, Reverend Rose and Sheriff Dunbar. The rest of the men crowded behind. For a foolish moment Isobel thought John may be here. She scanned the crowd for a friendly face and saw none. She shuddered when she saw Hugh Hay of Brightmoney, standing behind Reverend Rose.

A friendly face. Only Reverend Harry Forbes, who briefly placed his hand on Isobel's knee and said in a low voice. "Remember what we said, my child. Just take your time and tell it now. For your soul."

Isobel was subdued that 13th April. Weak, tired, frightened, confused and subdued. No bardic ballad this day. Guided only by Reverend Forbes and the questions of the principal prosecutors she wracked her mind to think what they most wanted to hear. She had been over long in the service of the Devil and wished only to repent. She saw Reverend Forbes relax a little in his chair and mouth "Well done." She told them how she had renounced her baptism and covenanted with the Devil. She knew on a good day she would have stood up to touch the crown of her head and the souls of her feet. This day her arms barely waved vaguely at each extremity.

"And did you ever have carnal dealings with the Devil?" Reverend Forbes asked. So many men in the room, staring at her expectantly. Isobel told them of one time. A meikle black roch man, whose nature inside her was as cold as spring well water. Then she caught Forbes's eye and said his feet were cloven or forked.

"And what maleficum did you do?" Reverend Rose asked. Isobel looked round at the questioner. The Minister from Nairn, she knew. Another man who in other times, would have looked wise and kindly. Janet Breadheid and I raised the corpse of an unchristened child out of its grave in the kirkyard in Nairn, she told him. To use the fingers, toes and nails for a charm to take the strength from the corn and kale in Broadley's Land in Nairn.

"How many of you are there, who take part in these practices?" This question was from the third man, Sheriff Dunbar. Isobel thought of the people she had seen on her flights and at the great feasts and dances after they took the nurture from the land or the food and drink from the houses. There are thirteen persons in my coven. She remembered Reverend Forbes telling her thirteen was an inauspicious number, being the number of the disciple Judas, he who betrayed the Lord Jesus Christ. A good number for worshippers of Satan. Isobel wanted to tell them of the mischievous and marvellous things they could do. Yoking a puddock to pull a plough. Taking meat and drink and refilling the barrels with our own pish. Even entering the great dining hall of the Earl of Moray at Darnaway Palace, eating and drinking only the best. Crying horse and hattock to fly on a cornstalk upon a fairy whirlwind, flicking elf arrows at our pleasure at any who are not quick enough to sanctify themselves.

Most magical of all, she told them, she entered the fairy kingdom under Downie Hill and was dined beyond sufficiency by the Queen and King of the Faerie, resplendent in all their finery. Yet for all Isobel was a welcome guest, she yet recounted a certain fear at the wild elf bulls who roared and snorted up and down.

Isobel told them how they took their neighbour's cow's milk and sheep's milk. Remembering to say, they did this in the Devil's name. She told them how they took their neighbour's ale, excepting that which had been sanctified, that ale they had no power over. We get all this power from the Devil and when we seek it from him, we call him our Lord.

Isobel asked then for some food and drink, for she had been given none for at least a day. Reverend Forbes instantly instructed that her wish should be granted. So grateful was he for the naming of the Devil as Lord, he took the plate and flagon from John Weir and handed them to Isobel himself. Isobel enjoyed the moment, in front of so many Lairds and kirk Elders, it was quite something for the Minister to serve a common parishioner like herself. She thought of the story she knew of Jesus washing the feet of his disciples. The room hushed and waited upon her as she wolfed down the food and drink. "Good, thank ye." Isobel said, as she wiped her mouth. The moment consumed with sheer animal gratification, as the room waited for her to finish. She took a final bite of one of the pastries Reverend Forbes had brought, that combined so well with a hunk of cheese. As she chewed appreciatively, Forbes asked,

"You have told us of riding in the fairy whirlwind, shooting those who pass by, have you ever directed your powers against an intended victim?"

The room, if possible, grew even quieter, except Hugh Hay of Brightmoney, who cleared his throat. Isobel finished the last swallow of food and took a last slurp of ale. "Hmm, yes" she said, her words delayed by the blessed entry of sustenance. John Taylor, Janet Breadheid, Bessie and Margaret Wilson and Isobel made a picture of clay to destroy the Laird of Park's male children. Isobel explained how John Taylor brought home the clay in his plaid neuk and the women worked it into the physical likeness of a child. Isobel found herself quite carried away by the description and how those involved had soon told all the other witches in the area. Suddenly Isobel was jolted by the jarring difference between all that she was describing and her present situation. "And our powers, which we had before we were taken, both Janet and I, but now we have no power at all."

Isobel felt a sudden nausea and great tiredness, both from her lack of food and sleep in the days before and from a growing anxiety about what she had already said. Her principal inquisitors sensed she was slipping away. Reverend Rose pressed for an answer he most wanted to hear. "Who else is in your coven or the neighbouring covens, describe them, so we may know them also?"

"Margaret Kylie is in one of the other covens. Meslie Hirdall, spouse to Alexander Ross in Loadhead is one of them. Her skin is firey." Other names followed, before Isobel recalled when she and Maggie Brodie had sought particular revenge on the skinflint Alexander Cummings, who had cheated them at his dye works. Isobel smiled at the memory of dancing widdershins about Cumming's vats, in the Devil's name, she said, with a particular nod to Reverend Forbes, until the whole strength of the vat was taken away until it could only blacken cloth. Black the Devil's colour.

With a great exhalation, Isobel hung her head. *"So very tired"* she thought. *"Enough. Enough. I hae gied them enough."* A few of the assembled men tried to cajole her with further questions until Reverend Forbes stood. "She is tired, gentlemen. I believe we have sufficient for now. Mister Innes, did you capture all that was said?"

The room fractured into various murmurs, until all agreed that they had heard sufficient for this day. Several had already promised to attend on the morrow at Inschoch to hear Janet Breadheid, the other accused. Almost tenderly, certainly solicitously, Harry Forbes took Isobel by the hand and led her through the pressing throng back into her cell. "See that she is well treated tonight, Mister Weir" were the last words Isobel heard.

• •

CHAPTER 38 : UNDER THE PANE OF DEID

Friday 5th July 1662

"Anentis Witchcraftis: as the Quenis Majestie and thre Estatis in this present Parliament being informit, that the havy and abominabill superstitioun usit be divers of the liegis of this Realme, be using of Witchcraftis, Sorsarie and Necromancie, and credence gevin thairto in tymes bygane aganis the Law of God: And for avoyding and away putting of all sic vane superstitioun in tymes to cum: It is statute and ordanit be the Quenis Majestie, and thre Estatis foirsaidis, that na maner of persoun nor persounis, of quhatsumever estate, degre or conditioun thay be of, tak upone handin ony tymes heirefter, to use ony maner of Witchcraftis, Sorsarie or Necromancie, nor gif thame selfis furth to have ony sic craft or knawlege thairof. Nor that na persoun seik ony help, response or casultatioun at ony sic usaris or abusaris foirsaidis of Witchcraftis, Sorsareis or Necromancie, under the pane of deid, alsweill to be execute aganis the usar, abusar, as the seikar of the response or consultatioun. And this to be put to executioun be the Justice, Schireffis, Stewartis, Baillies, Lordis of Regaliteis, thair Deputis, and uthers Ordinar Judges competent within this Realme, with all rigour, having powar to execute the samin. " **Witchcraft Act of Scotland 1563 (the even harsher 1649 Witchcraft Act being in recission in 1662)**

I was apoplectic with rage. At 10 am on Friday morning, Wattie and I were met at the door of Auldearn Tollbooth by young Tamas Dunbar who told us Isobel had been taken that morning to Nairn Tollbooth to receive the verdict of the Commissioners that afternoon. Much as young Tamas wished to close the Tollbooth door after imparting the information, my foot and Wattie's shoulder forced it open. We saw that Isobel's cell was truly empty. The gut-wrenching disappointment after working so hard to restore her to health. I need not dwell on the accusations I shouted at Tamas. Weir knew we were coming this day, he knew Isobel was improving, he knew the Commissioners' meeting was this afternoon. It was blatant obstruction of my access to the most important witness of all, the accused. Tamas cowered and said little. He did tell us that Isobel was much the same in her health as the day before and the transfer of a prisoner to place of trial was customary practice. I could not help but suspect these unfamiliar words had been taught to him that day.

I returned to my lodgings, carefully packed my best lawyer's clothing into my saddlebag and set off for Nairn. All that was left for me to do on the journey was to seek to control my anger and to think through what it was that we had found out, for, the truth was, I still was not sure. I could not talk this through with Wattie as I had tasked him to find and persuade William Bower to attend the Sheriff Principal's Chambers in Nairn that afternoon, to provide living proof that at least some of the maleficum confessed by Isobel, simply wasn't true. *"For why should he come?"* Wattie, reasonably, asked. *"Just bring him. Use your silver tongue. Just bring him!"* I replied, my voice a cross between exasperation and desperation.

So much jostled in my head. The only certainty I clung to was that the Devil did not come to Nairn to flick arrows at local Ministers and miss. Yet for all I knew it was absurd, I could not formulate the crucial argument to convince others, particularly those for whom the simplest and most plausible explanation of Isobel and Janet's words was that they were true. I knew she was a bard, steeped in fairy lore and that Forbes' had somehow twisted this to insert the Devil into the story but it still did not tell me what Isobel was describing when she spoke of having carnal copulation with the Devil or of being chased, begging for mercy, round the church of Auldearn. I could not let go that these most humanly possible descriptions must be the creation of Hugh Hay and his servant, Black John. Hay had access to the church and a motivation that stretched back to the previous witch trials, eliminate his older brothers and now his older brother's male descendants to inherit. This explanation accorded with the world as I knew it, more than Satan concerning himself, somewhat ineffectually, with the male posterity of the Laird of Park.

On arrival in Nairn I requested entry to the Tollbooth to meet with Isobel. My request was denied. A small shuttered opening in the thick wooden door allowed the keeper to state his refusal, without affording me an opportunity to force open the door. Damn these pious adherents of the Covenanted Kirk. Damn their manipulations. Their faith in their own piety meant that their every corruption was seen, by them, as an expression of God's will. Even as I exposed them in my own angry mind, I knew not how to penetrate their self-righteousness. How to construct an argument from the fragments of evidence I had collected that might change their minds. I would be more likely of success had I thrown my shoulder against the stout, barred Tollbooth door.

At two o'clock we gathered in the Sheriff Principal's Chambers in Nairn. They were tolerant of me, formally polite, these men who all exhibited such practiced ease in each other's company. All familiar with each other, most related through marriage, as the same few families clung onto their ancient patrimonies and estates. Sir Hugh Campbell of Cawdor, presiding, supported by John Stewart, Sheriff Depute of Moray, Hugh Rose of Kilravock, William Dallas of Cantray and Alexander Dunbar of Boath. Accompanied around the great oak table by the expert witnesses, Reverend Harry Forbes, Notary John Innes and, in a capacity not fully explained to me, Hugh Hay of Brightmoney. Hay and I glared at each other, or, in truth, he glared at me and I did my best to hold his eyes for a few seconds, as the ferment of doubt welled inside me. Did I have anything other than the most circumstantial evidence, to voice my suspicion that this man masqueraded as the Devil to command his tenantry in sexual excess and malicious rites, aimed at clearing his path to full inheritance of the senior Hay titles and holdings in the area?

Campbell was brusque and succinct. He touched a paper in front of him as he reminded the room that Alexander Colville, Justice Depute of Scotland had granted Commission to this assembled group to investigate and judge the confessed witchcraft of Janet Breadheid and Isobel Gowdie. Campbell opened his palm to indicate myself, when he added that this original Commission had acquiesced to a written request from Advocate Depute MacKenzie to permit Notary Kellas from Edinburgh to undertake his own investigation and conjoin his observations with the original Commission.

Sir Hugh Campbell kept his gaze upon me as he directed the order of business for the meeting. "Before we discuss our findings as original Commissioners, it would be best to dispense with the remit afforded to Mister Kellas. Mister Kellas, when we met a week past to discuss Advocate Depute Mackenzie's reasons for imposing yourself upon us, you informed me that he was concerned by the activity of Prickers and of confessions obtained through bodily mutilation and torture. That he was sceptical of convictions based upon the discovery of so-called witch's marks upon the body and concerned also about the arrest of those named by the accused, where there was no corroboration to condemn them. Tell me, Mister Kellas, in this past week, where you have been afforded open and frequent access to the accused and other witnesses, have you established any evidence for the specific practices that caused the Advocate Depute to intervene? Pricking, for example, have you found evidence that this was used in this case?"

I chose to rise to my feet, to reflect the legal propriety of the occasion. "Thank you, Sheriff Principal. I will say firstly, that although I have been granted access to conduct my inquiries, it has been imperfect access. One of the accused, Janet Breadheid died sometime in April and her body burned, so I have no direct knowledge of whether she was pricked or tortured." The room rumbled in dissent and disapproval. I decided to show that I was a scrupulous and evidence led man. I raised my right hand to calm the noise. "However, I doubt that either Janet, or Isobel were pricked. Certainly I have heard no-one talk of a pricker being involved in their detection or interrogation. My imperfect access," I said, raising my voice to return to my original theme, "has meant that I have also been denied reasonable access to second accused, Isobel Gowdie. I found her starved and in the insensible throws of ergotic stupor, caused by repeated exposure to tainted bread. I have done everything in my power to restore her to health, at least sufficient to speak with me, only to find my access to her denied this very morning. I find this sufficient reason to defer any verdict until I can complete my interrogation of Mistress Gowdie."

Once again, the objections erupted, *"out of the question!"*, *"an outrage"*, *"wha does he think he is!?"* Sir Hugh Campbell compelled them to silence with two upraised palms. "Mister Kellas, I yet preside here and I shall be the judge of whether we have sufficiency of evidence. I acknowledge your lesser access to the accused but crave that ye consider this, Isobel Gowdie has already given un-coerced testimony on four occasions, witnessed and attested under oath by the leading men of this community, her words recorded faithfully by Notary Innes, seated here. Is that not correct, John?" Innes nodded in agreement and Sir Hugh continued. "Even if you persuaded

Mistress Gowdie to recant, she has confessed so fully, as did her accomplice, Breadheid, I cannot think what might persuade any reasonable man of the Law to believe her fifth statement and discount her first four? Mister Kellas, there are gentlemen here among us who attended the confessions, such as Reverend Forbes , Hugh Hay, Hugh Rose and John Innes. With their own eyes and ears they witnessed Isobel Gowdie describe both her demonic compact and her earnest repentance. What possible reason can there be to contradict these honourable men? If ye ha'e uncovered evidence to deny the guilt of these women now is the time for you to declare it. Oot wi' it, man or keep your peace!"

I rose uncertainly to my feet, until I heard a commotion beyond the chamber door. Wattie's unmistakeable voice, persuading Sir Hugh's servant to permit him entrance. Seconds later the servant entered, followed swiftly by Wattie and a sheepish looking Willie Bower. All looked round to seek the reason for the interruption. The servant blurted an incoherent apology. I stepped toward the men who had just entered to take control of the explanation.

"Esteemed fellow Commissioners, here is your evidence!" I declared with a flourish of my arm toward Willie Bower. "If you do not already know him, let me introduce William Bower, miller at the Mill of Moynes. If you have read or heard Isobel's confessions, you will know this is the man she most regrets "killing". Regrets it so much she says it twice. Yet here is Mister Bower alive and well." I moved next to Willie Bower to clasp his arm to prove its corporeal reality. "We cannot trust Isobel Gowdie's confession in this matter or in any other. Mister Bower what is Isobel Gowdie's reputation in your community?"

For all his bulk, Willie Bower looked frightened both by the elevated company and the subject matter. "I willna say. Mister

Garland speerit I was jist tae come wi' him and prove a wisna deid."

"And I thank you for that. Just two simple questions and you may be on your way, with our thanks. Did Isobel Gowdie have a reputation among the folk o' the fermtouns as a teller of stories, a bard o' the baillie?"

To my great relief, Willie Bower's face lit up, changing from concerned frown to a smile of pleasant remembrance. "Aye, she was. Yin o' the finest."

"Thank you, Mister Bower. A teller of stories. One of the finest and did she also have a reputation as a healer, one who knew the old ways?"

Bower's smile faded and his anxious look returned. "I dinna ken. I jalouse she may be. I nivver went tae her."

Before I could thank Willie Bower, Reverend Harry Forbes called out, "And did she also have a reputation for maleficent curses? Come man, you are in no danger here. All ye maun dae is speak honestly."

Bower looked over, saw it was the Minister, saw also the Sheriff principal nod his head, indicating he should answer. "Aye," he said, more certainly, "she had that reputation, one wha rode wi' the faerie tae dae men harm." Then Bower's courage crumbled and he blurted out in a panic stricken voice. "I hope tae God nae harm comes tae me for speaking oot, nor harm for kenning she wished me harm. I want nae part o' sic devilry. I beg ye, let me be!"

Now it was Harry Forbes' turn to stride out from the table, just a practiced lawyer might do. He moved toward Willie Bower and took his hand in both of his own. "My son, my son. I can see you hae muckle fear in your eyes and ye hae every reason tae fear a witch." Forbes squeezed Bower's hand firmly, as he let the word hang in the air. "But fear nae mair, my son. The Devil has no power once exposed tae the light o' the Lord. No harm can come tae you for speaking the truth. Ken that the Lord will bless ye, keep ye and gie ye peace. Go from this room in peace, William Bower."

If Forbes had used his free hand to draw a cross in the air, the blessing could not have been more Romanish, yet it was utterly appropriate to the moment. The power of the Devil countered and overturned by the power of the Lord. I could see Bower felt so. He bowed to Forbes, thanked him profusely and departed the room, followed by Campbell's servant and Wattie, who only had time to give me the slightest shrugging gesture, indicating he had played his part and brought the man.

The fleeting control of proceedings I had gained evaporated as soon as Reverend Forbes intervened. Any skill I had in presentation was matched by the Reverend. Sir Hugh knew this too and instead of asking me to continue with my case he said, "Reverend Forbes, do you have an observation on the presence and words of Mister Bower?"

Forbes spoke as he slowly returned to his seat, "Isobel Gowdie has a fearsome reputation as a practitioner of maleficent curses. Curses by her own confession that invoke the Devil's name. Whether in some cases, as in the case of Mister Bower, they do not harm the victim is immaterial. Isobel Gowdie intended harm to William Bower. She intended harm to me! All know how greatly I sickened some two years back and survived only through prayer and my wife's loving care. Both Isobel Gowdie and Janet Breadheid confessed to renouncing their baptism and covenanting with the Devil. That of itself is enough to convict them. Whatever Mister Kellas says about the efficacy of these witches' curses, we have more than enough evidence to convict them. We cannot have our lives and our community threatened by having vile cursers, in league with the Devil in our midst."

I was left isolated out in the middle of the room. Sir Hugh asked if I had any further comment to make. I wanted to wail, *there is no Devil, you fools!* but knew this would only harm my case. Only harm Isobel. "The Devil wished to harm Reverend Forbes, had elf arrows flicked at him and had unseen acolytes enter his room when he was sick, yet Reverend Forbes is here in rude, good health, as we all can see! The Devil repeatedly wishes to harm the Laird of Park, yet the Laird still lives. William Bower still lives. I am sure if we visited the Earl of Moray the day after Isobel claims to have dined at Darnaway, we would find no food or drink consumed that was not consumed by the living guests the day before! This is truly a pitiful Devil! A creation, a fantasy, dreamt up by a pitiful woman. Does anyone here in this room truly believe the physical, corporeal Devil was able to repeatedly enter the sacred ground of Auldearn Kirk to perform his abominable rites? Did anyone witness these gatherings? These feasts, dances. These orgies!? The kirk is the most prominent building in the village, why did no-one see light from the kirk at night when it was not expected? There is no reality to these confessions. I do not believe anything occurred as Isobel Gowdie confessed it. No puddock pulled a plough. No-one flew on a corn stalk. No-one was chased by dogs while in the shape of a hare. She is a local storyteller and charmer, who, if not tortured, has been pressured through long captivity, into attributing these dreams and stories to a Devil, who does not exist. At least not as Isobel describes him. You cannot convict a pitiful storyteller for reciting a fantasy."

I had held the back of my chair as I spoke, when I finished I moved round and resumed my seat. I could sense my words had given the assembled group pause for thought, possibly even some doubt. It was Reverend Forbes who once again struck back. "Did we hear Mister Kellas say that the Devil does not exist? Yet the Devil very definitely does exist. Is described in the Holy Bible. Does Mister Kellas ask us to disbelieve or renounce the Word of the Lord? As for whether the Devil could enter Auldearn kirk, disturbing as the prospect may be, the disguises and powers of the Devil are many and mysterious. Was not the Devil able to appear before our Lord Jesus Christ to tempt him in the desert? I do not claim to know all the ways of the Devil but I do know the only safeguard against his temptation is our own piety, the strength of our resolve, our faith in the Lord and our courage to root out the Devil and his followers whenever we find them among us. I wonder if Mister Kellas is truly concerned to see due legal process done or whether he has some other reason to persuade us to keep a self-confessed witch practicing in our midst. Archibald Kellas who is well kent as an enemy of our kirk." Forbes was by now pointing his finger at me. "Dare we permit a self-confessed witch to live? Dare we take that risk? I, for one, know that we cannot."

Sir Hugh Campbell drew the Commission to try Isobel Gowdie to a close. "We have heard Mister Kellas's words and Reverend Forbes'. We have all studied the confessions and understand the character of the men who attest to their truth. Mister Innes, we have accepted your testimony as to the veracity of the words attributed to the accused, I would ask you also to confirm that in all five interviews that you saw no sign of physical injury, of torture, upon either accused. How say you, Mister Innes?"

"I saw no sign. My notes make clear that these were the words spoken by both Mistress Gowdie and Breadheid, confessed freely without pressure. I would not have written such, if such had been otherwise."

"Sheriff Stewart," Campbell asked, "considering all you have heard and read, what is your verdict?"

"Guilty" said John Stewart, "both Janet Breadheid and Isobel Gowdie are guilty as charged."

Such also was the verdict of William Dallas, Hugh Rose and Alexander Dunbar. Sir Hugh Campbell also concluded that he found both accused to be guilty of the heinous crime of witchcraft. "Mister Kellas, for the record, as additional Commissioner, what is your verdict?"

The matter was decided, unanimity was not needed just a majority. My verdict did not matter. I had a sudden melancholy feeling that my arguments had not mattered either. They were never going to sway the others. For all my rationalism, I retained a romantic, even fantastical streak and had thought my words might have saved Isobel. I had only one final card to play.

"My verdict is not proven. I retain too much doubt. Too much that makes no sense. I was sent by the Advocate Depute with the agreement of the King's Commissioner to the Scots Parliament. I am to report to them my findings, particularly if I harboured any doubt. I will write my report this very day and my man Wattie will take it to Edinburgh on the morrow. You may wish to write your own report for the attention of both Advocate Deputes MacKenzie and Colville. With the time needed for a reply to return, you must delay sentence for ten days. In that period I must retain my access to the accused and be permitted to present any significant new evidence I uncover. Nothing less will accord with the remit given to me in Edinburgh."

To my surprise there was no great opposition. Sir Hugh looked at Reverend Forbes who briefly nodded. Sir Hugh replied. "We have nothing to fear from your report. I am sure that a lawyer of the eminence and experience of George Mackenzie, will draw the same conclusions as we have done, even after he reads of your doubts. The women confessed without duress, man! You do but delay what must come to pass."

CHAPTER 39: ISOBEL CANNOT STOP

Auldearn, 16th April 1662

"The name of the seventh spirit is the red reiver and he is my owin spirit that waitis on my selfe and is still clothed in black......there will be many uther divellis waiting upon the maister divell bot he is bigger and more awfull than the rest of the divellis and they all reverence him. I will ken them all one by one from uthers quhen they appear lyk a man......In winter 1660 quhen Mr Harry Forbes minister at Auldearn wes seik, we maid an bagg of gull's flesh and guts of toadis pikles of bear pairingis of the naillis of fingeris and toes the liver of ane hare and bitts of clowts, we steipit this all together all night...Satan wes with us and learned us the wordis following to say thryse ower are thus; he is lyeing in his bed and he is lyeing seik and sore, let him lye intill his bed two months, three days more" **Isobel's second confession. 3rd May 1662**

Isobel cannot stop thinking about Reverend Harry Forbes. He is the only man. The only man who visits her. The only man who shows her any kindness. The only man who speaks to her. A small part of her mind knows that her husband, John and her other friends are not allowed to visit her. She remembers also that before her arrest she feared and doubted Reverend Forbes but he is different now she has begun to know him. "We are not so different, you and me, Isobel." He told her. "For all my robes and education and your lack thereof, we are both seekers after spiritual truth, I believe." He had been sitting on his chair, so very close to Isobel as she sat on her bed, in her simple grimy white shift, that was all that separated Isobel's nakedness from the Reverend. He had placed his hand on her left thigh, just above the knee to emphasise his point and their connection. "Do you not agree? Where we differ is that I have but one God but you, you commune with many. God in Heaven included. You must tell me of this, Isobel. You must speak to the kirk session of this. You must have no shame. You have called on many saints and spirits. Tell it with no shame."

Harry Forbes was the only person who told Isobel anything about the world beyond her four walls. The world of the fermtouns of Auldearn, Inshoch and Lochloy. The fermtouns that had been Isobel's world. The world she had lived in all her life and the world she had once walked through, as a woman unlike any other. How she longed for the tiny morsels of village gossip he gave her. Forbes told her that John Taylor and his mother Elspet Nishie, with all John's children, including baby Isobel and heavily pregnant Moira, had left Auldearn, headed to Inverness. *"Thank God they are safe,"* Isobel thought, *"especially my namesake, baby Isobel. No wonder John and Elspet have fled,"* Isobel thought, *"they were as much involved in the craft as Janet and I. Elspet had taken Janet as her Maiden, just as Janet had taken me."* "How was Janet?" Isobel asked.

Harry Forbes looked thoughtful. His right hand squeezed more firmly on Isobel's left thigh, even as it, almost imperceptibly, moved further up her upper leg. "Ah yes," he said. A flicker of disappointment in his eyes. "It is Janet I wanted to speak to you about. The Session interviewed her the day after we spoke with you." Forbes spoke the next words as a trusted advisor would offer counsel or as a fellow conspirator would whisper. "I am loathe to tell you this but in many ways her testimony was stronger and more vivid than yours. Do you know what that means?" Forbes ensured Isobel's eyes met with his. His right hand, now inches from Isobel's vagina lips, the hem of her shift pushed in upon itself. "I want the Session to understand you as I do, Isobel. We cannot have Janet appear more penitent. More revealing. You are but a seeker of the truth who has strayed. I ken also you are a performer of ballads, one who reaches out to draw-in others, as I do with my sermons. It is another way in which you and I are similar, Isobel. Do you not feel it?" Forbes' strong male hand now almost touching Isobel's vagina under her shift. "Promise me Isobel, next meeting with the Session, you will give them more. Give me more. Given them more for me. Can ye promise me, Isobel?"

Longing, such longing, Isobel saw in Reverend Forbes' eyes. Longing for what, she could not tell. Isobel reached down with her left hand and moved the Reverend's hand further down her leg. She made no sound or facial sign of anger or rejection. A simple assertion. It allowed Forbes to decide what he did with his hand without accusation. He did not push it forward once more but withdrew it to his own lap. Isobel could not promise anything, until she more fully understood what "more" Janet had given. What "more" Isobel was expected to give. She asked as much. Forbes answered.

"Janet told us of the coven in her day, when she first renounced her baptism and accepted Satan. She told us that her husband and her mother-in-law, Elspet Nishie, had taken her to kill a man, just to show her that it could be done. She spoke of the Devil, having carnal copulation with her, not just after she agreed to give herself to him but when he chose, for pleasure. Hers as well as his. You did not give us such a vivid picture, Isobel. You, my storyteller, Isobel." Forbes leant forward and placed his left hand on Isobel's right thigh. "You have as much in you and more, I know. If I were the Devil, Isobel, I ken who I would wish to have copulation wi'."

Isobel held Forbes's gaze for long seconds. The sensation of knowing his hand was so close to her inner-most place created a throbbing heartbeat between them. Isobel was not sure what she wanted, except her freedom and she knew Forbes would not, today, give her that. "Reverend. I am unclear whit ye want fae me? My testimony or something other? I would dae whate'er ye ask, for my freedom and I would gi'e my testimony true, for your continued kindness. What is it I can hope for? What is it ye would hae me dae?"

Harry Forbes removed his hand. He widened his eyes and he suddenly rose to his feet, as if remembering himself. As he rose, Isobel could see his erection pressing within his breeks. "Your testimony. Your testimony is what I seek. I wish to help you prove your sincere repentance. Prove it through honestly describing the mistaken path ye hae been on." Forbes returned to his seat, close to Isobel, this time taking both her hands within his. "I will pray wi' ye, Isobel. Guide ye and invigorate your soul with the strength and the truth of God's love that ye need." Forbes pressed Isobel's hands as an earnest suitor might when wooing, his face shone with a light akin to that of love. "Isobel, my brave, beautiful lass, the days ahead of you are truly the most important of your whole life. Your chance to outshine Janet in the eyes of the Session. Your chance to cleanse your soul of past error and for the first time let in the glorious light of the Lord! I envy you this moment. To know God's love anew! When next you are interrogated, you must respond as if you are reciting one of your ballads. You will never have another chance like this. To give the performance of your life!"

Isobel felt the passion flowing out of Harry Forbes, not just through his words, from his being. Beads of sweat formed on his brow. She saw that he had come away from his chair and was now kneeling before her, holding her hands in his. He may have assumed this position to join in prayer but in that instant it felt to Isobel like supplication. Forbes truly wanted her to tell her full story. She was silent for a few seconds, not wanting the moment to end, not wanting her realisation of this moment to end. This man from the top table wanted her testimony. Normally the Lairds and the educated folk took as much notice of the tenants and cottars as they did of their livestock. Forbes needed her.

"Reverend Forbes, Mister Harry, why dae ye wish me tae testify, sae sorely?" Isobel said the words so softly, that at first Forbes knew he had heard them but had not taken them in. He looked her in the eye, suddenly aware also that he was kneeling before her. He could have abruptly pulled away. Raised himself to his full height and strutted round the room delivering a sermon as a reply. Instead, he chose to stay exactly as he was. To keep them each, exactly as they were. He did not need the question repeated, he had heard it. "Isobel, I have tried so hard to explain to you. I thought, surely you would know." In that moment Isobel had the strangest feeling that the Reverend was about to say that he loved her. "I wish to save your soul." Isobel felt a sudden foolishness, as her thoughts jostled to reassert reality. "I truly believe you have been misled. Both when you were introduced to witchcraft and through the devil appearing in more helpful, less frightening forms. You must tell me of all your spirit guides, for they were all the devil under the cloak of disguise. Those who have been mis-led, I believe, can be properly led back down the path of penitence. I so desperately want to help you, Isobel, my parishioner, my child."

Isobel laughed, a self-depreciating mischievous laugh. "I hae called on many saints and spirits, it's true. A' o' them at once, when desperate enough. Saint Ninian for healing. Brigit, or Saint Bride, as ye ken her, for childbirth. Ye learn wa's best for what. The auld church had mair time for saints and Blessed Mary, my grandmother telt me. Your kirk is no so keen on them. I nivver understood the hairm."

Harry Forbes had waited years for a parish. Now he knew he had found his calling among the pious Lairds but also among these poor misguided folk. Their world was so narrow, full of ancient superstition, few had any conception of the great issues of the day. The great issues that were weighing so heavily upon Forbes himself, as he considered whether he could submit to Episcopal authority to save the livelihood he had striven so hard to attain. On another day he may have smiled with condescension at Isobel's naive pantheon or even fulminated at the heresy but today, sitting so close to her, the heat and scent of her body in his nostrils, he felt only the pity and the waste. Ignorance and misguided faith. One wrong step after another, leading her further and further into the Devil's clutches. Nothing now could save her mortal body, the evidence was too compelling but he could help her meet her end in a state of penitence, illuminated by the light of the Lord. He feared it was too late for her immortal soul also, no Catholic death-bed confession could help her join the elect but perhaps her penitence, proven through the fullness of her confession, might soften the eternal torments yet to come. Isobel, he sensed, need not be tortured into confession but rather cajoled, seduced even, by kindness and understanding.

"The Reformed Kirk," he explained, "has no need of intermediaries between God and man, save the Lord Jesus Christ and surely he is intermediary enough? I am not an ignorant man. I know that when you name Bride as Brigit, you are recalling an ancient Goddess and that is where the danger in all these saints and spirit guides arises. They depart from the true path and, as I have said, they can be the Devil in disguise. I do not condemn you for not knowing the difference. Until now, you have lacked proper guidance. I can give you that guidance, Isobel." Forbes removed his hands from clasping Isobel's and placed them both upon each thigh. From his position kneeling in front of her, he had but to push forward with his body and push apart with his hands to be able to penetrate her. Reverend Forbes knew he longed to do so. The image of consummating such an act, twisted and writhed alongside his desire to save Isobel's soul. Denying his forward surge, filled him with a delicious righteous passion. For many seconds Forbes maintained his stance, prolonging the intense pleasure of desire and sublimation. Isobel, her hands freed from the Reverend's embrace, placed her hands upon his. Whether to join with him or to impede their further movement, neither of them truly knew. "You are quite beautiful." Forbes said, tenderly and with that he pushed Isobel's hands aside and stood up. A deep inhalation by the Reverend marked the moment's end. The matter of her soul must take precedence. "Tell me, Isobel, did you have a particular spirit guide, who helped you commune with the Faerie, with the dead or with the Devil himself?"

Isobel worked to control her ragged breathing. Instinctively she pushed her shift back down to cover her upper thighs. Once again she allowed herself a small laugh at her memory. "Oh aye, I hae the Red Reiver. A bonny, yet mischievous, lad. A bit like me! He speerit me he wis a pirate wha kenned William Wallace, a thon yearis ago but he has been wi' the faerie sae mony yearis , he's mair like one o' them noo."

Forbes saw the fond memory in Isobel's face. The glory of her own personal spirit. It was wrong but he could sense the seduction. "And can you tell the difference between a spirit, like this Red Reiver and the Devil himself?" Forbes asked.

"Oh aye," Isobel replied. "The De'il is larger, even in the form o' a man. Mair stern and a' the lesser spirits look up tae him."

"Then you must say so next confession. It is the bridge that the Session needs to understand. How your more benign spirits acknowledge the Devil as their master and Lord. You see that now, don't you, Isobel. I sense you have been understanding everything I have explained to you in all my visits. Tell the session clearly of the familiar spirits and of the over-ruling Devil and your confession will be so much more complete. I will bring a cut of roasted meat and ale, if your next interview excels the first.

Isobel felt her moth moisten. She emitted her most mischievous half- smile, half- laugh yet. "Ken what? We even tried tae make you mair sick! We kenned ye would be a thorn in our side."

Harry Forbes felt a surge of excitement, tinged with fear. He had been right all along! "Fear not!" he exclaimed as he once again, leapt forward to kneel in front of Isobel. "You must include that. I promise you it is a sign of your desire to cleanse your soul of guilt, not an admission to be afraid of." Forbes smiled with joy. "Include that. I will ensure the others do not think more harshly of you, if ye do."

Isobel had a sudden thought that she had gone too far with her admissions, despite the Reverend's delighted response. Her thoughts darkened and with that a grim, pressing question pushed itself to the forefront of her mind. This time Isobel leant forward and took Forbes' hands in hers. "Might I be saved, Mister Harry? If I tell the truth as ye desire me to, might I not be burnt?"

Harry Forbes moved his enclosed hands and released them, so that they took each of Isobel's. He pressed them together, drew them to his lips and kissed them. "It is in God's hands, Isobel. I wish it were otherwise but I fear it is too late to save you in this world. I would not be your true confessor and guide, if I did not tell you so. I urge you to think on the state of your soul when you go to meet your maker. Before the next interview, think and pray on that. As I will pray for you too."

Isobel let the confirmed truth, sound within her head with every rise and fall of the breath within her bosom. *"They already hae enough tae condemn me. I will never get out of this place to see John, Janet or baby Isobel again. My only concern, now, is the fate o' my immortal soul."*

"Thank you, Reverend, "she said. "I will think hard on your words, when alane in my cell."

CHAPTER 40 : APPEAL TO EDINBURGH

Nairn: Friday 6th July 1662

"I am not of their opinion, who deny that there are Witches, though I think them not numerous; and though I believe that some are suffer'd by providence, to the end that the being of Spirits may not be deny'd; Yet I cannot think, that our Saviour, who came to dispossess the devil, who wrought more Miracles in his own time, upon possessed persons, than upon any else, at whose first appearances the oracles grew dumb, and all the devils forsook their temples; and who promised, (John 12) that the Prince of this World was now to be cast out, would yet suffer him to reign like a Sovereign, as our fabulous representations would now persuade us." **George MacKenzie: Pleadings on some remarkable cases before the supreme courts of Scotland since 1661.**

"Now is the judgment of this world: now shall the prince of this world be cast out. And I, if I be lifted up from the earth, will draw all men unto me." **John chapter 12 verses 31 and 32**

I wrote my letter by candlelight in our shared room in the Cawdor Inn. I knew my audience, George Mackenzie, Advocate Depute. He had schooled me in methodical, evidence-based law. I would present to him just such a report. In truth, I wrote little that I had not explained to my fellow Commissioners, a few hours before. I had to hope that minds would not be as closed in more enlightened Edinburgh.

I had found no evidence of actual harm committed by Isobel and Janet save that attested to in their confessions. William

Bower lived, the Laird of Park lived, Harry Forbes lived. The Laird of Park had a living male child. True, he had lost a child while yet young but which parent among us has not? If all children who die are to be attributed to witchcraft, we must concede that there are more witches than Christians in Scotland. All my fellow Commissioners had presented were the five confessions. Alexander Colville, Advocate Depute, was not sent testimony proving or even alleging that harm had been caused by these women. Reverend Harry Forbes remembers feeling sick in 1660. Who among us does not? If Janet and Isobel had kept their mouths shut, there would be no case against them at all.

I explained in my letter that the shape changing into animals and the flights with the faerie, whether to extract food and drink or to shoot elf arrows, did not, in my opinion, correspond to real events but to a form of deeply believed dream. Nothing else made sense. People do not change into hares or crows, under any extremis. Might not the men I rode down, who begged for their lives, not have done so, had it been possible? Might not I, when the English closed upon my shattered command at Worcester? I stated my belief that Reverend Harry Forbes had used his regular access to the women whilst imprisoned and his control over the conditions in which they were imprisoned, to shape their testimony. Repeating sections confessed by one into the testimony of the other, cajoling them to believe their spirit and faerie beliefs as encounters controlled by the Devil.

I gave my opinion that with all the greater concerns of the world, why would Satan be concerned with extinguishing the male inheritance of the impoverished estate of Park and Lochloy? If there was a human motivation for such a desire, the only beneficiary would be Hugh Hay, the Tutor and uncle, named as the nearest male relative. I wrote that Hay had control over Janet Breadheid within Inshoch Castle and had visited her before she died. Janet having given the clearest description of the Devil's wish to make heirless the current Laird of Park . My quill paused over my paper, as I considered whether to include the following. I thought to ask Wattie but decided to read to him the totality, once I had set it all down. That thought made up my mind, state plainly what I believe most probable. I wrote that if there was any truth to the more humanly possible descriptions, such as the carnal copulation and the chastising of the coven, then Hugh Hay was the most plausible candidate for the ritual leader of the coven and his negro manservant, John, the most likely human person who fulfilled the role attributed in the confessions to Black John. Having passed beyond the point of no return with my accusations. I wrote that Hugh Hay had been an adult in the 1640s, I myself had seen him, when two previous witches had been accused and convicted of actions to kill the previous Laird of Park and to kill Hugh Hay's two older brothers, deaths that brought him ever closer to inheritance. As his oldest brother had already sired a son, Hugh Hay had the galling task of acting as Tutor to the one person who stood between him and the Lairdship. Having seen that the use of witches could both further his ends and take the blame for his actions, in a previous generation, was it not possible that Hugh Hay was repeating the formula? The copulation, I assumed, was but a pleasurable additional benefit and a tool, a very large tool, to help bind the female followers. I thought to strike out what I had just written, particularly the bawdy innuendo but I felt it made such a compelling case that I left the comment as it was. Hugh Hay made much more sense as the person claiming to be the Devil in Janet and Isobel's testimonies, than did the Devil himself.

My final comment concerned the healing charms and the cursing charms. Did we not all use them at some point or another? A great many of Isobel's charms were in the name of the Father, Son and Holy Ghost. She had not renounced her baptism but turned on each occasion, to the spirit, or deity that best suited her purpose. I knew this was not according to doctrine, it was based on primitive superstition and the folk beliefs that still clung to the uneducated folk of our realm. I thought the prominence of the Devil in the final testimony was likely to be the imposition of Reverend Forbes' beliefs and preoccupations and not how Isobel had truthfully, spoken most of her charms. If Isobel called upon the Holy Trinity, the Devil, the Red Reiver, all the Saints and the Queen of the Faerie, what she needed was education, not execution.

If Scotland is to be a modern country, governed by just and scientific law, I concluded, then a conviction must be based on proven harm, not upon words cajoled out of a deluded woman during confession.

I felt tired yet elated when I set down my quill. My hand ached, as did my eyes. My elation ebbed when I read my report to Wattie. "Aye, that's whit we found out, Maister Archie. Richt enough. The only pity is we havena heard it fae Isobel and ye havenae a scrap o' actual proof agin Hugh Hay. Sorry for saying but ye did ask. For a' we ken it could be the De'il hisself wha cam tae Auldearn and Isobel could hae met wi' the King and Queen o' Faerie."

I stared at Wattie in disconsolate disbelief, before sinking my head into my hands. "Christ man, have I taught ye nothing." I muttered. When I pulled my face out of from my fingers' embrace, I defiantly blotted my letter. "This is what I am sending. My report. My findings. You will take it tae Edinburgh wi' all haste Wattie and present the arguments, answer any questions as you think I might. Wattie, ye understand? I will stay here and hope to have that conversation with Isobel that proves or no' that the Devil is really a flesh and blood man."

For all that he yet believed in faeries and the Devil, I knew that Wattie would fulfil the task just given to him, as faithfully as he could. I folded my parchment and sealed it in a letter. I had done all I could for Isobel, within the time permitted to me. What happened next would be within the hands of the Advocate Depute and the Royal Commissioner.

CHAPTER 41 : ISOBEL'S FINEST AND DARKEST HOUR

Auldearn: Third Confession 15th May 1662

"Isobel Gowdie appearing to be most penitent for her abominable sins of witchcraft most ingeniously proceeded in her confession."
John Innes' different introduction to the third confession.

It started the week before on 8th May. Reverend Harry Forbes visited Isobel in her cell. Instantly Isobel could sense a reticence in his manner, less ardently seeking a response from her. Isobel felt the loss, starved as she was of the human connection on which she thrived. When they assumed their accustomed positions, Isobel sitting on her bed, Forbes on his stool, she noticed he did not bring the stool close to her, as he usually did. Within the confines of their personal interactions in the last two months, she felt as if she had done something wrong but could not think what it was. She had spoken more fully at her second interrogation. She had heeded his gestures and prompts that reminded her to insert the Devil into more of the charms and activities. Forbes was guarded and uncertain when he explained.

"Isobel, I am sorry but I may not come to see you again very often, save for, well, save for ....You see, the Kirk Session believe we have gathered sufficient evidence. Your two confessions and Mistress Breadheid's have been transcribed by Notary Innes and copies sent to Edinburgh, to the Privy Council. The Laird of Brodie took them two days past." Forbes suddenly leant forward, stating the next as if were something he did not wish. "The Privy Council will grant a Commission to try you for witchcraft, of that I am certain. When the reply comes back, all that will remain will be for the appointed Commissioners to meet and pronounce a verdict. I have truly come to believe in your penitence, evidenced by your willingness to confess your former sins. I am sorry, Isobel, when I see you next, it is like to be to offer you the final comfort of God's love before your execution."

Isobel felt herself exhale a long breath, followed by a wave of sadness that pricked tears at the back of her eyes. She felt suddenly foolish that she had been worrying about displeasing Reverend Forbes. The word "execution" jarred with all other considerations. "Is there…is there nae hope for me?" she asked.

Harry Forbes was in his element. Appearing concerned and reluctant. Only speaking the harsh truth out of decency. He was thrilled. This was the culmination of his ministry. The exposure of the Devil's work in his own small, out of the way, parish. It could even attract national attention. If he acknowledged a visceral attraction to the woman in front of him, it only added to his sense of himself as a man who could take hard but necessary decisions. A man willing to sacrifice in the service of the Lord a woman he would have enjoyed copulating with. If he acknowledged an attraction to the woman sitting in front of him, it would only add to his pleasure when he watched her burn. *What a waste,* he might think, at that moment *but necessary for God's work.*

Forbes moved his stool forward and took Isobel's hands in his. "I am afraid, I believe, there is none. Your hope is in how God weighs your final days of penitence against your many years of sin."

Isobel closed her eyes, allowing her hands to feel the comforting touch of Reverend Forbes. She felt her breath rise and fall. She knew what that meant. She knew what she was letting go. The thought that she had brought this upon herself and that part of her had always known that this day might come, drowned out any pity for self. With eyes still closed, hands still clasped within Reverend Forbes', she knew each successive breath told her she felt sorry for her husband John, who loved her as best he could and she felt sorry for baby Isobel, whatever would become of her? Herself and Janet, her breaths told her, *what did you expect? Still*, the prick of tears at the back of her eyes replied, *she did not want it to end, not like this, not in the fire. Oh God, not in the fire.*

Isobel's eyes opened. She knew she was talking but it felt as if it might be someone else. Her eyes not only opened, they flared and plead. "Gie me yin ither chance, Mister Harry. No' tae save masel, I ken it's much too late but tae save my soul. Like ye said. I didna tell it as true nor as well as I could hae, thon last twa times. Arrange another hearing for me and I will speirit a'thing I ken."

Forbes' head had been lowered when Isobel's eyes had been closed. His own breathing had fallen into time with Isobel's exhalation of her life. Now, when her eyes opened and she spoke, Forbes raised his own head in keen interest. "You would speak more of the harm the Devil instructed you to do? Against leading members of our community, such as myself or the Laird o' Park?" Forbes stroked his fingers over Isobel's hands and wrists. "You would speak more of how the Devil used you, in cruel punishment and carnal copulation!?"

"Yes!" Isobel replied with enthusiasm, then more thoughtfully. "Aye, I would."

"Then I believe I can arrange it. In a moment we shall pray together, seeking God's guidance for your next confession and the Lord's comfort in your trials to come but before that, Isobel, is there ought else ye desireth of me?"

Isobel tilted her head and smiled an innocent smile. "Some

rouge, for my cheeks and lips, afore I meet the Session. I hae grown awfy pale locked in this cell these past months."

Forbes shook his head in a gesture of incredulous admiration. "Very well, my Bard o' Baillie, I will ensure you look your best for this third confession."

• •

They could all tell the difference. Men can smell the difference. Whatever their schooling in Reformed Faith, whatever the abominable subject of their interrogation. What they all saw enter the room was an attractive, confident woman. Not frightened, cowed and broken as the first time. Not frightened, cowed and broken as they expected. No gibbering peasant mumbling obstinate denial through recently broken teeth or admitting misdeeds under threat of further pricking from agonising foot long iron needles. It was the woman they saw first, then they had to remind themselves that this was a witch.

John Weir had treated Isobel well in the days leading up to this interrogation. She had been permitted to wash her body and her hair. Her simple white linen thigh-length dress was clean. Her long curly red hair tied back in a single loose tail. Her legs and arms were bare. Her striking features restored to pre-captivity beauty through skilled application of the rouge and of ash and lampblack on her eyelashes. Weir, under instruction from Reverend Forbes, allowed Isobel to walk into the room unshackled and without prodding. The effect transformed Weir into a guard of honour, rather than a cruel jailer. Notary Innes at his writing table uttered an involuntary "Oh my!" as, all in a fluster, he hastily caught the inkpot he knocked into with his hand.

This being an extraordinary meeting arranged by Reverend Forbes, neither Sir Hugh Campbell nor William Dallas, the Sheriff and Depute of Nairn, were present. Forbes had elected to have Isobel brought to Auldearn Kirk. Reverend Forbes would largely conduct this third examination. Along with Reverend Rose of Nairn and Notary Innes, fifteen respectable parishioners from Auldearn filled the front rows of pews. Isobel stood before them, even in her bare feet as tall as many and standing this day upright and alert, some thought almost defiant. Reverend Forbes asked if she acknowledged that she had renounced her baptism and compacted with the Devil. With a dismissive wave of her hand Isobel replied, "Aye, aye, hae I no' already said so" she turned to John Innes, who was busily scratching his notes at his table, Isobel inclined her head with a knowing smile and gestured permission with her right hand, "Mister Innes ye may write it doon in your wee bookie, just as I agreed it afore." Then Isobel turned to the assembled men, her hands on her hips, her breasts thrust forward, "Would ye no' wish tae ken what auld Nick, the De'il, and I did next!?"

Reverend Forbes motioned that she should proceed.

"Wi'in a few days o' *said baptism* he cam to me in the new wards of Inschoch and there had carnal copulation with me." Isobel arched her body, tilted her head back, closed her eyes and several times jerked her head back, emitting a series of breathy grunts, as her whole body rocked as if being penetrated by a man.

Reverend Rose exclaimed, "*Reverend Forbes is this fitting for a house of God?*" Forbes extended an open palm in a gesture of forestalling any intervention, "*Please Hugh, she is a performer of ballads, let her express as she sees fit. We may get more this way than any other.*" Forbes replied in a low, urgent whisper.

Isobel opened her eyes, returning to the room, after her dream of copulation with the Devil. "Dae ye want tae hear my story or no'?" she asked stepping toward and looking directly at Hugh Rose. Rose lowered his head and made a hesitant gesture with his hand that she should continue. "He was a very meikle, black, roch man." Isobel turned her back to the men, squatted upon her hunkers, while crossing her arms, as if a man was fiercely hugging her shoulders. "He will lie heavy upon us, when he has carnal dealings with us, heavy as a malt sack." She exhaled a long breath, intimating a woman experiencing the crushing embrace of a powerful man. Isobel turned to face the eager and appalled faces of the watching men. "A'thing about him is big, ye ken. His legs are great and long, no man's legs are as long and his nature, ken, is huge." Still squatting upon her parted thighs in front of the men, Isobel moaned and rocked again several times as she recalled the copulation. "He would be amongst us like a stud horse among mares." Isobel sprang to her feet, now imitating the Devil, moving here and there among his acolytes, grunting and pushing forward his pelvis in the act of multiple penetration. "He would lie with us in the presence of all the multitude." Isobel stood at her full height, facing the assembly of men, her head held high with defiant pride. "Neither had we or he any shame!"

A murmur of angry and embarrassed disapproval arose from the men. "For shame" whispered Reverend Rose, he so much wanted there to be shame. Reverend Forbes said nothing as he looked on eagerly. Notary Innes was aware that he now had an erection and was glad his writing table concealed the fact.

Isobel raised up her eyes and extended her arms. "But especially he has no shame with him at all. D'ye ken what it is tae be wi' sic a man? He would lie and have carnal dealing with all. Any time he pleased. A' kinds o' ways. Any shape he pleased. Like a wee deer licking. Like a dog hard and fast. Like a great beast. He would hae carnal dealing with us in any shape he would be in and we would never refuse him."

Isobel sat upon a chair, crossing her legs and leaning forward, like a storyteller confiding in each individual member of the audience. She gave a short laugh, then smiled with fond memory. "He would come to visit me at hame, ye ken. He could move through our fermtoun wi'out a soul seeing him." Isobel laughed again. "He would come to my house top in the shape of a crow, or a deer, or in any other shape, now and then and I would ken his voice at the first hearing of it." Isobel stood up from her seat and stepped forward before wrapping her arms around herself, mimicking the embrace of a lover. "And I would go furth to him and have carnal copulation with him."

Isobel walked along the front rank of the assembled men, challenging each to look her in the eye. If anyone looked away, it was the men. "Ye need tae understand, he was not like other men. The youngest and lustiest women will have very great pleasure in their carnal copulation with him. Yea! Much more than with their ain husbands. And they will have an exceeding great desire of it with him." Isobel stopped in front of Reverend Hugh Rose, she moved her two hands from her breasts into the very depths of her diaphragm, while closing her eyes in ecstasy "Do ye ken what desire is, Reverend?" Rose looked away. "We had exceeding great desire of it with him, as much as he had with us and more and never, never, think shame of it." Isobel trailed her hand close to Harry Forbes, as she stepped past him, before turning to look him in the eye. "He is more able for us that way than any man can be." Isobel moved next to John Innes who was desperately trying to concentrate on his note taking. Isobel closed her eyes and inhaled deeply twice, inhaling memory. "Alas" she whispered in Innes' ear, "that I should compare him to a man."

Exhausted from the recall of ecstasy, Isobel paused for several seconds, the palms of her hands resting upon John Innes' table. Reverend Rose took advantage of the respite to say, "Mister Forbes, Harry, for love of God, we have been informed sufficiently regarding the Devil's carnal ability!"

Harry Forbes had been intently watching Isobel, knowing she was breathing in sensual memory, he had to shake himself out of erotic empathy at Hugh Rose's words. "Uh, um yes. Mistress Gowdie, if ye please, speak now of some of the tasks the Devil would set you and how you would undertake them."

Isobel opened her eyes, slowly, languidly inhaled a great breath that arched her back, filled her diaphragm and thrust out her breasts. She lifted her two hands from Notary Innes's table. Innes was transfixed, barely able to write, his erection still hidden beneath his writing desk. "So, the men hae had enough o' the carnal pleasures? Just when I was enjoying masel! Typical!" Isobel said with a mischievous, mocking smile. She stepped back to the middle of the space in front of the gathered men. "Ye want tae ken what errands the De'il send me on and in what way?"

"He would send me now and then to Auldearn for errands to my neighbours. He would send me in the shape o' a hare!" Isobel laughed and squatted down with her thighs splayed and palms on the floor, in the shape of a hare. She twitched her nose. "It was on the morning, about the break of day" said the hare, "I was going to Auldearn in the shape of a hare." Isobel took a hop forward and sniffed the air, for predators. "Patrick Papley's servants were in Killhill, going to their labouring. And his hounds were with them." Isobel's hare froze, her face turning left and right, alert to danger. "Suddenly!" Isobel shouted and the men in the front row of the audience rocked back in shared fright. "They ran after me, me being in the shape of a hare." Isobel scampered across the floor, in the shape of a hare, fear and exertion expressed by her face, torso and limbs. "I ran very long," she panted, " but was feart being near at last to my own house, I was feart I might not make it. The door was left open." Isobel darted behind a chair, signifying she had entered a building. "I ran in behind a chest and the hounds followed me." Isobel stuck out her tongue to its full length and width and panted loudly several times to show the audience the sniffing, hungry hounds. "But they went to the other side of the chest." Isobel in hare shape smiled, then darted out from behind the chair. "I was forced to run furth again and ran and ran to another house and there, at last, took the leisure to say "Hare, Hare, God send the care, I am in a hare's likeness now but I shall be a woman even now. Hare, hare, God send the care." Slowly, with muscles stretching, Isobel rose from her hunkers and returned to a full standing woman, in front of the utterly absorbed men. "So I returned to my own shape." Isobel spread her arms and stepped forward, as a person might announce their arrival. "As I am before you all, this instant again, gentlemen." Isobel looked at her arms for scratches. She stuck out her lower lip, as child might when slightly injured. "The dogs will sometimes get some bites of us when we are shaped as hares but we will not get killed."

"You mean you can return to your own body and see physical injuries, after one of these adventures in the shape of a hare or another animal!?" Hugh Rose exclaimed.

"Oh aye," Isobel said as she moved to sit on her chair, once seated she examined her arms and legs. "When we turn out of a hare's likeness to our own shape, we will have the bites and scratches on our bodies. When we would be in the shape of a cat, we did nothing but cry and wraw and yowl and it was very worrying to each other." Isobel caterwauled like an injured, frightened cat. The noise came from the back of her throat and formed the perfect likeness of a cat. "When we come to our own shapes again we will find the scratches and cuts on our skins very sore."

"Mistress Gowdie you are talking of "we" and "each other", how do you meet with other people in the shape of an animal?" Alexander Dunbar, schoolmaster, asked.

Isobel turned and acknowledged with a brief bow of her head, the new questioner. "Dominee Dunbar, when one of us, or more than one of us, are in the shape of a cat and meet with any of our neighbours, we will say "Devil speed thee, go thou with me!" and immediately they will turn into the shape of a cat and go with us."

"Mistress Gowdie," interjected Reverend Rose, with some impatience in his voice, "but what did you actually do, when in animal form? What maleficum?"

Isobel turned to Rose, thought for a second, then nodded. "When we will be in the shape of crows," Isobel extended her arms, to reveal the great black feathered wings of a crow, "we will be larger than ordinary crows and we will sit upon the branches of trees." Isobel hopped onto her seat, extended her arms to show wings, then brought them to her sides and cawed, as crow does. As a large black bird she sat on the seat that was acting a branch and looked from side to side, as beady-eyed crow might look. Seeking prey, seeking mischief. "We went in the shape of rooks to Mister Robert Donaldson's house. The Devil and John Taylor and his wife, Janet Breidheid, went in by the kitchen chimney." Isobel hopped down from her seat and bounced across the floor, as a rook might. "It was about Lammas time in the year 1659. They opened a window and we all went into the house and got beef and drink there." Isobel bobbed her head to peck at the appropriated food. "But we did no more harm."

"Please Mistress Gowdie, Isobel, tell us something more substantial than stealing beef and drink." Harry Forbes implored.

Isobel returned, a woman, to her seat. She placed her chin upon her two hands, as she thought. "The maist grand place, the maist "substantial" was when we went into Downie hills.

The hill opened and we came to a fair and large and braw and marvellous room. The palace of the King and Queen o' the Faerie." Isobel's forehead creased at a frightening memory. "There are great bulls crowtting and skrylling there at the entry, which feared me."

"Please, Isobel, you have told us this already!" Reverend Forbes interrupted "Tell us something you did that you truly regret."

Isobel withdrew herself from the dazzling, yet frightening Faerie realm within Downie Hill. For long seconds she regarded the man who had just spoken, Harry Forbes. They had grown close in her weeks of captivity. The only man, the only person, who spoke to her. Yet for all that, she saw in that instant, that their view of the world could never be quite the same. For Isobel her journey into the Palace of the faerie Queen and King was the pinnacle of her experience, yet for Reverend Forbes it was an inconvenience that distracted from what he wanted to hear. Always the Devil with Harry Forbes. The Devil and the harm done to others. Forget the cures. Speak of the harm and the loftier the victim the better. Isobel closed her eyes, while on her seat and pressed the tips of the fingers of both hands into her mouth as she searched deep within herself. She was committed now. No way back. No way out.

"That which troubles my conscience most is the killing of several persons, with arrows which I got from the Devil" said Isobel. Her features registered sadness and regret. She was simply a woman in front of them now, talking about regret. "The first woman that I killed was at the plough lands. Also I killed in the east of Moray. At Candlemas last year, at that time Bessie Wilson in Auldearn killed one there and Margaret Wilson killed another. I killed also James Dick in Conniecavell but the death that I am most sorry for is the killing of William Bower in the Miltown of Moynes. We had been friends once, Willie and I." Isobel voice trailed away, as she thought of Willie

Bower. She recovered herself reciting several other instances of others who had killed. She concluded. "Janet Breidheid, spouse to John Taylor, told me a little before she was apprehended that Margaret Wilson shot Alexander Hutcheson in Auldearn."

"Tell us Isobel of the spells and charms you used to inflict harm on specific people. People you set out to harm with malice aforethought." Reverend Forbes requested.

"Bessie Wilson on the first Monday of the Reath, took a bag made of hare's livers, the flesh and guts of toads and clippings of finger and toenails and swung the bag at a young man called Thomas Reid and he died."

"Isobel, please, remember our agreement." Harry Forbes pressed. "Specific spells performed by yourself, under the guidance of the Devil, to cause harm to individuals of significance. You will address that, please."

Isobel tilted her head and spanned her left-hand fingers on her chin, in a thoughtful pose, a slight smile on her lips. "People o' significance, ye want is it?" she said quietly. "Bessie and Margaret Wilson, John Taylor and his wife, Margaret Brodie and I, oh, and the Devil were together" Isobel rose from her seat, extended a slender arm and pointed at Reverend Forbes "and Mister Harry Forbes, Minister of Auldearn, was going to Moynes. The Devil gave Margaret Brodie an arrow to shoot at him , which she did but it came short. Now why dae ye think Margaret Brodie might hae cause tae shoot at Harry Forbes?" Isobel looked at the stern male faces but none responded to her question. "The Devil bade Margaret to take an arrow again and she desired to shoot again but Mister Harry Forbes had moved too far away and the Devil said, "No, we will not get his life that time." And Mister Harry Forbes continued on his way." Isobel lowered her arm. "People o' significance, ye say? The Devil, aye him again, caused me to shoot at the Laird of Park, as he was crossing the Burn of Boath but I missed him."

"Thank you, Mistress Gowdie," Reverend Forbes said, as he stood to address the assembly. "As you can see, the Good Lord preserved and protected me. From the Devil's arrows and false accusation, alike." A murmur of supportive laughter and comment passed through the group. Forbes raised two hands to quieten the noise. It was his church and he was well versed in controlling proceedings therein. "Let us proceed. Mistress Gowdie tell us of some specific charms the Devil instructed you in and of occasions when you met as a gathering. A "coven" I recall you called it last time. Tell us of when you met with the Devil as a coven."

"The Devil ye say?" Isobel quietly sighed the words, with eyes that had lost some of their earlier lustre. "We were at Candlemas last year in Grangehill, where we got meat and drink enough. Meat and drink aplenty! The Devils sat at the heid of the table and all the coven about. That night he desired Alexander Elder in Earlseat to say grace before we partook of meat, which he did. His words were thus. "We eat this meat in the Devil's name, with sorrow and sighing and meikle shame. We shall destroy house and hold, both sheep and nold within the fold, little good shall come to the fore, of all the rest of little store" and then we began to eat." Isobel had risen again to her feet and faced the assembly defiantly. "And when we had endit eating, we looked steadfastly to the Devil and bowed ourselves to him. We said to the Devil, "We thank you our Lord for this meat and drink and all the diverse bounties and pleasures that…"

Reverend Rose interrupted "Stop! Please stop, Mistress Gowdie. Much as we welcome your testimony, there is a limit to the blasphemy that should be permitted in this, the House of our Lord. Tell us of the Devil's particular interest in the Laird of Park, both yourself and Janet Breidheid have spoken of it previously."

"Mak your mind up, Mister Rose. D'ye want tae hear my testimony or no?" Isobel muttered to herself as she took a step back, lifted the hem of her skirt and sat with her bare knees upon the floor. She began twisting and interweaving her hands in front of her. "The words we spoke when we made a picture for the destroying of the Laird of Park's male children were thus: "In the Devil's name we pour in this water among this meal, for land downing and ill-heall, we put it into the fire, that it be burnt both stick and stone. It shall be burnt with our will, as any stubble upon a kill." The Devil, himself, taught us the words and when we had learned them we all fell down upon our bare knees." Isobel was already kneeling on her bare knees but she reached back and pulled the loop that held the her long red hair in a bun and shook it free, When she lowered her chin upon her chest, the long red hair covered her face like a curtain. "And our hair about our eyes." Isobel raised her two arms in the air, then tilted back her head, tossing back her hair. "And our hands lifted up, looking steadfastly upon the Devil and saying the words thrice over, until it was made."

As Isobel continued to describe the making of the image to harm the Laird of Park's male children she felt tears begin to prick behind her eyes as she recalled her own babes that had not survived, "It wanted no mark of a baby child. Sweet little lips, chubby little cheeks, tiny little feet, perfect in every way, except for the breath of life. Its little baby hands folded down by its sides." Isobel paused in memory of closing the shroud on each of her babes. Isobel shook her head, took a deep breath and went on to explain how all the other members of the coven came to hear of the picture. When she had finished, she stood up, returned to her chair and sat limp and exhausted, waiting for the next question.

Harry Forbes sensed that Isobel had experienced emotion

not necessarily related to guilt about harming the Laird of Park's children. This third confession had already exceeded his expectations and surpassed the two previous interrogations, yet still Forbes suspected there may be even more that could be coaxed from his bard o' baillie. The Reverend now moved out from the assembled group, walked softly toward Isobel and gently said. "Isobel, you have already told and shown us so much. Your penitent desire to reveal your past sins has shone brightly today. The Devil had you ensnared but now it must be plain to all that you are striving to expose and denounce your former sin and admit the light of our Lord." Forbes placed his hand on the back of the chair where Isobel sat. "We have spoken, have we not, that it is like to be too late to save your physical body but you can yet confess, to cleanse, as far as possible, your conscience and your soul before you face Judgement. Is that not correct, Isobel?"

Isobel felt again the sensation of breathing away her life. Sadness and courage to let go. She lifted her head, turning to meet Harry Forbes' gaze as he looked down upon her. "Yes, Reverend," she said. "I hope the Lord hears my confession and kens the truth o' my penitence."

The men gathered in the church of Auldearn sat in silence. Whatever suspicions they harboured about Isobel's true penitence, they saw in that moment, that this woman was acknowledging her own impending death and was preparing her soul for transition. No hope of earthly reprieve. "Most penitent" John Innes wrote in his notes and found he had a lump in his throat.

"Thank you," said Forbes gently. He moved round Isobel in her chair and walked back to his place in the front row of the interrogation . "Tell me, Isobel, how was your coven organised and how did the Devil impose his control over you?"

Isobel searched for an answer and found that she emitted a laugh. "How did the De'il impose control?" she said to herself, as she sought the best example. "When we are at meat or any other place whatever, the Maiden of the Coven sits above the rest, next to the Devil. The De'il likes the beautiful young lasses. The Maiden serves the Devil for all the old people that he cares not for and are weak and unmeet for him. As I have said, he will be with her and us all like a stud horse after mares and sometimes as a man but always very wilful in carnal copulation at all times and they, we, even so, also wilful and desirous of him."

"Mistress Gowdie" interjected Reverend Rose, "you were asked about how he kept control o'er the coven, not about the carnal copulation. Please attend to the question."

Isobel glared at Hugh Rose before shaking her head and smiling. "Very well," she said softly as she stood. "Sometimes, among ourselves, we would be calling him "Black John" or the like," Isobel raised her hand to shield her mouth as person would do when sharing dangerous gossip in whisper, "and he would ken it and hear us well enough and he even then came to us" Isobel transformed her body into large strutting male, as she stepped toward the assembly. Her voice deepened. "and say "I ken weil aneugh what ye were saying of me!" Then" Isobel raised her right arm to deliver a series of whipping blows with a belt "he would beat and buffet us very sore." Isobel moved seamlessly from the aggressive Devil into the injured victim, rubbing a stinging arm. "We would be beaten if we were absent any time or neglect anything that would be appointed to be done." Isobel shrank her body through hunching her shoulders and timidly wringing her hands. "Alexander Elder in Earlseat would be very often beaten." Isobel cried like an injured schoolboy. "He is but soft and could never defend himself in the least but greet and cry when he would be scourging him." Isobel's body shook as if she experienced a brief involuntary tremor. She emerged stout and defiant with her hands bunched into fists and pressed into either side of her waist. "But Margaret Wilson in Auldearn would defend herself finely." Isobel's bunched fists went up and forward as a boxer might defend himself. "She would cast up her hands to keep the strokes of from her." The fists went back down to the waist and her mouth twisted to show a vituperative washerwoman. "And Bessie Wilson would speak crossly with her tongue, "Dinna you bluidy dare!" and she would be belling against him stoutly."

Isobel became animated, jumping around her allotted space, changing in an instant from the scourging, leaping Devil, into the scurrying, avoiding acolytes. "He would be beating and scourging us all up and down, with cords and other sharp scourges and we would be leaping to protect ourselves, running hither and thither like naked ghosts and we would still be crying "Pity, pity, mercy, mercy, our Lord!" but he would have neither pity nor mercy." Isobel stood now only as the Devils. Chest inflated, her body stretched as tall as it could stand, yet her feet strong planted on the ground. Her face contorted to show the Devil's rage. "When he would be angry at us, he would gurn at us, like a dog" Isobel's lips curled back to reveal her side teeth and a deep growl emanated from between her gritted teeth. "as if he would swallow us up!" Isobel lunged forward toward the seated men, snapping her mouth shut. Alexander Dunbar and Hugh Rose, being nearest flinched involuntarily. Isobel smiled, still as the strutting, animalistic Devil. "He would be like a stirk, or a bull, a deer, a rae or a dog. The scourging and the beating would inflame his desire and he would have dealings with us and when he was finished" Isobel stepped backward and turned her back to the assembly, bending away as she did, lifting the hem of her skirt. Lifting, lifting, her hem until her skirt passed over her hips revealing her bare behind. Her legs parted, to part also the cleavage between quim and anus. "He would lift up his tail and hold it there, until we would kiss his arse." Isobel let her skirt fall back to normal as she straightened and turned. Reverend Rose was too stunned to interject. "And each time when we would meet with him, we knew it behoovit us to rise and make our bows or curtsies to him and we would say, "Ye are welcome our Lord and how do ye do my Lord and three bags full, my Lord."

Isobel bobbed up in down in a series of bows and curtsies, mocking rather than obsequious. When she had finished, she said in a low voice, as she returned to her seat. "And that is how the De'il keeps control."

There followed several seconds of silence. The men needed to re-group. Isobel whispered to herself, *"If ye didnae wish tae ken, ye shouldnae hae asked."* Reverend Rose turned to confer with Reverend Forbes and found that Forbes had a distant, distracted look. Forbes was still thinking about the sight of Isobel's bare behind. Although she had been portraying a male Devil, it was most definitely a woman's arse that Harry Forbes had seen. When Forbes turned to respond to Rose he was momentarily lost, unable to formulate what he wished next from Isobel Gowdie. His absolute clarity, driven by religious certainty and ambition, had been weakened and challenged by the assault on his senses of Isobel's performance. By Isobel the woman. *"Harry are you well?"* Rose asked with concern, reaching out and shaking his colleague. *"Harry, we must conclude this session."* Forbes shook himself back to attentiveness and certainty. "God's grace, I maun gird myself. I fear I may have been bewitched!" He thought." *Finish this. Get her to acknowledge her sin"*

"Thank you, Hugh," said Forbes. "it has been a long afternoon. Quite extraordinary, in a diabolical way. Yes, let us conclude." Forbes stepped forward, drawing strength from the surroundings of the kirk where he was Minister, where he was Lord and master of ceremonies. "Mistress Gowdie, we will detain ye but a few minutes longer. Please answer with a bit less…em… a bit more pious decorum. We are in the House of God." Isobel heard the words and understood the tone of criticism. She felt a wave of confusion. The joy and certainty that filled her words and movements when she inhabited a ballad had been wonderfully strong with her that day but when she saw that Reverend Forbes may not be pleased, she had the strangest sensation of tumbling out of a dream. When she shook herself, she was a woman alone on a chair, in a church full of men who wished her dead. A woman, she now believed, who deserved to die. She could no more act out her final answers than fly through the air. In a seated position and flat voice, she answered Reverend Forbes' questions about further maleficum and the invocation of the Devil within its practice. *"we tak the strength from a person's midden or dunghill with the flesh of an un-christened child, in our Lord the Devil's name."* *" the Devil would give us the brawest like money that was ever coined, but within four and twentie hours it would be but horse-muck."* *"we take away the fruit of corn at Lammas and say "we cut this corn in our Lord the Devil's name" and we take the kale and lay it up until Yule or Holy days and divide it among us when we feast on it together."*

Forbes did not solicitously thank Isobel for her answers as he had done previously. He stood over her, sternly receiving each answer, tersely asking his next question. In such a manner he brought this third confession to a close. "Good God woman! There is no end to the evil you have done. No task you will not invoke the Devil's aid for, while acknowledging him to be your Lord. Isobel Gowdie, you have confessed to killing innocent people of conspiring and conjuring to harm leaders of the community like myself, of stealing from neighbours, of mutilating the flesh of un-christened infants to concoct your spells. Of having carnal relations with the Devil within this very kirk! Of renouncing your baptism in Christ and accepting instead the Devil as your Lord. Your sins are many and grievous, woman. What say ye to that!?"

Isobel's face contorted in anguish. No performance this, the thundering growth of realisation of her fate, the inrushing guilt at her life as laid bare by Reverend Forbes' words. He towered over her in his Ministerial garb, as the regret convulsed Isobel in her chair below him. She wailed,

"Alas I deserve not to be sitting here! For I have done so many evil deeds, especially the killing of men, women and children. I deserve to be riven upon iron harrows or worse, if it could be devised."

Notary Innes, breathing heavily, exhausted, exhilarated, wrote down Isobel's words.

After Isobel was returned to her cell, Reverend Forbes said in a low voice to John Weir. "Do what ye will wi' her now Weir, we've got what we need fae her."

John Weir's eyes widened as he grinned.

CHAPTER 42 :ISOBEL

Auldearn, Wednesday 11th July 1662

"And he rode upon a cherub, and did fly: yea, he did fly upon the wings of the wind. He made darkness his secret place; his pavilion round about him were dark waters and thick clouds of the skies. The LORD also thundered in the heavens, and the Highest gave his voice; hail stones and coals of fire. Yea, he sent out his arrows, and scattered them; and he shot out lightnings, and discomfited them."
Psalm 18

Isobel was halfway when I met with her. Halfway to recovering her senses. Halfway between repentance and defiance. Halfway toward feeling the full sadness and terror of her predicament. Halfway through the ten days agreed for word to return from Edinburgh.

John Weir hovered within the cell after showing me in. "I'm nae sure you did the lass ony favours," he said, with a sour grin, "helping her recover her senses, so she can truly fear what lies aheed." Isobel had so few visitors, she had been sleeping when I entered. Slowly, uncertainly, she pulled herself to sitting. "I will stay tae hear what she has tae say." Weir said. "The Commission has gi'en its verdict. I'm tae mak sure ye dinna put words in the lassie's mouth."

My anger and frustration had been growing throughout the week. I had been denied clear access to the accused at every turn. I was not wearing my rapier but I was carrying a needle point knife. In seconds the point of my knife was pressing at

Weir's throat. "I ha'e slit throats for less." I hissed. "You will wait outside. I canna stop you lurking and listening but I will not have you in this room."

Weir's eyes narrowed as Isobel's widened. With the pressing of my knife drawing the first prick of blood, Weir acquiesced. "Ye've no heard the last o' this," he threatened, as he exited the room. I believed it was something he felt compelled to say, to give way without losing too much face.

Isobel backed away against the cell wall as Weir closed the door. "Who are ye, sir?" she asked and I realised that for all that I had been immersed in her life and she had performed Thomas the Rhymer for me a week before, she had not been a well woman at the time. I looked down at the knife, yet in my hand, and tucked it back into its sheath in my belt, with a placatory, reassuring gesture of my face and hands.

"A friend." I said. "I have been paying for Mistress Duncan to treat you and for your improved food. I have been sent from Edinburgh to find out the truth of your case. We spoke last week….perhaps you do not remember?"

Isobel stretched out her arm and I realised she was wanting me to pass her a comb that I was sitting on. She did not say if she remembered me or not, instead she asked, "Will ye gie me a minute, sir, tae mak mysel mair presentable? There are no mony folk get tae meet wi' me."

Isobel tugged and brushed at her long red hair. She also pulled across her bowl of water and splashed her face. "Why are ye my friend fae Edinburgh, sir, if I hae ne'er met ye?" she asked, as she tugged her hair into a neat bun that she tied with a piece of ribbon.

"I am sent by the King's Commissioner to the Scots Parliament to see that justice is done. I would help you, Isobel, if I can. I have tried to help you, argue your defence but it would greatly help me if I could hear your account from yourself."

Isobel appeared content with her adjustments to her appearance, which had indeed transformed her. "You sent Mister Weir fae the room wi' a knife at his throat are ye here tae set me free?" The yearning in her face was heart-breaking. I briefly closed my eyes as I shared her pain of thwarted release.

"I am sorry, no." I said. "I can deal wi' bullies like Weir but I am not empowered to release you. Just hear your defence."

Isobel deflated as the breath escaped her body. "What is your name, kind sir?" and I felt so foolish, being at this stage, with the woman I hoped to save, days after a guilty verdict had been delivered.

"Archie, Archie Kellas. I thought you knew something of me, when we last met. You spoke of seven years and that was the span in which I was indentured in the Indies, as a prisoner after the war with Cromwell."

Isobel looked tired and confused. Her skin had cleared of the ergotic blotches and her mind appeared returned but her presentation was weary, small-voiced and timid. She did lean closer to me, the better to examine my face. "Did I? I canna remember. I was sae very sick. Seven year was how lang True Tamas had tae bide in the land o' the Faerie Queen." Isobel reached out and took hold of my hand. "It must hae been sae hard for ye, being shipped tae the Indies for so mony years."

"Yes it was, thank you for your concern." I brought across my left hand and patted Isobel's right hand that rested on mine. I had a thought that we were just two hurting people trying to find our way.

Isobel looked down at our clasped hands, with a gentle smile of empathy upon her lips and eyes. Gently she pulled her hand back. "What is to happen tae me, kind sir? Archie. Reverend Forbes has not cam tae visit me for sae lang. Weir" at the mention of the name Isobel's face twisted in anger and disgust, "Weir is a brute. He says the Commission has speerit me guilty o' witchcraft and I will burn wi'in the week. Is that true?"

Isobel leant forward again and reached out with her two hands, which I took in mine. "I am sorry lass, it is true. The Commission has found you guilty. I was part of the Commission. I found you not proven and have sent word tae Edinburgh, for the Advocate Deputes to give verdict upon the case. Their judgement should be back in a day or two. There is some small hope. A very slight chance your sentence will be commuted or overturned. You should prepare yourself for sentence being caried out, it is the more likely outcome."

Isobel's eyes blinked three times as I spoke and I understood it was an outward sign of a keen intelligence calculating the different strands of the information I had given her. She has been found guilty, there is a small hope of reprieve, she should prepare herself for execution. I thought she might ask me to explain the "small hope", instead she asked, "And was Janet found guilty also?"

I was still holding her two hands, perhaps that helped me understand the question. Janet had been found guilty posthumously but Isobel was asking with living concern, not barren curiosity. "Has no-one told you?" I searched Isobel's face as I asked. Her eyes widened with fear. "Janet died in custody more than two months back. No-one told me what of, poor treatment and sickness from being arrested so soon after giving birth, I believe."

Isobel let go of my hands and placed her right hand on her forehead. "Oh puir Janet and her puir bairns. Whate'er ye think o' us, she was a guid mither tae them. Oh puir Janet. No-one telt me."

Isobel's face hardened in an instant, "Reverend Forbes did not tell me, though he must hae kent." She said and I felt a surge of pleasure from seeing her, before my very eyes, begin to doubt Harry Forbes. "How is my John?" she asked.

It crossed my mind to say *which one? Black John or your husband John?* But our connection was such that I knew it was her husband she meant. "He is well. He is....brave. He has not left Auldearn as Janet's husband did. I saw your John in Auldearn Kirk. He attends service although he must know people suspect he was in league with your activities..."

"He was not!" Isobel interjected passionately, grabbing both my hands again. "If ye believe onything, sir, ken that John is innocent."

For some reason, I let the moment linger. Isobel on her knees, clasping my hands, her cleavage visible beneath her insubstantial shift, desperately wanting to know that I understood that John was innocent. After a few more seconds than necessary, I helped her rise back to sitting on her bed while saying, "I believe you, Isobel and I know of no plan to arrest John in connection with this." Isobel gave a half smile as she sniffed away the tears that had engulfed her expression of concern for John. I continued, "John loves you very much and he would have visited you in captivity but has not been allowed."

Isobel's hands were free of mine, she clasped them in front of her mouth, closing her eyes, "Oh God, what hae I done?" she said softly.

"Isobel. I am here to help you, if I can. Are you guilty of witchcraft?"

Isobel looked up at me. She looked tired and broken, all her losses overwhelming her. "What? What does it matter if I am or no? I am going tae burn either way."

"Please. Please, Isobel. I can still speak for you."

Isobel lent forward once more and placed her hand on mine. "Kind sir, an' I jalouse ye are a *kind* sir, I wouldna waste your breath. I hae invoked mony saints, spirits and devils in my charms and curses. I hae called on them tae curse an' cure. I hae ridden wild wi' the faerie, taking whit we please, no caring wha we hairm. Aye, I hae called upon Faither, Son and Holy Ghaist mair often than ony ither but Mister Harry, Reverend Forbes, has telt me, there can be ainly yin God and He's no happy tae share this world wi' ony ither. I hae made my peace, kind sir, aye, an' said my piece an' a'. I hae confessed a' an' mair. My ainly hope is that God kens my repentance. Your talk o' hope unsettles me. It wid be best if you just left."

It was my turn to beseech, bringing my left hand to rest on our joined hands. "Isobel, please, just a couple more questions to help me understand." Isobel looked utterly weary. She sighed and nodded almost imperceptibly. "Thank you." I said. I had a growing sense of intruding upon Isobel's remaining hours, my questions more for myself than for her. "Isobel, when you ride with the faerie, fire elf arrows or enter homes, is it real, in this world or is it in dream?"

Isobel's face changed. From being tearful and worn out, she looked up at me with a laugh. I could feel the energy flood through her hand into mine. She broke our clasp and raised herself to her full statuesque height. "Oh, puir kind sir. Ye will ne'er understand. It has been my pride and joy." Isobel ran her hands over the curving shape of her body as she undulated. "It has gi'en me the greatest plaisur in my life. I hae dined wi' the Queen o' Faerie an' danced wi' auld kings here on earth. Oh the riches and plaisur I hae kent and seen!"

Isobel was standing, smiling, full of joy in front of me while I still sat. I could not help a short laugh of empathy at her transformation. At her infectious pleasure. "But it's not real," I said softly, then I rose, so that my extra inch of height allowed me to look down on Isobel. "But it's not real!" I said more forcefully, grabbing her arm, not in the soft exchange of connection as before but in an attempt to shake her to understanding.

Isobel's eyes flared. Within the small confines of her cell, she shook her arm free of my grasp and moved as far from me as she could. "It's real tae me!" she countered angrily, then defiantly, "And no man is going tae tak it fae me." Now in the corner of her cell, she let her body slide down the wall, as it emptied of the power it had displayed seconds before. Slumped, small in the corner, she said softly. "It may be the ainly place I can go tae, when they cam tae burn me."

"I'm sorry," I said as I stepped toward her.

"Please go," she replied.

"Isobel, please. I am not your enemy. I may be the only friend you have. Please let me help you. How can I help you?" I plead as I stepped toward her, before squatting next to where she sat hugging her knees in the corner.

She had been engulfed in her own fear and misery but the word *help* struck a chord. "Dae tae help me?" she asked. "You could get Weir tae stop. I dinna want my last days in this world filled wi' that man."

I placed my hand on Isobel's shoulder. "Get Weir to stop what?" I asked, though I feared I already knew.

Isobel turned her sad and frightened face toward me. "Using me sexually. Sine I gi'ed my confession and Mister Harry stopped coming tae see me. I hae been sair sick but no' sae sick tae nae ken when a man is upon me. Inside me. "

"Jesus." I whispered. I already hated Weir but this information pushed me over the edge.

The bolt slid on the door and John Weir entered. He must have been listening and waiting to overhear such an accusation. He had also gone away, after my knife to his throat, and brought a loaded pistol which he held pointed at my chest. "No-one'll believe a witch and a whore. Mister Kellas, you will leave my tollbooth now and ye wid dae well tae no' repeat the witch's lies."

I rose to my feet yet hesitated to leave the room. "You'll no harm her, Weir." I hissed. "You'll no touch her again." Weir responded by pulling back the cocking mechanism, so that the pistol was fully ready to fire.

"If you dinna move now, Kellas, I will find that I was gied nae choice but tae shoot you as you tried tae help the prisoner escape. No-one here will miss ye. Move!"

I mouthed *sorry* to Isobel as I moved round Weir and out the small room. Isobel had closed her eyes and was hugging her knees once more. Perhaps her lips were moving in invocation or prayer. Weir ushered me out into the hallway. He moved the pistol to his left hand and kept it pointed toward me, in a wavering hand as he used his right hand to pull closed the bolt on Isobel's cell door. I pounced then, grabbing his left hand to direct the pistol away from me. My head slammed in a stunning butt into Weir's face. The pistol did not discharge, instead I wrestled it from his hand and moved the firing pin to an uncocked position. Weir staggered in front of me, clutching his face. I reversed the pistol and brought the wooden handle hard down upon his head. Weir fell to the ground.

I could in that moment have released Isobel. Set her free to face a fighting chance on the run or even aided her in that escape myself. I looked at the bolted door. I moved to the shutter, pulled it open and saw Isobel standing on the other side of the door. She must have sprung up at the sound of commotion. Her lips fell soundlessly open, her eyes widened in understanding and appeal. Whether she was about to ask to be released, I will never know. Weir was groaning on the floor and I did not wish to murder him with another blow. I did not wish to end my legal career through helping an accused prisoner escape. "You will no be harmed further." I called to Isobel through the shutter opening. "I will inform Sheriff Campbell and Reverend Forbes. I will ask to see you once sentence is known. You must stay strong till then and draw upon what comfort you can."

Isobel's face was at the shutter. She looked puzzled and lost. "Why did you beat him, if it wasn't tae set me free?" she asked.

I looked at Weir's pistol in my hand and set it down on the ground, near to its slowly waking owner. "I am sorry, Isobel. I will do everything in my power to help you within the law, not beyond. I knocked Mister Weir to the ground because of what he has done to you and because I do not take kindly to people holding pistols to my head."

"Tak me wi' you." Isobel said, her face pressed against the shutter. The question was asked. My refusal given. I would be forever part of her condemnation now.

Weir rose up on one elbow. I picked up the pistol and rammed the barrel into his mouth. "I am Archibald "Bluidy" Kellas. I have killed men like you for sport. You will not molest Isobel Gowdie again, you understand. I will learn of it and come to find you, if you do."

Weir's eyes were wide with fear, his breeks wet. He nodded his head, as most people would with a pistol shoved between their lips. I carried the pistol with me until I exited the tollbooth door, where I dropped it in the street.

Of all the images that stayed with me from the minutes just past, my mind would not let go of Isobel pleading at the shutter of her cell door, "Tak me wi' you" and I did not.

CHAPTER 43: GALLOWHILL, NAIRN.

Monday 16th July 1662

"We must then conclude, that these confessions of Witches, who affirm, that they have been transformed into beasts, is but an illusion of the fancy, wrought by the Devil upon their melancholy brains, whilst they sleep; and this we may rather believe, because it hath been oft seen, that some of these confessors were seen to be lying still in the room when they awak'd, and told where, and in what shapes they had travell'd many miles" **Sir George MacKenzie, Pleadings in some remarkable cases before the Supreme Courts of Scotland since the year 1661**

"Will ye look at the paps on thon!" Wattie exclaimed. "Christ, man, is it no a crying shame?"

We were riding our horses at a walk behind the crowd gathered around the pyre on Gallowhill. For all that it was unsuitable for the occasion, Wattie had been right to call out. Isobel looked beautiful, somehow transformed in this her final hour. Her face looked more youthful, her long red hair cascading about her shoulders and the ropes around her upper abdomen, that tied her to the stake, served to enhance the contours of her belly and breasts. That and gusts of warm wind that puffed out the white material of her dress at her cleavage. In the same moment, unbearably beautiful and tragic.

Reverend Forbes, bible in hand, was leading the assembled crowd nearest the pyre, in prayer. The people gathered beyond appeared to exhibit so many different emotions, some baying, some fearful, others grimly amused and yet others respectfully sad. Close by our horses a group of children laughed as they sang a rhyme, "Fi ye think ye ken, Fi the De'il ye dae, wa maist seems your friend, maks yer mannie oot o' clay!" Two children skipped along crying, "Horse and Hattock awa!" receiving a cuff round the lugs from their mother, for their mischief.

John Weir stood by a flaming brazier, a stout brand in his hand poised to ignite the piled wood. "God forgive me my mony sins!" Isobel called out, as Forbes concluded his prayer.

Wattie and I had walked our mounts a little further away to a small copse of trees, "Jesus, Archie, it's no richt. They're going tae burn her alive, wi'oot strangling her first! She's going tae be burnt alive, richt afore our eyes!" Wattie said, the anguish evident in his voice.

When Wattie looked round to see if I was answering, he found that I had dismounted and was reaching into my saddlebags. My intention becoming ever clearer as I pulled out my sword belt and sword within its scabbard. "Archie, no" he said in disbelief, as I fastened the buckle on my belt. I said nothing at all as I proceeded with quiet determination about my business. My business ever more certain as I withdrew my two dragoon pistols and my pouch of powder and shot.

"I'm no' asking ye tae come wi' me." I said, as I completed the loading of each pistol. Calmly, methodically, as I had learnt to do eighteen years before, when we had scattered every enemy we rode against.

"Archie, it's madness. Agin the law ye swore tae uphold. Christ, man, even if ye get awa wi' it, you'll be Scotland's maist wantit man. Think man, you've ainly just regained your life after years o' servitude. Dinna throw it a' awa."

After Forbes concluded his prayer, Sheriff Principal Campbell started explaining the finding of guilt of witchcraft. "I hae no more time, Wattie." I said as I used my stirrup to swing myself back into the saddle. "What they are doing is wrong. Thank you for a' ye hae done for me."

"Christ, Archie," Wattie said with a huge sigh, his forehead held in his right hand. "Ye ken I canna let ye dae this alane. Gie me one o' your pistols."

I looked across to my greatest friend, a lingering look to make sure he was certain about the course he had chosen. I need not have looked. Wattie held out his hand for my pistol. Beyond our exchange, I could hear Campbell finish his declaration of guilt and sentence. A murmur of tension ran through the crowd. Isobel must have been asked if she wished a final word, for she kept her head high, looking more beautiful than ever, "May God hae mercy on my soul!" she called out. John Weir pulled the burning brand from the brazier. The man who had raped Isobel moved to ignite the pyre that would end her life in unimaginable terror and pain.

"Mister Weir! You'll no' light that pyre!" I called as we pushed our horses through the least packed section of the crowd. Wattie warding folk away from our progress with his drawn sword and loaded pistol. "Release Mistress Gowdie, she'll no' burn today!"

Sheriff Cambell, Reverend Forbes and John Weir stared back in disbelief. I could just see a look of hope and recognition cross Isobel' face as we moved closer. There were four or five town guardsmen from Nairn around the pyre but they carried halberds, not loaded weapons. "Kellas! Desist now before you go beyond all hope of salvation." Sir Hugh Campbell shouted.

"Mister Weir will proceed with legal sentence and you will not stop him."

Weir looked quickly across to Reverend Forbes, over to me, then briefly up at Isobel, now straining on her ropes. It was if looking at Isobel decided him more than any words of authority. Weir plunged the flaming brand into the pyre.

My shot rang out, breaking open the back of Weir's head, sending him sprawling into the pyre he had just ignited. Wattie and I pushed our horses to within feet of the dead man and smouldering fire. "I am Archibald Bluidy Kellas! We will not hesitate to kill the next man that opposes us. This woman has been wrongly convicted. You," I pointed my sword as one of the guardsmen. "Cut her free, before the flames grow too great."

The people in the crowd could have rushed forward, their numbers overpowering us, instead they shuffled back, out of fear and perhaps sympathy. Campbell, Forbes and the guardsman I had commanded looked at each other uncertainly. "Thank you, Lord!" Isobel called out. "Hurry! The flames, I can feel them."

I moved my horse so my sword pointed at Sir Hugh Cambell, Wattie's two weapons covering the others around. "Sir Hugh, I will run you through first. Tell him!"

Sheriff Campbell looked at my sword and down at Weir's body, already scorching in the flames. "Cut her free, man. Quickly about it!" The guardsman stepped toward the part of the pyre furthest from where the brand was burning the dried wood. He reached in with his halberd and cut the ropes from round Isobel's wrists and waist. "You will not get away with this." Campbell hissed in belated defiance but by the time he said the words, Isobel was already scrambling down from the pyre and running toward my horse. I dropped my guard only long enough to help Isobel up onto my saddle in front of me. Wattie roared "Stand back!" and menacingly brandished both his pistol and sword to deter any foolhardy citizens at this critical point. "Thank you." Isobel said quietly to me, as she settled within the embrace of my left arm round her waist on the saddle. Now with the complication of holding the reins, my sword and gripping onto Isobel, my effectiveness as either a threat or a fighter was much reduced. We needed to make our escape immediately. Reverend Forbes stepped forward, "Both God and man will pursue you all, to the ends of your days." He said. Perhaps if I had not discharged my pistol to shoot John Weir, I would have shot Harry Forbes, not for the immediate physical threat he posed but for what he represented to me. I contented myself with making him the focal point of my horse's aggressive and alarming turn, to allow us to retrace our steps through the crowd. Forbes and those around him stumbled back. Wattie, following my lead, also turned his mount. "Clear the road!" Wattie yelled and we each kicked our mounts into a canter then a gallop as the people, yet stunned and frightened, scrambled out of our way.

We did not stop to look back. We did not see Sir Hugh Campbell's desperate attempts to resume control, ordering men to pull John Weir's protruding feet from the flames, ordering yet others to obtain pistols and muskets from the town armoury and tasking all the local gentry nearby to gather their horses. The majority of the crowd were not animated by coherent outrage or organisation to greatly aid the pursuit. They displayed instead an excited fatalism. "God could not have meant her to burn" someone said, a shout taken up enthusiastically by John Gilbert within the throng. There developed then a discordant cacophony as Reverend Forbes called back, "No! This is Satan's work! She has bewitched these men. They must be stopped! This is Satan's work!" While the children at the edge of the crowd capered with glee crying "Horse and hattock we flee, Horse and Hattock you'll no catch me!" The confusion allowed us all the time we needed to make clear of the immediate vicinity of Nairn.

We headed south. As the rescue had not been planned, I called across to Wattie as we rode, "We go south. We must avoid Inverness or Aberdeen, they will send word there first and avoid Edinburgh also. If we can reach Perth or Dundee and catch a boat, to anywhere." I saw Wattie raise his eyebrows. It had all happened so fast and now our lives were irrevocably changed. No going back. I was a murderer, Wattie an accessory and Isobel a condemned witch on the run. We would have a lot to talk about when we finally stopped.

We stopped early, just ten miles clear, by the village of Ferness on the River Findhorn, a chance to water the horses, fill our water pouches and take stock of our unexpected situation. Whatever Wattie wanted to say about my decision to ruin both our lives, was drowned out when Isobel slid down the saddle and off my horse. Ecstatic relief and delight to be still alive filled her face, all the more so, as it started with childish disbelief. "I'm alive!?" she said, running her hands down her breasts and body to verify her existence. "I'm alive!" she shouted joyfully, while leaping toward both of us. "Ye dinna ken how it feels. Tae be deid! Tae be ready tae die. Truly ready. An' now I'm no'. Oh ye bonny, bonny lads. I could kiss ye baith!"

And she did. Leapt into each of our arms and crushed us in ferocious embrace. The embrace of life. As it happened, I did know what it felt like to be sure I would die and yet, unexpectedly, live, as had happened to me at Philliphaugh but I had not been securely tied to a stake, surrounded by a smouldering pyre. I returned Isobel's embrace with the same infectious joy with which it was given. Wattie did also. Wattie may have had so much to say to me but now, there was so little to say. As in battle, in a split second, we had done what we chose to do. Each chose to do. Now there was nothing else to say except to agree what we must do next. What we *all* must do next, because there were three of us, who could never now return to their former lives.

Isobel went to the river and immersed herself. "Will I ne'er get rid o' this smell o' burning!?" she called out as she splashed blessed water over her soaking white dress. The fabric clung to her flesh, every curve of her body and thrust of nipple now laid as bare as was possible, without being exposed entire. Truth was, she did smell of smoke and burning. Not just the smoke that had threatened to engulf her but the scorched flesh of John Weir, as he had lain in the burning wood by Isobel's feet. A fearful, pungent reminder of the dreadful fate she had escaped. "He deserved tae die." she said, as if reading my mind. "Bastard!" she spat, as she emerged, dripping, from the water. "Raped me, sae mony times."

Bewildering, enchanting was the change in emotion. Within a step, angry, vengeful at the memory of Weir, the next, smiling, utterly grateful at the sight of our concerned faces. "I hae lived my life dreamin' o' flight, "she said, "I hae never kent it tae be as sweet as this." Soaking wet she pressed her body into each of ours once again and kissed us. I had heard Forbes' words as we rode way, "*Bewitched*" he had shouted. I knew in that moment, I did not care if I was.

"We must leave Scotland." I said when we had stopped in a small circle for a pause to breathe. "There is not the slightest hope for any o' us of reprieve. No matter what friends I hae in high places, my Lord Middleton for one, he cannot undo what I hae done. We cannot go back, to collect gear or speak wi' loved ones. We only hae each other now, we three. America or Europe, it is our only hope."

Wattie was slowly savouring a boiled egg we had brought as part of our provisions. He simply looked at me, as he twirled the egg in his hand before taking a bite. He had sacrificed so much, more than I, who yet had so little intimate life in Scotland. "Aye, I ken." was all Wattie said. "You gied me the chance no tae ride wi' you and I pulled oot my sword and kicked my nag on. Scotland's done for us. America or Europe, I ken."

Isobel had been staring intently at Wattie as he spoke. It was a sudden revelation to me that we had been immersed for weeks in her story, yet she knew so little of ours. "Oh ye beautiful, brave man," she said, as she moved across and planted a kiss upon Wattie's cheek. "Thank ye, for a' you chose tae dae for me and a' ye chose tae give up."

Wattie blushed as he smiled. "Truth is, lass, ye dinnae a'ways ken whit yer choosing tae gie up, when ye chose whit tae dae. No' beforehand. Otherwise nae buddy would e'er dae onything!" Wattie said with a laugh. Isobel laughed too, their worlds intwined in mutual understanding. "Ye only ken whit ye've bluidy weel gone and done afterwards!" Wattie concluded with another laugh and smile.

And with such, characteristic, humour and generosity, Wattie gave up his friends and family in Scotland for all time. *"Would I hae cast my first charm, if I kenned whaur it would end?"* Isobel said softly, looking down, as if speaking to herself. I had heard her. *"Would you?"* I asked. *"Could you have been anyone else?"*

Isobel had been biting on a hunk of bread, within our small circle seated on the ground. She stopped and regarded me. "You truly wish tae ken," she said and it took me a moment to realise, she had expressed a statement, not a question. "No, I wouldnae wish tae change. It has been the greatest pleasure o' my life tae fly wi' the faerie and tae use their wisdom tae help, aye, and sometimes tae hairm." Isobel raised her head until it perched proudly upon her slender neck. "Twa things I lo'ed in my life, when a story truly lit on fire through my telling. Became mair real than the puir wee hoose we were in. Mair real than the puir lives we were a' leading. Ye ken what that feels like?"

I thought of the conversations with Kate that had sustained me on the voyage to Barbados and through my long years in servitude. I spoke to her more in my head those years than I ever did in life. Loved her more also. The longing to be back with Kate and Mary was more real to me, more sustaining to me, than any reward the overseers might offer. "Yes." I said softly, looking down, as if speaking to myself. I looked up and saw that both Wattie and Isobel had heard me and were waiting for an explanation. "In my seven years of servitude, I spoke often with my wife. Hah!" I laughed, "she understood me better than anyone else during these years. Said the right things to me to help me carry on. It was, what you said, mair real."

"You have a wife?" Isobel asked. She looked from me to Wattie. "Yet you still did what you did. For me!?"

"My wife died when I was in captivity, as did my child. There has been no other." I replied and was dumbfounded by the sympathy in Isobel's face. My discomfort at this unexpected intimacy was rescued by Wattie.

"And I'm too smart tae hae a wife!" Wattie joked, "and too bonny as weel!"

"We can a' see that, Mister Garland!" Isobel replied with enthusiasm, yet I saw also a brief glance, with a more concerned expression, toward me.

"You said there were twa things, I mean two things, you loved about your life?" I reminded.

"Mair like three," Isobel replied with a hint of mischief in her eye, directed at Wattie. "But the ither thing I had in mind was being me, Isobel the charmer, Isobel the healer, Isobel the curser. It made me walk wi' my heid held high. Made me think I wasnae just breaking my back in the fields until the day I died. D'ye ken what it feels like tae feel blessit?"

"Always the past," Wattie had so often warned me not to dwell in the past, yet at Isobel's description, my mind could not stop itself from thinking back to that year with Montrose and MacColla when I had begun to feel like God's gift to Death. No-one could stop me, best me, kill me. And yet I could kill and plunder without harm. Without regret. I did not want to always return to Bluidy Kellas. I did not share my thoughts, instead I chose to answer Isobel's question with my own in return. It killed the moment. "Yet you must have known the church would not tolerate you, as Isobel the healer, the charmer, the curser. That they would see you as Isobel the witch?"

Isobel's expression darkened. She rose to her feet. "Please, can we be going? I hae had mair than sufficient for today o' what the kirk thinks o' me"

We all rose, breaking up our impromptu camp, me cursing myself silently for being so insensible of the terrible fear that Isobel must have experienced as she awaited a most horrible death. Someone, I did not notice who, suggested that Isobel ride with Wattie, to share the burden on the horses, Wattie explained. I agreed but when we were mounted and on our way I felt a stab of jealousy when I looked across at Isobel on Wattie's saddle, held within the curve of his arm and I felt the absence of her womanly body from my protective embrace.

On south we rode through the foothills of the Cairngorms. We stopped for night camp near the castle of Grant of Freuchie.

These Grants had fought alongside me for Montrose and we may well have been able to obtain a roof and succour had I called on the memory. *"We want to be seen by as few people as possible. We don't want any pursuers piecing together the details of our journey."* I explained, as we set up a rudimentary campfire and beds among a grove of trees. Thankfully the weather was blessedly warm and fine.

Before my impulsive decision to rescue Isobel, Wattie and I had set off with sufficient food and money for our journey home to Edinburgh, adding Isobel would not greatly change that and stopping at a port on the Tay, without crossing Fife and the Forth, would cut our expense. Having enough money for passage by boat out of Scotland would be our problem. We would have to work our passage or steal our fare. One thing for certain was I wasn't going to be indentured again.

What I could not be sure of was how swift would be the pursuit or if not pursuit, the spreading of word across the town crosses of Scotland. It was hard to imagine the crier calling out more captivating news. "Witch on the run! Two accomplices slay innocent town official as he was about to execute the accused! Satan is at work here. All citizens and Burgh guards to be on the alert for three fugitives."

Darkness was falling and the heat and light from our small campfire illuminated each of us as I explained my thoughts to Wattie and Isobel. *"Then we maun be on a boat an' awa afore the crier in the toon we're leaving fae cries oot that!"* Wattie said. Isobel was half in firelight, half in shadow. I suppose we all were, except hers was a lithe female form upon which the shadows were catching and curving. She bit her lip then said, *"You twa must leave me and make your ain way. I am the maist recognisable o' the three o' us. It will be me they maistly want. I can mak my ain way."* Although Wattie and I glanced at each other, he had already said, *"Dinna be daft, Isobel! We canna dae that."*

And I rose to my feet and placed my hand on Isobel's arm. *"No-one is going on their own. We are ahead of them and we do this together, the three of us, whate'er may betide."* I looked round at the two firelit faces beside me. *"Thank you, Isobel, for your offer but the three o' us are in this together, agreed!?"* Wattie nodded and said *"agreed".* Sparkling from the firelight I saw that Isobel had a tear in her eye. *"Thank you. I hae never kent twa sic guid men. I canna thank you enough."*

The night was thankfully dry again, we each settled for sleep in a circle round the embers of our fire. I could hear Wattie snoring when I heard a sound of movement. Alert to threat, I moved my hand to the sword and pistol that lay close to my side, when I saw through the darkness that it was Isobel crawling on hands and knees toward me. *"Shhh"* she motioned with a finger to her lips as she drew next to me. *"Shhh"* she motioned with her finger upon my lip, in response to my questioning look as she drew close enough to do so. *"Shhh"* she said, as her hand stroked my face. *"I would lie wi' you, if you would lie wi' me."* Our bodies were alongside each other, close enough to touch, with hands or without. We were each propped on one elbow. *"You do not have to..."* I said and I could see that there was a slight smile on her lips as her hand yet reached out to touch me. *"Dinna be daft, Archie. I ken I dinnae hae tae. I want tae."* She leaned her head forward and pressed her lips into mine in a lingering kiss. When she moved her head back I could see that she was still smiling as she trailed her free hand down my body to rest on my rising manhood. *"And ye want it tae! Archibald Kellas."* I allowed a few seconds for my eyes to widen, my lips to smile and my manhood to rise further, before we each dissolved in each-others' arms, no longer propped up but embracing , kissing, rolling once so that Isobel was on top of me, from where she rose to her knees to pull off her shift, my eyes, adjusting to the starlight, rewarded with my first sight of the glory of her breasts, arms, tumbling hair, smiling lips and eyes. Isobel shifted down to rest her buttocks on my thighs, to give me freedom to pull off my own sark and as two naked people, smiling, our bodies crying out our desire to be together, we met, in the darkness, as men and women do, dissolving, merging, stroking, inhaling, tasting, feeling, exploring, filling, sometimes one on top, then the other, joined in a most beautiful and intimate way.

It was wonderous. I could not help, after all I had read, to use the words, our *carnal copulation* was wonderous. Isobel, as if reading my mind, my seed inside her, as she sat astride me, popped a finger onto the end of my nose and said, "*Nae shame, mind.*" I pulled her to me, so our lips could meet again and our bodies roll once more so that we lay facing each other side by side. "*Nae shame,*" I repeated, once my lips were free to do so, "*only carnal plaisur.*"

"Mair, I think" Isobel said softly, as the palm of her hand stroked my chest above my heart, her face no longer smiling but thoughtful. "Mair" she whispered again, "but perhaps only in time. Archie, I must tell ye straight, tomorrow night I will lie with Wattie. He too has risked everything tae save me. It will be for plaisur and gratitude, as it was betwixt we too." Isobel lay naked on my blanket, my seed inside her, a sheen of sweat from our coupling yet dappling her skin, the palm of her right hand still resting upon my chest, her face neither angry, nor dismissive, rather respectful and determined. When I fought through my confusion to ask "*Why?*" she simply said, "I hae already told ye. Ye hae gi'en me my life back and I will choose whit I dae wi' it."

Isobel stirred to move away. In something like panic I grabbed the right hand that still touched my chest. "What about the "mair"? Can there be mair between us?"

Isobel prepared the rest of her body to rise and move away, while allowing me to hold her hand to my chest, above my heart. She leaned in and kissed my lips. "Perhaps, Archie. As I said, perhaps in time. Let us get awa safe and free, then let us each decide what we want. What our hearts' truly feel?"

And then she was away. Despite the lump in my throat and my furrowed brow, I watched every second of her bending to collect her shift, to raise her shapely arms to drop it over her body and then walk quietly back to her own blanket. *"Let us get awa safe and free, then let us each decide what we want. What our hearts' truly feel."* I repeated in my head. *"Let us get awa safe and free."*

The next day, the scenery should have been majestic as we followed a high mountain track to Tomintoul then down the other side to Cock Bridge, walking our mounts rather than riding them at the steepest parts. It was not the intermittent showers that dulled my spirits, it was my perplexed thoughts. Wattie asked at one point, *"Whit's wrang wi' you twa? Your face is tripping ye."* All I could grunt in return was, *"You'll find out tonight."*

To keep out the rain, we camped that night in an old shepherd's bothy. I tried to sleep, I swear I did but when I sensed Isobel creeping over to Wattie, I could not un-hear their whispered exchange, so similar to the wonderful surprise that had entranced me the night before. Then the movement and I found I had turned my head and opened my eyes to catch a glimpse of Isobel as she removed her shift and offered her nakedness to another man. I squeezed my eyes shut and rolled to my other side, my blanket over my ears, trying to dampen the sound of carnal copulation. That they were both giving and taking "plaisur" I had no doubt. To my shame, I rolled my body to allow me to face them and watched through narrowed eyes as Wattie mounted Isobel like a rutting beast from behind, all consideration for my presence in the room apparently forgot. I watched with a mixture of sadness and excitement, in my head, my heart and further down below. *"Let us get awa safe and free"* I repeated to myself, when I could watch no more and turned away.

The third day we rounded the brooding eminence of Lochnagar. We had spoken at breakfast, Wattie and I briefly when Isobel took herself off for her toilet, then the three of us, when she returned. There was little more to say, as Isobel had been so frank and open with each of us. She liked and admired us both. It had been her pleasure to lie with us both. It was also her thank you, freely given, for saving her life. Once we were safely out of Scotland, if she had to choose between us and we wished to be chosen, she would do so. Wattie and I shook hands in a gesture that said, the one not chosen would not impede the one who was. "Aye but it's a guy queer state o' affairs." Wattie opined and I said "aye" in agreement. Talk moved on to where we most wanted to go. Even England would be outside the purview of Scot's law but the accusation of witchcraft hanging over Isobel, not to mention the crime of murder attached to me, favoured a clean break to a more distant land where news from Scotland would be very slow in coming, if it came at all. Dundee had trade with the Low countries and the Baltic states, these were places we could go. We also spoke of how we might survive in a new land. My legal training would be of little use in a different jurisdiction, using a different language. Would Wattie and I really return to soldiering, eleven years since we were forced to give it up?

We camped that night near Spittal of Glenshee, now just one day's ride from the lowlands and the possibility of a boat from Dundee. Isobel said, *"Ye can lie close beside me, lads, either side, the nicht but no carnal copulation. D'ye jalouse whit I'm saying?"* We both nodded agreement like eager little puppies, although in a private moment Wattie said *"This is nae richt us being bossed around by a woman!"* I replied, *" I dinna ken, I quite like it"* To which Wattie came back with a grin, *"Aye me an' a'"*

We slept as arranged by Isobel. "This is nice." She murmured. "I feel sae safe and protectit." To our credit, we rarely tried to prod her and she only once, each, had to move straying hands, with a gentle "uh-uh"

We awoke with a shared feeling of communal bliss, like a family of animals who sleep huddled together, or a human family with a babe in the bed. As we packed our horses for the resumption of our journey, Wattie's only comment was a shrug, a smile and a widening of his eyes. We were both in a journey into the unknown in more ways than one. At least Isobel's unexpected behaviour had taken our minds off the danger of our situation and from dwelling on all that we had lost.

We skirted the town of Blairgowrie with Isobel taking her turn being held close on Wattie's saddle. At Coupar Angus the road forked either to Perth or Dundee. We settled on Dundee, with its great port at the mouth of the Tay. We were in good spirits, we each had skills, we would make a new living wherever fate decreed we should go. The strange exchange of everything for carnal copulation with a redheaded condemned witch simply made both me and Wattie just shake our heads with a stupefied smile. If it was bewitchment, it was of the most ancient and natural kind.

We approached Dundee from the northwest, past the village of Liff and the ruins of King Alexander's Palace at Hurly Hawkin. The land was wooded and dark as evening was falling. We emerged into a long strip of land cleared for agriculture when we saw them. Two hundred yards ahead, a group of fifteen to twenty horsemen. No ordinary travellers. Dragoons or mounted town guards by the look of them and unbelievably at their head, Sir Hugh Campbell of Cawdor and Reverend Harry Forbes.

It made no sense. Even if Campbell and Forbes and taken the quicker route by the Aberdeen to Dundee, they could only be here if they knew exactly where we were headed and we had spoken to no-one. It froze the blood in our veins. Warmth and happiness fled out, fear and dread of a destiny that demanded we be punished, flooded in. Commotion among the men in front of us told us we had been seen and recognised. Destiny or no, we had to go. "We maun be oot o' here!" I yelled as I turned my mount and grabbed hold of the horse carrying the double load of Wattie and Isobel, to encourage them to do the same.

The double load. It was that which sealed it. Wattie and Isobel would be slower and eventually overtaken and caught. We galloped half a mile back the way we came. I pulled us over into the overgrown ruins of Hurly Hawkin. The stones were too robbed away to hide us. There was little time for words, only actions. I vaulted off my horse. My sword was already scabbarded by my hip. I pulled out my two pistols and began loading them. Wattie made to do the same.

"No" I said, a Captain of Horse once again. "You two ride on, get away wherever you can. I will buy you the time you need to escape."

Wattie and Isobel stared at me, as I completed the loading of my pistols. "Ye ken it is the only way! Go!" I yelled. Isobel nodded, encouraging Wattie to leave. He held out his hand to me.

"Ye were the truest Captain I e'er kent, Maister Archie." He said, then kicked his mount around and away. I glanced for a second then knew I had to let them go, wherever and whatever fate held in store for only them.

I always knew there would be a price to pay for being Bluidy Kellas, the Captain who accepted no quarter. A price to be paid for that year being the greatest of my life. The dream of endless victory and killing with impunity that I returned to night after night. I spoke to Kathy my wife, when in captivity, when I needed to but once free, I longed to ride as an angel of death as once I had done.

I walked my horse out of the woodland that was slowly enveloping the ruins. The pursuing riders had overshot us but soon realised that there were no riders on the visible road up ahead. They were milling round looking for a trail to follow, when I kicked my horse into a canter and fired my first pistol into the nearest enemy I could find. My piece discharged with its beautiful flash and thunder. I saw the man fall.

With the aid of surprise, I was attacking en-caracole, riding perpendicular to a disorganised line, I fired my second pistol and another man fell. God, I was good at this, even after all these years. I disappeared into the trees, to reload. Kill Forbes and Campbell, I thought, and the others might give up. If they were the Dundee town guard, they would have no personal reason to die in the attempt to kill me. Through the trees to the right-hand side of the road, where my enemy tried to make sense of their position, I picked my horse, aiming to emerge at the opposite end of the grouping. Even in the growing dark of the evening and the dark of the trees, I found I could reload by instinct and memory. This was whom I was born to be.

Before I could emerge and fire again, I heard crunching through the undergrowth and the whinnying of a horse. Brave souls had come in after me. How many there were, I will never know. I held my mount under the command of my thighs behind a stout tree, until I saw the first rider approach. He had his weapon ready but not as ready as mine. I fired and he too recoiled and went bounding past me, either dead or dying, clinging to his fleeing mount by the stirrups.

My position exposed, I heard the crack of several dragoon

pistols firing in my direction. The balls thumped into trees nearby. I urged my mount into a swerving ride round the trees about me until I emerged upon the road, fifty feet from the rear of the men looking for me. Perhaps I could have kicked on and out-paced them in escape. My horse was tired after many days journey but it was not that which caused me not to attempt to break-off and ride away. It never crossed my mind. I was enjoying myself too much. I saw Forbes and Campbell shouting and pointing, men falling back from the woods where their comrade had just entered but not returned.

Back across their flank I rode. I levelled my pistol to fire at Forbes but at the last second, saw a horseman turn and level his own firearm at me. This became my target. Two shots discharged but the second was fired by the hand of a man already severely injured or dead from my shot. Into the woods on the left-hand side I plunged, seeking respite to reload.

How many remained? Twelve perhaps. I had kept them all with me. I had bought Wattie and Isobel their chance to escape. *"Mair, I think, in time"* Isobel's voice sounded in my head and for the first time my reloading faltered. *"No time for regret,"* I told myself, *"We all must choose our dream and I have chosen mine."* My hand steadied and both pistols were successfully loaded and primed.

I burst from the trees heading away from Dundee. I was surprised by a horseman, mere inches from my point of exit. A sword arm swiped at me and I dived sideways on my mount, with the same skill that had kept me alive seventeen years before. The same skill that allowed me to keep control of my horse, evade and fire all at once. Another enemy rocked back, yet as I made for the clear road beyond I heard the bark of pistols and the dreadful thud of impact as I realised my horse had been hit. She veered and whinnied, as I realised another living being was giving her life for others.

For all their losses, the sight of my horse buckling and skidding under the impact of a pistol ball, gave the men opposing me fresh courage. They all swung round to face me. Campbell and Forbes urging them on. "See, he's hit! We hae him, if we a' charge at once!" I heard Campbell cry.

I patted my horse's broad neck. "This is it, my darling," I told her, "It's the end o' the road for us. We've done a' we can." I could feel the strength ebbing from my mount. I pulled my sabre into my right hand and held my pistol in my left. "Harry Forbes!" I heard myself shout, as I urged my horse into a final charge. My pistol levelled on Forbes. Bluidy Kellas putting the enemy to flight once again.

A ragged volley erupted from the group of men I was heading toward.

Then I woke up.

CHAPTER 44: BURNING COMES IN FASHION.

Monday 15th July 1662. Auldearn.

"Since then these confessions are but the effects of melancholy, it follows necessarily, that the depositions of these Witches amounts to no more, but that they dreamed that my Client was there: and were it not a horrid thing, to condemn innocent persons upon mere dreams. I confess, that such confessions may be a ground to condemn the confessors, because though they were not actually where they dream'd, at these meetings, yet it infers that they had a desire to be there, and consented to the Worship, and believed that transformation to have been in the Devils power; but all these are but personal guilts in the confessors, and cannot reach others. Consider how much fancy does influence ordinary Judges in the trial of this crime, for none now labour under any extraordinary Disease, but it is instantly said to come by Witch-craft, and then the next old deform'd or envyed woman is presently charged with it; from this ariseth a confused noise of her guilt, called diffamatio by Lawyers, who make it a ground for seizure, upon which she being apprehended is imprisoned, starved, kept from sleep, and oft times tortured: To free themselves from which, they must confess; and having confest, imagine they dare not thereafter retreat. And then Judges allow themselves too much liberty, in condemning such as are accused of this crime, because they conclude they cannot be severe enough to the enemies of GOD; and Assisers are affraid to suffer such to escape as are remitted to them, lest they let loose an enraged Wizard in their neighbourhood. And thus poor Innocents die in multitudes by an unworthy Martyredom, and Burning comes in fashion" **Sir George MacKenzie , Pleadings in some remarkable cases before the Supreme Courts of Scotland since the year 1661. (published 1704 and not necessarily his views in 1662)**

Dreams. I understood how Isobel had come to live so much of her life within them. To believe them. To prefer them. To prefer the person she was within them. To enjoy the wild freedom.

On the day allotted for Isobel's execution, I read once more the letter that Wattie had brought back from Edinburgh, written by George MacKenzie, counter signed by Lord Middleton.

"Kellas, Though I have some sympathy with your argument that there is a deficiency of proven evidence of actual harm caused by the accused, it is not the central test of guilt or innocence within this matter. Both accused have been witnessed and attested by several leading citizens, to have confessed to covenanting with the Devil, of intending harm, whether they succeeded in causing it or no. You have not presented sufficient evidence that torture or pricking or reliance on witch's marks have been used in this case. These were the matters I counselled you to be concerned with. That you believe that Reverend Forbes has in some way influenced the testimony, through schooling the accused to replace folk belief with compacts with the Devil is vague and unsubstantiated. You have established no firm case upon which you, as the Privy Council representative, might overrule the otherwise unanimous verdict of the local Commission. You cannot overrule. You must not attempt to overrule. We require local justice to hold sway within its own domain and reserve the right to challenge this, only when the evidence is overwhelming that such local justice has been flawed or corrupted in its methods or dealings. We thank you for your report, your remit to intervene in this matter is concluded. You are commanded to return to Edinburgh at once. Your affectionate servant, George Mackenzie, Advocate Depute.

Middleton, Kings Commissioner to the Scots Parliament."

I was not Bluidy Kellas. Not any longer. That had been the creation of a few months of war, many years before. I was Archibald Kellas, public notary, with a career to consider, a life to rebuild after near death and indenture. On the day of the execution, as we packed our belongings to head back south, Wattie summed it up, saying, "You did your best Maister Archie." We would go home and Isobel would be publicly strangled, then her body burned to ensure the Devil could not revive it. I laughed grimly to myself, *the De'il will not revive her, he could not even lift a finger to help her when alive. Her only hope of salvation is in this room, packing up to leave.* The memory of my dream unsettled me deeply.

"Will we attend, Archie?" Wattie asked. "Doesnae seem richt efter getting tae ken her."

"We should be there," was all I said, "to see it done."

CHAPTER 45: ISOBEL FACES THE END.

Gallowhill Nairn, Monday 15th July 1662

'Be not dismayed, my brethren, for I am to die for the most exalted of causes. Led by the greatest of captains, Our Lord Jesus Christ, I have lived amongst the finest of companions. Not just those of you, here, today, who have remained steadfast for the Lord and his Covenant but also all the saints and martyrs who have gone before. I go to join them in blessed communion. Wherefore should I fear? Wherefore should I be dismayed?' **Final words before execution of Reverend James Guthrie, 1st June 1661**

We all converged on Gallowhill, on the outskirts of Nairn.

Reverend Harry Forbes carefully put on his best ministerial robes. He had already had a visit from the local Bishop. He must accept Episcopal authority or lose not only his parish but his ordination also. All appointments made during the period covered by the Act of Recission requiring to be confirmed and only those who accepted the new hierarchy would be confirmed. The execution this afternoon would now become the culmination of Forbes' ministry in Auldearn. His crowning glory. He had worked so hard and used skills that so few others possessed, to achieve the most complete demonic confession ever recorded. Perhaps his name would live on as a soldier of the faith against Satan. He brushed his white starched collar and cuffs. He must look his most splendid for such an occasion.

John Weir and Tamas Dunbar had prepared the wagon with a rudimentary cage, within which Isobel would travel the three miles from tollbooth to Gallowhill. Both men would be carrying loaded pistols. The chances of anyone attempting to rescue Isobel were remote but Weir yet brooded over his encounter with Bluidy Kellas. He could not shake the alternating waves of anger and fear, following having a pistol shoved in his mouth. Weir hoped that he would gain a measure of release and revenge when he performed his civic duty of turning the wooden baton threaded through the corded rope that would strangle Isobel Gowdie. Weir smiled to himself when he thought he might stop twisting while she was yet semi-conscious, leaving her alive to feel the flames. Yes that thought made him momentarily forget his feeling of victimhood at the hands of Kellas.

John Gilbert, Isobel's husband, walked apart from the throng of people heading toward the spectacle of execution. He both understood yet despised his neighbours for travelling to Isobel's gruesome death in such high spirits. This was his wife. A woman many of them had known, some had even consulted for the very charms for which she was about to die. All happy it was her, not them. After months of being denied access to his wife, John hoped he might be able to speak with her as the wagon took her to the place of execution. To say what? All he could say was that he loved her. He wanted her to hear that from his own lips before it was too late. Children were skipping along laughing. Some citizens carried baskets of fruit, as if they intended to make a picnic of it. John laughed bitterly to himself. *You hae gien all the folk for miles around a holiday, my Isobel.* He thought she might like that. Then he remembered the price she would pay and tears pricked his eyes once more.

Jean Martin, John and their master Hugh Hay also dressed in their Sunday best clothes and together boarded a small pony and trap. Although they were master and two house-servants, there was an odd familiarity about their interactions, a sense that they shared a secret. Heading to the execution of a woman who had named Jean as the Maiden of the coven and the youthful favourite of the Devil in his frequent carnal copulation. John was always most solicitous of Jean's welfare. "You should not feel sorry," he consoled her, "you did what you had tae dae. For all our sakes." Jean was often calculating in her emotions but today she was unnerved to see her one-time friend and mentor go to the flames. In her pocket she carried a small baked figure of a woman, which she would crush in her palm at the appropriate time to give Isobel a swift and pain free death. Hugh Hay did not know of the baked figure but he could sense Jean's conflicted emotion. "Come, my lass," he instructed, "keep your heid held high and show them a' ye hae naething tae be ashamed o'"

Wattie and I packed all our belongings in preparation for heading south as soon as we had seen sentence carried out. After the vividness of my dream I kept my rapier, knife and two pistols near the top of my belongings. Close to the surface but buried just deep enough not to show. Wattie and I had little to say to each other as we prepared to set off for Gallowhill. Although we had agreed that we had done all we could, an oppressive sense of failure and disappointment hung over us. Ours would be such a quiet and ineffectual departure. Forbes would preach his sermon, Campbell would pronounce sentence, Weir, the man who had raped Isobel, would be the agent of the Lord and of the Law, twisting the throttling cord round her neck. I longed for him to whisper some final obscenity in her ear and for me to ride forward pistol blazing, as in my dream. My disappointment was with myself, that I knew I would not.

Isobel prayed in the final moments before departure from Auldearn tollbooth. Reverend Forbes had attended her the day before, to offer her final comfort for her ordeal to come.

Although Harry Forbes' manner had been the same, Isobel could no longer respond to it as positively as she had done before. Not since she learned that Forbes had kept the news of Janet's death from her for two months. *A friend would not dae that,* she thought. She prayed to God and Jesus with Reverend Forbes and felt nothing. For the same reason, once Forbes had gone, she would not even contemplate calling on Satan for aid. Not because it was wrong but because there was no-one there. She just knew. Much of her life she had venerated so many spirits and they were so sternly quiet in her time of greatest fear and need. Isobel thought of John and of her first love, Sean the deserter, who had taught her the ways of physical love. She thought of her great friendship, Janet and the wild and bawdy nights she had had with the women o' the fermtouns. These thoughts made her smile. The echoes of these memories sounded louder in her head than waiting for any mighty deity to reply. *I wouldna hae it any other way,* she thought. *I wouldna have had my life any other way. That's no really proper repentance, is it?* she thought and made herself laugh out loud so much so that Weir opened the shutter to look. As Isobel was led, tied at the hands, into the caged cart for her journey to the appointed place, she was aware of people watching her. As they bumped along their journey, she watched their reactions, as if watching from somewhere outside her own body. She saw people jeering, others crossing themselves, which was surely against Reverend Forbes' rule. She saw mothers pulling their bairns into their skirts. She was only jolted out of her feeling of disconnect when the wagon reached the foot of Gallowhill. It took Isobel several seconds to realise the voice calling "Isobel, Isobel!" was not inside her head but was her husband John running alongside. "Oh God, John. I'm so sorry" Isobel managed to say. She could not reach out and John could not reach in, as Weir and Dunbar whipped the wagon into a trot. "Isobel, I love you!" John shouted, as the wagon outpaced him. "I love you, too, John" she shouted, as her heart was breaking, her strange calm deserting her. *Help me, Red Reiver* Isobel called within her head, as her panic rose at the sight of the massed crowd, the pyre and the platform on which she would be strangled before all watching eyes. *You hae been my true religion, tak me tae Elphane yin last time.*

Isobel was led, hands still tied behind her back onto the platform, where she was also tied to the wooden stake, on top of the pyre. The stake only reached as high as Isobel's shoulders, round her neck was placed a stout, tight corded rope, with a wooden baton threaded through loops at either cord end. This baton would be turned by John Weir to constrict Isobel's throat and break her neck. The flames, thereafter, were not to kill her but to stop the Devil reclaiming her. Reverend Forbes preached his sermon. Sir Hugh Campbell pronounced sentence. Isobel was asked if she had any final words. "I am sorry for anyone I hae hairmed and for anyone I didna lo'e well enough." Reverend Forbes was disappointed this was not the devout expression of repentance they had rehearsed. A hood was placed over Isobel's head, her auburn curls covered for the final time, as her life was silenced as well. Isobel saw the Reiver offer her his hand. Nearby, amid the haze of beauty that always accompanied them, the Queen and King of Faerie beckoned to Isobel with a smile. Weir began to twist the baton. Jean crumbled her baked figure. Weir's first twist broke Isobel's slender neck. Far more quickly than he hoped.

Hugh Hay sensed that Isobel had gone. "Now no-one will e'er ken" he said to John. Beside them Jean was crying, as beyond them, John Gilbert was also.

I turned my horse to face its head south, "Come on, Wattie" I said, "we've seen enough."

AUTHOR'S NOTE

Isobel Gowdie was a real woman, not a fantasy witch. The men who accused, investigated and tried her were real men, pious, honourable and educated within the standards of their day. It is unlikely they simply invented Isobel's testimony or that the words are the utterly random outpourings of a woman tortured beyond coherence and endurance. How then to explain Isobel's remarkable testimony?

My journey began with the Sensational Alex Harvey Band song "Isobel Gowdie". SAHB was big in my home when I was growing up. Years later I worked in Dudhope Castle, Dundee and gained a sense of the duality of so many people in the seventeenth century, where religion and politics mixed so potently. Dudhope's former owner, John Graham of Claverhouse was to some Bonnie Dundee and to others Bluidy Clavers. Similarly Sir George Mackenzie of Rosehaugh is Bluidy MacKenzie for his prosecution of Covenanters, yet also one of the leading figures in the modernisation of Scot's Law, including improving the evidence base for investigating witches.

I found online Robert Pitcairn's "Ancient Criminal Trials in Scotland" and one weekend set myself the task of reading Isobel's four original confessions and Janet's one, with a view to seeing what they said to me. I admit to reeling in confusion. Why were they saying these things? The changing into animals, flying on cornstalks and shooting people with elf arrows left me cold. The words that moved me were the descriptions of carnal copulation, in particular the repeated reference to "no shame" and our pleasure as well as his. Considering how few voices from ordinary people come down through history, and how even fewer ordinary women, this was powerful to me. We tend to assume that everyone held to the prevailing elite view of the world, yet the ordinary population of Scotland must have had an imperfect grasp of Protestant doctrine and an idiosyncratic mix of beliefs, just as people do today.

I was also struck by the Devil's obsession with ending the male inheritance of the Laird of Park. This led me to consider the old detective maxim of who had the means and motive. I could find little online about the Hays of Lochloy and Park but I settled on Hugh Hay of Brightmoney as my candidate for the man behind the devil. Finally I purchased and read Emma Wilby's "The Visions of Isobel Gowdie; Magic, Witchcraft and Dark Shamanism in Seventeenth-Century Scotland". This is an excellent book and Professor Wilby has had access to original documents from Nairnshire in the 1660s. She gave no credence to a possible human motivation for the Devil wanting to alter the inheritance of Park and Lochloy, instead she postulated that the tenants of Park had a debt ridden and unsympathetic landlord, who would have incurred the dislike of people living a relentless subsistence existence. Wilby proposed that Isobel was most likely an oral performer of Ballads at a time when this would have been a pre-eminent form of ordinary human expression and storytelling. She also built the argument for Isobel being a user of charms for both cure and harm and a practitioner who travelled within a shamanistic dream world. I have tried in my novel to be largely consistent with Emma Wilby's book and Hugh Hay of Brightmoney has been relegated to a suggestion as the Devil rather than a proven culprit.

The Kellases of Cabrach, Strathdon are my maternal ancestors. I have been to the bleak valley and cannot imagine what pre-technology life amid the heavily snowed winter must have been like. Perhaps they too turned to fireside ballads for intense, dark entertainment. My maternal ancestors were born into great poverty yet exhibited huge intellect and broke free through becoming a series of Ministers of the Church of Scotland.

Readers may be glad to know that the McLeans of Strathglass were released after the investigation byJohn Neilson. Their false accuser Chisholm went unpunished.

Reverend Harry Forbes resigned as Minister of Auldearn in 1663 being unable to accept Episcopacy. His fate thereafter is not known but it may have ended in some form of declined circumstances, perhaps through poverty, debauchery or ill-health. Alexander Brodie of Brodie wrote in his diary in 1678, "Sir Ludovic Gordon cam heir this night. He told me he had sein Mister H. Forbes in England. I considered this and was humbld."

Isobel Gowdie, whatever the outcome of her physical life, has gone on to become the most famous ordinary woman in seventeenth century Scotland.

The confessions of Isobel and Janet were lost for 168 years until they were discovered by Robert Pitcairn in 1833 and included in his book "Ancient Criminal Trials in Scotland". Many sections of the confessions are quoted within this novel but if you wish to read Isobel's four and Janet's single confession in their entirety then the are in an appendix at the end of the final volume (being outwith the time period of Pitcairn's book, yet included because he found them so fascinating). They start on page 602 in the volume I used.

Two chapters in the novel deserve special mention. Archie's dream in chapter 43 is the oldest personal-to-me story in this book. Rescuing an attractive witch was a late teen fantasy of mine. For all its flaws, it gave Isobel a better end than that which I believe she suffered.

Chapter 41 was a complete revelation to me. Until I established the context and set out how the third confession might be pro-actively and defiantly performed , I had no idea how exactly the words would fit such a scenario. It may just be what happened.

1661-2 saw an absolutely appaling wave of witch trials and executions throughout Scotland, I hope this novel does some justice to Isobel and Janet, two women, as real and non-fantastical as me or you, who lived and were persecuted in that cruel time.

Martin Dey
Dundee, Hallowe'en 2022

PRAISE FOR AUTHOR

"I cried. This incredible book. I fell in love with the characters. I always want the Scots to win. I learned so much. It really did make me cry and that may be why I liked it so much."

"Could not put the book down. I read endless historical fiction both as an escape and for perspective. This single work provided pleasure, insight and the desire to have more."

"I had to pry the story away from myself. It is the reason we read. Books such as this."

- WORLDWIDE REVIEWS OF "NO GREAT MISCHIEF IF THEY FALL."

" I am a voracious reader, though a picky one. I can really only tolerate books where I am held captive by the writing and the characters. This book has done both. I read and read, then became despondant when I finished. I loved this book. Thank you for such a thriilling journey."

"Immersed in history, geopolitics and loyalties; a great read that sticks with you. I was immersed in the sense of place, time and history. You can feel the author's need for authenticity. There are moments of elation and those of nerve wracking trauma. This would be magnificent on screen."

— WORLDWIDE REVIEWS OF "LIBERTY OR DEATH"

"Another great story by Martin Dey. The last of the trilogy is poignant and insightful. The creative concept of a soldier surviving four brutal wars spanning so many years makes the trilogy well worth reading and it would make a terrific television series."

"I have thoroughly enjoyed this series. The finale, like the other two books, has a great plot woven into historical events. A great read."

— WORLDWIDE REVIEWS OF "THE WORLD TURNED UPSIDE DOWN."

BOOKS BY THIS AUTHOR

No Great Mischief If They Fall

In 1745 young Ewan MacKenzie is caught up in Bonnie Prince Charlie's Jacobite Rebellion and sees his home destroyed by Redcoat soldiers, as they pacify the Highlands. Yet 12 years later Ewan becomes a Redcoat himself. "No Great Mischief If They Fall" explores why a man might make such a transition, while following Ewan's service with the 78th Fraser Highlanders from Louisbourg to Quebec. Ewan faces many dangers, none more so than when he finds himself in the same army as the Redcoat who harmed his family.

Liberty Or Death

Ewan MacKenzie has survived the Jacobite Rebellion and the French and Indian War but even these bitter conflicts do not prepare him for the terror and divided allegiance he is yet to face. The terror comes when he is a captive of the Seneca, while Pontiac's Rising ignites the frontier. Divided loyalty comes to the fore when 12 years later conflict looms between Britain and Ewan's adoptive home of America. How could a man fight against the comrades he once swore an oath to serve alongside?

The World Turned Upside Down

Ewan MacKenzie drags his injured and weary body through

the great American Revolutionary War battles of Brandywine, Germantown and Monmouth, while also having to endure the harsh winter camps at Morristown and Valley Forge, yet his time of greatest fear and guilt arises when his home and family are threatened by the British invasion of Virginia, with Ewan's sworn enemy, Malachi Cobden, in their midsts. An enthralling conclusion to the trilogy of stories charting Ewan's eventful life.

Printed in Great Britain
by Amazon